Praise for John Scalzi

'Scalzi's clever dialogue, fast-paced story and strong characters are reminiscent of Robert A. Heinlein, without his sometimes tedious lectures'
The Times

'John Scalzi's debt to Heinlein, Haldeman and Pohl is apparent, and it gladdens the reader's heart. A good old-fashioned future, and great fun'
Daily Telegraph

'It's a neat scenario, allowing Scalzi to pose questions of identity and morality while telling a fast-paced, entertaining action adventure story'
Guardian

'John Scalzi's *Old Man's War* (and, indeed, its sequels) was the best pure splash of science fiction I've read in ages'
Martin McGrath,
Vector Magazine (Best Books of 2007 feature)

'An unalloyed delight . . . appealing, well written and smart. You may have gathered that I loved it'
Daily Telegraph

John Scalzi's debut novel, *Old Man's War*, was a finalist for the Hugo Award for Best Novel. In 2006 he won the John W. Campbell Award for Best New Writer. His weblog is one of the longest-running and most widely read journals on the Internet. He lives in Ohio with his wife and daughter.

Also by John Scalzi

Agent to the Stars
Old Man's War
The Android's Dream
The Ghost Brigades
The Last Colony

ZOE'S TALE

John Scalzi

TOR

First published 2008 by Tor
an imprint of Tom Doherty Associates, LLC, New York

First published in Great Britain in paperback 2009 by Tor
an imprint of Pan Macmillan Ltd
Pan Macmillan, 20 New Wharf Road, London N1 9RR
Basingstoke and Oxford
Associated companies throughout the world
www.panmacmillan.com

ISBN 978-0-330-50603-8

For Karen Meisner and Anne KG Murphy
And most especially for Athena.

PROLOGUE

I lifted up my dad's PDA and counted off the seconds with the two thousand other people in the room.

"Five! Four! Three! Two! One!"

And then there was no noise, because everyone's attention—and I mean *everyone's*—was glued to the monitors peppered around the *Magellan's* common area. The screens, which had held starry skies in them, were blank and black, and everyone was holding their breath, waiting for what came next.

A world appeared, green and blue.

And we all went *insane*.

Because it was *our* world. It was Roanoke, our new home. We would be the first people to land there, the first people to settle there, the first people to live our lives there. And we celebrated seeing it for that first time, we two thousand settlers of Roanoke, all crammed into that common area, hugging and kissing and singing "Auld Lang Syne," because, well, what else do you sing when you come to a new world? A new world, new beginnings, a new year, a new life. New everything. I hugged my best friend Gretchen and we hollered into the microphone I had been using to count down the seconds, and hopped up and down like idiots.

When we stopped hopping, a whisper in my ear. "So beautiful," Enzo said.

I turned to look at him, at this gorgeous, beautiful boy who I was seriously considering making my boyfriend. He was a perfect combination: heart-flutteringly pretty and apparently entirely ignorant of the fact, because he'd been spending the last week trying to charm me with his *words*, of all things. Words! Like he didn't get the teenage boy manual on how to be completely inarticulate around girls.

I appreciated the effort. And I appreciated the fact that when he whispered his words, he was looking at me and not the planet. I glanced over at my parents about six meters away, kissing to celebrate the arrival. That seemed like a good idea. I reached my hand behind Enzo's head to draw him to me and planted one right on his lips. Our first kiss. New world, new life, new boyfriend.

What can I say. I was caught up in the moment.

Enzo didn't complain. " 'O brave new world, that has such people in it,' " he said, after I let him breathe again.

I smiled at him, my arms still around his neck. "You've been saving that up," I said.

"Maybe," he admitted. "I wanted you to have a quality first kiss moment."

See. Most sixteen-year-old boys would have used a kiss as an excuse to dive straight for the boobs. He used it as an excuse for Shakespeare. A girl could do worse.

"You're adorable," I said, kissed him again, then gave him a playful push and launched myself into my parents, breaking up their canoodling and demanding their attention. The two of them were our colony's leaders, and soon enough they would barely have time to breathe. It was best I get in some quality time while I could. We hugged and laughed and then Gretchen yanked me back toward her.

"Look what I have," she said, and thrust her PDA in my face. It showed a vidcap of me and Enzo kissing.

"You evil little *thing*," I said.

"It's amazing," Gretchen said. "It actually looks like you're trying to swallow his entire *face*."

"Stop it," I said.

"See? Look," Gretchen tapped a button, and the vidcap played in slow motion. "Right there. You're *mauling* him. Like his lips were made of *chocolate*."

I was trying very hard not to laugh, because she was actually right about that. "Wench," I said. "Give me that." I snatched the PDA from her with one hand, erased the file, and handed it back. "There. Thank you."

"Oh, no," Gretchen said, mildly, taking the PDA.

"Learned your lesson about violating the privacy of others?" I said.

"Oh, yes," Gretchen said.

"Good," I said. "Of course, you already forwarded it to everyone we know before you showed it to me, didn't you?"

"Maybe," Gretchen said, and put her hand to her mouth, eyes wide.

"Evil," I said, admiringly.

"Thank you," Gretchen said, and curtsied.

"Just remember I know where you live," I said.

"For the rest of our lives," Gretchen said, and then we did embarrassingly girly squeals and had another hug. Living the rest of your life with the same two thousand people ran the risk of being dead-bang boring, but not with Gretchen around.

We unhugged and then I looked around to see who else I wanted to celebrate with. Enzo was hovering in the background, but he was smart enough to know that I'd get back to him. I looked over and saw Savitri Guntupalli, my parents' assistant, conferring with my dad very seriously about something.

Savitri: She was smart and capable and could be wicked funny, but she was always working. I got between her and Dad and demanded a hug. Yes, I was all about the hugs. But, you know, look: You only get to see your new world for the first time once.

"Zoë," Dad said, "can I have my PDA back?"

I had taken Dad's PDA because he'd set the exact time the *Magellan* would skip from the Phoenix system to Roanoke, and used it to count off the last few minutes before the jump. I had my own PDA, of course; it was in my pocket. No doubt the vidcap of me smooching Enzo was waiting for me in my in-box, just like it was in the in-boxes of all our friends. I made a note to myself to plot revenge against Gretchen. Sweet, merciless revenge. Involving witnesses. And farm animals. But for now I gave Dad back his PDA, gave him a peck on his cheek, and found my way back to Enzo.

"So," Enzo said, and smiled. God, he was even charming when monosyllabic. The rational part of my brain was lecturing me about how infatuation makes everything seem better than it is; the irrational part (meaning, most of me) was telling the rational part to get well and truly stuffed.

"So," I said back, not nearly as charmingly, but Enzo didn't seem to notice.

"I was talking to Magdy," Enzo said.

"Uh-oh," I said.

"Magdy's not so bad," Enzo said.

"Sure, for certain values of 'not so bad,' meaning '*bad*,'" I said.

"And he said that he was talking to some of the *Magellan* crew," Enzo said, forging along (charmingly). "They told him about an observation lounge on the crew level that's usually empty. He says we could get a great view of the planet there."

I glanced over Enzo's shoulder, where Magdy was talking animatedly to Gretchen (or *at* her, depending on one's point of view). "I don't think the planet is what he's hoping to view," I said.

Enzo glanced back. "Maybe not," he said. "Although to be fair to Magdy, certain people aren't exactly trying hard not to be viewed."

I crooked an eyebrow at that; it was true enough, although I knew Gretchen was more into the flirting than anything else. "And what about you?" I said. "What are *you* hoping to see?"

Enzo smiled and held up his hands, disarmingly. "Zoë," he said. "I just got to *kiss* you. I think I want to work on that a little more before moving on to anything else."

"Ooh, nicely said," I said. "Do these lines work on all the girls?"

"You're the first girl I've tried them on," Enzo said. "So you'll have to let me know."

I actually blushed, and gave him a hug. "So far, so good," I said.

"Good," Enzo said. "Also, you know. I've seen your bodyguards. I don't think I want them to use me for target practice."

"What?" I said, mock-shocked. "You're not frightened of Hickory and Dickory, are you? They're not even here." Actually, Enzo has a perfectly good reason to be utterly terrified of Hickory and Dickory, who were already vaguely suspicious of him and would happily cycle him out an airlock if he did anything stupid with me. But there was no reason to let him know that yet. Good rule of thumb: When your relationship is minutes old, don't freak out the new squeeze.

And anyway, Hickory and Dickory were sitting out this celebration. They were aware they made most of the humans nervous.

"I was actually thinking of your parents," Enzo said. "Although they seem to be missing, too." Enzo motioned with his head to where John and Jane had been standing a few minutes before; now neither of them were there. I saw Savitri leaving the common area as well, as if she suddenly had someplace to be.

"I wonder where they went," I said, mostly to myself.

"They're the colony leaders," Enzo said. "Maybe now they have to start working."

"Maybe," I said. It was unusual for either John or Jane to disappear without telling me where they were going; it was just a common courtesy. I fought back the urge to message them on my PDA.

"So, the observation lounge," Enzo said, getting himself back to the topic at hand. "You want to check it out?"

"It's on the crew deck," I said. "You think we might get in trouble?"

"Maybe," Enzo said. "But what can they do? Make us walk the plank? At worst they'll just tell us to get lost. And until then we'll have a heck of a view."

"All right," I said. "But if Magdy turns into all tentacles, I'm leaving. There are some things I don't need to see."

Enzo laughed. "Fair enough," he said, and I snuggled into him a little. This new boyfriend thing was turning out just fine.

We spent some more time celebrating with our friends and their families. Then, after things had settled down enough, we followed Magdy and Gretchen through the *Magellan* and toward the crew observation lounge. I thought sneaking into the crew area might be a problem; not only was it easy, but a crew member coming out of an entrance held it open for us.

"Security is not a huge issue here on the *Magellan*," Gretchen said, back to me and Enzo, then looked down at our clasped hands and smiled at me. She was evil, sure, but she was also happy for me.

The observation lounge was where it was advertised to be, but alas for Magdy's nefarious plans, it was not empty as promised; four *Magellan* crew members sat at a table, intent in a conversation. I glanced over to Magdy, who looked like he had just swallowed a fork. I found this rather amusing myself. Poor, poor Magdy. Frustration became him.

"Look," Enzo said, and still holding my hand, guided me to a huge observation window. Roanoke filled the view, gorgeously green, fully illuminated with her sun behind us, more breathtaking in person than she was on the monitors. Seeing something with your own eyes makes a difference.

It was the most beautiful thing I think I'd ever seen. *Roanoke*. Our world.

"Wrong *place*," I heard, barely, from the conversation at the table to the left of me.

I glanced over at the table. The four *Magellan* crew there were so engaged in their conversation and so closed in to each other that it looked like most of their bodies were actually on the table rather than in their seats. One of the crew was sitting with his back to me, but I could see the other three, two men and a woman. The expression on their faces was grim.

I have a habit of listening in to other people's conversations. It's not a bad habit unless you get caught. The way not to get caught is to make sure it looks like your attention is somewhere else. I dropped my hand from Enzo's and took a step toward the observation lounge window. This got me closer to the table while at the same time keeping Enzo from whispering sweet nothings in my ear. I kept myself visually intent on Roanoke.

"You don't just *miss*," one of the crew members was saying. "And the *captain* sure as hell doesn't. He could put the *Magellan* in orbit around a pebble if he wanted to."

The crew member with his back to me said something low, which I couldn't hear.

"That's *crap*," said the first crew member. "How many ships have actually gone missing in the last twenty years? In the last fifty? No one gets *lost* anymore."

"What are you thinking?"

I jumped, which made Enzo jump. "Sorry," he said, as I turned to give him an exasperated look. I put a finger to my lips to shush him, and then motioned with my eyes at the table now behind me. Enzo glanced behind me and saw the table. *What?* he mouthed. I shook my head a tiny bit to tell him he shouldn't distract me anymore. He gave me a strange look. I took his hand again to let him know I wasn't upset with him, but then focused my attention back to the table.

"—calm. We don't know anything yet," said another voice, this one belonging (I think) to the woman. "Who else knows about this?"

Another mutter from the crew member facing away from me.

"Good. We need to keep it that way," she said. "I'll clamp down on things in my department if I hear anything, but it only works if we all do it."

"It won't stop the crew from talking," said someone else.

"No, but it'll slow down the rumors, and that's good enough until we know what's really happened," the woman said.

Yet another mutter.

"Well, if it's true, then we have bigger problems, don't we?" said the woman, and all the strain she was experiencing was suddenly clear in her voice. I shuddered a little; Enzo felt it through my hand and looked at me, concerned. I gave him a serious hug. It meant losing the rest of the conversational thread, but at the moment, it's what I wanted. Priorities change.

There was the sound of chairs pushing back. I turned and the crew members—it was pretty clear they were actually officers—were already heading toward the door. I broke away from Enzo to get the attention of the one closest to me, the one who had had his back to me earlier. I tapped him on the shoulder; he turned and seemed very surprised to see me.

"Who are you?" he said.

"Has something happened to the *Magellan*?" I asked. The best way to learn stuff is not to get distracted, for example, by questions relating to one's identity.

The man actually scowled, which is something I'd read about but had never actually seen someone do, until now. "You were listening to our conversation."

"Is the ship lost?" I asked. "Do we know where we are? Is something wrong with the ship?"

He took a step back, like the questions were actually hitting him. I should have taken a step forward and pressed him.

I didn't. He regained his footing and looked past me to Enzo and Gretchen and Magdy, who were all looking at us. Then he realized who we were, and straightened up. "You kids aren't supposed to be here. Get out, or I'll have ship's security throw you out. Get back to your families." He turned to go.

I reached toward him again. "Sir, wait," I said. He ignored me and walked out of the lounge.

"What's going on?" Magdy asked me, from across the room. "I don't want to get in trouble because you've pissed off some random crew member."

I shot Magdy a look, and turned to look out the window again. Roanoke still hung there, blue and green. But suddenly not as beautiful. Suddenly unfamiliar. Suddenly threatening.

Enzo put his hand on my shoulder. "What is it, Zoë?" he said.

I kept staring out the window. "I think we're lost," I said.

"Why?" Gretchen asked. She had come up beside me. "What were they talking about?"

"I couldn't hear it all," I said. "But it sounded like they were saying we're not where we're supposed to be." I pointed to the planet. "That this isn't Roanoke."

"That's crazy," Magdy said.

"Of course it's crazy," I said. "Doesn't mean it might not be true." I pulled out my PDA from my pocket and tried to connect with Dad. No answer. I tried connecting to Mom.

No answer.

"Gretchen," I said. "Would you try calling your dad?" Gretchen's dad was on the colonial council my parents headed up.

"He's not answering," she said, after a minute.

"It doesn't mean anything bad," Enzo said. "We did just skip to a new planet. Maybe they're busy with that."

"Maybe they're still *celebrating*," Magdy said.

Gretchen smacked him upside the head. "You really *are* childish, Magdy," she said. Magdy rubbed the side of his head and shut up. This evening was not going anything like he had planned. Gretchen turned to me. "What do you think we should do?"

"I don't know," I said. "They were talking about keeping the crew from talking. It means some of them might know what's going on. It won't take long to get to the colonists."

"It's already gotten to the colonists," Enzo said. "*We're* colonists."

"We might want to tell someone," Gretchen said. "I think your parents and my dad need to know, at least."

I glanced down at her PDA. "I think they might know already," I said.

"We should make sure," she said. So we left the observation lounge and went looking for our parents.

We didn't find them; they were in a council meeting. I did find Hickory and Dickory, or rather, they found me.

"I think I should go," Enzo said, after they'd stared at him, unblinking, for a minute. It wasn't meant as intimidation; they don't blink at all. I gave him a peck on the cheek. He and Magdy left.

"I'm going to listen around," Gretchen said. "See what people are saying."

"All right," I said. "Me too." I held up my PDA. "Let me know what you hear." She left.

I turned to Hickory and Dickory. "You two," I said. "You were in your room earlier."

"We came looking for you," Hickory said. It was the talker of the two. Dickory could talk, but it was always a surprise when it happened.

"Why?" I said. "I was perfectly safe before. I've been perfectly safe since we left Phoenix Station. The *Magellan* is entirely threat-free. The only thing you've been good for this entire trip is scaring the crap out of Enzo. Why are you looking for me now?"

"Things have changed," Hickory said.

"What do you mean?" I asked, but then my PDA vibrated. It was Gretchen.

"That was fast," I said.

"I just ran into Mika," she said. "You won't *believe* what she said a crew member just told her brother."

The adult colonists may have been either clueless or tight-lipped, but the Roanoke teenage rumor mill was in full swing. In the next hour, this is what we "learned":

That during the skip to Roanoke, the *Magellan* had wandered too close to a star and had been thrown out of the galaxy.

That there was a mutiny and the first officer had relieved Captain Zane of command because of incompetence.

That Captain Zane shot his own traitorous first officer right there on the bridge and said he'd shoot anyone who tried to help him.

That the computer systems had failed just before the skip, and we didn't know where we were.

That aliens had attacked the ship and were floating out there, deciding whether to finish us off.

That Roanoke was poisonous to human life and if we landed there we'd die.

That there was a core breach in the engine room, whatever that meant, and that the *Magellan* was this close to blowing up.

That ecoterrorists had hacked into the *Magellan*'s computer systems and sent us off in another direction so that we couldn't ruin another planet.

No, wait, it was wildcat colonists-turned-pirates who hacked in, and they were planning to steal our colony supplies because their own were running low.

No, wait, it was mutinous crew members who were going to steal our supplies and leave us stranded on the planet.

No, wait, it wasn't thieving crew, wildcat pirates or ecoterrorists, it was just some idiot programmer who messed up the code, and now we don't know where we are.

No, wait, nothing's wrong, this is just the standard operating procedure. There's not a thing wrong, now stop bothering the crew and let us *work*, damn it.

I want to be clear about something: We knew most of this was crap and nonsense. But what was underneath all the crap and nonsense was just as important: Confusion and unease had spread through the crew of the *Magellan*, and from them, to us. It moved fast. It told any number of lies—not to lie but to try to make sense of something. Something that happened. Something that shouldn't have happened.

Through all of this, nothing from Mom or Dad, or Gretchen's dad, or any of the colony council, all the members of which had suddenly found themselves called into a meeting.

The common room, previously deserted after the new world celebrations, began to fill up again. This time people weren't celebrating. They looked confused, and concerned and tense, and some of them were beginning to look angry.

"This isn't going to turn out well," Gretchen said to me when we reunited.

"How are you doing?" I said.

She shrugged. "Something's happening, that's for sure. Everyone's on edge. It's putting *me* on edge."

"Don't go crazy on me," I said. "Then there won't be anyone to hold me back when I lose it."

"Oh, well, for *your* sake then," Gretchen said, and rolled her eyes dramatically. "Well. At least now I'm not having to fight off Magdy."

"I like how you can see the bright side of any situation," I said.

"Thanks," she said. "How are you?"

"Honestly?" I asked. She nodded. "Scared as hell."

"Thank God," she said. "It's not only me." She held up her thumb and finger and marked the tiny space between them. "For the last half hour I've been this close to peeing myself."

I took a step back. Gretchen laughed.

The ship's intercom kicked on. "This is Captain Zane," a man's voice said. "This is a general message for passengers and crew. All crew will assemble in their respective department conference rooms in ten minutes, 2330 ship time. All passengers will assemble in the passenger common area in ten minutes, 2330 ship time. Passengers, this is a mandatory assembly. You will be addressed by your colony leaders." The intercom went dead.

"Come on," I said to Gretchen, and pointed to the platform where, earlier in the evening, she and I counted down the seconds until we were at our new world. "We should get a good place."

"It's going to get crowded in here," she said.

I pointed to Hickory and Dickory. "They'll be with us. You know how everyone gives them all the space they want." Gretchen looked up at the two of them, and I realized that she wasn't terribly fond of them either.

Minutes later the council came streaming in from one of the

common area side doors and made their way to the platform. Gretchen and I stood in the front, Hickory and Dickory behind us, and at least five feet on every side. Alien bodyguards create their own buffer zone.

A whisper in my ear. "Hey," Enzo said.

I looked over to him and smiled. "I wondered if you were going to be here," I said.

"It's an all-colonist meeting," he said.

"Not here, in general," I said. "*Here.*"

"Oh," Enzo said. "I took a chance that your bodyguards wouldn't stab me."

"I'm glad you did," I said. I took his hand.

On the platform, John Perry, the colony leader, my dad, came forward and picked up the microphone that still lay there from earlier in the evening. His eyes met mine as he reached down to pick it up.

Here's the thing to know about my dad. He's smart, he's good at what he does, and almost all the time, his eyes look like he's about to start laughing. He finds most things funny. He *makes* most things funny.

When he looked at me as he picked up the microphone, his eyes were dark, and heavy, and as serious as I had ever seen them. When I saw them I was reminded, no matter how young he looked, how old he really was. For as much as he could make light of things, he was a man who had seen trouble more than once in his life.

And he was seeing it again. Now, with us. *For* all of us.

Everyone else would know it as soon as he opened his mouth to tell them, but right then was when I knew—when I saw the truth of our situation.

We were lost.

PART I

ONE

The flying saucer landed on our front yard and a little green man got out of it.

It was the flying saucer that got my attention. Green men aren't actually unheard of where I come from. All the Colonial Defense Forces were green; it's part of the genetic engineering they do on them to help them fight better. Chlorophyll in the skin gives them the extra energy they need for truly first-class alien stomping.

We didn't get many Colonial Defense Force soldiers on Huckleberry, the colony I lived on; it was an established colony and we hadn't been seriously attacked in a couple of decades. But the Colonial Union goes out of its way to let every colonist know all about the CDF, and I knew more about them than most.

But the flying saucer, well. *That's* novel. New Goa is a farming community. Tractors and harvesters and animal-drawn wagons, and wheeled public buses when we wanted to live life on the edge and visit the provincial capital. An actual flying transport was a rare thing indeed. Having one small enough for a single passenger land on our lawn was definitely not an everyday occurrence.

"Would you like Dickory and me to go out and meet him?" asked Hickory. We watched from inside the house as the green man pulled himself out of the transport.

I looked over at Hickory. "Do you think he's an actual threat? I think if he wanted to attack us, he could have just dropped a rock on the house while he was flying over it."

"I am always for prudence," Hickory said. The unsaid portion of that sentence was *when you are involved.* Hickory is very sweet, and paranoid.

"Let's try the first line of defense instead," I said, and walked over to the screen door. Babar the mutt was standing at it, his front paws up on the door, cursing the genetic fate that left him without opposable thumbs or the brains to pull the door instead of pushing on it. I opened the door for him; he took off like a furry heat-seeking slobber missile. To the green man's credit, he took a knee and greeted Babar like an old friend, and was generously coated in dog drool for his pains.

"Good thing he's not soluble," I said to Hickory.

"Babar is not a very good watchdog," Hickory said, as it watched the green man play with my dog.

"No, he's really not," I agreed. "But if you ever need something really *moistened,* he's got you covered."

"I will remember that for future reference," Hickory said, in that noncommittal way designed for dealing with my sarcasm.

"Do that," I said, and opened the door again. "And stay in here for now, please."

"As you say, Zoë," Hickory said.

"Thanks," I said, and walked out to the porch.

By this time the green man had gotten to the porch steps, Babar bouncing behind him. "I like your dog," he said to me.

"I see that," I said. "The dog's only so-so about you."

"How can you tell?" he asked.

"You're not *completely* bathed in saliva," I said.

He laughed. "I'll try harder next time," he said.

"Remember to bring a towel," I said.

The green man motioned to the house. "This is Major Perry's house?"

"I hope so," I said. "All his stuff is here."

This earned me about a two-second pause.

Yes, as it happens, I *am* a sarcastic little thing. Thanks for asking. It comes from living with my dad all these years. He considers himself quite the wit; I don't know how I feel about *that* one, personally, but I will say that it's made me pretty forward when it comes to comebacks and quips. Give me a soft lob, I'll be happy to spike it. I think it's endearing and charming; so does Dad. We may be in the minority with that opinion. If nothing else it's interesting to see how other people react to it. Some people think it's cute. Others not so much.

I think my green friend fell into the "not so much" camp, because his response was to change the subject. "I'm sorry," he said. "I don't think I know who you are."

"I'm Zoë," I said. "Major Perry's daughter. Lieutenant Sagan's, too."

"Oh, right," he said. "I'm sorry. I pictured you as younger."

"I used to be," I said.

"I should have known you were his daughter," he said. "You look like him in the eyes."

Fight the urge, the polite part of my brain said. *Fight it. Just let it go.*

"Thank you," I said. "I'm adopted."

My green friend stood there for a minute, doing that thing people do when they've just stepped in it: freezing and putting a smile on their face while their brain strips its gears trying to figure how it's going to extract itself out of *this* faux pas. If I leaned in, I could probably hear his frontal lobes go *click click click click*, trying to reset.

See, now, that was just mean, said the polite part of my brain.

But come *on*. If the guy was calling Dad "Major Perry," then he probably knew when Dad was discharged from service, which was eight years ago. CDF soldiers can't make babies; that's part of their combat-effective genetic engineering, don't you know—no accidental kids—so his earliest opportunity to spawn would have been when they put him in a new, regular body at the end of his service term. And then there's the whole "nine months gestation" thing. I might have been a little small for my age when I was fifteen, but I assure you, I didn't look *seven*.

Honestly, I think there's a limit to how bad I should feel in a situation like that. Grown men should be able to handle a little basic math.

Still, there's only so long you can leave someone on the hook. "You called Dad 'Major Perry,' " I said. "Did you know him from the service?"

"I did," he said, and seemed happy that the conversation was moving forward again. "It's been a while, though. I wonder if I'll recognize him."

"I imagine he looks the same," I said. "Maybe a different skin tone."

He chuckled at that. "I suppose that's true," he said. "Being green would make it a little more difficult to blend in."

"I don't think he would ever quite blend in here," I said, and then immediately realized all the very many ways that statement could be misinterpreted.

And of course, my visitor wasted no time doing just that. "Does he not blend?" he asked, and then bent down to pat Babar.

"That's not what I meant," I said. "Most of the people here at Huckleberry are from India, back on Earth, or were born here from people who came from India. It's a different culture than the one he grew up in, that's all."

"I understand," the green man said. "And I'm sure he gets along very well with the people here. Major Perry is like that. I'm sure that's why he has the job he has here." My dad's job was as an ombudsman, someone who helps people cut through government bureaucracy. "I guess I'm just curious if he likes it here."

"What do you mean?" I asked.

"I was just wondering how he's been enjoying his retirement from the universe, is all," he said, and looked back up at me.

In the back of my brain something went *ping*. I was suddenly aware that our nice and casual conversation had somehow become something less casual. Our green visitor wasn't just here for a social call.

"I think he likes it fine," I said, and kept from saying anything else. "Why?"

"Just curious," he said, petting Babar again. I fought off the urge to call my dog over. "Not everyone makes the jump from military life to civilian life perfectly." He looked around. "This looks like a pretty sedate life. It's a pretty big switch."

"I think he likes it just fine," I repeated, putting enough emphasis on the words that unless my green visitor was an absolute toad, he'd know to move on.

"Good," he said. "What about you? How do *you* like it here?"

I opened my mouth to respond, and then shut it just as quickly. Because, well. *There* was a question.

The idea of living on a human colony is more exciting than the reality. Some folks new to the concept think that people out in the colonies go from planet to planet all the time, maybe living on one planet, working on another and then having vacations on a third: the pleasure planet of Vacationaria, maybe. The reality is, sadly, far more boring. Most colonists live their whole lives on their home planet, and never get out to see the rest of the universe.

It's not *impossible* to go from planet to planet, but there's usually a reason for it: You're a member of the crew on a trade ship, hauling fruit and wicker baskets between the stars, or you get a job with the Colonial Union itself and start a glorious career as an interstellar bureaucrat. If you're an athlete, there's the Colonial Olympiad every four years. And occasionally a famous musician or actor will do a grand tour of the colonies.

But mostly, you're born on a planet, you live on a planet, you die on a planet, and your ghost hangs around and annoys your descendants on that planet. I don't suppose there's really anything bad about that—I mean, most people don't actually go more than a couple dozen kilometers from their homes most of the time in day-to-day life, do they? And people hardly see most of their own planet when they do decide to wander off. If you've never seen the sights on your *own* planet, I don't know how much you can really complain about not seeing a whole *other* planet.

But it helps to be on an *interesting* planet.

In case this ever gets back to Huckleberry: I love Huckleberry, really I do. And I love New Goa, the little town where we lived. When you're a kid, a rural, agriculturally-based colony town is a lot of fun to grow up in. It's life on a farm, with goats and chickens and fields of wheat and sorghum, harvest celebrations and winter festivals. There's not an eight- or nine-year-old kid who's been invented who doesn't find all of that unspeakably fun. But then you become a teenager and you start thinking about everything you might possibly want to *do* with your life, and you look at the options available to you. And then all farms, goats and chickens—and all the same people you've known all your life and will know all your life—begin to look a little less than optimal for a total life experience. It's all still the same, of course. That's the point. It's *you* who's changed.

I know this bit of teenage angst wouldn't make me any different than any other small-town teenager who has ever existed throughout the history of the known universe. But when even the "big city" of a colony—the district capital of Missouri City—holds all the mystery and romance of watching compost, it's not unreasonable to hope for something else.

I'm not saying that there's anything *wrong* with Missouri City (there's nothing wrong with compost, either; you actually need it). Maybe it's better to say it's the sort of place you come back *to*, once you've gone out and had your time in the big city, or the big bad universe. One of the things I know about Mom is that she loved it on Huckleberry. But before she was here, she was a Special Forces soldier. She doesn't talk too much about all the things she's seen and done, but from personal experience I know a little bit about it. I can't imagine a whole life of it. I think she'd say that she'd seen enough of the universe.

I've seen some of the universe, too, before we came to Huckleberry. But unlike Jane—unlike Mom—I don't think I'm ready to say Huckleberry's all I want out of a life.

But I wasn't sure I wanted to say any of *that* to this green guy, who I had become suddenly rather suspicious of. Green men falling from the sky, asking after the psychological states of various family members including oneself, are enough to make a girl paranoid about what's going on. Especially when, as I suddenly realized, I didn't actually get the guy's *name*. He'd gotten this far into my family life without actually saying who he was.

Maybe this was just something he'd innocently managed to overlook—this wasn't a formal interview, after all—but enough bells were ringing in my head that I decided that my green friend had had enough free information for one day.

Green man was looking at me intently, waiting for me to respond. I gave him my best noncommittal shrug. I was fifteen years old. It's a quality age for shrugging.

He backed off a bit. "I don't suppose your dad is home," he said.

"Not yet," I said. I checked my PDA and showed it to him. "His workday finished up a few minutes ago. He and Mom are probably walking home."

"Okay. And your mom is constable here, right?"

"Right," I said. Jane Sagan, frontier law woman. Minus the frontier. It fit her. "Did you know Mom, too?" I asked. Special Forces was an entirely different thing from regular infantry.

"Just by reputation," he said, and again there was that studied casual thing.

Folks, a little tip: Nothing is more transparent than you try for casual and miss. My green friend was missing it by a klick, and I got tired of feeling lightly groped for information.

"I think I'll go for a walk," I said. "Mom and Dad are probably right down the road. I'll let them know you're here."

"I'll go with you," Green man offered.

"That's all right," I said, and motioned him onto the porch, and to our porch swing. "You've been traveling. Have a seat and relax."

"All right," he said. "If you're comfortable having me here while you're gone." I think that was meant as a joke.

I smiled at him. "I think it'll be fine," I said. "You'll have company."

"You're leaving me the dog," he said. He sat.

"Even better," I said. "I'm leaving you two of my friends." This is when I called into the house for Hickory and Dickory, and then stood away from the door and watched my visitor, so I wouldn't miss his expression when the two of them came out.

He didn't *quite* wet his pants.

Which was an accomplishment, all things considered. Obin—which is what Hickory and Dickory are—don't look *exactly* like a cross between a spider and a giraffe, but they're close enough to make some part of the human brain fire up the *drop ballast* alert. You get used to them after a bit. But the point is it takes a while.

"This is Hickory," I said, pointing to the one at the left of me, and then pointed to the one at my right. "And this is Dickory. They're Obin."

"Yes, I know," my visitor said, with the sort of tone you'd expect from a very small animal trying to pretend that being cornered by a pair of very large predators was not that big of a deal. "Uh. So. *These* are your friends."

"*Best* friends," I said, with what I felt was just the right amount of brainless gush. "And they *love* to entertain visitors. They'll be happy to keep you company while I go look for my parents. Isn't that right?" I said to Hickory and Dickory.

"Yes," they said, together. Hickory and Dickory are fairly monotone to begin with; having them be monotone in stereo offers an additional—and delightful!—creepy effect.

"Please say hello to our guest," I said.

"Hello," they said, again in stereo.

"Uh," said Green man. "Hi."

"Great, everybody's friends," I said, and stepped off the porch. Babar left our green friend to follow me. "I'm off, then."

"You *sure* you don't want me to come along?" Green man said. "I don't mind."

"No, please," I said. "I don't want you to feel like you have to get up for anything." My eyes sort of casually flicked over at Hickory and Dickory, as if to imply it would be a shame if they had to make steaks out of him.

"Great," he said, and settled onto the swing. I think he got the hint. See, *that's* how you do studied casual.

"Great," I said. Babar and I headed off down the road to find my folks.

TWO I climbed out onto the roof through my bedroom window and looked back at Hickory. "Hand me those binoculars," I said. It did—

(Obin: "it," not "he" or "she." Because they're hermaphrodites. That means male and female sex organs. Go ahead and have your giggle. I'll wait. Okay, done? Good.)

—and then climbed out the window with me. Since you've probably never seen it I'll have you know it's a pretty impressive sight to watch an Obin unfold itself to get through a window. Very graceful, with no real analogue to any human movement you might want to describe. The universe, it has *aliens* in it. And they *are*.

Hickory was on the roof with me; Dickory was outside the house, more or less spotting me in case I should trip or feel suddenly despondent, and then fall or leap off the roof. This is their standard practice when I climb out my window: one with me, one on the ground. And they're *obvious* about it; when I was a little kid Mom or Dad would see Dickory blow out the door and hang around just below the roof, and then yell up the stairs for me to get back into my room. Having paranoid alien pals has a downside.

For the record: I've never fallen off the roof.

Well, *once.* When I was ten. But there were extenuating circumstances. That doesn't count.

Anyway, I didn't have to worry about either John or Jane telling me to get back into the house this time. They stopped doing that when I became a teenager. Besides, they were the reason I was up on the roof in the first place.

"There they are," I said, and pointed for Hickory's benefit. Mom and Dad and my green friend were standing in the middle of our sorghum field, a few hundred meters out. I raised my binoculars and they went from being hash marks to being actual people. Green man had his back to me, but he was saying something, because both Jane and John were looking at him intently. There was a rustle at Jane's feet, and then Babar popped up his head. Mom reached down to scratch him.

"I wonder what he's talking to them about," I said.

"They're too far away," Hickory said. I turned to it to make a comment along the lines of *no kidding, genius.* Then I saw the consciousness collar around its neck and was reminded that in addition to providing Hickory and Dickory with sentience— with their idea of who they were—their collars also gave them expanded senses, which were mostly devoted to keeping me out of trouble.

I was also reminded that their consciousness collars were why they were here in the first place. My father—my biological father—created them for the Obin. I was also reminded that they were why *I* was here, too. Still here, I mean. Alive.

But I didn't go down that road of thought.

"I thought those things were useful," I said, pointing to the collar.

Hickory lightly touched the collar. "The collars do many things," it said. "Enabling us to hear a conversation hundreds of meters away, and in the middle of a grain field, is not one of them."

"So you're useless," I said.

Hickory nodded its head. "As you say," it said, in its non-committal way.

"It's no fun mocking you," I said.

"I'm sorry," Hickory said.

And the thing of it was, Hickory really *was* sorry. It's not easy being a funny, sarcastic thing when most of who you *were* depended on a machine you wore around your neck. Generating one's own prosthetic identity takes more concentration than you might expect. Managing a well-balanced sense of sarcasm above and beyond that is a little much to ask for.

I reached over and gave Hickory a hug. It was a funny thing. Hickory and Dickory were here for me; to know me, to learn from me, to protect me, and if need be to die for me. And here I was, feeling protective of *them*, and feeling a little sad for them, too. My father—my biological father—gave them consciousness, something the Obin had lacked and had been searching for, for the entire history of their species.

But he didn't make consciousness *easy* for them.

Hickory accepted my hug and tentatively touched my head; it can be shy when I'm suddenly demonstrative. I took care not to lay it on too thick with the Obin. If I get too emotional it can mess up their consciousness. They're sensitive to when I get overwrought. So I backed up and then looked toward my parents again with the binoculars. Now John was saying something, with one of his patented half-cocked smiles. His smile erased when our visitor started talking again.

"I wonder who he is," I said.

"He is General Samuel Rybicki," Hickory said.

This got another glance back from me. "How do you know that?" I said.

"It is our business to know about who visits you and your family," Hickory said, and touched its collar again. "We queried him the moment he landed. Information about him is in our database. He is a liaison between your Civil Defense Forces and your Department of Colonization. He coordinates the protection of your new colonies."

"Huckleberry isn't a new colony," I said. It wasn't; it had been colonized for fifty or sixty years by the time we arrived. More than enough time to flatten out all the scary bumps new colonies face, and for the human population to become too big for invaders to scrape off the planet. Hopefully. "What do you think he wants from my parents?" I asked.

"We don't know," Hickory said.

"He didn't say anything to you while he was waiting for John and Jane to show up?" I said.

"No," Hickory said. "He kept to himself."

"Well, sure," I said. "Probably because you scared the crap out of him."

"He left no feces," Hickory said.

I snorted. "I sometimes question your alleged lack of humor," I said. "I meant he was too intimidated by you to say anything."

"We assumed that was why you had us stay with him," Hickory said.

"Well, yeah," I said. "But if I knew he was a general, maybe I wouldn't have given him such a hard time." I pointed to my parents. "I don't want them getting any grief because I thought it would be fun to mess with this guy's head."

"I think someone of his rank would not come all this way to be deterred by you," Hickory said.

A list of snappy retorts popped in my head, begging to be used. I ignored them all. "You think he's here on some serious mission?" I asked.

"He is a general," Hickory said. "And he is here."

I looked back through the binoculars again. General Rybicki—as I now knew him—had turned just a bit, and I could see his face a little more clearly. He was talking to Jane, but then turned a bit to say something to Dad. I lingered on Mom for a minute. Her face was locked up tight; whatever was going on, she wasn't very happy about it.

Mom turned her head a bit and suddenly she was looking directly at me, like she knew I was watching her.

"How does she *do* that?" I said. When Jane was Special Forces, she had a body that was even more genetically modified than the ones regular soldiers got. But like Dad, when she left the service, she got put into a normal human body. She's not superhuman anymore. She's just scary observant. Which is close to the same thing. I didn't get away with much of *anything* growing up.

Her attention turned back to General Rybicki, who was addressing her again. I looked up at Hickory. "What I want to know is why they're talking in the sorghum field," I said.

"General Rybicki asked your parents if there was someplace they could speak in private," Hickory said. "He indicated in particular that he wanted to speak away from Dickory and me."

"Were you recording when you were with him?" I asked. Hickory and Dickory had recording devices in their collars that recorded sounds, images and emotional data. Those recordings were sent back to other Obin, so they could experience what it's like to have quality time with me. Odd? Yes. Intrusive? Sometimes, but not usually. Unless I start *thinking* about it, and then I focus on the fact that, why yes, an entire alien race got to experience my puberty through the eyes of Hickory and Dickory. There's nothing like sharing menarche with a billion hermaphrodites. I think it was *everyone's* first time.

"We were not recording with him," Hickory said.

"Okay, good," I said.

"I'm recording now," Hickory said.

"Oh. Well, I'm not sure you should be," I said, waving out toward my parents. "I don't want *them* getting in trouble."

"This is allowed under our treaty with your government," Hickory said. "We're allowed to record all you allow us to record, and to report everything that we experience. My government knew that General Rybicki had visited the moment Dickory and I sent our data query. If General Rybicki wanted his visit to remain secret, he should have met your parents elsewhere."

I chose not to dwell on the fact that significant portions of my life were subject to treaty negotiation. "I don't think he knew you were here," I said. "He seemed surprised when I sicced you on him."

"His ignorance of us or of the Obin treaty with the Colonial Union is not our problem," Hickory said.

"I guess not," I said, a little out of sorts.

"Would you like me to stop recording?" Hickory asked. I could hear the tremble on the edge of its voice. If I wasn't careful about how I showed my annoyance I could send Hickory into an emotional cascade. Then it'd have what amounted to a temporary nervous breakdown right there on the roof. That'd be no good. He could fall off and snap his snaky little neck.

"It's fine," I said, and I tried to sound more conciliatory than I really felt. "It's too late now anyway." Hickory visibly relaxed; I held in a sigh and gazed down at my shoes.

"They're coming back to the house," Hickory said, and motioned toward my parents. I followed its hand; my parents and General Rybicki were indeed heading back our way. I thought about going back into the house but then I saw Mom look directly at me, again. Yup, she'd seen me earlier. The chances were pretty good she knew we had been up there all that time.

Dad didn't look up the entire walk back. He was already lost in thought. When that happened it was like the world collapsing in around him; he didn't see anything else until he was done dealing with what he was dealing with. I suspected I wouldn't see much of him tonight.

As they cleared the sorghum field, General Rybicki stopped and shook Dad's hand; Mom kept herself out of handshaking distance. Then he headed back toward his floater. Babar, who had followed the three of them into the field, broke off toward the general to get in one last petting. He got it after the general got to the floater, then padded back to the house. The floater opened its door to let the general in.

The general stopped, looked directly at me, and waved. Before I could think what I was doing, I waved right back.

"*That* was smart," I said to myself. The floater, General Rybicki inside, winged off, taking him back where he came from.

What do you want with us, General? I thought, and surprised myself by thinking "us." But it only made sense. Whatever he wanted with my parents, I was part of it too.

THREE

"How do you like it here?" Jane asked me, as we were washing the dishes after dinner. "On Huckleberry, I mean."

"This is not the first time I've been asked that today," I said, taking the plate she handed me and drying it.

This got a slightly raised eyebrow from Mom. "General Rybicki asked you the question," she said.

"Yup," I said.

"And what did you tell him?" Jane asked.

"I told him I liked it just fine," I said. I put the dried plate into the cupboard and waited for the next one.

Jane was holding on to it. "But do you?" she asked.

I sighed, only slightly dramatically. "Okay, I give up," I said. "What's going on? Both you and Dad were like zombies at dinner tonight. I know you missed it, because you were wrapped up in your own heads, but I spent most of dinner trying to get either of you to talk more than a grunt. Babar was a better conversationalist than either of you."

"I'm sorry, Zoë," Jane said.

"You're forgiven," I said. "But I still want to know what's going *on*." I motioned to Jane's hand, to remind her I was still waiting on that plate.

She handed it over. "General Rybicki has asked your father and me to be the leaders of a new colony."

It was my turn to hold on to the plate. "A new colony."

"Yes," Jane said.

"As in, 'on another planet' new colony," I said.

"Yes," said Jane.

"Wow," I said.

"Yes," Jane said. She knew how to get mileage out of a single word.

"Why did he ask you?" I asked, and resumed drying. "No offense, Mom. But you're a constable in a tiny little village. And Dad's an ombudsman. It's kind of a leap."

"None taken," Jane said. "We had the same question. General Rybicki said that the military experience we had would cross over. John was a major and I was a lieutenant. And whatever other experience we need Rybicki believes we can pick up quickly, before we set foot on the new colony. As for why us, it's because this isn't a normal colony. The colonists aren't from Earth, they're from ten of the oldest planets in the Colonial Union. A colony of colonists. The first of its kind."

"And none of the planets contributing colonists want another planet to have a leadership role," I ventured.

Jane smiled. "That's right," she said. "We're the compromise candidates. The least objectionable solution."

"Got it," I said. "It's nice to be sort of wanted." We continued washing dishes in silence for a few minutes.

"You didn't answer my question," Jane said, eventually. "Do you like it here? Do you want to stay on Huckleberry?"

"I get a vote?" I asked.

"Of course you do," Jane said. "If we take this, it would mean leaving Huckleberry for at least a few standard years while we got the colony up and running. But realistically it would mean leaving here for good. It would mean *all* of us leaving here for good."

"*If*," I said, a little surprised. "You didn't say yes."

"It's not the sort of decision you make in the middle of a sorghum field," Jane said, and looked at me directly. "It's not something we can just say yes to. It's a complicated decision. We've been looking over the information all afternoon, seeing what the Colonial Union's plans are for the colony. And then we have to think about our lives here. Mine, John's and yours."

I grinned. "I have a life here?" I asked. This was meant as a joke.

Jane squashed it. "Be serious, Zoë," she said. The grin left my face. "We've been here for half of your life now. You have friends. You know this place. You have a future here, if you want it. You *can* have a life here. It's not something to be lightly tossed aside." She plunged her hands into the sink, searching under the soap suds for another dish.

I looked at Jane; there was something in her voice. This wasn't just about me. "*You* have a life here," I said.

"I do," Jane said. "I like it here. I like our neighbors and our friends. I like being the constable. Our life here suits me." She handed me the casserole dish she'd just cleaned. "Before we came here I spent all my life in the Special Forces. On ships. This is the first world I've actually lived *on*. It's important to me."

"Then why is this a question?" I said. "If you don't want to go, then we shouldn't do it."

"I didn't say I *wouldn't* go," Jane said. "I said I have a life here. It's not the same thing. There are good reasons to do it. And it's not just my decision to make."

I dried and put away the casserole dish. "What does Dad want?" I asked.

"He hasn't told me yet," Mom said.

"You know what *that* means," I said. "Dad's not subtle when there's something he doesn't want to do. If he's taking his time to think about it, he probably wants to do it."

"I know," Mom said. She was rinsing off the flatware. "He's trying to find a way to tell me what he wants. It might help him if he knew what *we* wanted first."

"Okay," I said.

"This is why I asked you if you liked it here," Jane said, again.

I thought about it as I dried the kitchen counter. "I like it here," I said, finally. "But I don't know if I want to have a *life* here."

"Why not?" Jane asked.

"There's not much *here* here, is there?" I said. I waved toward the general direction of New Goa. "The selection of life choices here is limited. There's farmer, farmer, store owner, and farmer. Maybe a government position like you and Dad."

"If we go to this new colony your choices are going to be the same," Jane said. "First wave colonist life isn't very romantic, Zoë. The focus is on survival, and preparing the new colony for the second wave of colonists. That means farmers and laborers. Outside of a few specialized roles that will already be filled, there's not much call for anything else."

"Yes, but at least it would be somewhere *new*," I said. "There we'd be building a new world. Here we're just maintaining an old one. Be honest, Mom. It's kind of slow around these parts. A big day for you is when someone gets into a fistfight. The highlight of Dad's day is settling a dispute over a goat."

"There are worse things," Jane said.

"I'm not asking for open warfare," I said. Another joke.

And once again, another stomping from Mom. "It'll be a brand-new colony world," she said. "They're the ones most at risk for attack, because they have the fewest people and the least amount of defense from the CDF. You know that as well as anyone."

I blinked, actually surprised. I *did* know it as well as anyone. When I was very young—before I was adopted by Jane and John—the planet I lived on (or above, since I was on a space station) was attacked. Omagh. Jane almost never brought it up, because she knew what it did to me to think about it. "You think that's what's going to happen here?" I asked.

Jane must have sensed what was going on in my head. "No, I don't," she said. "This is an unusual colony. It's a test colony in some ways. There will be political pressure for this colony to succeed. That means more and better defenses, among other things. I think we'll be better defended than most colonies starting out."

"That's good to know," I said.

"But an attack could still happen," Jane said. "John and I fought together at Coral. It was one of the first planets humans settled, and it was *still* attacked. No colony is totally safe. There are other dangers, too. Colonies can get wiped out by local viruses or predators. Bad weather can kill crops. The colonists themselves could be unprepared. Colonizing—*real* colonizing, not what we're doing here on Huckleberry—is hard, constant work. Some of the colonists could fail at it and take the rest of the colony with them. There could be bad leaders making bad decisions."

"I don't think we'd have to worry about that last one," I said. I was trying to lighten the mood.

Jane didn't take the bait. "I'm telling you this isn't without risk," she said. "It's there. A lot of it. And if we do this, we go in with our eyes open to that risk."

This was Mom all over. Her sense of humor wasn't as deprived as Hickory's and Dickory's—I *can* actually make her laugh. But it doesn't stop her from being one of the most serious people I've ever met in my life. When she wants to get your attention about something she thinks is important, she's going to get it.

It's a good quality to have, but right at the moment it was making me seriously uncomfortable. That was her plan, no doubt.

"Mom, I know," I said. "I know it has risks. I know that a lot of things could go wrong. I know it wouldn't be easy." I waited.

"But," Jane said, giving me the prompt she knew I was waiting for.

"But if you and Dad were leading it, I think it'd be worth the risk," I said. "Because I trust you. You wouldn't take the job if you didn't think you could handle it. And I know you wouldn't put me at risk unnecessarily. If you two decided to do it, I would want to go. I would definitely want to go."

I was suddenly aware that while I was speaking, my hand had drifted to my chest, and was lightly touching the small pendant there: a jade elephant, given to me by Jane. I moved my hand from it, a little embarrassed.

"And no matter what, starting a new colony wouldn't be *boring*," I said, to finish up, a little lamely.

Mom smiled, unplugged the sink and dried her hands. Then she took a step over to me and kissed the top of my head; I was short enough, and she was tall enough, that it was a natural thing for her. "I'll let your dad stew on it for a few more hours," she said. "And then I'll let him know where we stand."

"Thanks, Mom," I said.

"And sorry about dinner," she said. "Your dad gets wrapped up in himself sometimes, and I get wrapped up in noticing he's wrapped up in himself."

"I know," I said. "You should just smack him and tell him to snap out of it."

"I'll put that on the list for future reference," Jane said. She gave me another quick peck and then stepped away. "Now go do your homework. We haven't left the planet yet." She walked out of the kitchen.

FOUR

Let me tell you about that jade elephant.

My mother's name—my biological mother's name—was Cheryl Boutin. She died when I was five; she was hiking with a friend and she fell. My memories of her are what you'd expect them to be: hazy fragments from a five-year-old mind, supported by a precious few pictures and videos. They weren't that much better when I was younger. Five is a bad age to lose a mother, and to hope to remember her for who she was.

One thing I had from her was a stuffed version of Babar the elephant that my mother gave to me on my fourth birthday. I was sick that day, and had to stay in bed all day long. This did not make me happy, and I let everyone know it, because that was the kind of four-year-old I was. My mother surprised me with the Babar doll, and then we cuddled up together and she read Babar's stories to me until I fell asleep, lying across her. It's my strongest memory of her, even now; not so much how she looked, but the low and warm sound of her voice, and the softness of her belly as I lay against her and drifted off, her stroking my head. The sensation of my mother, and the feeling of love and comfort from her.

I miss her. Still do. Even now. Even right now.

After my mother died I couldn't go anywhere without

Babar. He was my connection to her, my connection to that love and comfort I didn't have anymore. Being away from Babar meant being away from what I had left of her. I was five years old. This was my way of handling my loss. It kept me from falling into myself, I think. Five is a bad age to lose your mother, like I said; I think it could be a good age to lose yourself, if you're not careful.

Shortly after my mother's funeral, my father and I left Phoenix, where I was born, and moved to Covell, a space station orbiting above a planet called Omagh, where he did research. Occasionally his job had him leave Covell on business trips. When that happened I stayed with my friend Kay Greene and her parents. One time my father was leaving on a trip; he was running late and forgot to pack Babar for me. When I figured this out (it didn't take long), I started to cry and panic. To placate me, and because he *did* love me, you know, he promised to bring me a Celeste doll when he returned from his trip. He asked me to be brave until then. I said I would, and he kissed me and told me to go play with Kay. I did.

While he was away, we were attacked. It would be a very long time before I would see my father again. He remembered his promise, and brought me a Celeste. It was the first thing he did when I saw him.

I still have her. But I don't have Babar.

In time, I became an orphan. I was adopted by John and Jane, who I call "Dad" and "Mom," but not "Father" and "Mother," because those I keep for Charles and Cheryl Boutin, my first parents. John and Jane understand this well enough. They don't mind that I make the distinction.

Before we moved to Huckleberry—just before—Jane and I went to a mall in Phoenix City, the capital city of Phoenix. We were on our way to get ice cream; when we passed a toy store I ran in to play hide-and-seek with Jane. This went smashingly until I went down an aisle with stuffed animals in it, and came face-to-face with Babar. Not *my* Babar, of course. But one close enough to him that all I could do was stop and stare.

Jane came up behind me, which meant she couldn't see my face. "Look," she said. "It's Babar. Would you like one to go with your Celeste doll?" She reached over and picked one out of the bin.

I screamed and slapped it out of her hand and ran out of the toy store. Jane caught up with me and held me while I sobbed, cradling me against her shoulder, stroking my head like my mother did when she read the Babar stories to me on my birthday. I cried myself out and then when I was done, I told her about the Babar my mother had given me.

Jane understood why I didn't want another Babar. It wasn't right to have a new one. It wouldn't be right to put something on top of those memories of her. To pretend that another Babar could replace the one she gave me. It wasn't the toy. It was everything *about* the toy.

I asked Jane not to tell John about Babar or what had just happened. I was feeling out of sorts enough having just gone to pieces in front of my new mom. I didn't want to drag my new dad into it too. She promised. And then she gave me a hug and we went to get ice cream, and I just about made myself throw up eating an entire banana split. Which to my eight-year-old mind was a *good* thing. Truly, an eventful day all around.

A week later Jane and I were standing on the observation deck of the CDFS *Amerigo Vespucci*, staring down at the blue and green world named Huckleberry, where we would live the rest of our lives, or so we thought. John had just left us, to take care of some last-minute business before we took our shuttle trip down to Missouri City, from where we would go to New Goa, our new home. Jane and I were holding hands and pointing out surface features to each other, trying to see if we could see Missouri City from geostationary orbit. We couldn't. But we made good guesses.

"I have something for you," Jane said to me, after we decided where Missouri City would be, or *ought* to be, anyway. "Something I wanted to give you before we landed on Huckleberry."

"I hope it's a puppy," I said. I'd been hinting in that direction for a couple of weeks.

Jane laughed. "No puppies!" she said. "At least not until we're actually settled in. Okay?"

"Oh, all right," I said, disappointed.

"No, it's this," Jane said. She reached into her pocket to pull out a silver chain with something that was a pale green at the end.

I took the chain and looked at the pendant. "It's an elephant," I said.

"It is," Jane said. She knelt down so that she and I were face-to-face. "I bought it on Phoenix just before we left. I saw it in a shop and it made me think of you."

"Because of Babar," I said.

"Yes," Jane said. "But for other reasons, too. Most of the people who live on Huckleberry are from a country on Earth called India, and many of them are Hindu, which is a religion. They have a god called Ganesh, who has the head of an elephant. Ganesh is their god of intelligence, and I think you're pretty smart. He's also the god of beginnings, which makes sense, too."

"Because we're starting our lives here," I said.

"Right," Jane said. She took the pendant and necklace from me and put the silver chain around my neck, fastening it in the back. "There's also the saying that 'an elephant never forgets.' Have you heard it?" I nodded. "John and I are proud to be your parents, Zoë. We're happy you're part of our life now, and will help us make our life to come. But I know neither of us would want you ever to forget your mother and father."

She drew back and then touched the pendant, gently. "This

is to remind you how much *we* love you," Jane said. "But I hope it will also remind you how much your mother and father loved you, too. You're loved by two sets of parents, Zoë. Don't forget about the first because you're with us now."

"I won't," I said. "I promise."

"The last reason I wanted to give you this was to continue the tradition," Jane said. "Your mother and your father each gave you an elephant. I wanted to give you one, too. I hope you like it."

"I love it," I said, and then launched myself into Jane. She caught me and hugged me. We hugged for a while, and I cried a little bit too. Because I was eight years old, and I could do that.

I eventually unhugged myself from Jane and looked at the pendant again. "What is this made of?" I asked.

"It's jade," Jane said.

"Does it mean anything?" I asked.

"Well," Jane said, "I suppose it means I think jade is pretty."

"Did Dad get me an elephant, too?" I asked. Eight-year-olds can switch into acquisition mode pretty quickly.

"I don't know," Jane said. "I haven't talked to him about it, because you asked me not to. I don't think he knows about the elephants."

"Maybe he'll figure it out," I said.

"Maybe he will," Jane said. She stood and took my hand again, and we looked out at Huckleberry once more.

About a week and a half later, after we were all moved in to Huckleberry, Dad came through the door with something small and squirmy in his hands.

No, it wasn't an elephant. Use your *heads*, people. It was a puppy.

I squealed with glee—which I was allowed to do, eight at the time, remember—and John handed the puppy to me. It immediately tried to lick my face off.

"Aftab Chengelpet just weaned a litter from their mother, so I thought we might give one of the puppies a home," Dad said. "You know, if you want. Although I don't recall you having any *enthusiasm* for such a creature. We could always give it back."

"Don't you *dare*," I said, between puppy licks.

"All right," Dad said. "Just remember he's your responsibility. You'll have to feed him and exercise him and take care of him."

"I will," I said.

"And neuter him and pay for his college," Dad said.

"What?" I said.

"John," Mom said, from her chair, where she had been reading.

"Never mind those last two," Dad said. "But you *will* have to give him a name."

I held the puppy at arm's length to get a good look at him; he continued to try to lick my face from a distance and wobbled in my grip as his tail's momentum moved him around. "What are some good dog names?" I asked.

"Spot. Rex. Fido. Champ," Dad said. "Those are the cliché names, anyway. Usually people try to go for something more memorable. When I was a kid I had a dog my dad called Shiva, Destroyer of Shoes. But I don't think that would be appropriate in a community of former Indians. Maybe something else." He pointed to my elephant pendant. "I notice you seem to be into elephants these days. You have a Celeste. Why not call him Babar?"

From behind Dad I could see Jane look up from her reading to look at me, remembering what happened at the toy store, waiting to see how I would react.

I burst out laughing.

"So that's a yes," Dad said, after a minute.

"I like it," I said. I hugged my new puppy, and then held him out again.

"Hello, Babar," I said.

Babar gave a happy little bark and then peed all over my shirt.

And that's the story of the jade elephant.

FIVE There was a tap on my door, a rat-a-tat that I gave Hickory to use when I was nine, when I made it a secret member of my secret club. I made Dickory a secret member of an entirely different secret club. Same with Mom, Dad and Babar. I was all about the secret clubs when I was nine, apparently. I couldn't even tell you what the name of that secret club was now. But Hickory still used the knock whenever my bedroom door was closed.

"Come in," I said. I was standing by my bedroom window.

Hickory came in. "It's dark in here," it said.

"That's what happens when it's late and the lights are out," I said.

"I heard you walking about," Hickory said. "I came to see if you needed anything."

"Like a warm glass of milk?" I said. "I'm fine, Hickory. Thank you."

"Then I'll leave you," Hickory said, backing out.

"No," I said. "Come here a minute. Look."

Hickory walked over to stand next to me at the window. He looked where I pointed, to two figures in the road in front of our house. Mom and Dad. "She has been out there for some time," Hickory said. "Major Perry joined her a few minutes ago."

"I know," I said. "I saw him walk out." I heard her walk out, too, about an hour earlier; the squeaking of the springs on the screen door had gotten me out of bed. I hadn't been sleeping, anyway. Thinking about leaving Huckleberry and colonizing somewhere new was keeping my brain up, and then made me pace around. The idea of leaving was sinking in. It was making me twitchier than I thought it would.

"You know about the new colony?" I asked Hickory.

"We do," Hickory said. "Lieutenant Sagan informed us earlier this evening. Dickory also filed a request to our government for more information."

"Why do you call them by their rank?" I asked Hickory. My brain was looking for tangents at the moment, it seemed, and this was a good one. "Mom and Dad. Why don't you call them 'Jane' and 'John' like everyone else?"

"It's not appropriate," Hickory said. "It's too familiar."

"You've lived with us for *seven years*," I said. "You *might* be able to risk a little familiarity."

"If you wish us to call them 'John' and 'Jane,' then we will do so," Hickory said.

"Call them what you want," I said. "I'm just saying that if you *want* to call them by their first names, you could."

"We will remember that," Hickory said. I doubted there would be a change in protocol anytime soon.

"You'll be coming with us, right?" I asked, changing the subject. "To the new colony." I hadn't assumed that Hickory and Dickory would *not* be joining us, which when I thought about it might not have been a smart assumption.

"Our treaty allows it," Hickory said. "It will be up to you to decide."

"Well, of course I want you to come," I said. "We'd just as soon leave Babar behind than not take you two."

"I am happy to be in the same category as your dog," Hickory said.

"I think that came out wrong," I said.

Hickory held up a hand. "No," it said. "I know you did not mean to imply Dickory and I are like pets. You meant to imply Babar is part of your household. You would not leave without him."

"He's not just part of the household," I said. "He's family. Slobbery, sort of dim family. But family. You're family, too. Weird, alien, occasionally obtrusive family. But family."

"Thank you, Zoë," Hickory said.

"You're welcome," I said, and suddenly felt shy. Conversations with Hickory were going weird places today. "That's why I asked about you calling my parents by rank, you know. It's not a usual *family* thing."

"If we are truly part of your family, then it is safe to say it's not a usual family," Hickory said. "So it would be hard to say what would be usual for us."

This got a snort from me. "Well, that's true," I said. I thought for a moment. "What *is* your name, Hickory?" I asked.

"Hickory," it said.

"No, I mean, what was your name *before* you came to live with us," I said. "You had to have been named something before I named you Hickory. And Dickory, too, before I named it that."

"No," it said. "You forget. Before your biological father, Obin did not have consciousness. We did not have a sense of self, or the need to describe ourselves to ourselves or to others."

"That would make it hard to do anything with more than two of you," I said. "Saying 'hey, you' only goes so far."

"We had descriptors, to help us in our work," Hickory said. "They were not the same as *names*. When you named Dickory and me, you gave us our true names. We became the first Obin to have names at all."

"I wish I had known that at the time," I said, after I took this in. "I would have given you names that weren't from a nursery rhyme."

"I like my name," Hickory said. "It's popular among other Obin as well. 'Hickory' and 'Dickory' both."

"There are other Obin Hickorys," I said.

"Oh, yes," Hickory said. "Several million, now."

I had no possible intelligible response to that. I turned my attention back to my parents, who were still standing in the road, entwined.

"They love each other," Hickory said, following my gaze.

I glanced back at it. "Not really where I was expecting the conversation to go, but okay," I said.

"It makes a difference," Hickory said. "In how they speak to each other. How they communicate with each other."

"I suppose it does," I said. Hickory's observation was an understatement, actually. John and Jane didn't just love each other. The two of them were nuts for each other, in exactly the sort of way that's both touching and embarrassing to a teenage daughter. Touching because who doesn't want their parents to love each other, right down to their toes? Embarrassing because, well. *Parents.* Not supposed to act like goofs about each other.

They showed it in different ways. Dad was the most obvious about it, but I think Mom felt it more intensely than he did. Dad was married before; his first wife died back on Earth. Some part of his heart was still with her. No one else had any claim on Jane's heart, though. John had all of it, or all of it that was supposed to belong to your spouse. No matter how you sliced it, though, there's nothing either of them wouldn't do for each other.

"That's why they're out here," I said to Hickory. "In the road right now, I mean. Because they love each other."

"How so?" Hickory asked.

"You said it yourself," I said. "It makes a difference in how they communicate." I pointed again to the two of them. "Dad wants to go and lead this colony," I said. "If he didn't, he would have just said no. It's how he works. He's been moody and out of sorts all day because he wants it and he knows there are complications. Because *Jane* loves it here."

"More than you or Major Perry," Hickory said.

"Oh, yeah," I said. "It's where she's been married. It's where she's had a family. Huckleberry is her homeworld. He'd say no if she doesn't give him permission to say yes. So that's what she's doing, out there."

Hickory peered out again at the silhouettes of my parents. "She could have said so in the house," it said.

I shook my head. "No," I said. "Look how she's looking up. Before Dad came out, she was doing the same thing. Standing there and looking up at the stars. Looking for the star our new planet orbits, maybe. But what she's really doing is saying good-bye to Huckleberry. Dad needs to *see* her do it. Mom knows that. It's part of the reason she's out there. To let him know she's ready to let this planet go. She's ready to let it go because he's ready to let it go."

"You said it was part of the reason she's out there," Hickory said. "What's the other part?"

"The other part?" I asked. Hickory nodded. "Oh. Well. She needs to say good-bye for herself, too. She's not just doing it for Dad." I watched Jane. "A lot of who she is, she became here. And we may never get back here. It's hard to leave your home. Hard for *her*. I think she's trying to find a way to let it go. And that starts by saying good-bye to it."

"And you?" Hickory said. "Do you need to say good-bye?"

I thought about it for a minute. "I don't know," I admitted. "It's funny. I've already lived on four planets. Well, three planets and a space station. I've been here longest, so I guess it's my home more than any of the rest of them. I know I'll miss some of the things about it. I know I'll miss some of my friends. But more than any of that . . . I'm *excited*. I want to do this. Colonize a new world. I *want* to go. I'm excited and nervous and a little scared. You know?"

Hickory didn't say anything to this. Outside the window, Mom had walked away a little from Dad, and he was turning to head back into the house. Then he stopped and turned back to Mom. She held out her hand to him. He came to her, took it. They began to walk down the road together.

"Good-bye, Huckleberry," I said, whispering the words. I turned away from the window and let my parents have their walk.

SIX "I don't know how you could *possibly* be bored," Savitri said to me, leaning on an observation deck rail as we looked out from Phoenix Station to the *Magellan*. "This place is *great*."

I looked over at her with mock suspicion. "Who *are* you, and what have you done with Savitri Guntupalli?"

"I don't know what you mean," Savitri said, blandly.

"The Savitri *I* know was sarcastic and bitter," I said. "*You* are all gushy, like a schoolgirl. Therefore: You're not Savitri. You are some horrible spunky camouflaged alien thing, and I hate you."

"Point of order," Savitri said. "You're a schoolgirl, and you hardly ever gush. I've known you for years and I don't believe I have ever seen you involved in a gushing incident. You are almost entirely gush-free."

"Fine, you gush even more than a schoolgirl," I said. "Which just makes it *worse*. I hope you're happy."

"I *am*," Savitri said. "Thank you for noticing."

"Hrrrumph," I said, rolled my eyes for extra effect, and applied myself to the observation deck rail with renewed moodiness.

I was not actually irritated with Savitri. She had an excellent reason to be excited; all her life she'd been on Huckleberry and now, finally, she was somewhere *else*: on Phoenix Station, *the* space station, the largest single thing humans had ever built, hovering above Phoenix, the home planet of the entire Colonial Union. For as long as I had known her—which was for as long as she had been my dad's assistant, back in New Goa, on Huckleberry—Savitri had cultivated an air of general smart-assery, which is one reason I adored her and looked up to her. One has to have role models, you know.

But after we had lifted from Huckleberry her excitement from finally getting to see more of the universe had gotten to her. She'd been unguardedly excited about everything; she even got up early to watch the *Magellan*, the ship that would take us to Roanoke, dock with Phoenix Station. I was happy for her that she was so excited about everything, and I mocked her mercilessly for it every chance I got. One day, yes, there would be payback—Savitri taught me much of what I know about being a smartass, but not everything *she* knew about it— but until then it was one of the few things keeping me enter-tained.

Listen: Phoenix Station is huge, it's busy, and unless you have an actual job—or like Savitri are just in from the sticks— there is *nothing going on*. It's not an amusement park, it's just a big dull combination of government offices, docks and military headquarters, all jammed into space. If it weren't for the fact that stepping outside to get some fresh air would kill you—no fresh air, just lung-popping vacuum—it could be any big, face-less, dead-boring civic center anywhere humans come to-gether to do big, faceless, dead-boring civic things. It is not designed for fun, or at least any sort of fun I was interested in having. I suppose I could have filed something. *That* would have been a kick.

Savitri, in addition to being insensibly excited not to be on Huckleberry, was also being worked like a dog by John and Jane: The three of them had spent nearly all their time since we arrived at Phoenix Station getting up to speed on Roanoke, learning about the colonists who would be with us, and overseeing the loading of supplies and equipment onto the *Magellan*. This didn't come as news to me, but it did leave me with not a whole lot to do, and no one much to do it with. I couldn't even do much with Hickory, Dickory, or Babar; Dad told Hickory and Dickory to lay low while we were on Phoenix Station, and dogs weren't really allowed the run of the station. We had to lay out paper towels for Babar to do his thing on. The first night I did this and tried to get him to take care of business, he gave me a look that said *you have* got *to be kidding*. Sorry, buddy. Now pee, damn it.

The only reason I was getting some time with Savitri at all was that through a clever combination of whining and guilt I had convinced her to take her lunch break with me. Even then she had brought her PDA and spent half of lunch going over manifests. She was even excited about that. I told her I thought she might be ill.

"I'm sorry you're bored," Savitri said, back in the present. "You might want to hint to your parents."

"Trust me, I did," I said. "Dad actually stepped up, too. He said he's going to take me down to Phoenix. Do some last-minute shopping and other things." The *other things* were the main reason for us to go, but I didn't want to bring them up to Savitri; I was moody enough as it was.

"You haven't come across any other colonists your own age yet?" Savitri asked.

I shrugged. "I've seen some of them."

"But you haven't spoken to any of them," Savitri said.

"Not really," I said.

"Because you're *shy*," Savitri said.

"Now your sarcasm comes back," I said.

"I'm sympathetic to your boredom," Savitri said. "But less so if you're just marinating in it." She looked around at the observation desk, which had a few other people in it, sitting or reading or staring out at the ships docked at the station. "What about her?" she said, pointing to a girl who looked about my age, who was looking out the deck window.

I glanced over. "What *about* her?" I said.

"She looks about as bored as you," Savitri said.

"Appearances can be deceiving," I said.

"Let's check," Savitri said, and before I could stop her called to the other girl. "Hey," Savitri said.

"Yes?" the girl said.

"My friend here thinks she's the most bored teenage girl on the entire station," Savitri said, pointing at me. I had nowhere to cringe. "I was wondering if you had anything to say about that."

"Well," the girl said, after a minute. "I don't want to brag, but the quality of my boredom is *outstanding*."

"Oh, I *like* her," Savitri said to me, and then waved the girl over. "This is Zoë," she said, introducing me.

"I can talk," I said to Savitri.

"Gretchen," she said, extending her hand to me.

"Hello," I said, taking it.

"I'm interested in your boredom and would like to hear more," Gretchen said.

Okay, I thought. *I like her too.*

Savitri smiled. "Well, since you two seem to be equally matched, I have to go," she said. "There are containers of soil conditioners that need my attention." She gave me a peck, waved to Gretchen, and left.

"Soil conditioners?" Gretchen said to me, after she had gone.

"It's a long story," I said.

"I've got nothing but time," Gretchen said.

"Savitri is the assistant to my parents, who are heading up a new colony," I said, and pointed to the *Magellan*. "That's the ship we're going on. One of Savitri's jobs is to make sure that everything that's on the manifest list actually gets put on the ship. I guess she's up to soil conditioners."

"Your parents are John Perry and Jane Sagan," Gretchen said.

I stared at her for a minute. "Yeah," I said. "How do you know?"

"Because my dad talks about them a lot," she said, and motioned toward the *Magellan*. "This colony your parents are leading? It was his idea. He was Erie's representative on the CU legislature, and for years he argued that people from established colonies should be able to colonize, not just people from Earth. Finally the Department of Colonization agreed with him—and then it gave the leadership of the colony to your parents instead of him. They told my dad it was a political compromise."

"What did your dad think about that?" I asked.

"Well, I just met you," Gretchen said. "I don't know what sort of language you can handle."

"Oh. Well, *that's* not good," I said.

"I don't think he *hates* your parents," Gretchen said, quickly. "It's not like that. He just assumed that after everything he did, he'd get to lead the colony. 'Disappointment' doesn't even begin to cover it. Although I wouldn't say he likes your parents, either. He got a file on them when they were appointed and then spent the day muttering to himself as he read it."

"I'm sorry he's disappointed," I said. In my head I was wondering if I needed to write Gretchen off as a possible friend; one of those stupid "our houses are at war" scenarios. The first person my age I meet, going to Roanoke, and we were already in different camps.

But then she said, "Yeah, well. At a certain point he got a little stupid about it. He was comparing himself to Moses, like, *Oh, I've led my people to the promised land but I can't enter*

myself"—and here she made little hand movements to accentu-
ate the point—"and that's when I decided he was overreacting.
Because we're *going*, you know. And he's on your parents' ad-
visory council. So I told him to suck it up."

I blinked. "You actually used those words?" I said.

"Well, no," Gretchen said. "What I actually said was I wondered if I kicked a puppy if it would whine more than he did."
She shrugged. "What can I say. Sometimes he needs to get over
himself."

"You and I are so totally going to be best friends," I said.

"Are we?" she said, and grinned at me. "I don't know. What
are the hours?"

"The hours are terrible," I said. "And the pay is even
worse."

"Will I be treated horribly?" she asked.

"You will cry yourself to sleep on a nightly basis," I said.

"Fed crusts?" she asked.

"Of course not," I said. "We feed the crusts to the dogs."

"Oh, very nice," she said. "Okay, you pass. We can be best
friends."

"Good," I said. "Another life decision taken care of."

"Yes," she said, and then moved away from the rail. "Now,
come on. No point wasting all this attitude on ourselves. Let's
go find something to point and laugh at."

Phoenix Station was a lot more interesting after that.

SEVEN

Here's what I did when my dad took me down to Phoenix: I visited my own grave.

Clearly, this needs an explanation.

I was born and lived the first four years of my life on Phoenix. Near where I lived, there is a cemetery. In that cemetery is a headstone, and on that headstone are three names: Cheryl Boutin, Charles Boutin and Zoë Boutin.

My mother's name is there because she is actually buried there; I remember being there for her funeral and seeing her shroud put into the ground.

My father's name is there because for many years people believed his body was there. It's not. His body lies on a planet named Arist, where he and I lived for a time with the Obin. There *is* a body buried here, though, one that looks like my father and has the same genes as he does. How it got there is a really complicated story.

My name is there because before my father and I lived on Arist, he thought for a time that I had been killed in the attack on Covell, the space station he and I had lived on. There was no body, obviously, because I was still alive; my father just didn't know it. He had my name and dates carved into the headstone before he was told I was still around.

And so there you have it: three names, two bodies, one

grave. The only place where my biological family exists, in any form, anywhere in the universe.

In one sense, I'm an orphan, and profoundly so: My mother and father were only children, and their parents were dead before I was born. It's possible I have second cousins twice removed somewhere on Phoenix, but I've never met them and wouldn't know what to say to them even if they existed. Really, what do you say? "Hi, we share about four percent of our genetic makeup, let's be friends"?

The fact is, I'm the last of my line, the last member of the Boutin family, unless and until I decide to start having babies. Now, *there's* a thought. I'm going to table it for now.

In one sense I was an orphan. But in another sense . . .

Well. First, my dad was standing behind me, watching me as I was kneeling down to look at the headstone my name was on. I don't know how it is with other adoptees, but I can say that there never was a time with John and Jane that I didn't feel cherished and loved and *theirs.* Even when I was going through that early puberty phase where I think I said "I hate you" and "Just leave me *alone*" six times daily and ten times on Sunday. *I* would have abandoned me at the bus stop, that's for sure.

John told me that back when he lived on Earth, he had a son, and his son had a boy, Adam, who would have been just about my age, which technically made me an aunt. I thought that was pretty neat. Going from having no family on the one hand to being someone's aunt on the other is a fun trick. I told that to Dad; he said "you contain multitudes," and then walked around with a smile for hours. I finally got him to explain it to me. That Walt Whitman, he knew what he was talking about.

Second, there were Hickory and Dickory to the side of me, twitching and trembling with emotional energy, because they were at the gravesite of my father, even if my father wasn't buried there, and never was. It didn't matter. They were worked up because of what it represented. Through my father, I guess you could say I was adopted by the Obin, too, although my relationship to them wasn't exactly like being someone's daughter, or their aunt. It was a little closer to being their goddess. A goddess for an entire race of people.

Or, I don't know. Maybe something that sounds less egotistical: patron saint, or racial icon or mascot or *something*. It was hard to put into words; it was hard to even wrap my brain around most days. It's not like I was put on a throne; most goddesses I know about don't have homework and have to pick up dog poop. If this is what being an icon is all about, on a day-to-day basis it's not terribly exciting.

But then I think about the fact that Hickory and Dickory live with me and have spent their lives with me because their government made it a demand of my government when the two of them signed a peace pact. I am actually a treaty condition between two intelligent races of creatures. What do you *do* with that sort of fact?

Well, I tried to use it once: When I was younger I tried to argue with Jane that I should be able to stay up late one night because I had special status under treaty law. I thought that was pretty clever. Her response was to haul out the entire thousand-page treaty—I didn't even know we *had* a physical copy—and invite me to find the part of the treaty that said I always got to have my way. I stomped over to Hickory and Dickory and demanded they tell Mom to let me do what I wanted; Hickory told me they would have to file a request to their government for guidance, and it would take several days, by which time I would already have to be in bed. It was my first exposure to the tyranny of bureaucracy.

What I do know that it means is that I belong to the Obin. Even at that moment in front of the grave, Hickory and Dickory were recording it into their consciousness machines, the machines my father made for them. They would be stored and sent to all the other Obin. Every other Obin would stand here with me, as I knelt at my grave and the grave of my parents, tracing their names and mine with my finger.

I belong. I belong to John and Jane; I belong to Hickory and Dickory and every Obin. And yet for all that, for all the connection I feel—for all the connection I *have*—there are times when I feel alone, and I have the sensation of drifting and not connecting at all. Maybe that's just what you do when you're this age; you have your stretches of alienation. Maybe to find yourself you've got to feel like you're unplugged. Maybe everyone goes through this.

What I knew, though, there at the grave, *my* grave, was that I was having one of those moments.

I had been here before, to this grave. First when my mother was buried, and then, a few years later, when Jane brought me here to say good-bye to both my mother and father. *All the people who know me have gone away,* I said to her. *All of my people are gone.* And then she came over to me and asked me to live with her and John, in a new place. Asked me to let her and John be my new people.

I touched the jade elephant at my neck and smiled, thinking of Jane.

Who am I? Who are my people? Who do I belong to? Questions with easy answers and no answers. I belong to my family and to the Obin and sometimes to no one at all. I am a daughter and goddess and girl who sometimes just doesn't know who she is or what she wants. My brain rattles around my head with this stuff and gives me a headache. I wish I were alone here. I'm glad John's with me. I want to see my new friend Gretchen and make sarcastic comments until we burst out laughing. I want to go to my stateroom on the *Magellan,* turn off the light, hug my dog, and cry. I want to leave this stupid cemetery. I don't ever want to leave it because I know I'm never coming back to it. This is my last time with my people, the ones who are already gone.

Sometimes I don't know if my life is complicated, or if it's that I just think too much about things.

I knelt at the grave, thought some more, and tried to find a way to say a last good-bye to my mother and father and to keep them with me, to stay and to go, to be the daughter and goddess and girl who doesn't know what she wants, all at once, and to belong to everyone and keep myself.

It took a while.

EIGHT

"You seem sad," Hickory said, as we took the shuttle back to Phoenix Station. Dickory sat next to Hickory, impassive as ever.

"I am sad," I said. "I miss my mother and father." I glanced over to John, who was sitting in the front of the shuttle with the pilot, Lieutenant Cloud. "And I think all this moving and leaving and going is getting to me a little bit. Sorry."

"No need to apologize," Hickory said. "This journey has been stressful for us, too."

"Oh, good," I said, turning back to the two of them. "Misery loves company."

"If you would like we would be happy to try to cheer you up," Hickory said.

"Really," I said. This was a new tactic. "How would you do that?"

"We could tell you a story," Hickory said.

"What story?" I asked.

"One that Dickory and I have been working on," Hickory said.

"You've been *writing*?" I said. I didn't bother to keep the incredulousness out of my voice.

"Is it that surprising?" Hickory said.

"Absolutely," I said. "I didn't know you had it in you."

"The Obin don't have stories of their own," Hickory said. "We learned about them through you, when you had us read to you."

I was puzzled for a minute, and then I remembered: When I was younger I asked Hickory and Dickory to read bedtime stories to me. It was a failed experiment, to say the least; even with their consciousness machines on, neither of them could tell a story to save their lives. The beats were all wrong—they didn't know how to read the emotions in the story is the best way I can put it. They could read the words, all right. They just couldn't tell the *story*.

"So you've been reading stories since then," I said.

"Sometimes," Hickory said. "Fairy tales and myths. We are most interested in myths, because they are stories of gods and creation. Dickory and I have decided to make a creation myth for the Obin, so we have a story of our own."

"And this is the story you want to tell me," I said.

"If you think it would cheer you up," Hickory said.

"Well, is it a *happy* creation myth?" I asked.

"It is for us," Hickory said. "You should know you play a part in it."

"Well, then," I said. "I definitely want to hear it now."

Hickory conferred with Dickory quickly, in their own language. "We will tell you the short version," Hickory said.

"There's a long version?" I said. "I'm really intrigued."

"The remainder of the shuttle ride will not be long enough for the long version," Hickory said. "Unless we then went back down to Phoenix. And then back up. And then back down again."

"The short version it is," I said.

"Very well," Hickory said, and began. "Once upon a time—"

"Really?" I said. " 'Once upon a time'?"

"What is wrong with 'once upon a time'?" Hickory asked. "Many of your stories and myths start that way. We thought it would be appropriate."

"There's nothing wrong with it," I said. "It's just a little old-fashioned."

"We will change it if you like," Hickory said.

"No," I said. "I'm sorry, Hickory, I interrupted you. Please start again."

"Very well," Hickory said. "Once upon a time . . ."

Once upon a time there were creatures who lived on a moon of a large gas planet. And these creatures did not have a name, nor did they know they lived on a moon, nor did they know that moon circled a gas planet, nor what a planet was, nor did they know anything in a way that could be said that they were knowing it. They were animals, and they had no consciousness, and they were born and lived and died, all their lives without thought or the knowledge of thought.

One day, although the animals knew nothing of the idea of days, visitors came to the moon that circled the gas planet. And these visitors were known as Consu, although the animals on the planet did not know that, because it was what the Consu called themselves, and the animals were not smart and could not ask the Consu what they called themselves, or know that things could have names.

The Consu came to the moon to explore and they did, noting all the things about the moon, from the air in its sky to the shape of its lands and waters to the shape and manner of all the life that lived in the moon's land, air and water. And when they came to these certain creatures who lived on this moon, the Consu became curious about them and how they lived their lives, and studied them and how they were born and lived and died.

After the Consu had watched the creatures for some time the Consu decided that they would change the creatures, and would give them something that the Consu possessed and that the creatures did not, which was intelligence. And the Consu took the genes of the creatures and changed them so that their brains, as they grew, would develop intelligence well beyond what the creatures would themselves achieve through experience or through many years of evolution. The Consu made these changes to a few creatures and then set them back on the moon and over many generations all the creatures became intelligent.

Once the Consu gave intelligence to the creatures they did not stay on the moon, nor shared themselves with the creatures, but departed and left machines above the sky, which the creatures would not see, to watch the creatures. And so the creatures for a very long time did not learn of the Consu and what they had done to the creatures.

And for a very long time these creatures who now had intelligence grew in number and learned many things. They learned how to make tools and create a language and work together for common goals and to farm the land and mine metals and create science. But although the creatures thrived and learned, they did not know that they among all intelligent creatures were unique, because they did not know there were other intelligent creatures.

One day, after the creatures had gained intelligence, another race of intelligent people came to visit the moon, the first since the Consu, although the creatures did not remember the Consu. And these new people called themselves the Arza and each of the Arza also had a name. And the Arza were amazed that the creatures on the moon, who were intelligent and who had built tools and cities, did not have a name and did not have names for each of their number.

And it was then the creatures discovered through the Arza

what made them unique: They were the only people in all the universe who were not conscious. Although every creature could think and reason, it could not know itself as every other intelligent creature could know itself. The creatures lacked awareness of who they were as individuals, even as they lived and thrived and grew on the face of the moon of the planet.

When the creatures learned this, and although no individual could know it felt this, there grew within the race of these creatures a hunger for that thing they did not have: for the consciousness that the creatures knew collectively they did not have as individuals. And this is when the creatures first gave themselves a name, and called themselves "Obin," which in their language meant "The ones who lack," although it might be better translated as "The deprived ones" or "The ones without gifts," and although they named their race they did not give names to each of their individual number.

And the Arza took pity on the creatures who now called themselves Obin, and revealed to them the machines that floated in the sky and that were put there by the Consu, who they knew to be a race of immense intelligence and unknowable aims. The Arza studied the Obin and discovered that their biology was unnatural, and so the Obin learned who had created them.

And the Obin asked the Arza to take them to the Consu, so they could ask why the Consu had done these things, but the Arza refused, saying the Consu met only with other races to fight them, and they feared what would happen to the Arza if they brought the Obin before the Consu.

So it was the Obin determined they must learn to fight. And while the Obin did not fight the Arza, who had been kind to the Obin and took pity on them and then left the Obin in peace, there came another race of creatures called the Belestier, who planned to colonize the moon on which the Obin lived and kill all the Obin because they would not live in peace with them. The Obin struggled with the Belestier, killing all those who landed on their moon, and in doing so found they had an advantage; because the Obin did not know themselves, they were not afraid of death, and had no fear where others had fear in abundance.

The Obin killed the Belestier, and learned from their weapons and technology. In time the Obin left their own moon to colonize other moons and grow their numbers and make war on other races when those other races chose to make war on the Obin.

And there came a day, after many years, when the Obin decided they were ready to meet the Consu, and found where they lived and set out to meet them. Although the Obin were strong and determined, they did not know the power of the Consu, who brushed them aside, killing any Obin who dared to call or attack, and there were many thousands of these.

Eventually the Consu became curious about the creatures they had made and offered to answer three questions for the Obin, if half the Obin everywhere would offer themselves up as a sacrifice to the Consu. And this was a hard bargain, because although no individual Obin would know its own death, such a sacrifice would wound the race, because by this time it had made many enemies among the intelligent races, and they would most certainly attack the Obin when they were weak. But the Obin had a hunger and needed answers. So one half of the Obin willingly offered themselves to the Consu, killing themselves in all manner of ways, wherever they were.

And the Consu were satisfied and answered our three questions. Yes, they had given the Obin intelligence. Yes, they could have given the Obin consciousness but did not, because they wanted to see what consciousless intelligence was like. No, they would not now give us consciousness, nor would they ever, nor would they allow us to ask again. And since that day the Consu have not allowed the Obin to speak to them again; each embassy to them since that day has been killed.

The Obin spent many years fighting many races as it returned itself to its former strength, and in time it became known to other races that to fight with the Obin meant death, for the Obin would not relent or show mercy or pity or fear, because the Obin did not know these things themselves. And for a long time this was the way of things.

One day a race known as the Rraey attacked a human colony and its space station, killing all the humans they could. But before the Rraey could complete their task, the Obin attacked them, because the Obin wanted the colony world for themselves. The Rraey were weakened after their first attack and were defeated and killed. The Obin took the colony and its space station, and because the space station was known as a scientific outpost, the Obin looked through its records to see what useful technology they could take.

It was then that the Obin discovered that one of the human scientists, who was named Charles Boutin, was working on a way to hold and store consciousness outside of the human body, in a machine based on technology the humans had stolen from the Consu. The work was not done, and the technology was not something the Obin at the space station could follow, nor the Obin scientists whom they had brought along. The Obin looked for Charles Boutin among the human survivors of the space station attacks, but he was not to be found, and it was discovered that he was away from the station when it was attacked.

But then the Obin learned that Charles Boutin's daughter Zoë had been on the space station. The Obin took her from the station and she alone was spared among the humans. And the Obin kept her and kept her safe and found a way to tell Charles Boutin that she was alive and offered to return her if he would give the Obin consciousness. But Charles Boutin was angry, not at the Obin but at the humans who he thought had let his daughter die, and demanded in exchange for giving the Obin consciousness, that the Obin would make war on the humans, and defeat them. The Obin could not do this themselves but allied with two other races, the Rraey, whom they had just attacked, and the Enesha, who were allies of the humans, to make war on the humans.

Charles Boutin was satisfied and in time joined the Obin and his daughter, and worked to create consciousness for the Obin. Before he could finish his task, the humans learned of the alliance between the Obin and the Rraey and the Enesha, and attacked. The alliance was broken and the Enesha were made to war on the Rraey by the humans. And Charles Boutin was killed and his daughter Zoë was taken from the Obin by the humans. And although no individual Obin could sense it, the entire nation despaired because in agreeing to give them consciousness Charles Boutin was their friend among all friends, who would do for them what even the great Consu would not: give them awareness of themselves. When he died, their hope for themselves died. To lose his daughter, who was of him and who was dear to them because of him, compounded this despair.

And then the humans sent a message to the Obin that they knew of Boutin's work and offered to continue it, in exchange for an alliance and the agreement by the Obin to war on the Enesha, who had allied with the Obin against the humans, once the Enesha had defeated the Rraey. The Obin agreed to this but added the condition that once the Obin were given consciousness that two of their number would be allowed to know Zoë Boutin, and to share that knowledge with all other Obin, because she was what remained of Charles Boutin, their friend and their hero.

And so it was that the Obin and the humans became allies, the Obin attacked and defeated the Enesha in due time, and the Obin, thousands of generations after their creation, were given consciousness by Charles Boutin. And among their number, the Obin selected two, who would become companions and protectors to Zoë Boutin and share her life with her new family. And when Zoë met them she was not afraid because she had lived with the Obin before, and she gave the two of them names: Hickory and Dickory. And the two of them became the first Obin to have names. And they were glad, and they know they are glad, because of the gift Charles Boutin gave them and all Obin.

And they lived happily ever after.

Hickory said something to me I didn't hear. "What?" I said.

"We are not sure 'and they lived happily ever after' is the appropriate ending," said Hickory, and then stopped and looked closely at me. "You are crying," it said.

"I'm sorry," I said. "I was remembering. The parts of it I was in."

"We told them wrong," Hickory said.

"No," I said, and put up my hand to reassure it. "You didn't tell it wrong, Hickory. It's just the way you tell it and the way I remember it are a little . . ." I wiped a tear off my face and searched for the right word. "They're just a little *different*, is all."

"You do not like the myth," Hickory said.

"I like it," I said. "I like it very much. It's just some things hurt me to remember. It happens that way for us sometimes."

"I am sorry, Zoë, for causing you distress," Hickory said, and I could hear the sadness in its voice. "We wanted to cheer you up."

I got up from my seat and went over to Hickory and Dickory and hugged them both. "I know you did," I said. "And I'm really glad you tried."

NINE

"Oh, look," Gretchen said. "Teenage boys, about to do something stupid."

"Shut *up*," I said. "That couldn't *possibly* happen." But I looked anyway.

Sure enough, across the *Magellan*'s common area, two clots of teenage males were staring each other down with that look of *we're so gonna fight about something lame*. They were all getting ready for a snarl, except for one of them, who gave every appearance of trying to talk some sense into one guy who looked particularly itchin' to fight.

"There's one who appears to have a brain," I said.

"One out of eight," Gretchen said. "Not a really excellent percentage. And if he really had a brain he'd probably be getting out of the way."

"This is true," I said. "Never send a teenage boy to do a teenage girl's job."

Gretchen grinned over to me. "We have that mind-meld thing going, don't we?"

"I think you know the answer to that," I said.

"You want to plan it out or just improvise?" Gretchen asked.

"By the time we plan it out, someone's going to be missing teeth," I said.

"Good point," Gretchen said, and then got up and started moving toward the boys.

Twenty seconds later the boys were startled to find Gretchen in the middle of them. "You're making me lose a bet," she said, to the one who looked the most aggressive.

The dude stared for a moment, trying to wrap whatever was passing for his brain around this sudden and unexpected appearance. "What?" he said.

"I said, you're making me lose a bet," Gretchen repeated, and then jerked a thumb over toward me. "I had a bet with Zoë here that no one would start a fight on the *Magellan* before we actually left dock, because no one would be *stupid* enough to do something that would get their entire family kicked off the ship."

"Kicked off the ship two hours before departure, even," I said.

"Right," Gretchen said. "Because what sort of *moron* would you have to be to do that?"

"A teenage *boy* moron," I suggested.

"Apparently," Gretchen said. "See—what's your name?"

"What?" the guy said again.

"Your *name*," Gretchen said. "What your mother and father will call you, *angrily*, once you've gotten them kicked off the ship."

The guy looked around at his friends. "Magdy," he said, and then opened his mouth as if to say something.

"Well, see, Magdy, I have *faith* in humanity, even the teenage male part of it," Gretchen said, plowing through whatever it was that our Magdy might have had to say. "I believed that not even teenage boys would be dumb enough to give Captain Zane an excuse to kick a bunch of them off the ship while he still could. Once we're under way, the worst he could do is put you in the brig. But right now he could have the crew drop you and your family at the loading bay. Then you could watch the rest of us wave good-bye. Surely, I said, no one could be that *incredibly dense*. But my friend Zoë disagreed. What did you say, Zoë?"

"I said that teenage boys can't think beyond or without their newly dropped testicles," I said, staring at the boy who had been trying to talk sense into his pal. "Also, they smell funny."

The boy grinned. He knew what we were up to. I didn't grin back; I didn't want to mess with Gretchen's play.

"And I was so convinced that I was right and she was wrong that I actually made a bet," Gretchen said. "I bet every single dessert I'd get here on the *Magellan* that no one would be that stupid. That's a serious bet."

"She loves her dessert," I said.

"It's true, I do," Gretchen said.

"She's a dessert *fiend*," I said.

"And now you are going to make me *lose* all my desserts," Gretchen said, poking Magdy in the chest. "This is not acceptable."

There was a snerk from the boy Magdy had been facing off with. Gretchen wheeled on him; the boy actually flinched backward. "I don't know why *you* think this is funny," Gretchen said. "Your family would have been thrown off the ship just like his."

"He started it," the boy said.

Gretchen blinked, dramatically. "'He started it'? Zoë, tell me I heard that wrong."

"You didn't," I said. "He really said it."

"It doesn't seem possible that anyone over the age of *five* would be using that as a rationale for *anything*," Gretchen said, examining the boy critically.

"Where's your faith in humanity *now*?" I asked.

"I'm losing it," Gretchen said.

"Along with all your desserts," I said.

"Let me guess," Gretchen said, and waved generally at the clot of boys in front of her. "You're all from the same planet." She turned and looked at the other boy clot. "And you're all from another planet." The boys shifted uncomfortably; she had gotten their number. "And so the first thing you do is you start picking fights because of where you *used* to live."

"Because that's the *smart* thing to do with people you're going to spend the rest of your life living with," I said.

"I don't remember that being in the new colonist orientation material," Gretchen said.

"Funny about that," I said.

"Indeed," Gretchen said, and stopped talking.

There was silence for several seconds.

"Well?" Gretchen said.

"What?" Magdy said. It was his favorite word.

"Are you going to fight now or what?" Gretchen said. "If I'm going to lose my bet, now's as good a time as any."

"She's right," I said. "It's almost lunchtime. Dessert is calling."

"So either get on with it or break it up," Gretchen said. She stepped back.

The boys, suddenly aware that whatever it was they were fighting about had been effectively reduced to whether or not some girl would get a cupcake, dispersed, each clot headed pointedly in a separate direction from the other. The sane boy glanced back at me as he walked off with his friends.

"*That* was fun," Gretchen said.

"Yeah, until they all decide to do it again," I said. "We can't use the dessert humiliation trick every time. And there are colonists from ten separate worlds. That's a hundred different possible idiotic teenage boy fight situations."

"Well, the colonists from Kyoto are Colonial Mennonites," Gretchen said. "They're pacifists. So it's only eighty-one possible idiotic teenage boy fight combinations."

"And yet still *only* two of us," I said. "I don't like the odds. And how did you know about the Kyoto folks, anyway?"

"When my father was still thinking he'd be running the colony, he made me read the reports on all the colonists and their original planets," Gretchen said. "He said I was going to be his *aide-de-camp*. Because, you know, that's really what I would have wanted to *do* with my time."

"Comes in handy, though," I said.

Gretchen pulled out her PDA, which was buzzing, and looked at the screen. "Speaking of which," she said, and showed me the screen. "Looks like Dad's calling."

"Go be aide de camp-y," I said.

Gretchen rolled her eyes. "Thanks. Want to get together for the departure? And then we can go have lunch. You'll have lost the bet by then. I'll get your dessert."

"Touch my dessert and you will die in horrible ways," I said. Gretchen laughed and left.

I pulled out my own PDA to see if there were messages from John or Jane; there was one from Jane telling me that Hickory and Dickory were looking for me about something. Well, they knew I was onboard, and they also knew how to reach me by PDA; it's not like I went anywhere without it. I thought about giving them a call but I figured they would find me sooner or later. I put the PDA away and looked up to find the sane boy standing in front of me.

"Hi," he said.

"Uh," I said, a testament to my smoothness.

"Sorry, I didn't mean to sneak up on you like that," he said.

"It's okay," I said, only a little flustered.

He stuck out his hand. "Enzo," he said. "And you're Zoë, I guess."

"I am," I said, taking his hand and shaking it.

"Hi," he said.

"Hi," I said.

"Hi," he said, and then seemed to realize he was back where he started. I smiled.

And then there was about, oh, *47 million seconds* of awkward silence. It was only actually a second or two, but as Einstein could tell you, some events have a way of stretching out.

"Thanks for that," Enzo said, finally. "For stopping the fight, I mean."

"You're welcome," I said. "I'm glad you didn't mind we stepped in on what you were doing."

"Well, I wasn't doing a great job of it anyway," Enzo said. "Once Magdy gets himself worked up, it's hard to get him to back down."

"What was that all about anyway?" I asked.

"It's kind of stupid," Enzo said.

"*That* I know," I said, and then wondered if Enzo would take it the wrong way. He smiled. Score one for Enzo. "I mean what caused it."

"Magdy's pretty sarcastic, and he's also pretty loud," Enzo said. "He made some snide remark about what those other guys were wearing as they passed by. One of them got upset and they got into it."

"So you guys nearly had a brawl over fashion," I said.

"I told you it was stupid," Enzo said. "But you know how it is. You get worked up, it's kind of hard to think rationally."

"But *you* were thinking rationally," I said.

"That's my job," Enzo said. "Magdy gets us into trouble, I get us out of it."

"So you've known each other for a while," I said.

"He's been my best friend since we were little," Enzo said. "He's really not a jerk, honest. He just sometimes doesn't think about what he's doing."

"You look out for him," I said.

"It goes both ways," Enzo said. "I'm not much of a fighter. A lot of kids we knew would have taken advantage of that fact if they didn't know Magdy would have punched them in the head."

"Why aren't you much of a fighter?" I asked.

"I think you have to like to fight a little," Enzo said. Then he seemed to realize this was challenging his own masculinity a bit, and this would get him kicked out of the teenage male club. "Don't get me wrong. I can defend myself just fine without Magdy around. We're just a good team."

"You're the brains of the outfit," I suggested.

"That's possible," he allowed, and then seemed to figure out that I'd gotten him to make a whole bunch of statements about himself without getting to find out anything about me. "What about you and your friend? Who is the brains of that outfit?"

"I think Gretchen and I both hold our own pretty well in the brains department," I said.

"That's a little scary," Enzo said.

"It's not a bad thing to be a little intimidating," I said.

"Well, you have that down," Enzo said, with just the right amount of offhandedness. I tried very hard not to blush. "So, listen, Zoë—" Enzo began, and then looked over my shoulder. I saw his eyes get very wide.

"Let me guess," I said, to Enzo. "There are two very scary-looking aliens standing directly behind me."

"How did you know?" Enzo said, after a minute.

"Because what you're doing now is the usual response," I said. I glanced back at Hickory and Dickory. "Give me a minute," I said to them. They took a step back.

"You *know* them?" Enzo said.

"They're sort of my bodyguards," I said.

"You need bodyguards?" Enzo asked.

"It's a little complicated," I said.

"Now I know why you and your friend can both work on being the brains of the outfit," Enzo said.

"Don't worry," I said, and turned to Hickory and Dickory. "Guys, this is my new friend Enzo. Say hello."

"Hello," they said, in their deadly monotone.

"Uh," Enzo said.

"They're perfectly harmless unless they think you're a threat to me," I said.

"What happens then?" Enzo asked.

"I'm not really sure," I said. "But I think it would involve you being turned into a large number of very small cubes."

Enzo looked at me for a minute. "Don't take this the wrong way," he said. "But I'm a little afraid of you right now."

I smiled at this. "Don't be," I said, and I took his hand, which seemed to surprise him. "I want us to be friends."

There was an interesting play across Enzo's face: pleasure at the fact I'd taken his hand, and apprehension that if he showed too much pleasure at the fact, he'd be summarily cubed. It was very cute. He was very cute.

As if on cue, Hickory audibly shifted its weight.

I sighed. "I need to talk to Hickory and Dickory," I said, to Enzo. "Will you excuse me?"

"Sure," Enzo said, and took his hand out of mine.

"Will I see you later?" I asked.

"I hope so," Enzo said, and then got that look that said his brain was telling him he was being too enthusiastic. Shut up, stupid brain. Enthusiasm is a *good* thing. He backed off and went away. I watched him go a little.

Then I turned to Hickory and Dickory. "This had better be good," I said.

"Who was that?" Hickory asked.

"That was Enzo," I said. "Which I already told you. He's a boy. A cute one, too."

"Does he have impure intentions?" Hickory asked.

"What?" I said, slightly incredulous. " 'Impure intentions'? Are you serious? No. I've only known him for about twenty minutes. Even for a teenage boy, that would be a pretty quick ramp-up."

"This is not what we have heard," Hickory said.

"From whom?" I asked.

"From Major Perry," Hickory said. "He said that he was once a teenage boy himself."

"Oh, God," I said. "Thank you so *very* much for the mental image of Dad as a teenage sack of hormones. That's the sort of image that takes therapy to get rid of."

"You have asked us to intercede for you with teenage boys before," Hickory said.

"That was a special case," I said. And it had been. Just before we left Huckleberry my parents had gone off on a planetary survey of Roanoke and I was given tacit permission to have a good-bye party for my friends, and Anil Rameesh had taken it upon himself to sneak into my bedroom and get naked, and upon discovery, to inform me that he was giving me his virginity as a good-bye gift. Well, he didn't put it that way; he was trying to avoid mentioning the whole "virginity" aspect of it at all.

Regardless, this was a gift I really didn't want, even though it was already unwrapped. I told Hickory and Dickory to escort him out; Anil responded by screaming, jumping out my window and down off the roof, and then running all the way home naked. Which was a sight. I had his clothes delivered home the next day.

Poor Anil. He wasn't a bad person. Just deluded and hopeful.

"I will let you know if Enzo presents any problems," I said. "Until then, you leave him alone."

"As you wish," Hickory said. I could tell it was not entirely pleased about this.

"What was it you wanted to talk to me about?" I asked.

"We have news for you from the Obin government," Hickory said. "An invitation."

"An invitation for what?" I asked.

"An invitation to visit our homeworld, and to tour our planets and colonies," Hickory said. "You are now old enough to travel unaccompanied, and while all Obin have known of you since you were young, thanks to our recordings, there is a great desire among all Obin to meet you in person. Our government asks you if you will not accede to this request."

"When?" I asked.

"Immediately," Hickory said.

I looked at them both. "You're asking me this *now*?" I said. "We're less than two hours from departing to Roanoke."

"We have only just now received the invitation," Hickory said. "As soon as it was sent to us, we came to find you."

"It couldn't wait?" I asked.

"Our government wished to ask you before your journey to Roanoke began," Hickory said. "Once you had established yourself on Roanoke, you might be hesitant to leave for such a significant amount of time."

"How much time?" I asked.

"We have sent a proposed itinerary to your PDA," Hickory said.

"I'm asking you," I said.

"The entire tour would take thirteen of your standard months," Hickory said. "Although if you were amenable, it could be extended."

"So, to recap," I said. "You want me to decide in the next *two hours* whether or not to leave my family and friends for at least a year, maybe longer, to tour the Obin worlds by myself."

"Yes," Hickory said. "Although of course Dickory and I would accompany you."

"No other humans, though," I said.

"We could find some if you wanted," Hickory said.

"Would you?" I said. "That would be swell."

"Very well," Hickory said.

"I'm being *sarcastic*, Hickory," I said, irritated. "The answer is no. I mean, *really*, Hickory. You're asking me to make a life-changing decision on two hours' notice. That's completely ridiculous."

"We understand that the timing of this request is not optimal," Hickory said.

"I don't think you do," I said. "I think you know it's short notice, but I don't think you understand that it's *offensive.*"

Hickory shrank back slightly. "We did not mean to offend," it said.

I was about to snap something off but I stopped and started counting in my head, because somewhere in there the rational part of my brain was letting me know I was heading into over-reaction territory. Hickory and Dickory's invitation was last-minute, but biting their heads off for it didn't make much sense. Something about the request was just rubbing me the wrong way.

It took me a minute to figure out why. Hickory and Dickory were asking me to leave behind everyone I knew, and everyone I had just met, for a year of being alone. I had already done that, long ago, when the Obin had taken me from Covell, in the time I had to wait before my father could find a way to reclaim me. It was a different time and with different circumstances, but I remember the loneliness and need for human contact. I loved Hickory and Dickory; they were family. But they couldn't offer me what I needed and could get from human contact.

And besides, I just said good-bye to a whole village of people I knew, and before that had said good-bye to family and friends, usually forever, a whole lot more than most people my age. Right now I had just found Gretchen, and Enzo was certainly looking interesting. I didn't want to say good-bye to them even before I properly got to know them.

I looked at Hickory and Dickory, who despite everything

they knew about me couldn't have understood why what they were asking me would affect me like this. *It's not their fault*, said the rational part of my brain. And it was right. Which was why it was the rational part of my brain. I didn't always *like* that part, but it was usually on point for stuff like this.

"I'm sorry, Hickory," I said, finally. "I didn't mean to yell at you. Please accept my apology."

"Of course," Hickory said. It unshrunk itself.

"But even if I wanted to go, two hours is not nearly enough time to think this through," I said. "Have you spoken to John or Jane about this?"

"We felt it best to come to you," Hickory said. "Your desire to go would have influenced their decision to let you go."

I smiled. "Not as much as I think you think it would," I said. "You may think I'm old enough to spend a year off touring the Obin worlds, but I guarantee you Dad will have a different opinion about that. It took both Jane and Savitri a couple of days to convince him to let me have that good-bye party while they were away. You think he'd say 'yes' to having me go away for a year when there's a two-hour time limit attached? That's *optimistic*."

"It is very important to our government," Dickory said. Which was surprising. Dickory almost never spoke about anything, other than to make one of its monochromatic greetings. The fact Dickory felt compelled to pipe up spoke volumes in itself.

"I understand that," I said. "But it's still too sudden. I *can't* make a decision like this now. I just can't. Please tell your government I'm honored by the invitation, and that I want to make a tour of the Obin worlds one day. I really do. But I can't do it like this. And I want to go to Roanoke."

Hickory and Dickory were silent for a moment. "Perhaps if Major Perry and Lieutenant Sagan were to hear our invitation and agree, you might be persuaded," Hickory said.

Rankle, rankle. "What is *that* supposed to mean?" I asked. "First you say you wanted me to say yes because then they might agree, and now you want to work it the other way? You asked me, Hickory. My answer is no. If you think asking my parents is going to get me to change my mind, then you don't understand human teenagers, and you certainly don't understand me. Even *if* they said yes, which, believe me, they won't, since the first thing they will do is ask me what I think of the idea. And I'll tell them what I told you. And *that* I told you."

Another moment of silence. I watched the two of them very closely, looking for the trembles or twitches that sometimes followed when they were emotionally wrung out. The two of them were rock steady. "Very well," Hickory said. "We will inform our government of your decision."

"Tell them that I will consider it some other time. Maybe in a year," I said. Maybe by that time I could convince Gretchen to go with me. And Enzo. As long as we were daydreaming here.

"We will tell them," Hickory said, and then it and Dickory did a little head bow and departed.

I looked around. Some of the people in the common area were watching Hickory and Dickory leave; the others were looking at me with strange expressions. I guess they'd never seen a girl with her own pet aliens before.

I sighed. I pulled out my PDA to contact Gretchen but then stopped before I accessed her address. Because as much as I didn't want to be alone in the larger sense, at that moment, I needed a time out. Something was going on, and I needed to figure what it was. Because whatever it was, it was making me nervous.

I put the PDA back in my pocket, thought about what Hickory and Dickory just said to me, and worried.

TEN There were two messages on my PDA after dinner that evening. The first was from Gretchen. "That Magdy character tracked me down and asked me out on a date," it read. "I guess he likes girls who mock the crap out of him. I told him okay. Because he is kind of cute. Don't wait up." This made me smile.

The second was from Enzo, who had somehow managed to get my PDA's address; I suspect Gretchen might have had something to do with that. It was titled "A Poem to the Girl I Just Met, Specifically a Haiku, the Title of Which Is Now Substantially Longer Than the Poem Itself, Oh, the Irony," and it read:

> *Her name is Zoë*
> *Smile like a summer breeze*
> *Please don't have me cubed.*

I laughed out loud at that one. Babar looked up at me and thumped his tail hopefully; I think he was thinking all this happiness would result in more food for him. I gave him a slice of leftover bacon. So I guess he was right about that. Smart dog, Babar.

After the *Magellan* departed from Phoenix Station, the colony leaders found out about the near-rumble in the common area, because I told them about it over dinner. John and Jane sort of looked at each other significantly and then changed the subject to something else. I guessed the problem of integrating ten completely different sets of people with ten completely different cultures had already come up in their discussions, and now they were getting the underage version of it as well.

I figured that they would find a way to deal with it, but I really wasn't prepared for their solution.

"Dodgeball," I said to Dad, over breakfast. "You're going to have all us kids play dodgeball."

"Not all of you," Dad said. "Just the ones of you who would otherwise be picking stupid and pointless fights out of boredom." He was nibbling on some coffee cake; Babar was standing by on crumb patrol. Jane and Savitri were out taking care of business; they were the brains of this particular setup. "You don't like dodgeball?" he asked.

"I like it just fine," I said. "I'm just not sure why you think it's an answer to this problem."

Dad set down his coffee cake, brushed off his hands, and started ticking off points with his fingers. "One, we have the equipment and it fits the space. We can't very well play football or cricket on the *Magellan*. Two, it's a team sport, so we can get big groups of kids involved. Three, it's not complicated, so we don't have to spend much time laying out the ground rules to everyone. Four, it's athletic and will give you guys a way to burn off some of your energy. Five, it's just violent enough to appeal to those idiot boys you were talking about yesterday, but not so violent that someone's actually going to get hurt."

"Any more points?" I asked.

"No," Dad said. "I've run out of fingers." He picked up his coffee cake again.

"It's just going to be that the boys are going to make teams with their friends," I said. "So you'll still have the problem of kids from one world staying with their own."

"I would agree with this, if not for the fact that I'm not a complete idiot," Dad said, "and neither is Jane. We have a plan for this."

The plan: Everyone who signed up to play was assigned to a team, rather than allowed to pick their own team. And I don't think the teams were entirely randomly assigned; when Gretchen and I looked over the team lists, Gretchen noted that almost none of the teams had more than one player from the same world; even Enzo and Magdy were put on different teams. The only kids who were on the same "team" were the Kyotoans; as Colonial Mennonites they avoided playing in competitive sports, so they asked to be the referees instead.

Gretchen and I didn't sign up for any teams; we appointed ourselves league managers and no one called us on it; apparently word of the intense mockery we laid on a wild pack of teenage boys had gotten around and we were feared and awed equally. "That makes me feel pretty," Gretchen said, once such a thing was told to her by one of her friends from Erie. We were watching the first game of the series, with the Leopards playing against the Mighty Red Balls, presumably named after the game equipment. I don't think I approved of the team name, myself.

"Speaking of which, how was your date last night?" I asked.

"It was a little grabby," Gretchen said.

"You want me to have Hickory and Dickory talk to him?" I asked.

"No, it was manageable," Gretchen said. "And besides which, your alien friends creep me out. No offense."

"None taken," I said. "They really are nice."

"They're your bodyguards," Gretchen said. "They're not supposed to be nice. They're supposed to scare the pee out of people. And they do. I'm just glad they don't follow you around all the time. No one would ever come talk to us."

In fact, I hadn't seen either Hickory or Dickory since the day before and our conversation about touring the Obin planets. I wondered if I had managed to hurt their feelings. I was going to have to check in on them to see how they were.

"Hey, your boyfriend just picked off one of the Leopards," Gretchen said. She pointed at Enzo, who was playing in the game.

"He's not my boyfriend, any more than Magdy is yours," I said.

"Is he as grabby as Magdy is?" Gretchen asked.

"What a question," I said. "How dare you ask. I'm madly offended."

"That's a yes, then," Gretchen said.

"No, it's not," I said. "He's been perfectly nice. He even sent me a poem."

"He did *not*," Gretchen said. I showed it to her on my PDA. She handed it back. "You get the poetry writer. I get the grabber. It's really *not* fair. You want to trade?"

"Not a chance," I said. "But he not's my boyfriend."

Gretchen nodded out to Enzo. "Have you asked him about that?"

I looked over to Enzo, who sure enough was sneaking looks my way while moving around the dodgeball field. He saw I was looking his way, smiled over at me and nodded, and as he was doing that he got nailed righteously hard in the ear by the dodgeball and went down with a *thump*.

I burst out laughing.

"Oh, *nice*," Gretchen said. "Laughing at your boyfriend's *pain*."

"I know! I'm so bad!" I said, and just about toppled over.

"You don't deserve him," Gretchen said, sourly. "You don't deserve his *poem*. Give them both to me."

"Not a chance," I said, and then looked up and saw Enzo there in front of me. I reflexively put my hand over my mouth.

"Too late," he said. Which of course made me laugh even more.

"She's mocking your pain," Gretchen said, to Enzo. "*Mocking* it, you hear me."

"Oh, God, I'm so sorry," I said, between laughs, and before I thought about what I was doing gave Enzo a hug.

"She's trying to distract you from her *evil*," Gretchen warned.

"It's working," Enzo said.

"Oh, fine," Gretchen said. "See if I warn you about her evil ways after this." She very dramatically focused back on the game, only occasionally glancing over and grinning at me.

I unhugged from Enzo. "I'm not *actually* evil," I said.

"No, just amused at the pain of others," Enzo said.

"You walked off the court," I said. "It can't have hurt that much."

"There's pain you can't see," Enzo said. "*Existential* pain."

"Oh, boy," I said. "If you're having existential pain from dodgeball, you're really just doing it wrong."

"I don't think you appreciate the philosophical subtleties of the sport," Enzo said. I started giggling again. "Stop it," Enzo said mildly. "I'm being serious here."

"I so hope you're not," I said, and giggled some more. "You want to get lunch?"

"Love to," Enzo said. "Just give me a minute to extract this dodgeball from my Eustachian tube."

It was the first time I had ever heard anyone use the phrase "Eustachian tube" in common conversation. I think I may have fallen a little bit in love with him right there.

"I haven't seen the two of you around much today," I said to Hickory and Dickory, in their quarters.

"We are aware that we make many of your fellow colonists uncomfortable," Hickory said. It and Dickory sat on stools that were designed to accommodate their body shape; otherwise their quarters were bare. The Obin may have gained consciousness and even recently tried their hand at storytelling, but the mysteries of interior decoration still clearly eluded them. "It was decided it would be best for us to stay out of the way."

"Decided by whom?" I asked.

"By Major Perry," Hickory said, and then, before I could open my mouth, "and we agree."

"You two are going to be living with us," I said. "With all of us. People need to get used to you."

"We agree, and they will have time," Hickory said. "But for now we think it's better to give your people time to get used to each other." I opened my mouth to respond, but then Hickory said, "Do you not benefit from our absence at the moment?"

I remembered Gretchen's comment earlier in the day about how the other teens would never come up to us if Hickory and Dickory were always hanging around, and felt a little bit ashamed. "I don't want you to think I don't want you around," I said.

"We do not believe that," Hickory said. "Please do not think that. When we are on Roanoke we will resume our roles. People will be more accepting of us because they will have had time to know you."

"I still don't want you to think you have to stay in here because of me," I said. "It would drive me crazy to be cooped up in here for a week."

"It is not difficult for us," Hickory said. "We disconnect our consciousnesses until we need them again. Time flies by that way."

"That was very close to a joke," I said.

"If you say so," Hickory said.

I smiled. "Still, if that's the only reason you stay in here—"

"I did not say it was the only reason," Hickory said, interrupting me, which it almost never did. "We are also spending this time preparing."

"For life on Roanoke?" I asked.

"Yes," Hickory said. "And how we will be of best service to you when we are there."

"I think by just doing what you do," I said.

"Possibly," Hickory said. "We think you might be underestimating how much different Roanoke will be from your life before, and what our responsibilities will be to you."

"I know it's going to be different," I said. "I know it's going to be harder in a lot of ways."

"We are glad to hear that," Hickory said. "It will be."

"Enough so that you're spending all this time planning?" I asked.

"Yes," Hickory said. I waited a second to hear if anything else was coming after that, but there wasn't.

"Is there anything you want me to do?" I asked Hickory. "To help you?"

Hickory took a second to respond. I watched it to see what I could sense from it; after this many years, I was pretty good at reading its moods. Nothing seemed unusual or out of place. It was just Hickory.

"No," Hickory said, finally. "We would have you do what you are doing. Meeting new people. Becoming friends with them. Enjoying your time now. When we arrive at Roanoke we do not expect you will have as much time for enjoyment."

"But you're missing out on all my fun," I said. "You're usually there to record it."

"This one time you can get along without us," Hickory said.

Another near joke. I smiled again and gave them both a hug just as my PDA vibrated to life. It was Gretchen.

"Your boyfriend really sucks at dodgeball," she said. "He just took a hit square on his nose. He says to tell you the pain isn't nearly as enjoyable if you're not around to laugh at it. So come on down and ease the poor boy's pain. Or add to it. Either works."

ELEVEN

Things to know about the life of Zoë, on the *Magellan*.

First, John and Jane's master plan to keep the teenage boys from killing themselves or others worked like a charm, which meant I grudgingly had to admit to Dad he'd done something smart, which he enjoyed probably more than he should have. Each of the dodgeball teams became their own little group, counterpointing with the already-established groups of kids from former colonies. It might have been a problem if everyone just switched their tribe allegiance to their teams, because then we'd have just substituted one sort of group stupidity for another. But the kids still felt allegiance to their homeworld friends as well, at least one of whom was likely to be on an opposing dodgeball team. It kept everyone friendly, or at least kept some of the more aggressively stupid kids in check until everyone could get over the urge to pick fights.

Or so it was explained to me by Dad, who continued to be pleased with himself. "So you can see how we weave a subtle web of interpersonal connection," he said to me, as we watched one of the dodgeball games.

"Oh, Lord," Savitri, who was sitting with us, said. "The self-satisfaction here is going to make me gag."

"You're just jealous that you didn't think it up," Dad said to Savitri.

"I *did* think it up," Savitri said. "Part of it, anyway. I and Jane helped with this plan, as I'm sure you recall. You're just taking all the credit."

"These are despicable lies," Dad said.

"Ball," Savitri said, and we all ducked as a runaway ball ricocheted into the crowd.

Whoever thought it up, the dodgeball scheme had side benefits. After the second day of the tournament, the teams started having their own theme songs, as team members riffled through their music collections to find tunes that would get them riled up. And this was where we discovered a real cultural gap: Music that was popular on one world was completely unheard of on another. The kids from Khartoum were listening to chango-soca, the ones from Rus were deep into groundthump and so on. Yes, they all had good beats, and you could dance to them, but if you want to get someone wild-eyed and frothy, all you have to do is suggest that your favorite music was better than theirs. People were whipping out their PDAs and queuing up their songs to make their points.

And thus began the Great *Magellan* Music War: All of us networked our PDAs together and furiously started making playlists of our favorite music to show how *our* music was indisputably the best music ever. In a very short time I was exposed to not just chango-soca and groundthump but also kill-drill, drone, haploid, happy dance (ironically named, as it turned out), smear, nuevopop, tone, *classic* tone, Erie stomp, doowa capella, shaker and some really whacked-out stuff alleged to be waltz but critically missing three-quarter time or indeed any recognizable time signature at all as far as I could tell. I listened to it all with a fair mind, then told all their proponents I pitied them because they had never been exposed to Huckleberry Sound, and sent out a playlist of my own.

"So you make your music by strangling cats," Magdy said, as he listened to "Delhi Morning," one of my favorite songs, with me, Gretchen and Enzo.

"That's *sitar*, you monkey," I said.

" 'Sitar' being the Huckleberry word for 'strangled cats,' " Magdy said.

I turned to Enzo. "Help me out here," I said.

"I'm going to have to go with the cat strangling theory," Enzo said.

I smacked him on the arm. "I thought you were my friend."

"I was," Enzo said. "But now I know how you treat your pets."

"Listen!" Magdy said. The sitar part had just risen out of the mix and was suspended, heartbreakingly, over the bridge of the song. "Annnd right *there* is when the cat died. Admit it, Zoë."

"Gretchen?" I looked over to my last, best friend, who would always defend me against Philistines.

Gretchen looked over to me. "That poor *cat*," she said, and then laughed. Then Magdy grabbed the PDA and pulled up some horrible shaker noise.

For the record, "Delhi Morning" does not sound like strangled cats. It really doesn't. They were all tone-deaf or something. Particularly Magdy.

Tone-deaf or not, however, the four of us were ending up spending a lot of time together. While Enzo and I were doing our slow, amused sizing up of each other, Gretchen and Magdy alternated between being interested in each other and trying to see just how low they could cut each other down verbally. Although you know how these things go. One probably led to the other and vice-versa. And I'm guessing hormones counted for a lot; both of them were good-looking examples of blossoming adolescence, which I think is the best way to put it. They both seemed willing to put up with a lot from each other in exchange for gawking and some light groping, which to be fair to Magdy was not entirely one-sided on his part, if Gretchen's reports were to be believed.

As for Enzo and me, well, this is how we were getting along:

"I made you something," I said, handing him my PDA.

"You made me a PDA," he said. "I always wanted one."

"Goof," I said. Of course he had a PDA; we all did. We would hardly be teens without them. "No, click on the movie file."

He did, and watched for a few moments. Then he cocked his head at me. "So, is the whole thing shots of me getting hit in the head with a dodgeball?" he asked.

"Of course not," I said. "Some of them are of you getting hit in other places." I took the PDA and ran my finger along the fast-forward strip on the video player. "See, look," I said, showing him the groin shot he took earlier in the day.

"Oh, great," he said.

"You're cute when you collapse in aching misery," I said.

"I'm glad you think so," he said, clearly not as enthused as I was.

"Let's watch it again," I said. "This time in slow motion."

"Let's *not*," Enzo said. "It's a painful memory. I had plans for those things one day."

I felt a blush coming on, and fought it back with sarcasm. "Poor Enzo," I said. "Poor squeaky-voiced Enzo."

"Your sympathy is overwhelming," he said. "I think you like watching me get abused. You could offer up some advice instead."

"Move faster," I said. "Try not to get hit so much."

"You're helpful," he said.

"There," I said, pressing the send button on the PDA. "It's in your queue now. So you can treasure it always."

"I hardly know what to say," he said.

"Did you get me anything?" I asked.

"As a matter of fact," Enzo said, and then pulled out his PDA, punched up something, and handed the PDA to me. On it was another poem. I read it.

"This is very sweet," I said. It was actually beautiful, but I didn't want to get mushy on him, not after just sharing video of him taking a hit to his nether regions.

"Yes, well," Enzo said, taking back the PDA. "I wrote it before I saw that video. Just remember that." He pressed his PDA screen. "There. In *your* queue now. So you can treasure it always."

"I will," I said, and would.

"Good," Enzo said. "Because I get a lot of abuse for those, you know."

"For the poems?" I said. Enzo nodded. "From whom?"

"From Magdy, of course," Enzo said. "He caught me writing that one to you and mocked the hell out of me for it."

"Magdy's idea of a poem is a dirty limerick," I said.

"He's not stupid," Enzo said.

"I didn't say he was stupid," I said. "Just vulgar."

"Well, he's my best friend," Enzo said. "What are you gonna do."

"I think it's sweet you stick up for him," I said. "But I have to tell you that if he mocks you out of writing poems for me, I'm going to have to kick his ass."

Enzo grinned. "You or your bodyguards?" he asked.

"Oh, I'd handle this one personally," I said. "Although I might get Gretchen to help."

"I think she would," Enzo said.

"There's no *think* involved here," I said.

"I guess I better keep writing you poems, then," Enzo said.

"Good," I said, and patted his cheek. "I'm glad we have these little conversations."

And Enzo was as good as his word; a couple of times a day I'd get a new poem. They were mostly sweet and funny, and only a little bit showing off, because he would send them in different poem formats: haiku and sonnets and sestinas and some forms I don't know what they're called but you could see that they were supposed to be something.

And naturally I would show them all to Gretchen, who tried very hard not to be impressed. "The scan's off on that one," she said, after she had read one I showed to her at one of the dodgeball games. Savitri had joined the two of us to watch. She was on her break. "I'd dump him for that."

"It's not off," I said. "And anyway he's not my boyfriend."

"A guy sends poems on the hour and you say he's not your boyfriend?" Gretchen asked.

"If he was her boyfriend, he wouldn't be sending poems anymore," Savitri said.

Gretchen smacked her forehead. "Of course," she said. "It all makes sense now."

"Give me that," I said, taking back my PDA. "Such cynicism."

"You're just saying that because you're getting sestinas," Savitri said.

"Which don't scan," Gretchen said.

"Quiet, both of you," I said, and turned the PDA around so it could record the game. Enzo's team was playing the Dragons in the quarter-final match for the league championship. "All your bitterness is distracting me from watching Enzo get slaughtered out there."

"Speaking of cynicism," Gretchen said.

There was a loud *pock* as the dodgeball smooshed Enzo's face into a not terribly appealing shape. He grabbed his face with both hands, cursed loudly, and dropped to his knees.

"There we go," I said.

"That poor boy," Savitri said.

"He'll live," Gretchen said, and then turned to me. "So you got that."

"It's going into the highlight reel for sure," I said.

"I've mentioned before that you don't deserve him," Gretchen said.

"Hey," I said. "He writes me poems, I document his physical ineptitude. That's how the relationship works."

"I thought you said he wasn't your boyfriend," Savitri said.

"He's not my boyfriend," I said, and saved the humiliating snippet into my "Enzo" file. "It doesn't mean we don't have a relationship." I put my PDA away and greeted Enzo as he came up, still holding his face.

"So you got that," he said to me. I turned and smiled at Gretchen and Savitri, as if to say, *See*. They both rolled their eyes.

In all, there was about a week between when the *Magellan* left Phoenix Station and when the *Magellan* was far enough away from any major gravity well that it could skip to Roanoke. Much of that time was spent watching dodgeball, listening to music, chatting with my new friends, and recording Enzo getting hit with balls. But in between all of that, I actually did spend a little bit of time learning about the world on which we would live the rest of our lives.

Some of it I already knew: Roanoke was a Class Six planet, which meant (and here I'm double-checking with the Colonial Union Department of Colonization Protocol Document, get it wherever PDAs have access to a network) that the planet was within fifteen percent of Earth standard gravity, atmosphere, temperature and rotation, but that the biosphere was not compatible with human biology—which is to say if you ate something there, it'd probably make you vomit your guts out if it didn't kill you outright.

(This made me mildly curious about how many classes of planet there were. Turns out there are eighteen, twelve of which are at least nominally humanly compatible. That said, if someone says you're on a colony ship headed to a Class Twelve planet, the best thing to do is to find an escape pod or volunteer to join the ship's crew, because you're not going to want to land on that world if you can avoid it. Unless you *like* weighing up to two and a half times your normal weight on a planet whose ammonia-choked atmosphere will hopefully smother you before you die of exposure. In which case, you know. Welcome home.)

What do you do on a Class Six planet, when you're a member of a seed colony? Well, Jane had it right when she said it on Huckleberry: You work. You only have so much food supply to go through before you have to add to it from what you've grown—but before you grow your food, you have to make over the soil so it can grow crops that can feed humans (and other species which started on Earth, like almost all our livestock) without choking to death on the incompatible nutrients in the ground. And you have to make sure that earlier-mentioned livestock (or pets, or toddlers, or inattentive adults who didn't pay attention during their training periods) don't graze or eat anything from the planet until you do a toxicology scan so see if it will kill them. The colonist materials we were given suggest this is more difficult than it sounds, because it's not like your livestock will listen to reason, and neither will a toddler or some adults.

So you've conditioned the soil and kept all your animals and dumb humans from gorging on the poisonous scenery: Now it's time to plant, plant, plant your crops like your life depended on it, because it *does*. To bring this point home, the colonist training material is filled with pictures of gaunt colonists who messed up their plantings and ended up a lot thinner (or worse) after their planet's winter. The Colonial Union won't bail you out—if you fail, you fail, sometimes at the cost of your own life.

You've planted and tilled and harvested, and then you do it again, and you keep doing it—and all the while you're also building infrastructure, because one of the major roles of a seed colony is to prepare the planet for the next, larger wave of colonists, who show up a couple of standard years later. I assume they land, look around at everything you've created, and say, "Well, colonizing doesn't look *that* hard." At which point you get to punch them.

And through this all, and in the back of your mind, is this little fact: Colonies are at their most vulnerable to attack when they're new. There's a reason humans colonize Class Six planets, where the biosystem might kill them, and even Class Twelve planets, where just about everything *else* will kill them too. It's because there are a lot of other intelligent races out there who have the same habitation needs as we have, and we all want as many planets as we can grab. And if someone else is already there, well. That's just something to *work* around.

I knew this very well. And so did John and Jane.

But it was something I wonder if other people—either my age or older—really understood; understood that Class Six planet or not, conditioned soil or not, planted crops or not, everything they've done and worked for doesn't matter much when a spacecraft shows up in your sky, and it's filled with creatures who've decided they want your planet, and you're in the way. Maybe it's not something you *can* understand until it happens.

Or maybe when it comes down to it people just don't think about it because there's nothing to do about it. We're not soldiers, we're colonists. Being a colonist means accepting the risk. And once you've accepted the risk, you might as well not think about it until you have to.

And during our week on the *Magellan*, we certainly didn't have to. We were having *fun*—almost too much fun, to be honest about it. I suspected we were getting an unrepresentative view of colony life. I mentioned this to Dad, while we watched the final game of the dodgeball tournament, in which the Dragons were raining rubbery red doom on the previously undefeated Slime Molds, the team Magdy was on. I was perfectly fine with this; Magdy had gotten insufferable about his team's winning streak. Humility would be a good thing for the boy.

"Of course this is unrepresentative," Dad said. "Do you think you're going to have time to be playing dodgeball when we get to Roanoke?"

"I don't just mean dodgeball," I said.

"I know," he said. "But I don't want you to worry about it. Let me tell you a story."

"Oh, goody," I said. "A story."

"So *sarcastic*," Dad said. "When I first left Earth and joined the Civil Defense Forces, we had a week like this. We were given our new bodies—those green ones, like General Rybicki still has—and we were given the order to have fun with them for an entire week."

"Sounds like a good way to encourage trouble," I said.

"Maybe it is," Dad said. "But mostly it did two things. The first was to get us comfortable with what our new bodies could do. The second was to give us some time to enjoy ourselves and make friends before we had to go to war. To give us a little calm before the storm."

"So you're giving us this week to have fun before you send us all to the salt mines," I said.

"Not to the salt mines, but certainly to the fields," Dad said, and motioned out to the kids still hustling about on the dodgeball court. "I don't think it's entirely sunk into the heads of a lot of your new friends that when we land, they're going to be put to work. This is a seed colony. All hands needed."

"I guess it's a good thing I got a decent education before I left Huckleberry," I said.

"Oh, you'll still go to school," Dad said. "Trust me on that, Zoë. You'll just work, too. And so will all your friends."

"Monstrously unfair," I said. "Work *and* school."

"Don't expect a lot of sympathy from us," Dad said. "While you're sitting down and reading, we're going to be out there sweating and toiling."

"Who's this 'we'?" I said. "You're the colony leader. You'll be administrating."

"I farmed when I was ombudsman back in New Goa," Dad said.

I snorted. "You mean you paid for the seed grain and let Chaudhry Shujaat work the field for a cut."

"You're missing the point," Dad said. "My point is that once we get to Roanoke we'll all be busy. What's going to get us through it all are our friends. I know it worked that way for me in the CDF. You've made new friends this last week, right?"

"Yes," I said.

"Would you want to start your life on Roanoke without them?" Dad asked.

I thought of Gretchen and Enzo and even Magdy. "Definitely not," I said.

"Then this week did what it was supposed to do," Dad said. "We're on our way from being colonists from different worlds to being a single colony, and from being strangers to being friends. We're all going to need each other now. We're in a better position to work together. And that's the practical benefit to having a week of fun."

"Wow," I said. "I can see how you weaved a subtle web of interpersonal connection here."

"Well, you know," Dad said, with that look in his eye that said that yes, he *did* catch that snarky reference. "That's why I *run* things."

"Is that it?" I asked.

"It's what I tell myself, anyway," he said.

The Dragons made the last out against the Slime Molds and started celebrating. The crowd of colonists watching were cheering as well, and getting themselves into the mood for the really big event of the night: the skip to Roanoke, which would happen in just under a half hour.

Dad stood up. "This is my cue," he said. "I've got to get ready to do the award presentation to the Dragons. A shame. I was pulling for the Slime Molds. I love that name."

"Try to make it through the disappointment," I said.

"I'll try," he said. "You going to stay around for the skip?"

"Are you kidding?" I said. "*Everyone's* going to stay around for the skip. I wouldn't miss it for anything."

"Good," Dad said. "Always a good idea to confront change with your eyes open."

"You think it's really going to be that different?" I asked.

Dad kissed the top of my head and gave me a hug. "Sweetie, I know it's going to be that different. What I don't know is how much more different it's going to be after *that*."

"I guess we'll find out," I said.

"Yes, and in about twenty-five minutes," Dad said, and then pointed. "Look, there's your mom and Savitri. Let's ring in the new world together, shall we?"

PART II

TWELVE

There was a rattle and then a thump and then a whine as the shuttle's lifters and engines died down. That was it; we had landed on Roanoke. We were home, for the very first time.

"What's that smell?" Gretchen said, and wrinkled her nose.

I took a sniff and did some nose wrinkling of my own. "I think the pilot landed in a pile of rancid socks," I said. I calmed Babar, who was with us and who seemed excited about something; maybe *he* liked the smell.

"That's the planet," said Anna Faulks. She was one of the *Magellan* crew, and had been down to the planet several times, unloading cargo. The colony's base camp was almost ready for the colonists; Gretchen and I, as children of colony leaders, were being allowed to come down on one of the last cargo shuttles rather than having to take a cattle car shuttle with everyone else. Our parents had already been on planet for days, supervising the unloading. "And I've got news for you," Faulks said. "This is about as pretty as the smells get around here. When you get a breeze coming in from the forest, then it gets really bad."

"Why?" I asked. "What does it smell like then?"

"Like everyone you know just threw up on your shoes," Faulks said.

"Wonderful," Gretchen said.

There was a grinding clang as the massive doors of the cargo shuttle opened. There was a slight breeze as the air in the cargo bay puffed out into the Roanoke sky. And then the smell really hit us.

Faulks smiled at us. "Enjoy it, ladies. You're going to be smelling it every day for the rest of your lives."

"So are you," Gretchen said to Faulks.

Faulks stopped smiling at us. "We're going to start moving these cargo containers in a couple of minutes," she said. "You two need to clear out and get out of our way. It would be a shame if your precious selves got squashed underneath them." She turned away from us and started toward the rest of the shuttle cargo crew.

"Nice," I said, to Gretchen. "I don't think now was a smart time to remind her that she's stuck here."

Gretchen shrugged. "She deserved it," she said, and started toward the cargo doors.

I bit the inside of my cheek and decided not to comment. The last several days had made everyone edgy. This is what happens when you know you're lost.

On the day we skipped to Roanoke, this is how Dad broke the news that we were lost.

"Because I know there are rumors already, let me say this first: We are safe," Dad said to the colonists. He stood on the platform where just a couple of hours earlier we had counted down the skip to Roanoke. "The *Magellan* is safe. We are not in any danger at the moment."

Around us the crowd visibly relaxed. I wondered how many of them caught the "at the moment" part. I suspected John put it in there for a reason.

He did. "But we are not where we were told we would be,"

he said. "The Colonial Union has sent us to a different planet than we had expected to go to. It did this because it learned that a coalition of alien races called the Conclave were planning to keep us from colonizing, by force if necessary. There is no doubt they would have been waiting for us when we skipped. So we were sent somewhere else: to another planet entirely. We are now above the real Roanoke.

"We are not in danger at the moment," John said. "But the Conclave is looking for us. If it finds us it will try to take us from here, again likely by force. If it cannot remove us, it will destroy the colony. We are safe now, but I won't lie to you. We are being hunted."

"Take us back!" someone shouted. There were murmurings of agreement.

"We can't go back," John said. "Captain Zane has been remotely locked out of the *Magellan's* control systems by the Colonial Defense Forces. He and his crew will be joining our colony. The *Magellan* will be destroyed once we have landed ourselves and all our supplies on Roanoke. We can't go back. None of us can."

The room erupted in angry shouts and discussions. Dad eventually calmed them down. "None of us knew about this. I didn't. Jane didn't. Your colony representatives didn't. And certainly Captain Zane didn't. This was kept from all of us equally. The Colonial Union and the Colonial Defense Forces have decided for reasons of their own that it is safer to keep us here than to bring us back to Phoenix. Whether we agree with this or not, this is what we have to work with."

"What are we going to do?" Another voice from the crowd.

Dad looked out in the direction the voice came from. "We're going to do what we came here to do in the first place," he said. "We're going to colonize. Understand this: When we all chose to colonize, we knew there were risks. You all know that seed colonies are dangerous places. Even without this Conclave searching for us, our colony would still have been at risk for attack, still a target for other races. None of this has changed. What *has* changed is that the Colonial Union knew ahead of time who was looking for us and why. That allowed them to keep us safe in the short run. It gives an advantage in the long run. Because now we know how to keep ourselves from being found. We know how to keep ourselves safe."

More murmurings from the crowd. Just to the right of me a woman asked, "And just how are we going to keep ourselves safe?"

"Your colonial representatives are going to explain that," John said. "Check your PDAs; each of you has a location on the *Magellan* where you and your former worldmates will meet with your representative. They'll explain to you what we'll need to do, and answer the questions you have from there. But there is one thing I want to be clear about. This is going to require cooperation from everyone. It's going to require sacrifice from everyone. Our job of colonizing this world was never going to be easy. It's just become a lot harder.

"*But we can do it*," Dad said, and the forcefulness with which he said it seemed to surprise some people in the crowd. "What's being asked of us is hard, but it's not impossible. We can do it if we work together. We can do it if we know we can rely on each other. Wherever we've come from, we all have to be Roanokers now. This isn't how I would have chosen for this to happen. But this is how we are going to have to make it work. We can do this. We *have* to do this. We have to do it together."

I stepped out of the shuttle, and put my feet on the ground of the new world. The ground's mud oozed over the top of my boot. "Lovely," I said. I started walking. The mud sucked at my feet. I tried not to think of the sucking as a larger metaphor.

Babar bounded off the shuttle and commenced sniffing his surroundings. He was happy, at least.

Around me, the *Magellan* crew was on the job. Other shuttles that had landed before were disgorging their cargo; another shuttle was coming in for a landing some distance away. The cargo containers, standard-sized, littered the ground. Normally, once the contents of the containers were taken out, the containers would be sent back up in the shuttles to be reused; waste not, want not. This time, there was no reason to take them back up to the *Magellan*. It wasn't going back; these containers wouldn't ever be refilled. And as it happened, some of these containers wouldn't even be unpacked; our new situation here on Roanoke didn't make it worth the effort.

But it didn't mean that the containers didn't have a purpose; they did. That purpose was in front of me, a couple hundred meters away, where a barrier was forming, a barrier made from the containers. Inside the barrier would be our new temporary home; a tiny village, already named Croatoan, in which all twenty-five hundred of us—and the newly-resentful *Magellan* crew—would be stuck while Dad, Mom and the other colony leaders did a survey of this new planet to see what we needed to do in order to live on it.

As I watched, some of the *Magellan* crew were moving one of the containers into place into the barrier, using top lifters to set the container in place and then turning off their power and letting the container fall a couple of millimeters to the ground with a thump. Even from this distance I felt the vibration in the ground. Whatever was in that container, it was heavy. Probably farming equipment that we weren't allowed to use anymore.

Gretchen had already gotten far ahead of me. I thought about racing to catch up with her but then noticed Jane coming out from behind the newly placed container and talking to one of the *Magellan* crew. I walked toward her instead.

When Dad talked about sacrifice, in the immediate term he was talking about two things.

First: no contact between Roanoke and the rest of the Colonial Union. Anything we sent back in the direction of the Colonial Union was something that could give us away, even a simple skip drone full of data. Anything sent to us could give us away, too. This meant we were truly isolated: no help, no supplies, not even any mail from friends and loved ones left behind. We were alone.

At first this didn't seem like much of a big deal. After all, we left our old lives behind when we became colonists. We said good-bye to the people who we weren't taking with us, and most of us knew it would be a very long time if ever until we saw those people again. But even for all that, the lines weren't completely severed. A skip drone was supposed to leave the colony on a daily basis, carrying letters and news and information back to the Colonial Union. A skip drone was supposed to arrive on a daily basis, too, with mail, and news and new shows and songs and stories and other ways that we could still feel that we were part of humanity, despite being stuck on a colony, planting corn.

And now, none of that. It was all gone. The no new stories and music and shows were what hit you first—a bad thing if you were hooked on a show or band before you left and were hoping to keep up with it—but then you realized that what it really meant was from now on you wouldn't know anything about the lives of the people you left behind. You wouldn't see a beloved baby nephew's first steps. You wouldn't know if your grandmother had passed away. You wouldn't see the recordings your best friend took of her wedding, or read the stories that another friend was writing and desperately trying to sell, or see pictures of the places you used to love, with the people you still love standing in the foreground. All of it was gone, maybe forever.

When that realization hit, it hit people hard—and an even harder hit was the realization that everyone else that any of us ever cared about knew nothing about what happened to us. If the Colonial Union wasn't going to tell us where we were going in order to fool this Conclave thing, they certainly weren't going to tell everyone else that they had pulled a fast one with our whereabouts. Everyone we ever knew thought we were lost. Some of them probably thought we had been killed. John and Jane and I didn't have much to worry about on this score—we were each other's family, and all the family we had—but everyone else had someone who was even now mourning them. Savitri's mother and grandmother were still alive; the expression on her face when she realized that they probably thought she was dead made me rush over to give her a hug.

I didn't even want to think about how the *Obin* were handling our disappearance. I just hoped the Colonial Union ambassador to the Obin had on clean underwear when the Obin came to call.

The second sacrifice was harder.

"You're here," Jane said, as I walked up to her. She reached down to pet Babar, who had come bounding up to her.

"Apparently," I said. "Is it always like this?"

"Like what?" Jane said.

"Muddy," I said. "Rainy. Cold. Sucky."

"We're arriving at the beginning of spring here," Jane said. "It's going to be like this for a little while. I think things will get better."

"You think so?" I asked.

"I hope so," Jane said. "But we don't know. The information we have on the planet is slim. The Colonial Union doesn't seem to have done a normal survey here. And we won't be able to put up a satellite to track weather and climate. So we have to hope it gets better. It would be better if we could know. But hoping is what we have. Where's Gretchen?"

I nodded in the direction I saw her go. "I think she's looking for her dad," I said.

"Everything all right between you two?" Jane said. "You're rarely without each other."

"It's fine," I said. "Everyone's twitchy these last few days, Mom. So are we, I guess."

"How about your other friends?" Jane asked.

I shrugged. "I haven't seen too much of Enzo in the last couple of days," I said. "I think he's taking the idea of being stranded out here pretty badly. Even Magdy hasn't been able to cheer him up. I went to go visit him a couple of times, but he doesn't want to say much, and it's not like I've been that cheerful myself. He's sending me poems, still, though. On paper. He has Magdy deliver them. Magdy hates that, by the way."

Jane smiled. "Enzo's a nice boy," she said.

"I know," I said. "I think I didn't pick a great time to decide to make him my boyfriend, though."

"Well, you said it, everyone's twitchy the last few days," Jane said. "It'll get better."

"I hope so," I said, and I did. I did moody and depressed with the best of them, but even I have my limits, and I was getting near them. "Where's Dad? And where's Hickory and Dickory?" The two of them had gone down in one of the first shuttles with Mom and Dad; between them making themselves scarce on the *Magellan* and being away for the last few days, I was starting to miss them.

"Hickory and Dickory we have out doing a survey of the surrounding area," Jane said. "They're helping us get a lay of the land. It keeps them busy and useful, and keeps them out of the way of most of the colonists at the moment. I don't think any of them are feeling very friendly toward nonhumans at the moment, and we'd just as soon avoid someone trying to pick a fight with them."

I nodded at this. Anyone who tried to pick a fight with Hickory or Dickory was going to end up with something broken, at least. Which would not make the two of them popular, even (or maybe especially) if they were in the right. Mom and Dad were smart to get them out of the way for now.

"Your dad is with Manfred Trujillo," Jane said, mentioning Gretchen's dad. "They're laying out the temporary village. They're laying it out like a Roman Legion encampment."

"We're expecting an attack from the Visigoths," I said.

"We don't know what to expect an attack from," Jane said. The matter-of-fact way she said it did absolutely nothing to cheer me up. "I expect you'll find Gretchen with them. Just head into the encampment and you'll find them."

"It'd be easier if I could just ping Gretchen's PDA and find her that way," I said.

"It would be," Jane agreed. "But we don't get to do that anymore. Try using your eyes instead." She gave me a quick peck on the temple and then walked off to talk to the *Magellan* crew. I sighed and then headed into the encampment to find Dad.

The second sacrifice: Every single thing we had with a computer in it, we could no longer use. Which meant we couldn't use most things we had.

The reason was radio waves. Every piece of electronic equipment communicated with every other piece of electronic equipment through radio waves. Even the tiny radio transmissions they sent could be discovered if someone was looking hard enough, as we were assured that they were. But just turning off the connecting capability was not enough, since we were told that not only did our equipment use radio waves to communicate with each other, they used them internally to have one part of the equipment talk to other parts.

Our electronics couldn't *help* transmitting evidence that we were here, and if someone knew what frequencies they used to work, they could be detected simply by sending the radio signal that turned them on. Or so we were told. I'm not an engineer. All I knew was that a huge amount of our equipment was no longer usable—and not just unusable, but a *danger* to us.

We had to risk using this equipment to land on Roanoke and set up the colony. We couldn't very well land shuttles without using electronics; it wasn't the trip down that would be a problem, but the landings would be pretty tricky (and messy). But once everything was on the ground, it was over. We went dark, and everything we had in cargo containers that contained electronics would stay in those containers. Possibly forever.

This included data servers, entertainment monitors, modern farm equipment, scientific tools, medical tools, kitchen appliances, vehicles and toys. And PDAs.

This was *not* a popular announcement. Everyone had PDAs, and everyone had their lives in them. PDAs were where you kept your messages, your mail, your favorite shows and music and reading. It's how you connected with your friends, and played games with them. It's how you made recordings and video. It's how you shared the stuff you loved, to the people you liked. It was everyone's outboard brain.

And suddenly they were gone; every single PDA among the colonists—slightly more than one per person—was collected and accounted for. Some folks tried to hide them; at least one colonist tried to sock the *Magellan* crew member who'd been assigned to collect them. That colonist spent the night in the *Magellan* brig, courtesy of Captain Zane; rumor had it the captain cranked down the temperature in the brig and the colonist spent the night shivering himself awake.

I sympathized with the colonist. I'd been without my PDA for three days now and I still kept catching myself reaching for it when I wanted to talk to Gretchen, or listen to some music, or to check to see if Enzo had sent me something, or any one of a hundred different things I used my PDA for on a daily basis. I suspected that part of the reason people were so cranky was because they'd had their outboard brains amputated; you don't realize how much you use your PDA until the stupid thing is gone.

We were all outraged that we didn't have our PDAs anymore, but I had this itchy feeling in the back of my brain that one of the reasons people were so worked up about their PDAs was that it kept them from having to think about the fact that so much of the equipment we needed to use to survive, we couldn't use at all. You can't just disconnect the computers from our farm equipment; it can't run without it, it's too much a part of the machine. It'd be like taking out your brain and expecting your body to get along without it. I don't think anyone really wanted to face the fact of just how deep the trouble was.

In fact, only one thing was going to keep all of us alive: the two hundred and fifty Colonial Mennonites who were part of our colony. Their religion had kept them using outdated and antique technology; none of their equipment had computers, and only Hiram Yoder, their colony representative, had used a PDA at all (and only then, Dad explained to me, to stay in contact with other members of the Roanoke colonial council). Working without electronics wasn't a state of deprivation for them; it's how they *lived*. It made them the odd folks out on the *Magellan*, especially among us teens. But now it was going to save us.

This didn't reassure everyone. Magdy and a few of his less appealing friends pointed to the Colonial Mennonites as evidence that the Colonial Union had been planning to strand us all along and seemed to resent them for it, as if they had known it all along rather than being just as surprised as the rest of us. Thus we confirmed that Magdy's way of dealing with stress was to get angry and pick nonexistent fights; his near-brawl at the beginning of the trip was no fluke.

Magdy got angry when stressed. Enzo got withdrawn. Gretchen got snappish. I wasn't entirely sure how I got.

"You're mopey," Dad said to me. We were standing outside the tent that was our new temporary home.

"So *that's* how I get," I said. I watched Babar wander around the area, looking for places to mark his territory. What can I say. He's a dog.

"I'm not following you," Dad said. I explained how my friends were acting since we'd gotten lost. "Oh, okay," Dad said. "That makes sense. Well, if it's any comfort, if I have the time to do anything else but work, I think I would be mopey, too."

"I'm thrilled it runs in the family," I said.

"We can't even blame it on genetics," Dad said. He looked around. All around us were cargo containers, stacks of tents under tarps and surveyor's twine, blocking off where the streets of our new little town will be. Then he looked back to me. "What do you think of it?"

"I think this is what it looks like when God takes a dump," I said.

"Well, yes, *now* it does," Dad said. "But with a lot of work and a little love, we can work our way up to being a festering pit. And what a day that will be."

I laughed. "Don't make me laugh," I said. "I'm trying to work on this mopey thing."

"Sorry," Dad said. He wasn't actually sorry in the slightest. He pointed at the tent next to ours. "At the very least, you'll be close to your friend. This is Trujillo's tent. He and Gretchen will be living here."

"Good," I said. I had caught up with Dad with Gretchen and her dad; the two of them had gone off to look at the little river that ran near the edge of our soon-to-be settlement to find out the best place to put the waste collector and purifier. No indoor plumbing for the first few weeks at least, we were told; we'd be doing our business in buckets. I can't begin to tell you how excited I was to hear that. Gretchen had rolled her eyes a little bit at her dad as he dragged her off to look at likely locations; I think she was regretting taking the early trip. "How long until we start bringing down the other colonists?" I asked.

Dad pointed. "We want to get the perimeter set up first," he said. "We've been here a couple of days and nothing dangerous has popped out of those woods over there, but I think we want to be safer rather than sorrier. We're getting the last containers out of the cargo hold tonight. By tomorrow we should have the perimeter completely walled and the interior blocked out. So two days, I think. In three days everyone will be down. Why? Bored already?"

"Maybe," I said. Babar had come around to me and was grinning up at me, tongue lolling and paws caked with mud. I could tell he was trying to decide whether or not to leap up on two legs and get mud all over my shirt. I sent him my best *don't even* think *about it* telepathy and hoped for the best. "Not that it's any less boring on the *Magellan* right now. Everyone's in a foul mood. I don't know, I didn't expect colonizing to be like this."

"It's not," Dad said. "We're sort of an exceptional case here."

"Oh, to be like everyone else, then," I said.

"Too late for that," Dad said, and then motioned at the tent. "Jane and I have the tent pretty well set up. It's small and crowded, but it's also cramped. And I know how much you like that." This got another smile from me. "I've got to join Manfred and then talk to Jane, but after that we can all have lunch and try to see if we can't actually enjoy ourselves a little. Why don't you go in and relax until we get back. At least that way you don't have to be mopey *and* windblown."

"All right," I said. I gave Dad a peck on the cheek, and then he headed off toward the creek. I went inside the tent, Babar right behind.

"Nice," I said to Babar, as I looked around. "Furnished in tasteful Modern Refugee style. And I love what they've done with those cots."

Babar looked up at me with that stupid doggy grin of his and then leaped up on one of the cots and laid himself down.

"You idiot," I said. "You could have at least wiped off your paws." Babar, notably unconcerned with criticism, yawned and then closed his eyes.

I got on the cot with him, brushed off the chunkier bits of mud, and then used him as a pillow. He didn't seem to mind. And a good thing, too, since he was taking up half my cot.

"Well, here we are," I said. "Hope you like it here."

Babar made some sort of snuffling noise. *Well said,* I thought.

Even after everything was explained to us, there were still some folks who had a hard time getting it through their heads that we were cut off and on our own. In the group sessions headed by each of the colonial representatives, there was always someone (or someones) who said things couldn't be as bad as Dad was making them out to be, that there had to be some way for us to stay in contact with the rest of humanity or at least use our PDAs.

That's when the colony representatives sent each colonist the last file their PDAs would receive. It was a video file, shot by the Conclave and sent to every other race in our slice of space. In it, the Conclave leader, named General Gau, stood on a rise overlooking a small settlement. When I first saw the video I thought it was a human settlement, but was told that it was a settlement of Whaid colonists, the Whaid being a race I knew nothing about. What I did know was that their homes and buildings looked like ours, or close enough to ours not to matter.

This General Gau stood on the rise just long enough for you to wonder what it was he was looking at down there in the settlement, and the settlement disappeared, turned into ash and fire by what seemed like a thousand beams of light stabbing down from what we were told were hundreds of spaceships floating high above the colony. In just a few seconds there was nothing left of the colony, or the people who lived in it, other than a rising column of smoke.

No one questioned the wisdom of hiding after that.

I don't know how many times I watched the video of the Conclave attack; it must have been a few dozen times before Dad came up to me and made me hand over my PDA—no special privileges just because I was the colony leader's kid. But I wasn't watching because of the attack. Or, well, I should say that wasn't really what I was looking at when I watched it. What I was looking at was the figure, standing on the rise. The creature who ordered the attack. The one who had the blood of an entire colony on his hands. I was looking at this General Gau. I was wondering what he was thinking when he gave the order. Did he feel regret? Satisfaction? Pleasure? Pain?

I tried to imagine what it would take to order the deaths of thousands of innocent people. I felt happy that I couldn't wrap my brain around it. I was terrified that this general could. And that he was out there. Hunting us.

THIRTEEN

Two weeks after we landed on Roanoke, Magdy, Enzo, Gretchen and I went for a walk.

"Watch where you land," Magdy told us. "There are some big rocks down here."

"Great," Gretchen said. She shined her pocket light—acceptable technology, no computer equipment in it, just an old-fashioned LED—at the ground, looking for a place to land, and then hopped down from the edge of the container wall, aiming for her preferred spot. Enzo and I heard the *oof* as she landed, and then a bit of cursing.

"I told you to watch where you landed," Magdy said, shining his light on her.

"Shut it, Magdy," she said. "We shouldn't even be out here. You're going to get us all in trouble."

"Yeah, well," Magdy said. "Your words would have more moral authority if you weren't actually out here with me." He flicked his light up off of Gretchen and toward me and Enzo, still up on the container wall. "You two planning to join us?"

"Will you please stop with the light?" Enzo said. "The patrol is going to see it."

"The patrol is on the other side of the container wall," Magdy said. "Although if you don't hurry it up, that's not going to be the case for long. So move it." He flicked the light back and forth quickly in Enzo's face, making an annoying strobe effect. Enzo sighed and slid down off the container wall; I heard the muffled thump a second later. Which left me, feeling suddenly very exposed on the top of the containers that were the defensive perimeter around our little village—and also the frontier beyond which we were not allowed to go at night.

"Come on," Enzo whispered up to me. He, at least, remembered we weren't supposed to be out and modulated his voice accordingly. "Jump down. I'll catch you."

"Are you dumb?" I asked, also in a whispery voice. "You'll end up with my shoes in your eye sockets."

"It was a joke," Enzo said.

"Fine," I said. "Don't catch me."

"Jeez, Zoë," Magdy said, in a definite nonwhisper. "Will you *jump* already?"

I hopped off the container wall, down the three meters or so from the top, and tumbled a little when I landed. Enzo flicked his light on me, and offered me a hand up. I took it and squinted up at him as he pulled me up. Then I flicked my own light over to where Magdy was. "Jerk," I told him.

Magdy shrugged. "Come on," he said, and started along the perimeter of the wall toward our destination.

A few minutes later we were all flashing our lights into a hole.

"Wow," Gretchen said. "We've just broken curfew and risked being accidentally shot by the night guard for this. A hole in the ground. I'm picking our next field trip, Magdy."

Magdy snorted and knelt down into the hole. "If you actually paid attention to anything, you'd know that this *hole* has the council in a panic," Magdy said. "Something dug this out the other night while the patrol wasn't watching. Something was trying to get *in* to the colony from out *here*." He took his light and moved it up the nearest container until he spotted something. "Look. There are scratches on the container. Something tried to go over the top, and then when it couldn't it tried to go under."

"So what you're saying is that we're out here now with a bunch of predators," I said.

"It doesn't have to be a predator," Magdy said. "Maybe it's just something that likes to dig."

I flicked my light back up to the claw marks. "Yeah, that's a *reasonable* theory."

"We couldn't have seen this during the day?" Gretchen asked. "When we could see the things that can leap out and eat us?"

Magdy motioned his light over to me. "Her mom had her security people around it all day long. They weren't letting anybody else near it. Besides, whatever made this hole is long gone now."

"I'll remind you that you said that when something tears out your throat," Gretchen said.

"Relax," Magdy said. "I'm prepared. And anyway, this hole is just the opening act. My dad is friends with some of the security folks. One of them told him that just before they closed everything up for the night, they saw a herd of those fanties over in the woods. I say we go look."

"We should get back," Enzo said. "We shouldn't even be out here, Magdy. If they find us out there, we're all going to catch hell. We can see the fanties tomorrow. When the sun is up, and we can actually see them."

"Tomorrow they'll be awake and foraging," Magdy said. "And there's no way we're going to be able to do anything other than look at them through binoculars." Magdy pointed at me again. "Let me remind you that her parents have kept us cooped up for two weeks now, waiting to find out if anything might bruise us on this planet."

"Or kill us," I said. "Which would be a problem."

Magdy waved this away. "My point is that if we actually

want to *see* these things—actually get close enough to them that we can get a good look at them—we have to do it now. They're asleep, no one knows we're gone, and we'll be back before anyone misses us."

"I still think we should go back," Enzo said.

"Enzo, I know this is taking away from valuable make-out time with your girlfriend," Magdy said, "but I thought you *might* want to explore something other than Zoë's tonsils for once."

Magdy was *very* lucky he wasn't in arm's reach when he made that comment. Either my arm or Enzo's.

"You're being an ass again, Magdy," Gretchen said.

"Fine," Magdy said. "You guys go back. I'll see you later. I'm going to see me some fanties." He started toward the woods, waving his pocket light in the grass (or grasslike ground cover) as he walked. I shined my light over to Gretchen. She rolled her eyes in exasperation and started walking after Magdy. After a minute Enzo and I followed.

Take an elephant. Make it just a little smaller. Lose the ears. Make its trunk shorter and tentaclly at the end. Stretch out its legs until it almost but not quite seems impossible that they could support the weight. Give it four eyes. And then do other assorted weird things to its body until it's not that it looks like an elephant, it's just that it looks more like an elephant than it looks like anything else you can think of.

That's a fantie.

In the two weeks we'd been trapped in the colony village, waiting for the "all clear" to actually begin colonization, the fanties had been spotted several times, either in the woods near the village or just barely in the clearing between the village and the woods. A fantie spotting would bring up a mad rush of children to the colony gate (a gap in the container wall, closed up at night) to look and gawk and wave to the creatures. It would also bring a somewhat more studiously casual wave of us teenagers, because we wanted to see them too, we just didn't want to seem *too* interested, since that would mess with our credibility with all our new friends.

Certainly Magdy never gave any indication of actually caring about the fanties at all. He'd allow himself to be dragged to the gate by Gretchen when a herd passed by, but then he spent most of his time talking to the other guys who were also happy to make it look like they had gotten dragged to the gate. Just goes to show, I suppose. Even the self-consciously cool had a streak of kid in them.

There was some argument as to whether the fanties we saw were a local group that lived in the area, or whether we'd seen a number of herds that were just migrating through. I had no idea which theory was right; we'd only been on planet for a couple of weeks. And from a distance, all the fanties looked pretty much the same.

And up close, as we quickly discovered, they smelled horrible.

"Does *everything* on this planet smell like crap?" Gretchen whispered to me as we glanced up at the fanties. They waved back and forth, ever so slightly, as they slept standing on their legs. As if to answer her question, one of the fanties closest to where we were hiding let rip a monumental fart. We gagged and giggled equally.

"Shhhh," Enzo said. He and Magdy were crouched behind another tall bush a couple of meters over from us, just short of the clearing where the fantie herd had decided to rest for the night. There were about a dozen of them, all sleeping and farting under the stars. Enzo didn't seem to be enjoying the visit very much; I think he was worried about us accidentally waking the fanties. This was not a minor concern; fantie legs looked spindly from a distance but up close it was clear they could trample any one of us without too much of a problem, and there were a dozen fanties here. If we woke them up and they panicked, we could end up being pounded into mince-meat.

I think he was also still a little sore about the "exploring tonsils" comment. Magdy, in his usual less-than-charming way, had been digging at Enzo ever since he and I officially started going out. The taunts rose and fell depending on what Magdy's relationship with Gretchen was at the moment. I was guessing at the moment Gretchen had cut him off. Sometimes I thought I needed a graph or maybe a flow chart to understand how the two of them got along.

Another one of the fanties let off an epic load of flatulence.

"If we stay here any longer, I'm going to suffocate," I whispered to Gretchen. She nodded and motioned me to follow her. We snuck over to where Enzo and Magdy were.

"Can we go now?" Gretchen whispered to Magdy. "I know you're probably enjoying the smell, but the rest of us are about to lose dinner. And we've been gone long enough that some-one might start wondering where we went."

"In a minute," Magdy said. "I want to get closer to one."

"You're joking," Gretchen said.

"We've come this far," Magdy said.

"You really are an idiot sometimes, you know that?" Gretchen said. "You don't just go walking up to a herd of wild animals and say hello. They'll kill you."

"They're asleep," Magdy said.

"They won't be if you walk right into the middle of them," Gretchen said.

"I'm not *that* stupid," Magdy said, his whispered voice be-coming louder the more irritated he became. He pointed to the one closest to us. "I just want to get closer to that one. It's not going to be a problem. Stop worrying."

Before Gretchen could retort Enzo put his hand up to quiet

them both. "Look," he said, and pointed halfway down the clearing. "One of them is waking up."

"Oh, wonderful," Gretchen said.

The fantie in question shook its head and then lifted it, spreading the tentacles on its trunk wide. It waved them back and forth.

"What's it doing?" I asked Enzo. He shrugged. He was no more an expert on fanties than I was.

It waved its tentacles some more, in a wider arc, and then it came to me what it was doing. It was *smelling* something. Something that shouldn't be there.

The fantie bellowed, not from its trunk like an elephant, but from its mouth. All the other fanties were instantly awake and bellowing, and beginning to move.

I looked over to Gretchen. *Oh, crap,* I mouthed. She nodded, and looked back over at the fanties. I looked over at Magdy, who had made himself suddenly very small. I don't think he wanted to get any closer now.

The fantie closest to us wheeled about and scraped against the bush we were hiding behind. I heard the thud of its foot as the animal maneuvered itself into a new position. I decided it was time to move but my body overruled me, since it wasn't giving me control of my legs. I was frozen in place, squatting behind a bush, waiting for my trampling.

Which never came. A second later the fantie was gone, run off in the same direction as the rest of its herd: away from us.

Magdy popped up from his crouching position, and listened to the herd rumbling off in the distance. "All right," he said. "What just *happened*?"

"I thought they smelled us for sure," I said. "I thought they'd found us."

"I told you you were an idiot," Gretchen said to Magdy. "If you'd been out there when they woke up, we'd be scooping what was left of you into a bucket."

The two of them started sniping at each other; I turned to

look at Enzo, who had turned to face the opposite direction from where the fanties had run. He had his eyes closed but it looked like he was concentrating on something.

"What is it?" I asked.

He opened his eyes, looked at me, and then pointed in the direction he was facing. "The breeze is coming from this direction," he said.

"Okay," I said. I wasn't following him.

"Have you ever gone hunting?" Enzo asked. I shook my head. "We were upwind of the fanties," he said. "The wind was blowing our scent away from them." He pointed to where the first fantie to wake up had been. "I don't think that fantie would have smelled us at all."

Click. "Okay," I said. "Now I get it."

Enzo turned to Magdy and Gretchen. "Guys," he said. "It's time to leave. Now."

Magdy flashed his pocket light at Enzo and seemed ready to say something sarcastic, then caught the expression on Enzo's face in the pocket light's circle. "What is it?"

"The fanties didn't run off because of us," Enzo said. "I think there's something else out there. Something that hunts the fanties. And I think it's coming this way."

It's a cliché of horror entertainments to have teenagers lost in the woods, imagining they're being chased by something horrible that's *right behind them.*

And now I know why. If you ever want to feel like you're on the verge of total, abject bowel-releasing terror, try making your way a klick or two out of a forest, at night, with the certain feeling you're being hunted. It makes you feel alive, it really does, but not in a way you *want* to feel alive.

Magdy was in the lead, of course, although whether he was leading because he knew the way back or just because he was running fast enough that the rest of us had to chase him was up for debate. Gretchen and I followed, and Enzo took up the rear. Once I slowed down to check on him and he waved me off. "Stay with Gretchen," he said. Then I realized that he was intentionally staying behind us so whatever might be following us would have to get through him first. I would have kissed him right then if I hadn't been a quivering mess of adrenaline, desperately running to get home.

"Through here," Magdy said to us. He pointed at an irregular natural path that I recognized as being the one we used to get into the forest in the first place. I was focusing on getting on that path and then something stepped in behind Gretchen and grabbed me. I screamed.

There was a bang, followed by a muffled thump, followed by a shout.

Ezno launched himself at what grabbed at me. A second later he was on the forest floor, Dickory's knife at his throat. It took me longer than it should have to recognize who it was holding the knife.

"Dickory!" I yelled. "Stop!"

Dickory paused.

"Let him go," I said. "He's no danger to me."

Dickory removed the knife and stepped away from Enzo. Enzo scrambled away from Dickory, and away from me.

"Hickory?" I called. "Is everything all right?"

From ahead, I heard Hickory's voice. "Your friend had a handgun. I have disarmed him."

"He's choking me!" Magdy said.

"If Hickory wanted to choke you, you wouldn't be able to talk," I yelled back. "Let him go, Hickory."

"I am keeping his handgun," Hickory said. There was a rustle in the darkness as Magdy picked himself up.

"Fine," I said. Now that we stopped moving, it was like someone pulled a stopper, and all the adrenaline in my body was falling out from the bottom of my feet. I crouched down to keep from falling over.

"No, *not* fine," Magdy said. I saw him emerge out of the gloom, stalking toward me. Dickory interposed itself between me and Magdy. Magdy's stalking came to a quick halt. "That's my dad's gun. If he finds it missing, I'm dead."

"What were you doing with the gun in the first place?" Gretchen asked. She had also come back to where I was standing, Hickory following behind her.

"I told you I was prepared," Magdy said, and then turned to me. "You need to tell your *bodyguards* that they need to be more careful." He pointed at Hickory. "I almost took off that one's head."

"Hickory?" I said.

"I was not in any serious danger," Hickory said, blandly. His attention seemed elsewhere.

"I want my gun back," Magdy said. I think he was trying for threatening; he failed when his voice cracked.

"Hickory will give you your dad's gun back when we get back to the village," I said. I felt a fatigue headache coming on.

"*Now,*" Magdy said.

"For God's sake, Magdy," I snapped. I was suddenly very tired, and angry. "Will you please just shut up about your damn gun. You're lucky you didn't kill one of us with it. And you're lucky you didn't hit one of *them*"—I waved at Dickory and then Hickory—"because then *you* would be dead, and the rest of us would have to explain how it happened. So just shut up about the stupid gun. Shut *up* and let's go *home.*"

Magdy stared at me, then stomped off into the gloom, toward the village. Enzo gave me a strange look and then followed his friend.

"Perfect," I said, and squeezed my temples with my hands. The monster headache I was on the verge of had arrived, and it was a magnificent specimen.

"We should return to the village," Hickory said to me.

"You *think*?" I said, and then stood up and stomped off, away from it and Dickory, back to the village. Gretchen, suddenly left with my two bodyguards for company, was not far behind me.

"I don't want one word of what happened tonight to get back to John and Jane," I said to Hickory, as it, Dickory and I stood in the common area of the village. At this time of night there were only a couple of other people who were loitering there, and they quickly disappeared when Hickory and Dickory showed up. Two weeks had not been enough time for people to get used to them. We had the common area to ourselves.

"As you say," Hickory said.

"Thank you," I said, and started walking away from them again, toward the tent I shared with my parents.

"You should not have been in the woods," Hickory said.

That stopped me. I turned around to face Hickory. "Excuse me?" I said.

"You should not have been in the woods," Hickory said. "Not without our protection."

"We had protection," I said, and some part of my brain didn't believe those words had actually come out of my mouth.

"Your protection was a handgun wielded by someone who did not know how to use it," Hickory said. "The bullet he fired went into the ground less than thirty centimeters from him. He almost shot himself in the foot. I disarmed him because he was a threat to himself, not to me."

"I'll be sure to tell him that," I said. "But it doesn't matter. I don't need your *permission*, Hickory, to do what I please. You and Dickory aren't my parents. And your *treaty* doesn't say you can tell me what to do."

"You are free to do as you will," Hickory said. "But you took an unnecessary risk to yourself, both by going into the forest and by not informing us of your intent."

"That didn't stop you from coming in after me," I said. It came out like an accusation, because I was in an accusatory mood.

"No," Hickory said.

"So you took it on yourself to follow me around when I didn't give you permission to do so," I said.

"Yes," Hickory said.

"Don't do that again," I said. "I know privacy is an *alien* concept to you, but sometimes I don't want you around. Can you understand that? You"—I pointed at Dickory—"nearly cut my boyfriend's throat tonight. I know you don't *like* him, but that's a little much."

"Dickory would not have harmed Enzo," Hickory said.

"*Enzo* doesn't know that," I said, and turned back to Dickory. "And what if he had gotten in a good hit on you? You might have hurt him just to keep him down. I don't *need* this kind of protection. And I don't want it."

Hickory and Dickory stood there silently, soaking up my anger. After a couple of seconds, I got bored with this. "Well?" I said.

"You were running out of the forest when you came by us," Hickory said.

"Yeah? So?" I said. "We thought we might be being chased by something. Something spooked the fanties we were watching and Enzo thought it might have been a predator or something. It was a false alarm. There was nothing behind us or else it would have caught up with us when you two leaped out of nowhere and scared the crap out of all of us."

"No," Hickory said.

"No? You *didn't* scare the crap out of us?" I said. "I beg to differ."

"No," Hickory said. "You were being followed."

"What are you talking about?" I said. "There was nothing behind us."

"They were in the trees," Hickory said. "They were pacing you from above. Moving ahead of you. We heard them before we heard you."

I felt weak. "Them?" I said.

"It is why we took you as soon as we heard you coming," Hickory said. "To protect you."

"What were they?" I asked.

"We don't know," Hickory said. "We did not have the time to make any good observation. And we believe your friend's gunshot scared them off."

"So it wasn't necessarily something hunting us," I said. "It could have been anything."

"Perhaps," Hickory said, in that studiously neutral way it had when it didn't want to disagree with me. "Whatever they were, they were moving along with you and your group."

"Guys, I'm tired," I said, because I didn't want to think about any of this anymore, and if I did think about it anymore—about the idea that some pack of creatures was following us in the trees—I might have a collapse right there in the common area. "Can we have this conversation tomorrow?"

"As you wish, Zoë," Hickory said.

"Thank you," I said, and started shuffling off toward my cot. "And remember what I said about not telling my parents."

"We will not tell your parents," Hickory said.

"And remember what I said about not following me," I said. They said nothing to this. I waved at them tiredly and went off to sleep.

I found Enzo outside his family's tent the next morning, reading a book.

"Wow, a real book," I said. "Who did you kill to get that?"

"I borrowed it from one of the Mennonite kids," he said. He showed the spine to me. "*Huckleberry Finn*. You heard of it?"

"You're asking a girl from a planet named Huckleberry if she's heard of *Huckleberry Finn*," I said. I hoped the incredulous tone of my voice would convey amusement.

Apparently not. "Sorry," he said. "I didn't make the connection." He flipped the book open to where he had been reading.

"Listen," I said. "I wanted to thank you. For what you did last night."

Enzo looked up over his book. "I didn't do anything last night."

"You stayed behind Gretchen and me," I said. "You put yourself between us and whatever was following us. I just wanted you to know I appreciated it."

Enzo shrugged. "Not that there was anything following us after all," he said. I thought about telling him about what Hickory told me, but kept it in. "And when something did come out at you, it was ahead of me. So I wasn't much help, actually."

"Yeah, about that," I said. "I wanted to apologize for that. For the thing with Dickory." I didn't really know how to put that. I figured saying *Sorry for when my alien bodyguard very nearly took your head off with a knife* wouldn't really go over well.

"Don't worry about it," Enzo said.

"I do worry about it," I said.

"Don't," Enzo said. "Your bodyguard did its job." For a second it seemed like Enzo would say something more, but then he cocked his head and looked at me like he was waiting for me to wrap up whatever it was I was doing, so he could get back to his very important book.

It suddenly occurred to me that Enzo hadn't written me any poetry since we landed on Roanoke.

"Well, okay then," I said, lamely. "I guess I'll see you a little later, then."

"Sounds good," Enzo said, and then gave me a friendly wave and put his nose into Huck Finn's business. I walked back to my tent and found Babar inside and went over to him and gave him a hug.

"Congratulate me, Babar," I said. "I think I just had my first fight with my boyfriend."

Babar licked my face. That made it a little better. But not much.

FOURTEEN

"No, you're still too low," I said to Gretchen. "It's making you flat. You need to be a note higher or something. Like this." I sang the part I wanted her to sing.

"I *am* singing that," Gretchen said.

"No, you're singing lower than that," I said.

"Then *you're* singing the wrong note," Gretchen said. "Because I'm singing the note you're singing. Go ahead, sing it."

I cleared my throat, and sang the note I wanted her to sing. She matched it perfectly. I stopped singing and listened to Gretchen. She was flat.

"Well, nuts," I said.

"I told you," Gretchen said.

"If I could pull up the song for you, you could hear the note and sing it," I said.

"If you could pull up the song, we wouldn't be trying to sing it at all," Gretchen said. "We'd just listen to it, like civilized human beings."

"Good point," I said.

"There's nothing good about it," Gretchen said. "I swear to you, Zoë. I knew coming to a colony world was going to be hard. I was ready for that. But if I knew they were going to take my PDA, I might have just stayed back on Erie. Go ahead, call me shallow."

"Shallow," I said.

"Now tell me I'm *wrong*," Gretchen said. "I dare you."

I didn't tell her she was wrong. I knew how she felt. Yes, it *was* shallow to admit that you missed your PDA. But when you'd spent your whole life able to call up everything you wanted to amuse you on a PDA—music, shows, books and friends—when you had to part with it, it made you miserable. Really miserable. Like "trapped on a desert island with nothing but coconuts to bang together" miserable. Because there was nothing to replace it with. Yes, the Colonial Mennonites had brought their own small library of printed books, but most of that consisted of Bibles and agricultural manuals and a few "classics," of which *Huckleberry Finn* was one of the more recent volumes. As for popular music and entertainments, well, they didn't much truck with that.

You could tell a few of the Colonial Mennonite teens thought it was funny to watch the rest of us go through entertainment withdrawal. Didn't seem very Christian of them, I have to say. On the other hand, they weren't the ones whose lives had been drastically altered by landing on Roanoke. If I were in their shoes and watching a whole bunch of other people whining and moaning about how horrible it was that their toys were taken away, I might feel a little smug, too.

We did what people do in situations where they go without: We adjusted. I hadn't read a book since we landed on Roanoke, but was on the waiting list for a bound copy of *The Wizard of Oz*. There were no recorded shows or entertainments but Shakespeare never fails; there was a reader's theater performance of *Twelfth Night* planned for a week from Sunday. It promised to be fairly gruesome—I'd heard some of the read-throughs—but Enzo was reading the part of Sebastian, and he was doing well enough, and truth be told it would be the first time I would have ever experienced a Shakespeare play—or any play other than a school pageant—live. And it's not like there would be anything else to do anyway.

And as for music, well, this is what happened: Within a couple days of landing a few of the colonists hauled out guitars and accordions and hand drums and other such instruments and started trying to play together. Which went horribly, because nobody knew anyone else's music. It was like what happened on the *Magellan*. So they started teaching each other their songs, and then people showed up to sing them, and then people showed up to listen. And thus it was, at the very tail end of space, when no one was looking, the colony of Roanoke reinvented the "hootenanny." Which is what Dad called it. I told him it was a stupid name for it, and he said he agreed, but said that the other word for it—"wingding"—was worse. I couldn't argue with that.

The Roanoke Hootenanners (as they were now calling themselves) took requests—but only if the person requesting sang the song. And if the musicians didn't know the song, you'd have to sing it at least a couple of times until they could figure out how to fake it. This led to an interesting development: singers started doing a cappella versions of their favorite songs, first by themselves and increasingly in groups, which might or might not be accompanied by the Hootenanners. It was becoming a point of pride for people to show up with their favorite songs already arranged, so everyone else in the audience didn't have to suffer through a set of dry runs before it was all listenable.

It was safe to say that some of these arrangements were more *arranged* than others, to put it politely, and some folks sang with the same vocal control as a cat in a shower. But now, a couple of months after the hootenannies had begun, people were beginning to get the hang of it. And people had begun coming to the hoots with new songs, arranged a cappella. One of the most popular songs at the recent hoots was "Let Me Drive the Tractor"—the tale of a colonist being taught to drive a manual tractor by a Mennonite, who, because they were the only ones who knew how to operate noncomputerized farm machinery, had been put in charge of planting crops and teaching the rest of us how to use their equipment. The song ends with the tractor going into a ditch. It was based on a true story. The Mennonites thought the song was pretty funny, even though it came at the cost of a wrecked tractor.

Songs about tractors were a long way from what any of us had been listening to before, but then, we were a long way from where any of us were before, in any sense, so maybe that fit. And to get all sociological about it, maybe what it meant was that twenty or fifty standard years down the line, whenever the Colonial Union decided to let us get in contact with the rest of the human race, Roanoke would have its own distinct musical form. Maybe they'll call it Roanokapella. Or Hootenoke. Or *something*.

But at this particular moment, all I was trying to do was to get the right note for Gretchen to sing so she and I could go to the next hoot with a halfway decent version of "Delhi Morning" for the Hootenanners to pick up on. And I was failing miserably. This is what it feels like when you realize that, despite a song being your favorite of maybe all time, you don't actually know every little nook and cranny of it. And since my copy of the song was on my PDA, which I could no longer use or even had anymore, there was no way to correct this problem.

Unless. "I have an idea," I said to Gretchen.

"Does it involve you learning to sing on key?" Gretchen asked.

"Even better," I said.

Ten minutes later we were on the other side of Croatoan, standing in front of the village's information center—the one place on the entire planet that you'd still find a functioning piece of electronics, because the inside was designed to completely block any radio or other signals of any sort. The technology to do this, sadly, was rare enough that we only had enough of it for a converted cargo container. The good news was, they were making more. The bad news was, they were only making enough for a medical bay. Sometimes life stinks. Gretchen and I walked into the receiving area, which was pitch black because of the signal-cloaking material; you had to close the outer door to the information center before you could open the inner door. So for about a second and a half it was like being swallowed by grim, black, featureless death. Not something I'd recommend.

And then we opened the inner door and found a geek inside. He looked at the both of us, a little surprised, and then got that *no* look.

"The answer is no," he said, confirming the look.

"Aw, Mr. Bennett," I said. "You don't even know what we're going to ask."

"Well, let's see," said Jerry Bennett. "Two teenage girls— daughters of the colony leaders, incidentally—just *happen* to walk into the only place in the colony where one could play with a PDA. Hmmm. Are they here to beg to play with a PDA? Or are they here because they enjoy the company of a chunky, middle-aged man? This is not a hard question, Miss Perry."

"We just want to listen to one song," I said. "We'll be out of your hair in just a minute."

Bennett sighed. "You know, at least a couple times a day someone just like you gets the bright idea to come in here and ask if I could just let them borrow a PDA to watch a movie, or listen to some music or read a book. And, oh, it'll just take a minute. I won't even notice they're there. And if I say yes, then other people will come in asking for the same time. Eventually

I'll spend so much time helping people with their PDAs that I won't have time to do the work your parents, Miss Perry, have assigned me to do. So you tell me: What should I do?"

"Get a lock?" said Gretchen.

Bennett glanced over to Gretchen, sourly. "Very amusing," he said.

"What are you doing for my parents?" I asked.

"Your parents are having me slowly and painstakingly locate and print every single Colonial Union administration memo and file, so they can refer to them without having to come in here and bother me," Bennett said. "In one sense I appreciate that, but in a more immediate sense I've been doing it for the last three days and I'm likely to be doing it for another four. And since the printer I have to work with jams on a regular basis, it does actually require someone to pay attention to it. And that's me. So there you have it, Miss Perry: Four years of technical education and twenty years of professional work have allowed me to become a printer monkey at the very ass end of space. Truly, my life's goal has been achieved."

I shrugged. "So let us do it," I said.

"I beg your pardon," Bennett said.

"If all you're doing is making sure the printer doesn't jam, that's something we could do for you," I said. "We'll work for you for a couple of hours, and in exchange you let us use a couple of PDAs while we're here. And then you can do whatever else you need to do."

"Or just go have lunch," Gretchen said. "Surprise your wife."

Bennett was silent for a minute, considering. "Offering to actually *help* me," he said. "No one's tried that tactic before. Very sneaky."

"We try," I said.

"And it is lunchtime," Bennett said. "And it is just printing."

"It is," I agreed.

"I suppose if you mess things up horribly it won't be too bad for me," Bennett said. "Your parents won't punish me for your incompetence."

"Nepotism working for you," I said.

"Not that there will be a problem," Gretchen said.

"No," I agreed. "We're excellent printer monkeys."

"All right," Bennett said, and reached across his worktable to grab his PDA. "You can use my PDA. You know how to use this?"

I gave him a look.

"Sorry. Okay." He punched up a queue of files on the display. "These are files that need to go through today. The printer is there"—he motioned to the far end of the worktable—"and the paper is in that bin. Feed it into the printer, stack the finished documents next to the printer. If it jams, and it will, several times, just yank out the paper and let it autofeed a new one. It'll automatically reprint the last page it was working on. While you're doing that you can sync up to the Entertainment archive. I downloaded all those files into one place."

"You downloaded everyone's files?" I asked, and felt ever so slightly violated.

"Relax," Bennett said. "Only public files are accessible. As long as you encrypted your private files before you turned in your PDA, like you were told to, your secrets are safe. Now, once you access a music file the speakers will kick on. Don't turn them up too high or you won't be able to hear the printer jam."

"You have speakers already set up?" Gretchen asked.

"Yes, Miss Trujillo," Bennett said. "Believe it or not, even chunky middle-aged men like to listen to music."

"I know that," Gretchen said. "My dad loves his."

"And on that ego-deflating note, I'll be off," Bennett said. "I'll be back in a couple of hours. Please don't destroy the place.

And if anyone comes in asking if they can borrow a PDA, tell them the answer is no, and no exceptions." He set off.

"I hope he was being ironic there," I said.

"Don't care," Gretchen said, and grabbed for the PDA. "Give me that."

"Hey," I said, holding it away from her. "First things first." I set up the printer, queued the files, and then accessed "Delhi Morning." The opening strains flowed out of the speakers and I soaked them in. I swear I almost cried.

"It's amazing how badly you remembered this song," Gretchen said, about halfway though.

"Shhhhh," I said. "Here's that part."

She saw the expression on my face and kept quiet until the song was done.

Two hours is *not* enough time with a PDA if you haven't had access to one in months. And that's all I'm going to say about that. But it was enough time that both Gretchen and I came out of the information center feeling just like we'd spent hours soaking in a nice hot bath—which, come to think of it, was something that we hadn't done for months either.

"We should keep this to ourselves," Gretchen said.

"Yes," I said. "Don't want people to bug Mr. Bennett."

"No, I just like having something over everyone else," Gretchen said.

"There aren't a lot of people who can carry off petty," I said. "Yet somehow you do."

Gretchen nodded. "Thank you, madam. And now I need to get back home. I promised Dad I'd weed the vegetable garden before it got dark."

"Have fun rooting in the dirt," I said.

"Thanks," Gretchen said. "If you were feeling nice, you could always offer to help me."

"I'm working on my evil," I said.

"Be that way," Gretchen said.

"But let's get together after dinner tonight to practice," I said. "Now that we know how to sing that part."

"Sounds good," Gretchen said. "Or will, hopefully." She waved and headed off toward home. I looked around and decided today would be a good day for a walk.

And it was. The sun was up, the day was bright, particularly after a couple of hours in the light-swallowing information center, and Roanoke was deep into spring—which was really pretty, even if it turned out that all the native blooms smelled like rotten meat dipped in sewer sauce (that description courtesy of Magdy, who could string together a phrase now and then). But after a couple of months, you stop noticing the smell, or at least accept there's nothing you can do about it. When the whole planet smells, you just have to deal with it.

But what really made it a good day for a walk was how much our world has changed in just a couple of months. John and Jane let us all out of Croatoan not too long after Enzo, Gretchen, Magdy and I had our midnight jog, and the colonists had begun to move into the countryside, building homes and farms, helping and learning from the Mennonites who were in charge of our first crops, which were already now growing in the fields. They were genetically engineered to be fast-growing; we'd be having our first harvest in the not too far future. It looked like we were going to survive after all. I walked past these new houses and fields, waving to folks as I went.

Eventually I walked past the last homestead and over a small rise. On the other side of it, nothing but grass and scrub and the forest in a line to the side. This rise was destined to be part of another farm, and more farms and pastures would cut up this little valley even further. It's funny how even just a couple thousand humans could start to change a landscape. But at the moment there was no other person in it but me; it was my private spot, for as long as it lasted. Mine and mine alone. Well, and on a couple of occasions, mine and Enzo's.

I laid back, looked up at the clouds in the sky, and smiled to myself. Maybe we were in hiding at the farthest reaches of the galaxy, but right now, at this moment, things were pretty good. You can be happy anywhere, if you have the right point of view. And the ability to ignore the smell of an entire planet.

"Zoë," said a voice behind me.

I jerked up and then saw Hickory and Dickory. They had just come over the rise.

"Don't *do* that," I said, and got up.

"We wish to speak to you," Hickory said.

"You could do that at home," I said.

"Here is better," Hickory said. "We have concerns."

"Concerns about what?" I said, and rose to look at them. Something wasn't quite right about either of them, and it took me a minute to figure out what it was. "Why aren't you wearing your consciousness modules?" I asked.

"We are concerned about the increasing risks you are taking with your safety," Hickory said, answering the first but not the second of my questions. "And with your safety in a general sense."

"You mean, being here?" I said. "Relax, Hickory. It's broad daylight, and the Hentosz farm is just over the hill. Nothing bad is going to happen to me."

"There are predators here," Hickory said.

"There are *yotes*," I said, naming the dog-sized carnivores that we'd found lurking around Croatoan. "I can handle a yote."

"They move in packs," Hickory said.

"Not during the day," I said.

"You do not only come here in the day," Hickory said. "Nor do you always come alone."

I reddened a bit at that, and thought about getting angry with Hickory. But it wasn't wearing its consciousness. Getting angry with it wouldn't do anything. "I thought I told the two of you not to follow me when I want to have some private time," I said, as evenly as I could.

"We do not follow you," Hickory said. "But neither are we stupid. We know where you go and with whom. Your lack of care is putting you at risk, and you do not always allow us to accompany you anymore. We cannot protect you as we would prefer to, and are expected to."

"We have been here for months, guys." I said. "There hasn't been a single attack on anyone by anything."

"You would have been attacked that night in the woods had Dickory and I not come to find you," Hickory said. "Those were not yotes in the trees that night. Yotes cannot climb or move through trees."

"And you'll notice I'm nowhere near the forest," I said, and waved in the direction of the tree line. "And whatever was in there doesn't seem to come out here, because we'd have seen them by now if they did. We've been over this before, Hickory."

"It is not only the predators here that concern us," Hickory said.

"I'm not following you," I said.

"This colony is being searched for," Hickory said.

"If you saw the video, you'll remember that this Conclave group blasted that colony from the sky," I said. "If the Conclave finds us, I don't think even you are going to be able to do much to protect me."

"It is not the Conclave we are concerned about," Hickory said.

"You're the only ones, then," I said.

"The Conclave is not the only one who will seek this colony," Hickory said. "Others will search for it, to win favor from the Conclave, or to thwart it, or to take the colony for its own. They will not blast this colony from the sky. They will take it in the standard fashion. Invasion and slaughter."

"What is with the two of you today?" I said. I was trying to lighten the mood.

I failed. "And then there is the matter of who you are," Hickory said.

"What does that mean?" I said.

"You should know well," Hickory said. "You are not merely the daughter of the colony leaders. You are also important to *us*. To the Obin. That fact is not unknown, Zoë. You have been used as a bargaining chip your entire life. We Obin used you to bargain with your father to build us consciousness. You are a treaty condition between the Obin and the Colonial Union. We have no doubt that any who would attack this colony would try to take you in order to bargain with the Obin. Even the Conclave could be tempted to do this. Or they would kill you to wound us. To kill a symbol of ourselves."

"That's crazy," I said.

"It has happened before," Hickory said.

"What?" I said.

"When you lived on Huckleberry, there were no fewer than six attempts to capture or kill you," Hickory said. "The last just a few days before you left Huckleberry."

"And you never *told* me this?" I asked.

"It was decided by both your government and ours that neither you nor your parents needed to know," Hickory said. "You were a child, and your parents wished to give you as unremarkable a life as possible. The Obin wished to be able to provide them that. None of these attempts came close to success. We stopped each long before you would have been in danger. And in each case the Obin government expressed its displeasure with the races who made such attempts on your well-being."

I shuddered at that. The Obin were not people to make enemies of.

"We would not have told you at all—and we have violated

our standing orders not to do so—were we not in our current situation," Hickory said. "We are cut off from the systems we had in place to keep you safe. And you are becoming increasingly independent in your actions and resentful of our presence in your life."

Those last words hit me like a slap. "I'm not resentful," I said. "I just want my own time. I'm sorry if that hurts you."

"We are not hurt," Hickory said. "We have responsibilities. How we fulfill those responsibilities must adapt to circumstance. We are making an adaptation now."

"I don't know what you mean," I said.

"It is time for you to learn how to defend yourself," Hickory said. "You want to be more independent from us, and we do not have all the resources we once had to keep you safe. We have always intended to teach you to fight. Now, for both of those reasons, it is necessary to begin that training."

"What do you mean, teach me to fight?" I asked.

"We will teach you to defend yourself physically," Hickory said. "To disarm an opponent. To use weapons. To immobilize your enemy. To kill your enemy if necessary."

"You want to teach me how to kill other people," I said.

"It is necessary," Hickory said.

"I'm not sure John and Jane would approve of that," I said.

"Major Perry and Lieutenant Sagan both know how to kill," Hickory said. "Both, in their military service, have killed others when it was necessary for their survival."

"But it doesn't mean that they want *me* to know," I said. "And also, I don't know that *I* want to know. You say you need to adapt how you fulfill your responsibilities. Fine. Figure out how to adapt them. But I'm not going to learn how to *kill* something else so you can feel like you're doing a better job doing something I'm not even sure I *want* you to do anymore."

"You do not wish us to defend you," Hickory said. "Or learn to defend yourself."

"I don't *know*!" I said. I yelled it in exasperation. "Okay? I hate having my face pushed into all of this. That I'm some special *thing* that needs to be defended. Well, you know what? *Everyone* here needs to be defended, Hickory. We're *all* in danger. Any minute hundreds of ships could show up over our heads and kill us all. I'm sick of it. I try to forget about it a little every now and then. That's what I was doing out here before the two of you showed up to crap over it all. So thank you very much for *that*."

Hickory and Dickory said nothing to that. If they had been wearing their consciousness, they'd probably be all twitchy and overloaded at that last outburst. But they were just standing there, impassive.

I counted to five and tried to get myself back under control. "Look," I said, in what I hoped was a more reasonable tone of voice. "Give me a couple of days to think about this, all right? You've dropped a lot on me all at once. Let me work it through in my head."

They still said nothing.

"Fine," I said. "I'm heading back." I brushed past Hickory.

And found myself on the ground.

I rolled and looked up at Hickory, confused. "What the hell?" I said, and made to stand up.

Dickory, who had moved behind me, roughly pushed me back into the grass and dirt.

I scrambled backward from the two of them. "Stop it," I said.

They drew their combat knives, and came toward me.

I grunted out a scream and bolted upright, running at full speed toward the top of the hill, toward the Hentosz farm. But Obin can run faster than humans. Dickory flanked me, got in front of me, and drew back its knife. I backpedaled, falling backward as I did. Dickory lunged. I screamed and rolled again and sprinted back down the side of the hill I came up.

Hickory was waiting for me and moving to intercept me. I tried to fake going left but it was having none of it, and grabbed for me, getting a grip on my left forearm. I hit at it with my right fist. Hickory deflected it easily, and then in a quick reversal slapped me sharply on the temple, releasing me as it did so. I staggered back, stunned. Hickory looped a leg around one of mine and jerked upward, lifting me completely off the ground. I fell backward and landed on my head. A white blast of pain flooded my skull, and all I could do was lie there, dazed.

There was heavy pressure on my chest. Hickory was kneeling on me, immobilizing me. I clawed desperately at it, but it held its head away from me on its long neck and ignored everything else. I shouted for help as loudly as I could, knowing no one could hear me, and yelling anyway.

I looked over and saw Dickory, standing to the side. "Please," I said. Dickory said nothing. And could feel nothing. Now I knew why the two of them came to see me without their consciousness.

I grabbed at Hickory's leg, on my chest, and tried to push it off. It pushed it in harder, offered another disorienting slap with one hand, and with the other raised it and then plunged it toward my head in one terrible and fluid move. I screamed.

"You are unharmed," Hickory said, at some point. "You may get up."

I stayed on the ground, not moving, eyes turned toward Hickory's knife, buried in the ground so close to my head that I couldn't actually focus on it. Then I propped myself up on my elbows, turned away from the knife, and threw up.

Hickory waited until I was done. "We offer no apology for this," it said. "And will accept whatever consequences for it that you may choose. Know only this: You were not physically harmed. You are unlikely even to bruise. We made sure of this. For all of that you were at our mercy in seconds. Others who will come for you will not show you such consideration. They will not hold back. They will not stop. They will have no concern for you. They will not show you mercy. They will seek to kill you. And they will succeed. We knew you would not believe us if we only told you this. We had to show you."

I rose to my feet, barely able to stay upright, and staggered back from the two of them as best I could. "God *damn* you," I said. "God damn you both. You stay away from me from now on." I headed back to Croatoan. As soon as my legs could do it, I started running.

"Hey," Gretchen said, coming into the information center and sealing the inside door behind her. "Mr. Bennett said I could find you here."

"Yeah," I said. "I asked him if I could be his printer monkey a little more today."

"Couldn't keep away from the music?" Gretchen said, trying to make a little joke.

I shook my head and showed her what I was looking at.

"These are classified files, Zoë," she said. "CDF intelligence reports. You're going to get in trouble if anyone ever finds out. And Bennett definitely won't let you back in here."

"I don't *care*," I said, and my voice cracked enough that Gretchen looked at me in alarm. "I have to know how bad it is. I have to know who's out there and what they want from us. From *me*. Look." I took the PDA and pulled a file on General Gau, the leader of the Conclave, the one who ordered the destruction of the colony on the video file. "This general is going to kill us all if he finds us, and we know *next to nothing* about him. What makes someone do this? Killing innocent people? What happened in his life that gets him to a place where wiping out entire planets seems like a good idea? Don't you think we should know? And we don't. We've got statistics on his military service and that's it." I tossed the PDA back on the table, carelessly, alarming Gretchen. "I want to know *why* this general wants me to die. Why he wants us *all* to die. Don't you?" I put my hand on my forehead and slumped a little against the worktable.

"Okay," Gretchen said, after a minute. "I think you need to tell me what happened to you today. Because this is not how you were when I left you this afternoon."

I glanced over at Gretchen, stifled a laugh, and then broke down and started crying. Gretchen came over to give me a hug, and after a good long while, I told her everything. And I do mean everything.

She was quiet after I had unloaded. "Tell me what you're thinking," I said.

"If I tell you, you're going to hate me," she said.

"Don't be silly," I said. "I'm not going to hate you."

"I think they're right," she said. "Hickory and Dickory."

"I hate you," I said.

She pushed me lightly. "Stop that," she said. "I don't mean they were right to attack you. That was just over the line. But, and don't take this the wrong way, you're not an ordinary girl."

"That's not true," I said. "Do you see me acting any different than anyone else? Ever? Do I hold myself out as someone special? Have you ever once heard me talk about any of this to people?"

"They know anyway," Gretchen said.

"I know that," I said. "But it doesn't come from *me*. I work at being normal."

"Okay, you're a perfectly normal girl," Gretchen said.

"Thank you," I said.

"A perfectly normal girl who's had six attempted assassinations," Gretchen said.

"But that's not *me*," I said, poking myself in the chest. "It's *about* me. About someone else's *idea* of who I am. And that doesn't matter to me."

"It would matter to you if you were dead," Gretchen said, and then held her hand up before I could respond. "And it would matter to your parents. It would matter to me. I'm pretty sure it would matter to Enzo. And it seems like it would matter a whole lot to a couple billion aliens. Think about *that*. Someone even thinks about coming after you, they bomb a planet."

"I don't want to think about it," I said.

"I know," Gretchen said. "But I don't think you have a choice anymore. No matter what you do, you're still who you are, whether you want to be or not. You can't change it. You've got to work with it."

"Thanks for that uplifting message," I said.

"I'm trying to help," Gretchen said.

I sighed. "I know, Gretchen. I'm sorry. I don't mean to bite your head off. I'm just getting tired of having my life be about other people's choices for me."

"This makes you different than any of the rest of us how, exactly?" Gretchen asked.

"My *point*," I said. "I'm a perfectly normal girl. Thank you for finally noticing."

"Perfectly normal," Gretchen agreed. "Except for being Queen of the Obin."

"Hate you," I said.

Gretchen grinned.

"Miss Trujillo said that you wanted to see us," Hickory said. Dickory and Gretchen, who had gotten the two Obin for me, stood to its side. We were standing on the hill where my bodyguards had attacked me a few days earlier.

"Before I say anything else, you should know I am still incredibly angry at you," I said. "I don't know that I will ever forgive you for attacking me, even if I understand why you did it, and why you thought you had to. I want to make sure you know that. And I want to make sure you *feel* it." I pointed to Hickory's consciousness collar, secure around its neck.

"We feel it," Hickory said, its voice quivering. "We feel it enough that we debated whether we could turn our consciousness back on. The memory is almost too painful to bear."

I nodded. I wanted to say *good,* but I knew it was the wrong thing to say, and that I would regret saying it. Didn't mean I couldn't *think* it, though, for the moment, anyway.

"I'm not going to ask you to apologize," I said. "I know you won't. But I want your word you will never do something like that again," I said.

"You have our word," Hickory said.

"Thank you," I said. I didn't expect they would do something like that again. That sort of thing works once if it works at all. But that wasn't the point. What I wanted was to feel like I could trust the two of them again. I wasn't there yet.

"Will you train?" Hickory asked.

"Yes," I said. "But I have two conditions." Hickory waited. "The first is that Gretchen trains with me."

"We had not prepared to train anyone other than you," Hickory said.

"I don't care," I said. "Gretchen is my best friend. I'm not going to learn how to save myself and not share that with her. And besides, I don't know if you've noticed, but the two of you aren't exactly human shaped. I think it will help to practice with another human as well as with you. But this is nonnegotiable. If you won't train Gretchen, I won't train. This is my choice. This is my condition."

Hickory turned to Gretchen. "Will you train?"

"Only if Zoë does," she said. "She's my best friend, after all."

Hickory looked over to me. "She has your sense of humor," it said.

"I hadn't noticed," I said.

Hickory turned back to Gretchen. "It will be very difficult," it said.

"I know," Gretchen said. "Count me in anyway."

"What is the other condition?" Hickory asked me.

"I'm doing this for the two of you," I said. "This learning to fight. I don't want it for myself. I don't think I need it. But you think I need it, and you've never asked me to do something you didn't know was important. So I'll do it. But now you have to do something for me. Something I want."

"What is it that you want?" Hickory asked.

"I want you to learn how to sing," I said, and gestured to Gretchen. "You teach us to fight, we teach you to sing. For the hootenannies."

"Sing," Hickory said.

"Yes, sing," I said. "People are still frightened of the two of you. And no offense, but you're not brimming with personality. But if we can get the four of us to do a song or two at the hootenannies, it could go a long way to making people comfortable with you."

"We have never sung," Hickory said.

"Well, you never wrote stories before either," I said. "And you wrote one of those. It's just like that. Except with singing. And then people wouldn't wonder why Gretchen and I are off with the two of you. Come on, Hickory, it'll be fun."

Hickory looked doubtful, and a funny thought came to me: *Maybe Hickory is shy.* Which seemed almost ridiculous; someone about to teach another person sixteen different ways to kill getting stage fright singing.

"I would like to sing," Dickory said. We all turned to Dickory in amazement.

"It speaks!" Gretchen said.

Hickory clicked something to Dickory in their native tongue; Dickory clicked back. Hickory responded, and Dickory replied, it seemed a bit forcefully. And then, God help me, Hickory actually *sighed*.

"We will sing," Hickory said.

"Excellent," I said.

"We will begin training tomorrow," Hickory said.

"Okay," I said. "But let's start singing practice today. Now."

"Now?" Hickory said.

"Sure," I said. "We're all here. And Gretchen and I have just the song for you."

FIFTEEN

The next several months were very tiring.

Early mornings: physical conditioning.

"You are soft," Hickory said to me and Gretchen the first day.

"Despicable lies," I said.

"Very well," Hickory said, and pointed to the tree line of the forest, at least a klick away. "Please run to the forest as quickly as you can. Then run back. Do not stop until you return."

We ran. By the time I got back, it felt like my lungs were trying to force themselves up my trachea, the better to smack me around for abusing them. Both Gretchen and I collapsed into the grass gasping.

"You are soft," Hickory repeated. I didn't argue, and not just because at the moment I was totally incapable of speaking. "We are done for today. Tomorrow we will truly begin with your physical conditioning. We will start slowly." It and Dickory walked away, leaving Gretchen and me to imagine ways we were going to murder Hickory and Dickory, once we could actually force oxygen back into our bodies.

Mornings: school, like every other kid and teen not actively working in a field. Limited books and supplies meant sharing with others. I shared my textbooks with Gretchen, Enzo, and

Magdy. This worked fine when we were all speaking to each other, less so when some of us were not.

"Will you two *please* focus?" Magdy said, waving his hands in front of the two of us. We were supposed to be doing calculus.

"Stop it," Gretchen said. She had her head down on our table. It had been a hard workout that morning. "God, I miss coffee," she said, looking up at me.

"It would be nice to get to this problem sometime today," Magdy said.

"Oh, what do you care," Gretchen said. "It's not like any of us are going to college anyway."

"We still have to do it," Enzo said.

"You do it, then," Gretchen said. She leaned over and pushed the book toward the two of them. "It's not me or Zoë who has to learn this stuff. We already know it. You two are always waiting for us to do the work, and then just nodding like you actually know what we're doing."

"That's not true," Magdy said.

"Really? Fine," Gretchen said. "Prove it. Impress me."

"I think someone's morning exertions are making her a little grumpy," Magdy said, mockingly.

"What's that supposed to mean?" I said.

"It means that since the two of you started whatever it is you're doing, you've been pretty useless here," Magdy said. "Despite what Gretchen the Grump is hinting at, it's the two of us who have been carrying the two of you lately, and you know it."

"You're carrying us in math?" Gretchen said. "I don't think so."

"Everything else, sweetness," Magdy said. "Unless you think Enzo pulling together that report on the early Colonial Union days last week doesn't count."

"That's not 'we,' that's Enzo," Gretchen said. "And thank

you, Enzo. Happy, Magdy? Good. Now let's all shut up about this." Gretchen put her head back down on the table. Enzo and Magdy looked at each other.

"Here, give me the book," I said, reaching for it. "I'll do this problem." Enzo slid the book over to me, not quite meeting my gaze.

Afternoons: training.

"So, how is the training going?" Enzo asked me one early evening, catching me as I limped home from the day's workout.

"Do you mean, can I kill you yet?" I asked.

"Well, no," Enzo said. "Although now that you mention it I'm curious. Can you?"

"It depends," I said, "on what it is you're asking me to kill you with." There was an uncomfortable silence after that. "That was a joke," I said.

"Are you sure?" Enzo said.

"We didn't even get around to how to kill things today," I said, changing the subject. "We spent the day learning how to move quietly. You know. To avoid capture."

"Or to sneak up on something," Enzo said.

I sighed. "Yes, okay, Enzo. To sneak up on things. To kill them. Because I like to kill. Kill and kill again, that's me. Little Zoë Stab Stab." I sped up my walking speed.

Enzo caught up with me. "Sorry," he said. "That wasn't fair of me."

"Really," I said.

"It's just a topic of conversation, you know," Enzo said. "What you and Gretchen are doing."

I stopped walking. "What kind of conversation?" I asked.

"Well, think about it," Enzo said. "You and Gretchen are spending your afternoons preparing for the apocalypse. What do you think people are talking about?"

"It's not like that," I said.

"I know," Enzo said, reaching out and touching my arm, which reminded me we spent less time touching each other lately. "I've told people that, too. Doesn't keep people from talking, though. That and the fact that it's you *and* Gretchen."

"So?" I said.

"You're the daughter of the colony leaders, she's the daughter of the guy everyone knows is next in line on the colony council," Enzo said. "It looks like you're getting special treatment. If it was just you, people would get it. People know you've got that weird thing you have with the Obin—"

"It's not weird," I said.

Enzo looked at me blankly.

"Yeah, okay," I said.

"People know you've got that thing with the Obin, so they wouldn't think about it if it was just you," Enzo said. "But the two of you is making people nervous. People wonder if you guys know something we don't."

"That's ridiculous," I said. "Gretchen is my best friend. That's why I asked her. Should I have asked someone else?"

"You could have," Enzo said.

"Like who?" I said.

"Like me," Enzo said. "You know, your boyfriend."

"Yeah, because people wouldn't talk about *that*," I said.

"Maybe they would and maybe they wouldn't," Enzo said. "But at least I'd get to see you every once in a while."

I didn't have any good answer to that. So I just gave Enzo a kiss.

"Look, I'm not trying to make you feel bad or guilty or whatever," Enzo said, when I was done. "But I would like to see more of you."

"That statement can be interpreted in many different ways," I said.

"Let's start with the innocent ones," Enzo said. "But we can go from there if you want."

"And anyway, you see me every day," rewinding the conversation just a little. "And we always spend time together at the hootenannies."

"I don't count doing schoolwork together as time together," Enzo said. "And as much fun as it is to admire how you trained Hickory to imitate a sitar solo—"

"That's Dickory," I said. "Hickory does the drum sounds."

Enzo gently put a finger to my lips. "As much fun as it is," he repeated. "I'd rather have some time for just you and me." He kissed me, which was pretty effective punctuation.

"How about now?" I said, after the kiss.

"Can't," Enzo said. "On my way home to babysit Maria and Katherina so my parents can have dinner with friends."

"Waaah," I said. "Kiss me, tell me you want to spend time together, leave me hanging. Nice."

"But I have tomorrow afternoon free," Enzo said. "Maybe then. After you're done with your stabbing practice."

"We already did stabbing," I said. "Now we're on to strangulation."

Silence.

"Joke," I said.

"I only have your word for that," Enzo said.

"Cute." I kissed him again. "See you tomorrow."

The next day training went long. I skipped dinner to head to Enzo's parents' homestead. His mother said he'd waited around, and then headed over to Magdy's. We didn't talk to each other much the next day during school.

Evenings: study.

"We have reached an agreement with Jerry Bennett to allow you to use the information center in the evenings twice a week," Hickory said.

I suddenly felt sorry for Jerry Bennett, who I had heard was more than a little terrified of Hickory and Dickory, and probably would have agreed to anything they asked just so long as they left him alone. I made a mental note to invite Bennett to the next hootenanny. There's nothing to make an Obin look less threatening than to see one in front of a crowd, bobbing its neck back and forth and making like a tabla drum.

Hickory continued. "While you are there, you will study the Colonial Union files of other sentient species."

"Why do you want us to learn about them?" Gretchen asked.

"To know how to fight them," Hickory said. "And how to kill them."

"There are hundreds of species in the Conclave," I said. "Are we supposed to learn about each of them? That's going to take more than two nights a week."

"We will be focusing on species who are not members of the Conclave," Hickory said.

Gretchen and I looked at each other. "But they're not the ones planning to kill us," Gretchen said.

"There are many trying to kill you," Hickory said. "And some may be more motivated than others. For example, the Rraey. They recently lost a war with the Enesha, who took control of most of their colonies before they were themselves defeated by the Obin. The Rraey are no longer a direct threat to any established race or colony. But if they were to find you here, there is no doubt what they would do."

I shuddered. Gretchen noticed. "You okay?" she asked.

"I'm fine," I said, too quickly. "I've met the Rraey before." Gretchen looked at me strangely but didn't say anything after that.

"We have a list for you," Hickory said. "Jerry Bennett has already prepared the files you have access to for each species. Take special note of the physiology of each race. This will be important in our instruction."

"To learn how to fight them," I said.

"Yes," Hickory said. "And to learn how to kill them."

Three weeks into our studies I pulled up a race who were not on our list.

"Wow, they're scary-looking," Gretchen said, looking over my shoulder after she noticed I had been reading for a while.

"They're Consu," I said. "They're scary, period." I handed my PDA over to Gretchen. "They're the most advanced race we know about. They make us look like we're banging rocks together. And they're the ones who made the Obin what they are today."

"Genetically engineered them?" Gretchen asked. I nodded. "Well, maybe next time they can code for personality. What are you looking at them for?"

"I'm just curious," I said. "Hickory and Dickory have talked to me about them before. They're the closet thing the Obin have to a higher power."

"Their gods," Gretchen said.

I shrugged. "More like a kid with an ant farm," I said. "An ant farm and a magnifying glass."

"Sounds lovely," Gretchen said, and handed back the PDA. "Hope I never get to meet them. Unless they're on my side."

"They're not on a side," I said. "They're above."

"Above is a side," Gretchen said.

"Not our side," I said, and switched the PDA back to what I was supposed to be reading.

Late evening: everything else.

"Well, this is a surprise," I said to Enzo, who was sitting on my doorstep as I came back from another thrilling night at the information center. "I haven't seen you too much recently."

"You haven't seen much of anybody recently," Enzo said, standing up to greet me. "It's just you and Gretchen. And you've been avoiding me since we broke up the study group."

"I'm not avoiding you," I said.

"You haven't been going out of your way to look for me," Enzo said.

Well, he had me there.

"I don't blame you for it," I said, changing the subject a little. "It's not your fault Magdy threw that fit of his." After several weeks of increased sniping, things between Magdy and Gretchen finally reached toxic levels; the two of them had a shouting match in class and Magdy ended up saying some fairly not forgivable things and then stomping off, Enzo trailing behind. And that was the end of our little band.

"Yeah, it's all Magdy's fault," Enzo said. "Gretchen's poking at him until he snapped didn't have anything to do with it at all."

Already this conversation had gone twice to places I didn't want it to go, and the rational part of my brain was just telling me to let it go and change the subject. But then there was the not quite rational part, which was suddenly getting really annoyed. "So are you hanging out on my doorstep just to dump on my best friend, or is there some other reason you dropped by?"

Enzo opened his mouth to say something, and then just shook his head. "Forget it," he said, and started to walk off.

I blocked his path. "No," I said. "You came here for a reason. Tell me what it is."

"Why don't I see you anymore?" Enzo said.

"Is that what you came here to ask me?" I said.

"No," Enzo said. "It's not what I came here to say. But it's what I'm asking you now. It's been two weeks since Magdy and Gretchen did their thing, Zoë. It was between the two of them, but I've hardly seen you since then. If you're not actually avoiding me, you're faking it really well."

"If it was between Gretchen and Magdy, why did you leave when he did?" I said.

"He's my friend," Enzo said. "Someone had to calm him down. You know how he gets. You know I'm his heat sink. What kind of question is that?"

"I'm just saying it's not just between Magdy and Gretchen,"

I said. "It's between all of us. You and me and Gretchen and Magdy. When was the last time you did anything without Magdy?"

"I don't remember him being there when *we* spend time together," Enzo said.

"You know what I mean," I said. "You're always following him, keeping him from getting hit by someone or breaking his neck or doing something stupid."

"I'm not his *puppy*," Enzo said, and for that minute he actually got a little angry. Which was new.

I ignored it. "You're his friend," I said. "His best friend. And Gretchen is mine. And right now our best friends can't stand the sight of each other. And that leaks into *us*, Enzo. Let me ask you, right now, how do you feel about Gretchen? You don't like her very much, do you?"

"We've had better days," Enzo said.

"Right. Because she and your best friend are at it. I feel the same way about Magdy. I guarantee you he feels the same way about me. And Gretchen isn't feeling very friendly to you. I want to spend time with you, Enzo, but most of the time, both of us are a package deal. We come with our best friends attached. And I don't want the drama right now."

"Because it's easier just not to bother," Enzo said.

"Because I'm *tired*, Enzo," I said, spitting out the words. "Okay? I'm *tired*. Every morning I wake up and I have to run or do strength exercises or something that tires me out right after I've gotten out of bed. I'm tired before the rest of you are even *awake*. Then school. Then an entire afternoon of getting physically beat up in order to learn how to defend myself, on the chance some aliens want to come down here and kill us all. Then I spend my evenings reading up on every single race out there, not because it's *interesting*, but just in case I need to *murder* one of them, I'll know where its soft spots are. I hardly have time to think about anything else, Enzo. I am *tired*.

"Do you think all of this is *fun* for me? Do you think it's fun for me not to see you? To spend all my time learning to hurt and kill things? Do you think it's fun for me that every single day I get my nose rubbed in the fact there's a whole universe out there just waiting to murder us? When was the last time *you* thought about it? When was the last time Magdy thought about it? I think about it *every day*, Enzo. My time is spent doing nothing but. So don't tell me that it's just *easier* for me not to bother with the drama. You have *no* idea. I'm sorry. But you don't."

Enzo stared at me for a minute, and then reached over to wipe my cheeks. "You could *tell* me, you know," he said.

I laughed a small laugh. "I don't have *time*," I said. That got a smile from Enzo. "And anyway, I don't want you to worry."

"It's a little late for that," Enzo said.

"I'm sorry," I said.

"It's all right," he said.

"I miss it, you know," I said, wiping my own face. "Spending time with you. Even when it meant spending time with Magdy. I miss having the time to really talk to you. I miss watching you fail at dodgeball. I miss you sending me poems. I miss *all* of it. I'm sorry that we've gotten mad at each other lately, and that we didn't do something to fix it. I'm sorry and I miss you, Enzo."

"Thank you," Enzo said.

"You're welcome," I said.

We stood there for a minute, looking at each other.

"You came here to break up with me, didn't you," I said, finally.

"Yeah," said Enzo. "Yeah, I did. Sorry."

"Don't be," I said. "I haven't been a very good girlfriend."

"Yes you have," Enzo said. "When you've had the time."

Another shaky laugh from me. "Well, that's the problem, isn't it," I said.

"Yes," Enzo said, and I know he was sorry he felt he had to say it.

And just like that my first relationship was over, and I went to bed, and I didn't sleep.

And then I got up when the sun came up and walked out to our exercise area, and started everything again. Exercise. School. Training. Study.

A very tiring time.

And this is how my days went, most days, for months, until we had been at Roanoke for almost an entire year.

And then things started happening. Fast.

SIXTEEN

"We're looking for Joe Loong," Jane said, to the assembled search team, at the edge of the forest by Joe's house. Dad, who was standing with her and Savitri, was letting her run the show. "He's been missing for the last two days. Therese Arlien, his companion, tells me that he was excited about the return of the fanties to the area and told her he was thinking of trying to get close to one of the herds. We're working under the assumption that's what he did, and then either got lost, or perhaps got injured by one of the animals."

Jane motioned at the line of trees. "We're going to search the area in teams of four, spreading out in a line from here. Everyone in a group stays in voice contact with the group members on either side; every one at the left or right of a group also stays in voice contact with your opposite number from the next group over. Call to each other every couple of minutes. We'll do this slow and careful; I don't want any of us adding to the number of the lost, understand? If you lose voice contact with the other members of your group, *stop* and stay where you are, and let your group members reestablish contact. If the person next to you doesn't respond when you call, *stop* and alert those you *are* in contact with. Again, let's not lose anyone else, especially when we're trying to find Joe. Now, you all know who we are looking for?"

There were general nods; most of the hundred and fifty or so folks who'd showed up to look for Loong were friends of his. I personally had only the vaguest of ideas of what he looked like, but I was going on the idea that if someone came running toward us, waving his hands and saying, "Thank God you found me," it was likely to be him. And joining the search party was getting me a day out of school. You can't argue with that.

"All right, then," Mom said. "Let's organize into teams." People started grouping together in fours; I turned to Gretchen and figured she and I would be a team with Hickory and Dickory.

"Zoë," Mom said. "You're with me. Bring Hickory and Dickory."

"Can Gretchen come with us?" I asked.

"No," Jane said. "Too large. Sorry, Gretchen."

"It's all right," Gretchen said to Mom, and then turned back to me. "Try to survive without me," she said.

"Stop," I said. "It's not like we're dating." She grinned and wandered off to join another group.

After several minutes three dozen groups of four were spread out over more than half a klick of tree line. Jane gave the signal and we started in.

Then came the boring: three hours of stomping through the woods, slowly, searching for signs that Joe Loong had wandered in this direction, calling out to each other every few minutes. I found nothing, Mom to my left found nothing, Hickory to my right found nothing, and Dickory to its right found nothing either. Not to be hopelessly shallow about it, but I thought it would be at least a little more interesting than it was.

"Are we going to take a break anytime soon?" I asked Jane, walking up to her when she wandered into visual range.

"You're tired?" she said. "I would think that after all the training you do, a walk in the woods would be an easy thing."

I paused at this comment; I didn't make any secret of my training with Hickory and Dickory—it would be hard to hide, given how much time I gave to it—but it's not something that the two of us talked about much. "It's not a stamina issue," I said. "It's a boredom issue. I've been scanning the forest floor for three hours. I'm getting a little punchy."

Jane nodded. "We'll take a rest soon. If we don't find something in this area in the next hour, I'll regather people on the other side of Joe's homestead and try over there," she said.

"You don't mind me doing what I do with Hickory and Dickory, do you?" I asked. "It's not like I talk about it to you much. Either with you or Dad."

"It worried us the first couple of weeks, when you came in covered with bruises and then went to sleep without actually saying hello to us," Jane said. She kept walking and scanning as she talked. "And I was sorry it broke up your friendship with Enzo. But you're old enough now to make your own choices about what you want to do with your time, and we both decided that we weren't going to breathe down your neck about it."

I was about to say, *Well, it wasn't entirely my own choice to do this,* but Jane kept talking. "Beside that, we think it's smart," she said. "I don't know when we'll be found, but I think we will be. I can take care of myself; John can take care of himself. We were soldiers. We're happy to see that you're learning to take care of yourself, too. When it comes down to it, it might be the thing that makes a difference."

I stopped walking. "Well, *that* was a depressing thing to say," I said.

Jane stopped and came back to me. "I didn't mean it that way," she said.

"You just said I might be alone at the end of all this," I said.

"That each of us will have to take care of ourselves. That's not exactly a *happy* thought, you know."

"I didn't mean it that way," Jane said. She reached over and touched the jade elephant pendant she had given me years ago. "John and I will never leave you, Zoë. Never abandon you. You need to know that. It's a promise we made to you. What I am saying is that we will need each other. Knowing how to take care of ourselves means we are better able to help each other. It means that you will be able to help *us*. Think about that, Zoë. Everything might come down to what you are able to do. For us. And for the colony. That's what I'm saying."

"I doubt it's going to come to that," I said.

"Well, I doubt it too," Jane said. "Or at least I hope it doesn't come to that."

"Thanks," I said, wryly.

"You know what I mean," Mom said.

"I do," I said. "I think it's funny how bluntly you put it."

To the left of us there was a faint scream. Jane swiveled in its direction and then turned back to face me; her expression left very little doubt that whatever mom-daughter bonding moment we'd been having was at a very abrupt end. "Stay here," she said. "Send word down the line to halt. Hickory, come with me." The two of them sped off in the direction of the scream quietly at what seemed like an almost impossible high speed; I was suddenly reminded that, yes, in fact, my mom *was* a veteran warrior. There's a thought for you. It was just now I finally had the tools to really appreciate it.

Several minutes later Hickory returned to us, clicked something to Dickory in their native tongue as he passed, and looked at me.

"Lieutenant Sagan says that you are to return to the colony with Dickory," Hickory said.

"Why?" I asked. "Have they found Joe?"

"They have," Hickory said.

"Is he all right?" I asked.

"He is dead," Hickory said. "And Lieutenant Sagan believes there is reason to worry that the search parties may be in danger if they stay out here much longer."

"Why?" I asked. "Because of the fanties? Was he trampled or something?"

Hickory looked at me levelly. "Zoë, you do not need me to remind you of your last trip into the forest and what followed you then."

I went very cold. "No," I said.

"Whatever they are, they appear to follow the fantie herds as they migrate," Hickory said. "They have followed those herds back here. And it appears that they found Joseph Loong in the woods."

"Oh my God," I said. "I have to tell Jane."

"I assure you, she has figured it out," Hickory said. "And I am to find Major Perry now, so he will know presently. This is being taken care of. The lieutenant asks for you to return to Croatan. As do I. Dickory will accompany you. Go now. And I advise silence until your parents speak of this publicly." Hickory strode off into the distance. I watched it go, and then headed home, fast, Dickory matching my strides, both of us moving quietly, as we had practiced so many times.

The fact that Joe Loong was dead spread fast in the colony. Rumors of *how* he died spread even faster. Gretchen and I sat in front of Croatan's community center and watched a revolving cast of rumormongers offer up their takes.

Jun Lee and Evan Black were the first to talk; they had been part of the group that had found Loong's body. They were enjoying their moment in the spotlight as they told everyone who would listen about how they found Loong, and how he had been attacked, and how whatever had attacked him had eaten part of him. Some people speculated that a pack of yotes, the local carnivores, had cornered Joe Loong and brought him down, but Jun and Evan laughed at that. We'd all seen the yotes; they were the size of small dogs and ran from the colonists whenever they saw them (and for good reason, since the colonists had taken to shooting at them for bothering the livestock). No yote, or even a pack of yotes, they said, could have done to Joe what they'd seen had been done to him.

Shortly after these gory tidbits had gotten around, the entire colony council met in Croatoan's medical bay, where Loong's body had been taken. The fact that the *government* was being pulled into it made people suspect it might actually have been murder (the fact that the "government" in this case was just twelve people who spent most of their time hoeing rows like everyone else didn't matter). Loong had been seeing a woman who'd recently dumped her husband, so now the husband was a prime suspect; maybe he'd followed Loong into the woods, killed him, and then yotes had at him.

This theory made Jun and Evan unhappy—their version with a mysterious predator was much more sexy—but everyone else seemed to like it better. The inconvenient fact that the presumed murderer in this case had already been in Jane's custody on a different charge and couldn't possibly have done the deed seemed to escape most people's notice.

Gretchen and I knew the murder rumor had nothing to it, and that Jun and Evan's theory was closer to reality than not, but we kept our mouths shut. Adding what we knew wouldn't make anyone feel less paranoid at the moment.

"*I* know what it is," Magdy said, to a bunch of male friends.

I nudged Gretchen with an elbow and motioned with my head at Magdy. She rolled her eyes and very loudly called him over before he could say anything else.

"Yes?" he said.

"Are you stupid?" Gretchen asked.

"See, this is what I miss about you, Gretchen," Magdy said. "Your charm."

"Just like what I miss about you is your brains," Gretchen said. "What were you about to say to your little group of friends, I wonder?"

"I was going to tell them about what happened when we followed the fanties," Magdy said.

"Because you think it would be *smart* at the moment to give people another reason to panic," Gretchen said.

"No one's panicking," Magdy said.

"Not yet," I said. "But if you start telling that story, you're not going to *help* things, Magdy."

"I think people should know what we're up against," Magdy said.

"We don't know what we're up against," I said. "We never actually *saw* anything. You're just going to be adding to the rumors. Let my parents and Gretchen's dad and the rest of the council do their jobs right now and figure out what's actually going on and what to tell people without you making their job harder."

"I'll take that under advisement, Zoë," Magdy said, and turned to go back to his pals.

"Fine," Gretchen said. "Take this under advisement, too: You tell your pals there about what followed us out there in the woods, and I'll tell them the part where you ended up eating dirt because Hickory dropped you to the ground after you panicked and took a shot at him."

"A really lousy shot," I said. "One where you almost blew off your own toe."

"Good point," Gretchen said. "We'll have *fun* telling that part."

Magdy narrowed his eyes at both of us and stomped off toward his pals without another word.

"Think it'll work?" I asked.

"Of course it'll work," Gretchen said. "Magdy's ego is the size of a planet. The amount of time and effort he puts into doing things to make himself look good is astounding. He's not going to let us mess with that."

As if on cue, Magdy glanced over at Gretchen. She waved and smiled. Magdy surreptitiously flipped her off and started talking to his friends. "See," Gretchen said. "He's not that hard to understand."

"You liked him once," I reminded her.

"I still like him," Gretchen said. "He's *very* cute, you know. And funny. He just needs to pull his head out of a certain part of his anatomy. Maybe in another year he'll be tolerable."

"Or two," I said.

"I'm optimistic," Gretchen said. "Anyway, that's one rumor squashed for now."

"It's not really a rumor," I said. "We really were followed that night. Hickory said so."

"I know," Gretchen said. "And it's going to come out sooner or later. I'd just rather not have it involve *us*. My dad still doesn't know I did all that sneaking out, and he's the sort of guy that believes in retroactive punishment."

"So you're not really worried about avoiding panic," I said. "You're just covering your own tail."

"Guilty," Gretchen said. "But avoiding panic is how I'm rationalizing it."

But as it happens, we didn't avoid panic for long.

Paulo Gutierrez was a member of the colonial council, and it was there he found out that Joe Loong had not only been killed, but that he'd been murdered—and not by a human being. There really was something else out there. Something smart enough to make spears and knives. Something smart enough to turn poor Joe Loong into food.

The council members had been ordered by my parents not to talk about this fact yet, in order to avoid a panic. Paulo Gutierrez ignored them. Or, actually, defied them.

"They told me it was covered by something called the State Secrets Act, and that I couldn't tell you about it," Gutierrez told a group that surrounded him and a few other men, all carrying rifles. "I say to hell with that. There's something that's out there right now, killing us. They have weapons. They say they follow the fantie herds, but I think they could have just been in the woods all this time, sizing us up, so they would know how to hunt us. They hunted Joe Loong. Hunted him and killed him. Me and the boys here are planning to return the favor." And then Gutierrez and his hunting party tromped off in the direction of the woods.

Gutierrez's declaration and news of his hunting party raced through the colony. I heard about it as kids came running up to the community center with all the latest; by that time Gutierrez and his crew had already been in the woods for a while. I went to tell my parents, but John and Jane were already off to bring back the hunting party. The two of them were former military; I didn't think they would have any trouble bringing them back.

But I was wrong. John and Jane found the hunting party, but before they could drag them back, the creatures in the woods ambushed them all. Gutierrez and all his men were killed in the attack. Jane was stabbed in the gut. John chased after the fleeing creatures and caught up with them at the tree line, where they attacked another colonist at his homestead. That colonist was Hiram Yoder, one of the Mennonites who helped save the colony by training the rest of us how to plant and farm without the help of computerized machinery. He was a pacifist and didn't try to fight the creatures. They killed him anyway.

In the space of a couple of hours, six colonists were dead,

and we learned that we weren't alone on Roanoke—and what was here with us was getting used to hunting us.

But I was more worried about my mom.

"You can't see her yet," Dad said to me. "Dr. Tsao is working on her right now."

"Is she going to be okay?" I asked.

"She'll be okay," Dad said. "She said it was not as bad as it looked."

"How bad did it look?" I asked him.

"It looked bad," Dad said, and then realized that honesty wasn't really what I was looking for at the moment. "But, look, she ran after those things after she'd been wounded. If she had been really injured, she wouldn't have been able to do that, right? Your mom knows her own body. I think she'll be fine. And anyway, she's being worked on right now. I wouldn't be at all surprised if she's walking around like nothing happened by this time tomorrow."

"You don't have to lie to me," I said, although per the previous comment he was actually telling me what I wanted to hear.

"I'm not lying," Dad said. "Dr. Tsao is excellent at what she does. And your mom is a very fast healer these days."

"Are you okay?" I asked.

"I've had better days," he said, and something flat and tired in his voice made me decide not to press the matter any further. I gave him a hug and told him I was going to visit Gretchen and would be over there for a while, in order to stay out of his hair.

Night was falling as I stepped out of our bungalow. I looked out toward Croatoan's gate and saw colonists streaming in from their homesteads; no one, it seemed, wanted to spend the night outside the walls of the colony village. I didn't blame them one bit.

I turned to head to Gretchen's and was mildly surprised to see her striding up under full steam. "We have a problem," she said to me.

"What is it?" I said.

"Our idiot friend Magdy has taken a group of his friends into the forest," Gretchen said.

"Oh, God," I said. "Tell me Enzo isn't with him."

"Of course Enzo's with him," Gretchen said. "Enzo's always with him. Trying to talk sense to him even as he's following him right off a cliff."

SEVENTEEN

The four of us moved as silently as we could into the forest, from the place where Gretchen had seen Magdy, Enzo and their two friends go into the tree line. We listened for their sounds; none of them had been trained to move quietly. It wasn't a good thing for them, especially if the creatures decided to hunt them. It was better for us, because we wanted to track them. We listened for our friends on the ground, we watched and listened for movement in the trees. We already knew whatever they were could track us. We hoped we might be able to track them, too.

In the distance, we heard rustling, as if of quick, hurried movement. We headed that direction, Gretchen and I taking point, Hickory and Dickory fast behind.

Gretchen and I had been training for months, learning how to move, how to defend ourselves, how to fight and how to kill, if it was necessary. Tonight, any part of what we learned might have to be used. We might have to fight. We might even have to kill.

I was so scared that if I stopped running, I think I would have collapsed into a ball and never gotten up.

I didn't stop running. I kept going. Trying to find Enzo and

Magdy before something else did. Trying to find them, and to save them.

"After Gutierrez left, Magdy didn't see any point in keeping our story quiet anymore, so he started blabbing to his friends," Gretchen had told me. "He was giving people the idea that he'd actually faced these things and had managed to keep them off while the rest of us were getting away."

"Idiot," I said.

"When you parents came back without the hunting party, a group of his friends came to him about organizing a search," Gretchen said. "Which was actually just an excuse for a bunch of them to stalk through the forest with guns. My dad caught wind of this and tried to step on its head. He reminded them that five adults just went into the forest and didn't come out. I thought that was the end of it, but now I hear that Magdy just waited until my dad went to go visit yours before gathering up some like-minded idiots to head off into the woods."

"Didn't anyone notice them heading off?" I asked.

"They told people they were going to do a little target practice on Magdy's parents' homestead," Gretchen said. "No one's going to complain about them doing that right about now. Once they got there they just took off. The rest of Magdy's family is here in town like everyone else. No one knows they're missing."

"How'd you find out about this?" I asked. "It's not like Magdy would tell you this right now."

"His little group left someone behind," Gretchen said. "Isaiah Miller was going to go with him, but his dad wouldn't let him have the rifle for 'target practice.' I heard him complaining about that and then basically intimidated the rest of it out of him."

"Has he told anybody else?" I asked.

"I don't think so," Gretchen said. "Now that he's had time to think about it I don't think he wants to get in trouble. But *we* should tell someone."

"We'll cause a panic if we do," I said. "Six people have already died. If we tell people four more people—four kids—have gone off into the woods, people will go insane. Then we'll have more people heading off with guns and more people dying, either by these things or by accidentally shooting each other because they're so wired up."

"What do you want to do, then?" Gretchen asked.

"We've been training for this, Gretchen," I said.

Gretchen's eyes got very wide. "Oh, no," she said. "Zoë, I love you, but that's loopy. There's no way you're getting me out there to be a target for these things again, and there's no way I'm going to let *you* go out there."

"It wouldn't just be us," I said. "Hickory and Dickory—"

"Hickory and Dickory are going to tell you you're nuts, too," Gretchen said. "They just spent months teaching you how to defend yourself, and you think they're going to be at all happy with you putting yourself out there for something to use as spear practice. I don't think so."

"Let's ask them," I said.

"Miss Gretchen is correct," Hickory said to me, once I called for it and Dickory. "This is a very bad idea. Major Perry and Lieutenant Sagan are the ones who should deal with this matter."

"My dad's got the whole rest of the colony to worry about at the moment," I said. "And Mom's in the medical bay, getting fixed from when she dealt with this the last time."

"You don't think that tells you something?" Gretchen said. I turned on her, a little angry, and she held up a hand. "Sorry, Zoë. That came out wrong. But think about it. Your mom was a

Special Forces soldier. She fought things for a living. And if she came out of this with a wound bad enough for her to spend her night in the medical bay, it means that whatever is out there is serious business."

"Who else can do this?" I asked. "Mom and Dad went after that hunting party on their own for a reason—they had been trained to fight and deal with experiences like that. Anyone else would have gotten themselves killed. They can't go after Magdy and Enzo right now. If anyone else goes after them, they're going to be in just as much danger as those two and their other friends. We're the only ones who can do this."

"Don't get angry at me for saying this," Gretchen said. "But it sounds like you're *excited* to do this. Like you want to go out there and fight something."

"I want to find Enzo and Magdy," I said. "That's all I want to do."

"We should inform your father," Hickory said.

"If we inform my father he'll tell us no," I said. "And the longer we talk about this the longer it's going to take to find our friends."

Hickory and Dickory put their heads together and clacked quietly for a minute. "This is not a good idea," Hickory said, finally. "But we will help you."

"Gretchen?" I asked.

"I'm trying to decide if Magdy is worth it," she said.

"Gretchen," I said.

"It's a joke," she said. "The sort you make when you're about to wet your pants."

"If we are to do this," Hickory said. "We must do it on the assumption that we will engage in combat. You have been trained with firearms and hand weapons. You must be prepared to use them if necessary."

"I understand," I said. Gretchen nodded.

"Then let us get ready," Hickory said. "And let us do so quietly."

Any confidence that I had any idea what I was doing left me the moment we entered the forest, when the running through the trees brought me back to the last time I raced through them at night, some unknown thing or things pacing us invisibly. The difference between now and then was that I had been trained and prepared to fight. I thought it would make a difference in how I felt.

It didn't. I was scared. And not just a little.

The rustling, rushing sound we had heard was getting closer to us and heading right for us, on the ground and moving fast. The four of us halted and hid and prepared ourselves to deal with whatever was coming at us.

Two human forms burst out of the brush and ran in a straight line past where Gretchen and I were hiding. Hickory and Dickory grabbed them as they passed by them; the boys screamed in terror as Hickory and Dickory took them down. Their rifles went skidding across the ground.

Gretchen and I rushed over to them and tried to calm them down. Being human helped.

Neither was Enzo or Magdy.

"Hey," I said, as soothingly as I could, to the one closest to me. "Hey. Relax. You're safe. Relax." Gretchen was doing the same to the other one. Eventually I recognized who they were: Albert Yoo and Michel Gruber. Both Albert and Michel were people I had long filed away under the "kind of a twit" category, so I didn't spend any more time with them than I had to. They had returned the favor.

"Albert," I said, to the one closest to me. "Where are Enzo and Magdy?"

"Get your thing off of me!" Albert said. Dickory was still restraining him.

"Dickory," I said. It let Albert go. "Where are Enzo and Magdy?" I repeated.

"I don't know," Albert said. "We got separated. Those things in the trees started chanting at us and Michel and I got spooked and took off."

"Chanting?" I asked.

"Or singing or clicking or whatever," Albert said. "We were walking along, looking for these things when all these noises started coming out of the trees. Like they were trying to show us that they had snuck up on us without us even knowing."

This worried me. "Hickory?" I asked.

"There is nothing significant in the trees," it said. I relaxed a little.

"They surrounded us," Albert said. "And then Magdy took a shot at them. And then things really got loud. Michel and I got out of there. We just ran. We didn't see where Magdy and Enzo went."

"How long ago was this?" I asked.

"I don't know," Albert said. "Ten minutes, fifteen. Something like that."

"Show us where you came from," I said. Albert pointed. I nodded. "Get up," I said. "Dickory will take you and Michel back to the tree line. You can get back from there."

"I'm not going anywhere with that *thing*," Michel said, his first contribution to the evening.

"Okay, then you have two choices," I said. "Stay here and hope we come back for you before these things do, or hope that you make it to the tree line before they catch up with you. Or you can let Dickory help you and maybe *survive*. Your choice." I said it a little more forcefully than I had to, but I was annoyed that this idiot didn't want help staying alive.

"Okay," he said.

"Good," I said. I picked up their rifles and handed them to Dickory, and took his. "Take them to the tree line near Magdy's homestead. Don't give them back their rifles until you get there. Come back and find us as soon as you can." Dickory nodded, intimidated Albert and Michel into movement, and headed off.

"I never liked them," Gretchen said as they left.

"I can see why," I said, and gave Dickory's rifle to Hickory. "Come on. Let's keep going."

We heard them before we saw them. Actually, Hickory, whose hearing goes above human range, heard them—trilling and chirping and chanting. "They *are* singing," Hickory said quietly, and led Gretchen and me to them. Dickory arrived, silently, just before we found them. Hickory handed over its rifle.

In the small clearing were six figures.

Enzo and Magdy were the first I recognized. They knelt on the ground, heads down, waiting for whatever was going to happen to them. The light was not good enough for me to see any expression on either of their faces, but I didn't have to see their faces to know that they were scared. Whatever had happened to the two of them had gone badly, and now they were just waiting for it to end. However it would end.

I took in Enzo's kneeling form and remembered in a rush why I loved him. He was there because he was trying to be a good friend for Magdy. Trying to keep him out of trouble, or at the very least to share his trouble if he could. He was a *decent* human being, which is rare enough but is something of a miracle in a teenage boy. I came out here for him because I still loved him. It had been weeks since we'd said anything more than a simple "hello" at school—when you break up in a small community you have to make some space—but it didn't matter. I was still connected to him. Some part of him stayed in my heart, and I imagined would for as long as I lived.

Yes, it was a really *inconvenient* place and time to realize all of this, but these things happen when they happen. And it didn't make any noise, so it was all right.

I looked over at Magdy, and this is the thought I had: *When all of this is through, I am seriously going to kick his ass.*

The four other figures . . .

Werewolves.

It was the only way to describe them. They looked feral, and strong, and carnivorous and nightmarish, and with all of that was movement and sound that made it clear that there were brains in there to go along with everything else. They shared the four eyes of all the Roanoke animals we had seen so far, but other than that they could have been lifted right out of folklore. These were werewolves.

Three of the werewolves were busy taunting and poking Magdy and Enzo, clearly toying with them and threatening them. One of them held a rifle that it had taken off of Magdy, and was jabbing him with it. I wondered if was still loaded, and what would happen to Magdy or the werewolf if it went off. Another held a spear and occasionally poked Enzo with it. The three of them were chirping and clicking at each other; I don't doubt they were discussing what to do with Magdy and Enzo, and how to do it.

The fourth werewolf stood apart from the other three and acted differently. When one of the other werewolves went to poke Enzo or Magdy, it would step in and try to keep them from doing it, standing between the humans and the rest of the werewolves. Occasionally it would step in and try to talk to one of the other werewolves, gesturing back to Enzo and Magdy for emphasis. It was trying to convince the other were-wolves of something. To let the humans go? Maybe. Whatever it was, the other werewolves weren't having any of it. The fourth werewolf kept at it anyway.

It suddenly reminded me of Enzo, the first time I saw him, trying to keep Magdy from getting into an idiotic fight for no reason at all. It didn't work that time; Gretchen and I had to step in and do something. It wasn't working now, either.

I glanced over and saw that Hickory and Dickory had both taken up positions where they could get clean shots at the werewolves. Gretchen had moved off from me and was setting up her own shot.

Between the four of us we could take all of the werewolves before they even knew what had happened to them. It would be quick and clean and easy, and we'd get Enzo and Magdy out of there and back home before anyone knew anything had happened.

It was the smart thing to do. I quietly moved and readied my weapon, and took a minute or two to stop shaking and steady up.

I knew we'd take them in sequence, Hickory on the far left taking the first of the three group werewolves, Dickory taking the second, Gretchen the third, and I the last one, standing away from the rest. I knew the rest of them were waiting for me to make the shot.

One of the werewolves moved to poke Enzo again. My werewolf hurried, too late, to stop the assault.

And I knew. I didn't want to. I just didn't. Didn't want to kill it. Because it was trying to save my friends, not kill them. It didn't deserve to die just because that was the easiest way to get back Enzo and Magdy.

But I didn't know what else to do.

The three werewolves started chittering again, first in what seemed like a random way, but then together, and to a beat. The one with a spear began thumping it into the ground in time, and the three of them started working off the beat, playing against each other's voices for what was clearly a victory chant of some sort or another. The fourth werewolf started gesturing more frantically. I had a terrible fear of what was going to happen at the end of the chant.

They kept singing, getting closer to the end of that chant.

So I did what I had to do.

I sang back.

I opened my mouth and the first line of "Delhi Morning" came out of it. Not well, and not on key. Actually, it was really bad—all those months of practicing it and playing it at hootenannies were not paying off. It didn't matter. It was doing what I needed it to do. The werewolves immediately fell silent. I kept singing.

I glanced over to Gretchen, who was not so far away that I couldn't read the *Are you completely insane?* look that she had on her face. I gave her a look that said, *Help me out please*. Her face tightened up into something unreadable and she sighted down her rifle to keep one of the werewolves squarely in target—and started to sing the counterpoint of the song, dipping above and below my part, like we had practiced so many times. With her help I found the right key to sing and homed in.

And now the werewolves knew there was more than one of us.

To the left of Gretchen, Dickory chimed in, mimicking the sitar of the song as he did so well. It was funny to watch, but when you closed your eyes it was hard to tell the difference between it and the real thing. I drank in the twang of his voice and kept singing. And to the left of Dickory, Hickory finally came in, using its long neck to sound off like a drum, finding the beat and keeping it from then on.

And now the werewolves knew there were as many of us as them. And that we could have killed them anytime. But we didn't.

My stupid plan was working. Now all I had to do was figure what I had planned to do next. Because I really didn't know what I was doing here. All I knew was that I didn't want to shoot my werewolf. The one, in fact, who had now stepped off entirely away from the rest of his pack and was walking toward where he thought my voice was coming from.

I decided to meet him halfway. I set down my rifle and stepped into the clearing, still singing.

The werewolf with the spear began to raise it, and suddenly my mouth was very dry. I think my werewolf noticed something on my face, because it turned and chattered madly at the spear carrier. The spear went down; my werewolf didn't know it, but he'd just saved his friend a bullet in the head from Gretchen.

My werewolf turned back to me and started walking toward me again. I kept singing until the song was through. By that time, my werewolf was standing right next to me.

Our song was finished. I stood there, waiting to see what my werewolf would do next.

What he did next was point to my neck, to the jade elephant pendant Jane had given me.

I touched it. "Elephant," I said. "Like your fanties."

He stared at it again and then stared at me again. Finally it chirped out something.

"Hello," I said back. What else was I going to say?

We had a couple more minutes of sizing each other up. Then one of the three other werewolves chirped something. He chirped something back, and then tilted his head at me, as if to say, *It would really help me if you actually did something here.*

So I pointed to Enzo and Magdy. "Those two belong to me," I said, making what I hoped were appropriate hand signals, so my werewolf would get the idea. "I want to take them back with me." I motioned back in the direction of the colony. "Then we'll leave you alone."

The werewolf watched all my hand signals; I'm not sure how many of them he actually got. But when I was done, he pointed to Enzo and Magdy, then to me, and then in the direction of the colony, as if to say, *Let me make sure I've got this right*.

I nodded, said "yes," and then repeated all the hand signals again. We were actually having a conversation.

Or maybe we weren't, because what followed was an explosion of chittering from my werewolf, along with some wild gesticulating. I tried to follow it but I had no idea what was going on. I looked at him helplessly, trying to get what he was saying.

Finally he figured out I had no clue what he was doing. So he pointed at Magdy, and then pointed at the rifle one of the other werewolves was holding. And then he pointed at his side, and then motioned at me as if to take a closer look. Against my better judgment, I did, and noticed something I missed before: My werewolf was injured. An ugly furrow was carved into his side, surrounded by raw welts on either side.

That idiot Magdy had shot my werewolf.

Barely, sure. Magdy was lucky that his aim continued to be bad, otherwise he'd probably already be dead. But even grazing it was bad enough.

I backed up from the werewolf and let him know I'd seen enough. He pointed at Enzo, pointed at me, and pointed back to the colony. Then he pointed at Magdy and pointed at his werewolf friends. This was clear enough: He was saying Enzo was free to go with me, but his friends wanted to keep Magdy. I didn't doubt that would end badly for Magdy.

I shook my head and made it clear I needed the both of them. My werewolf made it equally clear they wanted Magdy. Our negotiations had just hit a really big snag.

I looked my werewolf up and down. He was stocky, barely taller than me, and covered only in a sort of short skirt cinched up with a belt. A simple stone knife hung from the belt. I'd seen pictures of knives like it from history books detailing the

Cro-Magnon days back on Earth. The funny thing about the Cro-Magnons was that despite the fact that they were barely above banging rocks together, their brains were actually larger than our brains are now. They were cavemen, but they weren't stupid. They had the ability to think about serious stuff.

"I sure hope you have a Cro-Magnon brain," I said to my werewolf. "Otherwise I'm about to get in trouble."

He tilted his head again, trying to figure out what I was trying to say to him.

I motioned again, trying to make it clear I wanted to talk to Magdy. My werewolf didn't seem happy about this, and chattered something to his friends. They chattered back, and got pretty agitated. But in the end, my werewolf reached out to me. I let him take my wrist and he dragged me over to Magdy. His three friends fanned themselves out behind me, ready if I should try anything stupid. I knew outside the clearing Hickory and Dickory, at least, would be moving to get better sight lines. There were still lots of ways this could go very very wrong.

Magdy was still kneeling, not looking at me or anything else but a spot on the ground.

"Magdy," I said.

"Kill these stupid things and get us out of here already," he said, quietly and fast, still not looking at me. "I know you know how. I know you have enough people out there to do it."

"Magdy," I said again. "Listen to me carefully and don't interrupt me. These things want to kill you. They're willing to let Enzo go, but they want to keep you because you shot one of them. Do you understand what I'm saying to you?"

"Just kill them," Magdy said.

"No," I said. "*You* went after these guys, Magdy. *You* were hunting them. *You* shot at them. I'm going to try to keep you from getting killed. But I'm not going to kill them because you put yourself in their way. Not unless I have to. Do you understand me?"

"They're going to kill us," Magdy said. "You and me and Enzo."

"I don't think so," I said. "But if you don't shut up and actually listen to what I'm trying to say to you, you're going to make that more likely."

"Just shoot—" Magdy began.

"For God's sake, Magdy," Enzo said suddenly, from Magdy's side. "One person on the entire planet is risking her own neck for you and all you can do is *argue* with her. You really are an ungrateful piece of crap. Now would you please *shut up* and *listen* to her. I'd like to get out of this alive."

I don't know who was more surprised by that outburst, me or Magdy.

"Fine," Magdy said, after a minute.

"These things want to kill you because you shot one of them," I said. "I'm going to try to convince them to let you go. But you're going to have to trust me and follow my lead and not argue and *not fight back*. For the last time: Do you understand me?"

"Yes," Magdy said.

"Okay," I said. "They think I'm your leader. So I need to give them the idea I'm angry with you for what you did. I'm going to have to punish you in front of them. And just so you know, this is going to hurt. A *lot*."

"Just—" Magdy began.

"Magdy," I said.

"Yeah, all right, whatever," Magdy said. "Let's just do this."

"Okay," I said. "Sorry about this." Then I kicked him in the ribs. Hard.

He collapsed with a *whoosh* and fell flat to the ground. Whatever he was expecting, he wasn't expecting that.

After he had gasped on the ground for a minute I grabbed him by the hair. He clutched at my hand and tried to get away.

"Don't *fight* me," I said, and gave him a quick punch in the ribs to make the point. He got it and stopped. I pulled his head back and yelled at him for shooting the werewolf, pointing at his rifle and then the wounded werewolf and back and forth several times to make the point. The werewolves seemed to make the connection and chittered among themselves about it.

"Apologize," I told Magdy, still holding his head.

Magdy reached out to the wounded werewolf. "I'm sorry," he said. "If I had known that shooting would mean Zoë got to beat the crap out of me, I would never have done it."

"Thanks," I said, and then let go of his hair and smacked him hard across the face. Magdy went down again. I looked over to the werewolf to see if this was sufficient. He didn't look like he was quite there yet.

I loomed over Magdy. "How are you doing?" I asked.

"I think I'm going to throw up," he said.

"Good," I said. "I think that would work. Need any help?"

"I got it," he said, and retched all over the ground. This got impressed chirps from the werewolves.

"Okay," I said. "Last part, Magdy. You *really* have to trust me on this one."

"Please stop hurting me now," Magdy said.

"Almost done," I said. "Stand up, please."

"I don't think I can," he said.

"Sure you can," I said, and wrenched his arm to give him motivation. Magdy inhaled and stood up. I marched him over to my werewolf, who eyed the both of us, curiously. I pointed at Magdy, and then to the werewolf's wound. Then I pointed to the werewolf, and made a slashing motion on Magdy's side, and then pointed at the werewolf's knife.

The werewolf gave me yet another head tilt, as if to say, *I want to be sure we understand each other, here.*

"Fair's fair," I said.

"You're going to let him *stab* me?" Magdy said, his voice rising dramatically at the end of that sentence.

"You shot him," I said.

"He could *kill* me," Magdy said.

"You could have killed him," I said.

"I hate you," Magdy said. "I really really really hate you now."

"Shut up," I said, and then nodded to the werewolf. "Trust me," I said to Magdy.

The werewolf drew his knife, and then looked back at his companions, who were all chattering loudly and beginning to chant what they were chanting earlier. I was all right with that. The difference now was that it was my werewolf who would do whatever violence would be done.

My werewolf stood there for a minute, soaking in the chant of his fellow werewolves. Then without warning he sliced at Magdy so quickly that I only got him moving back, not forward. Magdy hissed in pain. I let him go and he fell to the ground, clutching his side. I moved in front of him and grabbed his hands. "Let me see," I said. Magdy moved his hands and winced preemptively, expecting a gush of blood.

There was only the thinnest red line on his side. The werewolf had cut Magdy just enough to let him know he could have cut him a lot worse.

"I knew it," I said.

"You knew what?" Magdy said.

"That I was dealing with a Cro-Magnon," I said.

"I *really* don't understand you," Magdy said.

"Stay down," I said. "Don't get up until I tell you."

"I'm not moving," he said. "Really."

I stood up and faced the werewolf, who had put his knife back on his belt. He pointed to Magdy, and then pointed to me, and then pointed back toward the colony.

"Thank you," I said, and gave the werewolf a little nod of my head, which I hoped would convey the idea. When I looked up again, I saw him staring at my jade elephant again. I wondered if he'd ever seen jewelry before, or if it was simply because an elephant looks like a fantie. These werewolves followed the fantie herds; they would be a main source of food for them. They were their lives.

I took off my necklace and handed it to my werewolf. He took it and gently touched the pendant, making it twirl and glitter in the dim light of the night. He cooed at it appreciatively. Then he handed it back to me.

"No," I said. I held up a hand, and then pointed to the pendant, and to him. "It's for you. I'm giving it to you." The werewolf stood there for a moment, and then uttered a trill, which caused his friends to crowd around him. He held up the pendant for them to admire.

"Here," I said, after a minute, and motioned to him to hand me the necklace. He did, and I—*very* slowly, so I wouldn't surprise him—put it around his neck and fastened it. The pendant touched his chest. He touched it again.

"There," I said. "That was given to me by someone very important, so I would remember the people who loved me. I'm giving it to you, so you'll remember that I'm thanking you for giving me back people I love. Thank you."

The werewolf gave me another of his head tilts.

"I know you don't have any idea what I'm saying," I said. "Thank you anyway."

The werewolf reached to his side, pulled his knife. Then he laid it flat on his hand and offered it to me.

I took it. "Wow," I said, and admired it. I was careful not to touch the actual blade; I'd already seen how sharp it was. I tried to return it but he held up his hand or claw or whatever you want to call it, in a mirror of what I did for him. He was giving it to me.

"Thank you," I said again. He chirped, and with that he returned to his friends. The one holding Magdy's rifle dropped it, and then without looking back they walked to the nearest trees, scaled them at an unbelievable speed and were gone almost instantly.

"Holy crap," I said, after a minute. "I can't believe that actually *worked*."

"*You* can't believe it," Gretchen said. She came out of hiding and stalked right up to me. "What the hell is wrong with you? We come out all this way and you *sing* at them. *Sing*. Like you're at a hootenanny. We are not doing this again. Ever."

"Thank you for following my lead," I said. "And for trusting me. I love you."

"I love you too," Gretchen said. "It still doesn't mean this is *ever* going to happen again."

"Fair enough," I said.

"It was almost worth it to see you beat the crap out of Magdy, though," Gretchen said.

"God, I feel horrible about that," I said.

"Really?" Gretchen said. "It wasn't just a little bit of fun?"

"Oh, all right," I said. "Maybe a little."

"I'm right *here*," Magdy said, from the ground.

"And you need to thank Zoë you are," Gretchen said, and bent down to kiss him. "You stupid, exasperating person. I am *so* happy you are still alive. And if you *ever* do anything like this again, I will kill you myself. And you know I can."

"I know," he said, and pointed to me. "And if you can't, she will. I get it."

"Good," Gretchen said. She stood up and then held out her hand to Magdy. "Now get up. We've got a long way to go to get home, and I think we just blew all our dumb luck for the year."

"What are you going to tell your parents?" Enzo asked me, as we walked home.

"Tonight? Not a thing," I said. "Both of them have enough

to worry about tonight. They don't need me coming in and saying that while they were out I faced down four werewolves who were about to kill two more colonists, and defeated them using only the power of *song*. I think I might wait a day or two to drop *that* one. That's a hint, by the way."

"Hint taken," Enzo said. "Although you are going to tell them something."

"Yes," I said. "We have to. If these werewolves are following the fantie herds then we're going to have problems like this every year, and every time they come back. I think we need to let people know they're not actually murdering savages, but we're all still better off if we just leave them alone."

"How did you know?" Enzo asked me, a minute later.

"Know what?" I said.

"That those werewolf thingies weren't just murdering savages," Enzo said. "You held Magdy and let that werewolf take a shot at him. You thought he wouldn't stab Magdy to death. I heard you, you know. After it did it, you said 'I knew it.' So how did you know?"

"I didn't," I said. "But I hoped. He had just spent God knows how long keeping his friends from killing the two of you. I don't think he was just doing it because he was a nice guy."

"Nice werewolf," Enzo said.

"Nice whatever he is," I said. "Thing is, the werewolves have killed some of us. I know John and Jane killed some of them trying to get our people back. Both of us—the colonists and the werewolves—showed we were perfectly able to kill each other. I think we needed to show that we were capable of *not* killing each other, too. We let them know that when we sang at them instead of shooting them. I think my werewolf got that. So when I offered him a chance to get back at Magdy, I guessed he wouldn't really hurt him. Because I think he wanted us to know he was smart enough to know what would happen if he did."

"You still took a big risk," Enzo said.

"Yeah, I did," I said. "But the only other alternative was to kill him and his friends, or have them kill all of us. Or all of us kill each other. I guess I hoped I could do something better. Besides, I didn't think it was too big a risk. What he was doing when he was keeping the others away from you two reminded me of someone I knew."

"Who?" Enzo asked.

"You," I said.

"Yes, well," Enzo said. "I think tonight marks the official last time I tag along with Magdy to keep him out of trouble. After this he's on his own."

"I have nothing bad to say about this idea," I said.

"I didn't think you would," Enzo said. "I know Magdy gets on your last nerve sometimes."

"He does," I said. "He really, really does. But what can I do? He's my friend."

"He belongs to you," Enzo said. "And so do I."

I looked over at him. "You heard that part, too," I said.

"Trust me, Zoë," Enzo said. "Once you showed up, I never stopped listening to you. I'll be able to recite everything you said for the rest of my life. Which I now have, thanks to you."

"And Gretchen and Hickory and Dickory," I said.

"And I will thank them all, too," Enzo said. "But right now I want to focus on you. Thank you, Zoë Boutin-Perry. Thank you for saving my life."

"You're welcome," I said. "And stop it. You're making me blush."

"I don't believe it," Enzo said. "And now it's too dark to see."

"Feel my cheeks," I said.

He did. "You don't feel especially blushy," he said.

"You're not doing it right," I said.

"I'm out of practice," he said.

"Well, fix that," I said.

"All right," Enzo said, and kissed me.

"That was supposed to make you blush, not cry," he said, after we stopped.

"Sorry," I said, and tried to get myself back together. "I've just really missed it. That. Us."

"It's my fault," Enzo started.

I put a hand up to his lips. "I don't care about any of that," I said. "I really don't, Enzo. None of that matters to me. I just don't want to miss you anymore."

"Zoë," Enzo said. He took my hands. "You saved me. You have me. You *own* me. I belong to you. You said it yourself."

"I did," I admitted.

"So that's settled," Enzo said.

"Okay," I said, and smiled.

We kissed some more, in the night, outside Enzo's front gate.

EIGHTEEN

The conversation Hickory was having with Dad about the Conclave and the Colonial Union was really interesting, right up until the point where Hickory said it and Dickory were planning to kill my parents. Then, well. I sort of lost it.

To be fair, it had been a really *long* day.

I had said good night to Enzo, dragged my butt home, and could barely think straight enough to hide the stone knife in my dresser and fend off Babar's lick attack on my face before I collapsed onto my cot and passed out without even bothering to get all the way undressed. At some point after I lay down, Jane came home from the medical bay, kissed me on the forehead and slipped off my boots, but I barely remember that other than murmuring something to her about how happy I was she was better. At least, that's what I was saying inside my head; I don't know if my mouth formed the actual words. I think it did. I was very tired at the time.

Not too much after that, though, Dad came in and gently nudged me awake. "Come on, hon," he said. "I need you to do something for me."

"I'll do it in the morning," I mumbled. "I *swear*."

"No, sweetheart," he said. "I need you to do it now." The tone of his voice, gentle but insistent, told me he really did need me to get up. I did, but with enough grumbling to maintain my honor. We went to the living room of our bungalow; Dad steered me to the couch, which I sat on and tried to maintain a semiconscious state that would allow me to go back to sleep when we were done with whatever it was we were doing. Dad sat down at his desk; Mom stood next to him. I smiled sleepily at her but she seemed not to notice. Between me and my parents were Hickory and Dickory.

Dad spoke to Hickory. "Can you two lie?" he asked it.

"We have not yet lied to you," Hickory said. Which even in my sleepy state I recognized as not being an actual answer to the question that was asked. Dad and Hickory bantered back and forth a little about what being able to lie brings to a conversation (in my opinion, mostly the ability to not have to argue about stupid things it's just better to lie about, but no one asked me), and then Dad asked me to tell Hickory and Dickory to answer all his questions without any lies or evasions.

This finally woke me all the way up. "Why?" I asked. "What's going on?"

"Please do it," Dad said.

"All right," I said, and then turned to Hickory. "Hickory, please answer my dad without lying to him or evading his questions. All right?"

"As you wish, Zoë," Hickory said.

"Dickory too," I said.

"We will both answer truthfully," Hickory said.

"Thank you," Dad said, and then turned back to me. "You can go back to bed now, sweetie."

This annoyed me. I was a human being, not a truth serum. "I want to know what's going on," I said.

"It's not something you need to worry about," Dad said.

"You order me to have these two tell you the truth, and you want me to believe it's not something I need to worry about?" I asked. The sleep toxins were taking their time leaving my system, because even as I was saying this I realized it came out showing a little more attitude to my parents than was entirely warranted at the moment.

As if to confirm this, Jane straightened herself up a bit. "Zoë," she said.

I recalibrated. "Besides, if I leave there's no guarantee they won't lie to you," I said, trying to sound a bit more reasonable. "They're emotionally equipped to lie to you, because they don't care about disappointing you. But they don't want to disappoint *me*." I didn't know if this was actually true or not. But I was guessing it was.

Dad turned to Hickory. "Is this true?"

"We would lie to you if we felt it was necessary," Hickory said. "We would not lie to Zoë."

There was a really interesting question here of whether Hickory was saying this because it was actually true, or whether it was saying it in order to back me up on what I said, and if the latter, what the actual truth value of the statement was. If I were more awake, I think I would have thought about it more at the time. But as it was, I just nodded and said, "There you go," to my dad.

"Breathe a word of this to anyone and you're spending the next year in the horse stall," Dad said.

"My lips are sealed," I said, and almost made a lip-locking motion, but thought better of it at the last second.

And a good thing, too, because suddenly Jane came up and loomed over me, bearing her *I am as serious as death* expression. "No," she said. "I need you to understand that what you're hearing here you absolutely cannot share with anyone else. Not Gretchen. Not any of your other friends. Not anyone. It's not a game and it's not a fun secret. This is dead serious business, Zoë. If you're not ready to accept that, you need to leave this room right now. I'll take my chances with Hickory and Dickory lying to us, but not you. So do you understand that when we tell you not to share this with anyone, that you cannot share it with anyone else? Yes or no."

Several thoughts entered my mind at that moment.

The first is that it was times like this when I had the smallest inkling of how *terrifying* Jane must have been as a soldier. She was the best mom a girl could ever have, make no mistake about it, but when she got like this, she was as hard and cold and direct as any person could be. She was, to use a word, intimidating. And this was just with words. I tried to imagine her stalking across a battlefield with the same expression on her face she had now, and standard-issue Defense Forces rifle. I think I actually felt at least three of my internal organs contract at the thought.

The second is I wondered what she would think of my ability to keep a secret if she had known what I had just done with my evening.

The third was maybe she *did*, and that was what this was about.

I felt several other of my internal organs contract at *that* thought.

Jane was still looking at me, cold like stone, waiting for my answer.

"Yes," I said. "I understand, Jane. Not a word."

"Thank you, Zoë," Jane said. Then she bent down and kissed the top of my head. Just like that, she was my mom again. Which in its way made her even more terrifying, if you ask me.

That settled, Dad started asking Hickory about the Conclave and what it and Dickory knew about that group. Since we had made the jump to Roanoke, we had been waiting for the Conclave to find us, and when they found us, to destroy us, like they had destroyed the Whaid colony in the video the Colonial Union had given us. Dad wanted to know if what Hickory knew about the Conclave was different than what we knew.

Hickory said yes, basically. They knew quite a bit about the Conclave, based on the Obin government's own files on them—and that their own files, contrary to what we had been told by the Colonial Union, showed that when it came to colonies, the Conclave much preferred to evacuate the colonies they confronted, rather than destroying them.

Dad asked Hickory why, if they had different information, they had not shared it earlier. Hickory said because they had been ordered not to by their government; neither Hickory nor Dickory would have lied about having the information if Dad had asked them, but he had never asked them about it before. I think this struck Dad as a bit weaselly on the part of Hickory and Dickory, but he let it go.

Dad asked Hickory if it'd seen the video the Colonial Union had given us, of the Conclave destroying the Whaid colony. Hickory said that it and Dickory had their own version. Dad asked if their version was different; Hickory said it was—it was longer and showed General Gau, who had ordered the destruction of the Whaid colony, trying to convince the Whaidi colony leader to let the Conclave evacuate the colonists, only to have the Whaid refuse to leave before the destruction of their colony. Hickory said that other times, on other colony worlds, colonists *did* ask to be evacuated, and the Conclave carried them off the planet, and sent them back to their homeworlds or allowed them to join the Conclave as citizens.

Jane asked for numbers. Hickory said they knew of seventeen colony removals by the Conclave. Ten of those had the Conclave returning colonists to their former homes. Four of those had the colonists joining the Conclave. Only three involved the destruction of the colonies, after the colonists refused to move. The Conclave was dead serious about not allowing anyone else to start new colonies, but—unlike what we were told by the Colonial Union—didn't insist on killing everyone on those new colonies to make the point.

This was fascinating stuff—and disturbing. Because if what Hickory was saying was true—and it was, because Hickory would not lie to me, or to my parents against my will—then it meant that either the Colonial Union had been wildly wrong about the Conclave, and its leader General Gau, or that the CU had lied to us when it told us what would happen if the Conclave found us. The first of these was certainly possible, I suppose; the Colonial Union was in a state of active hostility with almost every other alien race that we knew about, which I would guess would make intelligence gathering harder than it might be if we had more friends. But it was really more likely that the second of these was the truth: Our government lied to us.

But if the Colonial Union lied to us, why did it do it? What did it get from lying to us, punting us to who knows where in the universe, and making us live in fear of being discovered—and putting all of us in danger?

What was our own government up to?

And what would the Conclave really do to us if it found us?

This was such an interesting thing to think about that I almost missed the part where Hickory explained the reason why it and Dickory actually had detailed files about the Conclave's other colony removals: in order to convince Mom and Dad, should the Conclave come knocking, to surrender our colony rather than to let it be destroyed. And why would they want to convince Mom and Dad of this?

"Because of Zoë?" Dad asked Hickory.

"Yes," Hickory said.

"Wow," I said. This was news.

"Quiet, sweetheart," Dad said, and then gave his attention back to Hickory. "What would happen if Jane and I chose not to surrender the colony?" he asked.

"We would prefer not to say," Hickory said.

"Don't evade," Dad said. "Answer the question."

I caught Hickory giving me a quick look before it answered.

"We would kill you and Lieutenant Sagan," Hickory said. "You and any other colony leader who would authorize the destruction of the colony."

Dad said something to this and Hickory said something back, but I missed most of it because my brain was trying to process what I had just heard, and it was absolutely and completely utterly failing. I knew I was important to the Obin. I had always known it abstractly, and then Hickory and Dickory had pounded the point into me months ago, when they had attacked me and showed me what it felt to be hunted, and showed me why I had to learn to defend myself. But in no formulation of my importance was even the conception that I was so important to the Obin that if it came to it, they would kill my parents to save me.

I didn't even know how to *think* about something like that. Didn't know how to *feel* about it. The idea kept trying to hook into my brain, and it just wasn't working. It was like having an out of body experience. I floated up over the conversation, and listened to Jane interject herself into the discussion, asking Hickory if even after admitting this as their plan, if it and Dickory would still kill her and John. Kill my mom and dad.

"If you choose to surrender the colony, yes," Hickory said.

I actually felt a *snap* as I reeled myself back into my head, and I'm happy to say that I quite suddenly knew exactly how to feel about all of this: absolutely enraged.

"Don't you *dare*," I said, and I flung out the words. "Under no circumstances *will you do that.*" I was surprised to find myself standing when I said it; I didn't remember getting up. I was shaking so hard with anger I wasn't sure how I was still standing.

Hickory and Dickory both flinched at my anger, and trembled. "This one thing we must refuse you," Hickory said. "You are too important. To us. To all Obin."

To all Obin.

If I could have spat, I would.

Here it was again. All of my life, bounded by the Obin. Bounded not in *who* I was, but *what* I was. By what I *meant* to them. There was nothing about my own life that mattered in this, except what entertainment I could give them as billions of Obin played the records of my life like it was a funny show. If any other girl had been Charles Boutin's daughter, they would have happily watched her life instead. If any other girl's adopted parents had gotten in the way of the Obin's plan for her, they would have slaughtered them, too. Who I was meant nothing. The only thing that mattered was that I just happened to have been one man's daughter. A man who the Obin had thought could give them something. A man whose daughter's life they had bargained with to get that thing. A man who ended up *dying* because of the work he'd done for them. And now they wanted more sacrifices.

So I let Hickory and Dickory know how I felt. "I've already lost one parent because of the *Obin*," I said, and loaded everything I could into that last word. All my anger and disgust and horror and rage, at the idea they should so casually decide to take from me two people who had only ever shown me love and affection and honor, and flick them aside like they were nothing more than an inconvenience.

I hated Hickory and Dickory that minute. Hated them in that way that comes only when someone you love takes that love and betrays it, completely and totally. Hated them because they would betray me because they believe they loved me.

I hated them.

"Everybody calm down," John said. "No one is killing anyone. All right? This is a nonissue. Zoë, Hickory and Dickory aren't going to kill us because we're not going to let the colony be destroyed. Simple as that. And there is no way I would let anything happen to you, Zoë. Hickory and Dickory and I *all* agree that you are too important for that."

I opened my mouth to say something to that and just started sobbing instead. I felt like I'd gone numb from the legs; suddenly Jane was there, holding me and leading me back to the couch. I sobbed on her like I did so many years ago outside that toy store, trying to sort out everything I was thinking.

I heard Dad make Hickory and Dickory swear to protect me, always, under all circumstances. They swore. I felt like I didn't want their help or protection ever again. I knew it would pass. Even now I knew it was because of the moment that I felt this way. It didn't change the fact that I still felt it. I was going to have to live with it from now on.

Dad talked with Hickory more about the Conclave and asked to see the Obin's files on the other colony removals. Hickory said they would need to go to the information center to do it. Even though it was now so late it was almost morning, Dad wanted to do it right then. He gave me a kiss and headed out the door with the Obin; Jane held back a second.

"Are you going to be okay?" she asked me.

"I'm having a really intense day, Mom," I said. "I think I want it to be over."

"I'm sorry you had to hear what Hickory said," Jane said. "I don't think there would have been any good way to handle it."

I sniffled out a small grin. "*You* seem to have taken it well," I said. "If someone was telling me they had plans to kill me, I don't think I would have taken it anywhere as calmly."

"Let's just say I wasn't entirely surprised to hear Hickory say that," Jane said. I looked up at her, surprised. "You're a treaty condition, remember," she said. "And you are the Obin's main experience of what it's like to live."

"They all live," I said.

"No," Jane said. "They *exist*. Even with their consciousness implants they hardly know what to do with themselves, Zoë. It's all too new to them. Their race has no experience with it. They don't just watch you because you entertain them. They watch you because you're teaching them how to be. You're teaching them how to live."

"I've never thought about it that way," I said.

"I know you haven't," Jane said. "You don't *have* to. Living comes naturally to you. More naturally than to some of the rest of us."

"It's been a year since any of them have seen me," I said. "Any of them but Hickory and Dickory. If I've been teaching them how to live, I wonder what they've been doing for the last year."

"They've been missing you," Mom said, and kissed the top of my head again. "And now you know why they'll do anything to have you back. And to keep you safe."

I didn't have a good answer to that. Mom gave me one last quick hug and headed to the door to join Dad and the Obin. "I don't know how long this is going to take us," she said. "Try going to bed again."

"I'm too worked up to get back to sleep," I said.

"If you get some sleep you'll probably be less worked up when you wake up," Jane said.

"Trust me, Mom," I said. "It's going to take something pretty big to get me over being worked up about all of this."

NINETEEN

And wouldn't you know. Something big was arranged. The Colonial Union showed up.

The shuttle landed and a little green man popped out. And I thought, *This seems familiar.* It was even the same little green man: General Rybicki.

But there were differences. The first time I saw General Rybicki, he was in my front yard, and it was just him and me. This time his shuttle landed in the grassy area right in front of Croatoan's gate, and a large chunk of the colony had turned out to see him land. He was our first visitor since we came to Roanoke, and his appearance seemed to give the idea that maybe we would finally be out of exile.

General Rybicki stood in front of the shuttle and looked at the people in front of him. He waved.

They cheered wildly. This went on for several minutes. It's like people had never seen someone wave before.

Finally the general spoke. "Colonists of Roanoke," he said. "I bring you good news. Your days of hiding are over." This was interrupted by another gout of cheering. When it calmed down, the general continued. "As I speak to you, my ship above is installing your communications satellite. Soon you will be able to send messages to friends and loved ones back on your home planets. And from here on out, all the electronic and communication equipment you had been ordered to stop using will be returned to you." This got a huge whoop from the teenage sectors of the crowd.

"We know that we have asked much from you," Rybicki said. "I am here to tell you that your sacrifice has not been wasted. We believe that very soon now the enemy that has threatened you will be contained—and not just contained, but defeated. We couldn't have done this without you. So for all of the Colonial Union, I thank you."

More cheering and nonsense. The general seemed to be enjoying his moment in the sun.

"Now I must speak with your colony leaders to discuss how to reintegrate you into the Colonial Union. Some of this may take some time, so I ask you to be a little patient. But until then, let me just say this: Welcome back to civilization!"

Now the crowd really went nuts. I rolled my eyes and looked down at Babar, who went with me to the landing. "This is what happens when you spend a year out in the wilderness," I said. "Any dumb thing looks like entertainment." Babar looked up at me and lolled his tongue out; I could tell he agreed with me. "Come on, then," I said. And we walked through the crowd to the general, who I was supposed to escort back to my dad.

General Rybicki saw Babar before he saw me. "Hey!" he said, and bent down for his slobbering, which Babar duly and enthusiastically applied. He was a good dog but not a hugely accurate judge of character. "I remember you," he said to Babar, petting him. He looked up and saw me. "I remember you, too."

"Hello, General," I said, politely. The crowd was still milling around us but quickly dispersing as folks raced to all corners of the colony to pass on what they were told.

"You look taller," he said.

"It's been a year," I said. "And I am a growing girl. This despite being kept in the dark all this time."

The general seemed not to catch this. "Your mother said that you would be escorting me to see them. I'm a little surprised that they didn't come out themselves," he said.

"They've had a busy couple of days," I said. "As have we all."

"So colony life is more exciting than you thought it would be," the general said.

"Something like that," I said, and then motioned. "I know my dad is very interested in talking to you, General. Let's not keep him waiting."

I held my PDA in my hand. There was something not quite right about it.

Gretchen noticed it too. "It feels *weird*," she said. "It's been so long since we carried one around. It's like I've forgotten how to do it."

"You seemed to remember pretty well when we were using the ones in the information center," I said, reminding her of how we'd spent a fair amount of the last year.

"It's different," she said. "I didn't say I'd forgotten how to use one. I'm saying I've forgotten what it was like to carry one around. Two different things."

"You could always give it back," I said.

"I didn't say that," Gretchen said, quickly. Then she smiled. "Still, you have to wonder. In the last year people here actually *did* manage to get along without them just fine. All the hootenannies and the plays and the other stuff." She looked at her PDA. "Makes you wonder if they're all going to go away now."

"I think they're part of who we are now," I said. "As Roanokers, I mean."

"Maybe," Gretchen said. "It's a nice thought. We'll have to see if it's actually true."

"We could practice a new song," I said. "Hickory says Dickory's been wanting to try something new for a while now."

"That's funny," Gretchen said. "One of your bodyguards has become a musical fiend."

"He's a Roanoker too," I said.

"I guess he is," Gretchen said. "*That's* funny, too."

My PDA blinked; something happened with Gretchen's as well. She peered at hers. "It's a message from Magdy," she said. "This is going to be bad." She touched the PDA to open it. "Yup," she said, and showed me the picture. Magdy sent a short video of him mooning us.

"Some people are getting back into the swing of things sooner than others," I said.

"Unfortunately," Gretchen said. She tapped onto her PDA. "There," she said. "I made a note to kick his ass the next time I see him." She motioned at my PDA. "He send it to you, too?"

"Yes," I said. "I think I'll refrain from opening it."

"Coward," Gretchen said. "Well, then, what is going to be your first official act on your PDA?"

"I'm going to send a message to a certain two someones," I said. "And tell them that I want to see them alone."

"We apologize for being late," Hickory said to me, as it and Dickory stepped into my bedroom. "Major Perry and General Rybicki gave us priority status on a data packet so that we could communicate with our government. It took some time to prepare the data."

"What did you send?" I asked.

"Everything," Hickory said.

"*Everything*," I said. "Every single thing you two and I did in the last year."

"Yes," Hickory said. "A digest of events now, and a more comprehensive report as soon as we can. Our people will be desperate to know what has happened with you since they last heard from us. They need to know you are well and unharmed."

"This includes what happened last night," I said. "All of it. Including the part where you oh so lightly mentioned your plans to murder my parents."

"Yes," Hickory said. "We are sorry to have upset you, Zoë. We would not have wished to do that. But you offered us no alternative when you told us to speak the truth to your parents."

"And what about to me?" I asked.

"We have always told you the truth," Hickory said.

"Yes, but not all of it, have you?" I said. "You told Dad that you had information about the Conclave that you didn't tell him about. But you didn't tell it to me, either. You kept secrets from me, Hickory. You and Dickory both."

"You never asked," Hickory said.

"Oh, don't give me that crap," I said. "We're not playing word games here, Hickory. You kept us in the dark. You kept me in the dark. And the more I've thought about it, the more I realize how you acted on what you knew without telling me. All those alien races you had me and Gretchen study in the information center. All the races you trained us how to fight. Hardly any of them were in the Conclave. Because you knew that if the Conclave found us first, they'd try everything *not* to fight us."

"Yes," Hickory said.

"Don't you think I should have known that?" I asked. "Don't you think it would have mattered to me? To all of us? To the entire colony?"

"We are sorry, Zoë," Hickory said. "We had orders from our government not to reveal information to your parents that they did not already know, until such time as it became absolutely necessary. That would have only been if the Conclave were to appear in your sky. Until then, we were required to exercise care. If we had spoken to you about it, you would have naturally informed your parents. And so we decided that we would not bring these things up with you, unless you asked us directly about them."

"And why would I do that?" I asked.

"Indeed," Hickory said. "We regret the necessity. But we saw no other alternative."

"Listen to me, both of you," I said, and then stopped. "You're recording this now, aren't you."

"Yes," Hickory said. "We always record, unless you tell us otherwise. Would you like us to stop recording?"

"No," I said. "I actually want all of you to hear this. First, I forbid you to harm my parents in any way. Ever."

"Major Perry has already informed us that he would surrender the colony rather than destroy it," Hickory said. "Since this is true there is no reason to harm either him or Lieutenant Sagan."

"It doesn't matter," I said. "Who knows if there's going to be another time you decide it's going to be necessary to try to get rid of John and Jane?"

"It seems unlikely," Hickory said.

"I don't care if it's more likely that I was going to sprout wings," I said. "I didn't think it was *ever* possible that you might think to *kill my parents*, Hickory. I was wrong about that. I'm not going to be wrong about it again. So swear it. Swear you will never harm my parents."

Hickory spoke briefly to Dickory in their own language. "We swear it," Hickory said.

"Swear it for all Obin," I said.

"We cannot," Hickory said. "That is not something we can promise. It is not within our power. But neither Dickory nor I will seek to harm your parents. And we will defend them against all those who would try to harm them. Even other Obin. This we swear to you, Zoë."

It was the last part of this that made me believe Hickory. I hadn't asked him to defend John and Jane, just not harm them. Hickory added it in. They both did.

"Thank you," I said. I felt as if I were suddenly coming unwound; until that second I didn't realize how worked up I was just sitting there, talking about this. "Thank you both. I really needed to hear that."

"You are welcome, Zoë," Hickory said. "Is there something else you want to ask us?"

"You have files on the Conclave," I said.

"Yes," Hickory said. "We have already given them to Lieutenant Sagan for analysis."

That made perfect sense; Jane had been an intelligence officer when she was in the Special Forces. "I want to see them, too," I said. "Everything you have."

"We will provide them to you," Hickory said. "But there is a lot of information, and not all of it is easy to understand. Lieutenant Sagan is far more qualified to work with this information."

"I'm not saying give it to me and not her," I said. "I just want to see it too."

"If you wish," Hickory said.

"And anything else that you might get from your government on the Conclave," I said. "And I mean *all* of it, Hickory. None of this 'you didn't ask directly' junk from now on. We're done with that. Do you understand me?"

"Yes," Hickory said. "You understand that the information we receive might in itself be incomplete. We are not told everything."

"I know," I said. "But you still seem to know more than we do. And I want to understand what we're up against. Or were, anyway."

"Why do you say 'were'?" Hickory asked.

"General Rybicki told the crowd today that the Conclave

was about to be defeated," I said. "Why? Do you know any different?"

"We do not know any different," Hickory said. "But we do not think that just because General Rybicki says something in public to a large crowd, it means he is telling the truth. Nor does it mean that Roanoke itself is entirely out of danger."

"But that doesn't make any sense," I said. I held up my PDA to Hickory. "We were told we can use these again. That we can use all of our electronics again. We had stopped using them because they would give us away. If we're allowed to use them again, we don't have to worry about being given away."

"That is one interpretation of the data," Hickory said.

"There's another?" I asked.

"The general did not say that the Conclave had been defeated, but that he believed they would be defeated," Hickory said. "That is correct?"

"Yes," I said.

"Then it is possible that the general means for Roanoke to play a part in the defeat of the Conclave," Hickory said. "In which case, it is not that you are being allowed to use your electronics because it is safe. You are being allowed to use them because you are now bait."

"You think the Colonial Union is leading the Conclave here," I said, after a minute.

"We offer no opinion one way or another," Hickory said. "We note only that it is possible. And it fits what data we have."

"Have you told my dad about this?" I asked.

"We have not—" Hickory began, but I was already out the door.

"Close the door behind you," Dad said.

I did.

"Who have you talked to about this?" he asked.

"Hickory and Dickory, obviously," I said. "No one else."

"No one?" Dad asked. "Not even Gretchen?"

"No," I said. Gretchen had gone off to harass Magdy for sending her that video. I was beginning to wish I had gone with her instead of making Hickory and Dickory come to my room.

"Good," Dad said. "Then you need to keep quiet about it, Zoë. You and the alien twins."

"You don't think what Hickory is saying is going to happen, do you?" I asked.

Dad looked directly at me, and once again I was reminded how much older he was than he appeared. "It *is* going to happen," he said. "The Colonial Union has laid a trap for the Conclave. We disappeared a year ago. The Conclave has been looking for us all that time, and the CU has spent all that time preparing the trap. Now it's ready, so we're being dragged back into view. When General Rybicki's ship goes back, they're going to let it leak where we are. The news will get back to the Conclave. The Conclave will send its fleet here. And the Colonial Union will destroy it. That's the plan, anyway."

"Is it going to work?" I asked.

"I don't know," Dad said.

"What happens if it doesn't?" I asked.

Dad laughed a very small and bitter laugh. "If it doesn't, then I don't think the Conclave is going to be in any mood for negotiations," he said.

"Oh, God," I said. "We have to tell people, Dad."

"I know we do," he said. "I tried keeping things from the colonists before, and it didn't work very well." He was talking about the werewolves there, and I reminded myself that when all this was done I needed to come clean to him about my own adventures with them. "But I also don't need another panic on our hands. People have been whipsawed enough in the last couple of days. I need to figure out a way to tell people what the CU has planned without putting them in fear for their lives."

"Despite the fact they should be," I said.

"That is the catch," Dad said, and gave another bitter chuckle. Then he looked at me. "It's not right, Zoë. This whole colony is built on a lie. Roanoke was never intended to be a real colony, a viable colony. It exists because our government needed a way to thumb its nose at the Conclave, to defy its colonization ban, and to buy time to build a trap. Now that it's had that time, the only reason our colony exists is to be a goat at a stake. The Colonial Union doesn't care about us for who we are, Zoë. It only cares about us for what we are. What we represent to them. What they can use us for. Who we are doesn't actually enter into it."

"I know the feeling," I said.

"I'm sorry," Dad said. "I'm getting both abstract and depressed."

"It's not abstract, Dad," I said. "You're talking to the girl whose life is a treaty point. I know what it means to be valued for what I am rather than who I am."

Dad gave me a hug. "Not here, Zoë," he said. "We love you for you. Although if you want to tell your Obin friends to get off their asses and help us, I wouldn't mind."

"Well, I did get Hickory and Dickory to swear not to kill you," I said. "So that's progress, at least."

"Yes, baby steps in the right direction," Dad said. "It'll be nice not to have to worry about being knifed by members of my household."

"There's always Mom," I said.

"Trust me, if I ever annoyed her that much, she wouldn't use something as painless as a knife," Dad said. He kissed me on the cheek. "Thanks for coming to tell me what Hickory said, Zoë," he said. "And thanks for keeping it to yourself for now."

"You're welcome," I said, and then headed for the door. I stopped before I turned the handle. "Dad? How long do you think it will take before the Conclave is here?"

"Not long, Zoë," he said. "Not long at all."

In fact, it took just about two weeks.

In that time, we prepared. Dad found a way to tell everyone the truth without having them panic: He told them that there was still a good chance the Conclave would find us and that the Colonial Union was planning on making a stand here; that there was still danger but that we had been in danger before, and that being smart and prepared was our best defense. Colonists called up plans to build bomb shelters and other protections, and used the excavation and construction machinery we'd kept packed up before. People kept to their work and stayed optimistic and prepared themselves as best they could, readying themselves for a life on the edge of a war.

I spent my time reading the stuff Hickory and Dickory gave me, watching the videos of the colony removals, and poring through the data to see what I could learn. Hickory and Dickory were right, there was just too much of it, and lots of it in formats I couldn't understand. I don't know how Jane managed to keep it all straight in her head. But what was there was enough to know a few different things.

First, the Conclave was huge: Over four hundred races belonged to it, each of them pledging to work together to colonize new worlds rather than compete for them. This was a wild idea; up until now all the hundreds of races in our part of space fought with each other to grab worlds and colonize them, and then once they created a new colony they all fought tooth and nail to keep their own and wipe out everyone else's. But in the Conclave setup, creatures from all sorts of races would live on the same planet. You wouldn't have to compete. In theory, a great idea—it beats having to try to kill everyone else in the area—but whether it would actually work was still up in the air.

Which brought up the second point: It was still incredibly new. General Gau, the head of the Conclave, had worked for more than twenty years to put it together, and for most of those years it kept looking like it was going to fall apart. It didn't help that the Colonial Union—us humans—and a few others expended a lot of energy to break it up even before it got together. But somehow Gau made it happen, and in the last couple of years had actually taken it from planning to practicality.

That wasn't a good thing for everyone who wasn't part of the Conclave, especially when the Conclave started making decrees, like that no one who wasn't part of the Conclave could colonize any new worlds. Any argument with the Conclave was an argument with every member of the Conclave. It wasn't a one-on-one thing; it was a four-hundred-on-one thing. And General Gau made sure people knew it. When the Conclave started bringing fleets to remove those new colonies that other races planted in defiance, there was one ship in that fleet for every race in the Conclave. I tried to imagine four hundred battle cruisers suddenly popping up over Roanoke, and then remembered that if the Colonial Union's plan worked, I'd see them soon enough. I stopped trying to imagine it.

It was fair to wonder if the Colonial Union was insane for trying to pick a fight with the Conclave, but as big as it was, its newness worked against it. Every one of those four hundred allies had been enemies not too long ago. Each of them came in to the Conclave with its own plans and agenda, and not all of them, it seemed, were entirely convinced this Conclave thing was going to work; when it all came down, some of them planned to scoop up the choice pieces. It was still early enough for it all to fall apart, if someone applied just the right amount of pressure. It looked like the Colonial Union was planning to do that, up above Roanoke.

Only one thing was keeping it all together, and that was the third thing I learned: That this General Gau was in his way a remarkable person. He wasn't like one of those tin-pot dictators who got lucky, seized a country and gave themselves the title of Grand High Poobah or whatever. He had been an actual general for a people called the Vrenn, and had won some important battles for them when he decided that it was wasteful to fight over resources that more than one race could easily and productively share; when he started campaigning with this idea, he was thrown into jail. No one likes a troublemaker.

The ruler who tossed him in jail eventually died (Gau had nothing to do with it; it was natural causes) and Gau was offered the job, but he turned it down and instead tried to get other races to sign on to the idea of the Conclave. He had the disadvantage that he didn't get the Vrenn to go along with the idea at first; all he had to his name was an idea and a small battle cruiser called the *Gentle Star*, which he had gotten the Vrenn to give him after they decommissioned it. From what I could read, it seemed like the Vrenn thought they were buying him off with it, as in "here, take this, thanks for your service, go away, no need to send a postcard, bye."

But he didn't go away, and despite the fact that his idea was insane and impractical and nuts and could never possibly work because every race in our universe hated every other race too much, it worked. Because this General Gau made it work, by using his own skills and personality to get people of all different races to work together. The more I read about him, the more it seemed like the guy was really admirable.

And yet he was also the person who had ordered the killing of civilian colonists.

Yes, he'd offered to move them and even offered to give them space in the Conclave. But when it came right down to it, if they wouldn't move and they wouldn't join, he wiped them out. Just like he would wipe us all out, if despite everything

Dad told Hickory and Dickory we didn't surrender the colony—or if, should the attack the Colonial Union had planned on the Conclave fleet go wrong, the general decided that the CU needed to be taught a lesson for daring to defy the Conclave and wiped us out just on general principles.

I wasn't so sure just how admirable General Gau would be, if at the end of the day he wouldn't stop from killing me and every single person I cared about.

It was a puzzle. *He* was a puzzle. I spent those two weeks trying to sort it out. Gretchen got grumpy with me that I'd been locked away without telling her what I was up to; Hickory and Dickory had to remind me to get out and work on my training. Even Jane wondered if I might not need to get outside more. The only person not to give me much grief was Enzo; since we got back together he was actually very accommodating about my schedule. I appreciated that. I made sure he knew. He seemed to appreciate that.

And then just like that we all ran out of time. The *Gentle Star*, General Gau's ship, appeared above our colony one afternoon, disabled our communications satellite so Gau could have some time to chat, and then sent a message to Roanoke asking to meet with the colony leaders. John replied that he would meet with him. That evening, as the sun set, they met on the ridge outside the colony, about a klick away.

"Hand me the binoculars, please," I said to Hickory, as we climbed out to the roof of the bungalow. It obliged me. "Thanks," I said. Dickory was below us, on the ground; old habits die hard.

Even with the binoculars General Gau and Dad were little more than dots. I looked anyway. I wasn't the only one; on other roofs, in Croatoan and in the homesteads, other people sat on roofs with binoculars and telescopes, looking at Dad and the general, or scanning the sky, looking in the dusk for the *Gentle Star*. As night finally fell, I spotted the ship myself;

a tiny dot between two stars, shining unblinkingly where the other stars twinkled.

"How long until the other ships arrive, do you think?" I asked Hickory. The *Gentle Star* always arrived first, alone, and then at Gau's command, the hundreds of other ships would appear, a not-at-all-subtle bit of showmanship to get a reluctant colony leader to agree to get his or her people to leave their homes. I had watched it on previous colony removal videos. It would happen here, too.

"Not long now," Hickory said. "By now Major Perry will have refused to surrender the colony."

I took down my binoculars and glanced over to Hickory in the gloom. "You don't seem concerned about this," I said. "That's a different tune than you were singing before."

"Things have changed," Hickory said.

"I wish I had your confidence," I said.

"Look," Hickory said. "It has begun."

I glanced up. New stars had begun to appear in the sky. First one or two, then small groups, and then entire constellations. So many had begun to appear it was impossible to track every single appearance. I knew there were four hundred. It seemed like thousands.

"Dear God," I said, and I was afraid. Truly afraid. "Look at them all."

"Do not fear this attack, Zoë," Hickory said. "We believe this plan will work."

"You know the plan?" I asked. I didn't take my eyes off the sky.

"We learned of it this afternoon," Hickory said. "Major Perry told us, as a courtesy to our government."

"You didn't tell me," I said.

"We thought you knew," Hickory said. "You said you had spoken to Major Perry about it."

"We talked about the Colonial Union attacking the Conclave fleet," I said. "But we didn't talk about how."

"My apologies, Zoë," Hickory said. "I would have told you."

"Tell me now," I said, and then something happened in the sky.

The new stars started going nova.

First one or two, then small groups, and then entire constellations. So many expanded and brightened that they had begun to blend into each other, forming an arm of a small and violent galaxy. It was beautiful. And it was the worst thing I had ever seen.

"Antimatter bombs," Hickory said. "The Colonial Union learned the identity of the ships in the Conclave fleet. It assigned members of your Special Forces to locate them and plant the bombs just before the jump here. Another Special Forces member here activated them."

"Bombs on how many ships?" I asked.

"All of them," Hickory said. "All but the *Gentle Star.*"

I tried to turn to look at Hickory but I couldn't move my eyes from the sky. "That's impossible," I said.

"No," Hickory said. "Not impossible. Extraordinarily difficult. But not impossible."

From other roofs and from the streets of Croatoan, cheers and shouts lifted into the air. I finally turned away, and wiped the tears off my face.

Hickory noticed. "You cry for the Conclave fleet," it said.

"Yes," I said. "For the people on those ships."

"Those ships were here to destroy the colony," Hickory said.

"I know," I said.

"You are sorry they were destroyed," Hickory said.

"I am sorry that we couldn't think of anything better," I said. "I'm sorry that it had to be us or them."

"The Colonial Union believes this will be a great victory,"

Hickory said. "It believes that destroying the Conclave's fleet in one engagement will cause the Conclave to collapse, ending its threat. This is what it has told my government."

"Oh," I said.

"It is to be hoped they are correct," Hickory said.

I was finally able to look away and face Hickory. The afterimages of the explosions placed blotches all around it. "Do you believe they are correct?" I asked. "Would your government believe it?"

"Zoë," Hickory said. "You will recall that just before you left for Roanoke, my government invited you to visit our worlds."

"I remember," I said.

"We invited you because our people longed to see you, and to see you among us," Hickory said. "We also invited you because we believed that your government was going to use Roanoke as a ruse to open a battle against the Conclave. And while we did not know whether this ruse would be successful, we believed strongly that you would have been safer with us. There is no doubt that your life has been in danger here, Zoë, both in ways we had foreseen and in ways that we could not. We invited you, Zoë, because we feared for you. Do you understand what I am saying to you?"

"I do," I said.

"You asked me if I believe the Colonial Union is correct, that this is a great victory, and if my government would believe the same," Hickory said. "My response is to say that once again my government extends an invitation to you, Zoë, to come visit our worlds, and to travel safe among them."

I nodded, and looked back to the sky, where stars were still going nova. "And when would you want this trip to begin?" I asked.

"Now," Hickory said. "Or as close to now as possible."

I didn't say anything to that. I looked up to the sky, and then closed my eyes and for the first time, started to pray. I prayed for the crews of the ships above me. I prayed for the colonists below me. I prayed for John and Jane. For Gretchen and her father. For Magdy and for Enzo and their families. For Hickory and Dickory. I prayed for General Gau. I prayed for everyone.

I prayed.

"Zoë," Hickory said.

I opened my eyes.

"Thank you for the invitation," I said. "I regret I must decline."

Hickory was silent.

"Thank you, Hickory," I said. "Really, thank you. But I am right where I belong."

PART III

TWENTY

"Admit it," Enzo said, through the PDA. "You forgot."

"I did not," I said, with what I hoped was just the right amount of indignation to suggest that I had not forgotten, which I had.

"I can hear the fake indignation," he said.

"Rats," I said. "You're on to me. Finally."

"Finally? There's no *finally*," Enzo said. "I've been on to you since I met you."

"Maybe you have," I allowed.

"And anyway, that doesn't solve *this* problem," Enzo said. "We're about to sit down for dinner. You're supposed to be here. Not to make you feel guilty or anything."

This was the difference between me and Enzo now and then. There used to be a time when Enzo would have said those words and they would have come out sounding like he was accusing me of something (besides, of course, being late). But right now they were gentle and funny. Yes, he was exasperated, but he was exasperated in a way that suggested I might be able to make it up to him. Which I probably would, if he didn't push it.

"I am in fact wracked with guilt," I said.

"Good," Enzo said. "Because you know we put a whole extra potato in the stew for you."

"Gracious," I said. "A whole potato."

"And I promised the twins they could throw their carrots at you," he said, referring to his little sisters. "Because I know how much you love carrots. Especially when they're kid-hurled."

"I don't know why anyone would eat them any other way," I said.

"And after dinner I was going to read you a poem I wrote for you," Enzo said.

I paused. "Now that's not fair," I said. "Injecting something real into our witty banter."

"Sorry," Enzo said.

"Did you really?" I asked. "You haven't written me a poem in ages."

"I know," he said. "I thought I might get back into practice. I remember you kind of liked it."

"You jerk," I said. "Now I really *do* feel guilty for forgetting about dinner."

"Don't feel too guilty," Enzo said. "It's not a very good poem. It doesn't even rhyme."

"Well, that's a relief," I said. I still felt giddy. It's nice to get poems.

"I'll send it to you," Enzo said. "You can read it instead. And then, maybe if you're nice to me, I'll read it to you. Dramatically."

"What if I'm mean to you?" I asked.

"Then I'll read it melodramatically," he said. "I'll wave my arms and everything."

"You're making a case for me being mean to you," I said.

"Hey, you're already missing dinner," Enzo said. "That's worth an arm wave or two."

"Jerk," I said. I could almost hear him smile over the PDA.

"Gotta go," Enzo said. "Mom's telling me to set the table."

"Do you want me to try to make it?" I asked. All of a sudden I really did want to be there. "I can try."

"You're going to run across the entire colony in five minutes?" Enzo said.

"I could do it," I said.

"Maybe Babar could," Enzo said. "But he has two legs more than you."

"Fine," I said. "I'll send Babar to have dinner with you."

Enzo laughed. "Do that," he said. "I'll tell you what, Zoë. Walk here at a reasonable pace, and you'll probably make it in time for dessert. Mom made a pie."

"Yay, pie," I said. "What kind?"

"I think it's called 'Zoë gets whatever kind of pie she gets and likes it' pie," Enzo said.

"Mmmm," I said. "I always like that kind of pie."

"Well, yeah," Enzo said. "It's right there in the title."

"It's a date," I said.

"Good," Enzo said. "Don't forget. I know that's a problem for you."

"Jerk," I said.

"Check your mail queue," Enzo said. "There might be a poem there."

"I'm going to wait for the hand waving," I said.

"That's probably for the best," Enzo said. "It'll be better that way. And now my mom is glaring at me with laser eyeballs. I have to go."

"Go," I said. "See you soon."

"Okay," Enzo said. "Love you." We had started saying that to each other recently. It seemed to fit.

"Love you too," I said, and disconnected.

"You two make me want to vomit so hard," Gretchen said. She'd been hearing my side of the conversation and had been rolling her eyes the whole time. We were sitting in her bedroom.

I set down the PDA and whacked her with a pillow. "You're just jealous Magdy never says that to you."

"Oh, dear Lord," Gretchen said. "Leaving aside the fact that

I *so do not* want to hear that from him, if he ever *did* try to say that to me, his head would actually *explode* before the words could even get out of his mouth. Which now that I think about it might be an excellent reason to try to get him to say it."

"You two are so cute," I said. "I can see you two standing at the altar and getting into it right before saying 'I do.'"

"Zoë, if I ever get anywhere near an altar with Magdy, I authorize you to make a flying tackle and drag me away," Gretchen said.

"Oh, fine," I said.

"Now let's never speak of this again," Gretchen said.

"You're so in denial," I said.

"At least I'm not the one who forgot her dinner date," Gretchen said.

"It gets worse," I said. "He wrote me poetry. He was going to read it to me."

"You missed dinner *and* a show," Gretchen said. "You are the worst girlfriend ever."

"I know," I said. I reached for my PDA. "I'll write him an apology note saying that."

"Make it extra grovelly," Gretchen said. "Because that's sexy."

"That comment explains a lot about you, Gretchen," I said, and then my PDA took on a life of its own, blasting an alarm sound from its speaker and scrolling an air attack notice on its screen. Over on Gretchen's desk, her PDA made the same alarm sound and scrolled the same message. Every PDA in the colony did the same. In the distance, we heard the sirens, posted near the Mennonite homesteads, alerting them because they didn't use personal technology.

For the first time since the defeat of the Conclave fleet, Roanoke was under attack. Missiles were on their way.

I rushed to the door of Gretchen's room. "Where are you going?" she asked. I ignored her and went outside, where people were bursting out of their homes and running for cover, and looked into the sky.

"What are you doing?" Gretchen said, catching up with me. "We need to get to a shelter."

"Look," I said, and pointed.

In the distance, a bright needle of light was tracing across the sky, aiming at something we couldn't quite see. Then there was a flash, blinding white. There was a defense satellite above Roanoke; it had fired on and hit one of the missiles coming for us. But others were still on their way.

The sharp pop of the missile explosion reached us, with not nearly enough time lag.

"Come *on*, Zoë," Gretchen said, and started tugging at me. "We've got to go."

I stopped looking at the sky and ran with Gretchen to one of the community shelters we had recently excavated and built; it was filling up quickly with colonists. As I ran I saw Hickory and Dickory, who had spotted me; they closed in and took either side of me as we got into the shelter. Even in the panic, people still made room for them. Gretchen, Hickory, Dickory, about four dozen other colonists, and I all hunched down in the shelter, straining to hear what was going on above us through nearly a dozen feet of dirt and concrete.

"What do you think is happ—" someone said and then there was unspeakable wrenching noise, like someone had taken one of the cargo containers that made up the colony wall and peeled it apart, right on top of our eardrums and then I was tumbling to the ground because there was an earthquake and I screamed and bet that everyone else in the shelter did too but I couldn't hear it because then came the single loudest noise I had ever heard, so loud that my brain surrendered and the noise became the absence of noise, and the only way I knew that I, at least, was still screaming was that I could feel my throat getting raw. Either Hickory or Dickory grabbed me and held me steady; I could see Gretchen being held the same way by the other Obin.

The lights in the shelter flickered but stayed on.

Eventually I stopped screaming and the ground stopped shaking and something similar to my hearing came back to me and I could hear others in the shelter crying and praying and trying to calm children. I looked over at Gretchen, who looked stricken. I disentangled from Dickory (it turned out) and went over to her.

"You okay?" I asked. My voice sounded like it was pushed through cotton from a distance. Gretchen nodded but didn't look at me. It occurred to me it was the first time she'd been in an attack.

I looked around. Most of the people in the shelter looked like Gretchen. It was the first time any of these people had been in an attack. Of all these people, I was the one who was the veteran of a hostile attack. I guess that put me in charge.

I saw a PDA on the floor; someone had dropped it. I picked it up and activated it and read what was there. Then I stood up and waved my hands back and forth and said "Excuse me!" until people started looking at me. I think enough people recognized me as the daughter of the colony leaders that they decided I might know something after all.

"The emergency information on the PDA says that the attack seems to be over," I said when enough people were looking my way. "But until we get an 'all clear' signal we need to stay here in the shelter. We need to stay here and stay calm. Is anyone here injured or sick?"

"I can't hear very well," someone said.

"I don't think any of us can hear well right now," I said. "That's why I'm yelling." It was an attempt at a joke. I don't think people were going for it. "Are there any injuries here besides hearing loss?" No one said anything or raised their hand. "Then let's just sit tight here and wait for the 'all clear.'"

I held up the PDA I was using. "Whose is this?" Someone raised their hand; I asked if I could borrow it.

"Someone took 'in charge' lessons when I wasn't looking," Gretchen said when I sat back down next to her. The words were classic Gretchen, but the voice was very, very shaky.

"We were just under attack," I said. "If someone doesn't pretend like she knows what she's doing, people are going to start freaking out. That would be bad."

"Not arguing," Gretchen said. "Just impressed." She pointed to the PDA. "Can you send any messages? Can we find out what's happening?"

"I don't think so," I said. "The emergency system overrides usual messaging, I think." I signed out the owner on the PDA and signed in under my account. "See. Enzo said he sent that poem to me but it's not there yet. It's probably queued and will get sent once we have the all clear."

"So we don't know if everyone else is okay," Gretchen said.

"I'm sure we'll get an all clear signal soon," I said. "You worried about your dad?"

"Yes. Aren't you worried about *your* parents?" Gretchen asked.

"They were soldiers," I said. "They've done this before. I'm worried about them, but I'm betting they're fine. And Jane is the one running the emergency messages. As long as they're updating, she's fine." The PDA switched over from my mail queue to a scrolling note; we were being given the "all clear." "See," I said.

I had Hickory and Dickory check the entrance of the shelter for any falling debris; it was clear. I signed out from the PDA and gave it back to its owner, and then folks started shuffling out. Gretchen and I were the last to head up.

"Watch your step," Gretchen said as we came up, and pointed to the ground. Glass was everywhere. I looked around. All the houses and buildings were standing, but almost all the windows were blown out. We'd be picking glass out of everything for days.

"At least it's been nice weather," I said. No one seemed to hear me. Probably just as well.

I said good-bye to Gretchen and headed to my house with Hickory and Dickory. I found more glass in surprising places and Babar cowering in the shower stall. I managed to coax him out and gave him a big hug. He licked my face with increasing franticness. After I petted him and calmed him down, I reached for my PDA to call Mom or Dad, and then realized I had left it over at Gretchen's. I had Hickory and Dickory stay with Babar—he needed their company more than I did at the moment—and walked over to Gretchen's. As I walked to her house, her front door swung open and Gretchen burst through it, saw me and ran to me, her PDA in one hand and mine in the other.

"Zoë," she said, and then her face tightened up, and whatever she had to say was lost for a minute.

"Oh, no," I said. "Gretchen. Gretchen. What is it? Is it your dad? Is your dad okay?"

Gretchen shook her head, and looked up at me. "It's not my dad," she said. "My dad is fine. It's not Dad. Zoë, Magdy just called me. He says something hit. Hit Enzo's homestead. He said the house is still there but there's something big in the yard. He thinks it's part of a missile. Says he tried to call Enzo but he's not there. No one's there. No one's answering there. He said they just built a bomb shelter, away from the house. In the yard, Zoë. Magdy says he keeps calling and no one answers. I just called Enzo, too. I don't get anything, Zoë. It doesn't even connect. I keep trying. Oh God, Zoë. Oh God, Zoë. Oh, God."

Enzo Paulo Gugino was born on Zhong Guo, the first child of Bruno and Natalie Gugino. Bruno and Natalie had known each other since they were children and everyone who knew them knew that from the first moment they laid eyes on each other that they would be together for every single moment of their lives. Bruno and Natalie didn't argue with this idea. Bruno and Natalie, as far as anyone ever knew, never argued about anything, and certainly didn't argue with each other. They married young, even for the deeply religious culture they lived in on Zhong Guo, in which people often married early. But no one could imagine the two of them not being together; their parents gave their consent and the two of them were married in one of the best-attended weddings anyone could remember in their hometown of Pomona Falls. Nine months later, almost to the day, there was Enzo.

Enzo was sweet from the moment he was born; he was always happy and only occasionally fussy, although (as was frequently explained, much to his later mortification) he had a marked tendency to take off his own diapers and smear the contents of them against the nearest available wall. This caused a real problem one time in a bank. Fortunately he was toilet-trained early.

Enzo met his best friend Magdy Metwalli in kindergarten. On the first day of school, a third-grader had tried to pick on Enzo, and pushed him hard down to the ground; Magdy, whom Enzo had never seen before in his life, launched himself at the third-grader and started punching him in the face. Magdy, who at the time was small for his age, did no real damage other than scaring the pee out of the third-grader (literally); it was Enzo who eventually pulled Magdy off the third-grader and calmed him down before they were all sent to the principal's office and then home for the day.

Enzo showed a flair for words early and wrote his first story when he was seven, entitled "The horrible sock that smelled bad and ate Pomona Falls except for my house," in which a large sock, mutated by its own horrible unwashed smell, started eating its way through the contents of an entire town and was thwarted only when the heroes Enzo and Magdy first punched it into submission and then threw it into a swimming pool filled with laundry soap. The first part of the story (about the origin of the sock) took three sentences; the climactic battle scene took three pages. Rumor is Magdy (the one reading the story, not the one in it) kept asking for more of the fight scene.

When Enzo was ten his mother became pregnant for a second time, with twins Maria and Katherina. The pregnancy was difficult, and complicated because Natalie's body had a hard time keeping two babies in it at once; the delivery was a near thing and Natalie came close to bleeding out more than once. It took Natalie more than a year to fully recover, and during that time the ten- and eleven-year-old Enzo helped his father and mother to care for his sisters, learning to change diapers and feed the girls when his mom needed a rest. This was the occasion of the only real fight between Magdy and Enzo: Magdy jokingly called Enzo a sissy for helping his mom, and Enzo smacked him in the mouth.

When Enzo was fifteen the Guginos and the Metwallis and two other families they knew entered a group application to be part of the very first colony world made up of citizens of the Colonial Union rather than citizens of Earth. For the next few months every part of Enzo's life, and the life of his family, was opened up to scrutiny, and he bore it with as much grace as anyone who was fifteen and who mostly just wanted to be left alone could have. Every member of every family was required to submit a statement explaining why they wanted to be part of the colony. Bruno Gugino explained how he had been a fan of the American Colonization era, and the early history of the Colonial Union; he wanted to be part of this new chapter of history. Natalie Gugino wrote about wanting to raise her family on a world where everyone was working together. Maria and Katherina drew pictures of them floating in space with smiley moons.

Enzo, who loved words more and more, wrote a poem, imagining himself standing on a new world, and titled it "The

Stars My Destination." He later admitted he'd taken the title from an obscure fantasy adventure book that he'd never read but whose title stayed with him. The poem, meant only for his application, was leaked to the local media and became something of a sensation. It eventually became sort of an official unofficial anthem for the Zhong Guo colonization effort. And after all that, Enzo and his family and co-applicants really couldn't *not* be chosen to go.

When Enzo had just turned sixteen, he met a girl, named Zoë, and for some reason that passes understanding, he fell for her. Zoë was a girl who seemed like she knew what she was doing most of the time and was happy to tell you that this was in fact the case, all the time, but in their private moments, Enzo learned that Zoë was as nervous and uncertain and terrified that she would say or do something stupid to scare away this boy she thought she might love, as he was nervous and uncertain and terrified that he would do something stupid, too. They talked and touched and held and kissed and learned how not to be nervous and uncertain and terrified of each other. They did say and do stupid things, and they did eventually scare each other away, because they didn't know any better. But then they got over it, and when they were together again, that second time, they didn't wonder whether they might love each other. Because they knew they did. And they told each other so.

On the day Enzo died he talked to Zoë, joked with her about her missing the dinner she was supposed to have with his family, and promised to send her a poem he had written for her. Then he told her he loved her and heard her tell him she loved him. Then he sent her the poem and sat down with his family to dinner. When the emergency alert came, the Gugino family, father Bruno, mother Natalie, daughters Maria and Katherina, and son Enzo, went together into the attack shelter Bruno and Enzo had made just a week before, and sat together close, holding each other and waiting for the "all clear."

On the day Enzo died he knew he was loved. He knew he was loved by his mother and father who, like everyone knew, never stopped loving each other until the very moment they died. Their love for each other became their love for him, and for their daughters. He knew he was loved by his sisters, who he cared for when they were small, and when he was small. He knew he was loved by his best friend, who he never stopped getting out of trouble, and who he never stopped getting into trouble with. And he knew he was loved by Zoë—by me—who he called his love and who said the words back to him.

Enzo lived a life of love, from the moment he was born until the moment he died. So many people go through life without love. Wanting love. Hoping for love. Hungering for more of it than they have. Missing love when it was gone. Enzo never had to go through that. Would never have to.

All he knew all his life was love.

I have to think it was enough.

It would have to be, now.

I spent the day with Gretchen and Magdy and all of Enzo's friends, of whom there were so many, crying and laughing and remembering him, and then at some point I couldn't take any more because everyone had begun to treat me like Enzo's widow and though in a way I felt like I was, I didn't want to have to share that with anyone. It was mine and I wanted to be greedy for it for just a little while. Gretchen saw I had reached some sort of breaking point, and walked me back to her room and told me to get some rest, and that she'd check on me later. Then she gave me a fierce hug, kissed me on the temple and told me she loved me and closed the door behind me. I lay there in Gretchen's bed and tried not to think and did a pretty good job of it until I remembered Enzo's poem, waiting for me in my mail queue.

Gretchen had put my PDA on her desk and I walked over,

took the PDA and sat back down on the bed, and pulled up my mail queue and saw the mail from Enzo. I reached to press the screen to retrieve it and then called up the directory instead. I found the folder titled "Enzo Dodgeball" and opened it and started playing the files, watching as Enzo flailed his way around the dodgeball court, taking hits to the face and tumbling to the ground with unbelievable comic timing. I watched until I laughed so hard that I could barely see, and had to put the PDA down for a minute to concentrate on the simple act of breathing in and out.

When I had mastered that again, I picked up the PDA, called up the mail queue, and opened the mail from Enzo.

Zoë:
Here you are. You'll have to imagine the arm waving for now. But the live show is coming! That is, after we have pie. Mmmm . . . pie.

BELONG

    You said I belong to you
And I agree
But the quality of that belonging
Is a question of some importance.
    I do not belong to you
Like a purchase
Something ordered and sold
And delivered in a box
To be put up and shown off
To friends and admirers.
    I would not belong to you that way
And I know you would not have me so.
    I will tell you how I belong to you.
    I belong to you like a ring on a finger
A symbol of something eternal.

I belong to you like a heart in a chest
Beating in time to another heart.
I belong to you like a word on the air
Sending love to your ear.
I belong to you like a kiss on your lips
Put there by me, in the hope of more to come.
　　And most of all I belong to you
Because in where I hold my hopes
I hold the hope that you belong to me.
It is a hope I unfold for you now like a gift.
　　Belong to me like a ring
And a heart
And a word
And a kiss
And like a hope held close.
　　I will belong to you like all these things
And also something more
Something we will discover between us
And will belong to us alone.
　　You said I belong to you
And I agree.
Tell me you belong to me, too.
I wait for your word
And hope for your kiss.

Love you.
Enzo.

　I love you, too, Enzo. I love you.
　I miss you.

TWENTY-ONE

The next morning I found out Dad was under arrest.

"It's not exactly arrest," Dad said at our kitchen table, having his morning coffee. "I've been relieved of my position as colony leader and have to travel back to Phoenix Station for an inquiry. So it's more like a trial. And if *that* goes badly then I'll be arrested."

"Is it going to go badly?" I asked.

"Probably," Dad said. "They don't usually have an inquiry if they don't know how it's going to turn out, and if it was going to turn out well, they wouldn't bother to have it." He sipped his coffee.

"What did you do?" I asked. I had my own coffee, loaded up with cream and sugar, which was sitting ignored in front of me. I was still in shock about Enzo, and this really wasn't helping.

"I tried to talk General Gau out of walking into the trap we set for him and his fleet," Dad said. "When we met I asked him not to call his fleet. Begged him not to, actually. It was against my orders. I was told to engage in 'nonessential conversation' with him. As if you can have nonessential conversation with someone who is planning to take over your colony, and whose entire fleet you're about to blow up."

"Why did you do it?" I asked. "Why did you try to give General Gau an out?"

"I don't know," Dad said. "Probably because I didn't want the blood of all those crews on my hands."

"You weren't the one who set off the bombs," I said.

"I don't think that matters, do you?" Dad said. He set down his cup. "I was still part of the plan. I was still an active participant. I still bear some responsibility. I wanted to know that at the very least I tried in some small way to avoid so much bloodshed. I guess I was just hoping there might be a way to do things other than the way that ends up with everyone getting killed."

I got up out of my chair and gave my dad a big hug. He took it, and then looked at me, a little surprised, when I sat back down. "Thank you," he said. "I'd like to know what that was about."

"It was me being happy that we think alike," I said. "I can tell we're related, even if it's not biologically."

"I don't think anyone would doubt we think alike, dear," Dad said. "Although given that I'm about to get royally shafted by the Colonial Union, I'm not sure it's such a good thing for you."

"I think it is," I said.

"And biology or not, I think we're both smart enough to figure out that things are not going well for anyone," Dad said. "This is a real big mess, nor are we out of it."

"Amen," I said.

"How are you, sweetheart?" Dad asked. "Are you going to be okay?"

I opened my mouth to say something and closed it again. "I think right now I want to talk about anything else in the world besides how I'm doing," I said, finally.

"All right," Dad said. He started talking about himself then, not because he was an egotist but because he knew listening to him would help me take my mind off my own worries. I listened to him talk on without worrying too much about what he said.

Dad left on the supply ship *San Joaquin* the next day, with Manfred Trujillo and a couple other colonists who were going as representatives of Roanoke, on political and cultural business. That was their cover, anyway. What they were really doing, or so Jane had told me, was trying to find out anything about what was going on in the universe involving Roanoke and who had attacked us. It would take a week for Dad and the others to reach Phoenix Station; they'd spend a day or so there and then it would take another week for them to return. Which is to say, it'd take another week for everyone but Dad to return; if Dad's inquiry went against him, he wouldn't be coming back.

We tried not to think about that.

Three days later most of the colony converged on the Gugino homestead and said good-bye to Bruno and Natalie, Maria, Katherina, and Enzo. They were buried where they had died; Jane and others had removed the missile debris that had fallen on them, reshaped the area with new soil, and set new sod on top. A marker was placed to note the family. At some point in the future, there might be another, larger marker, but for now it was small and simple: the family name, the name of the members, and their dates. It reminded me of my own family marker, where my biological mother lay. For some reason I found this a little bit comforting.

Magdy's father, who had been Bruno Gugino's closest friend, spoke warmly about the whole family. A group of singers came and sang two of Natalie's favorite hymns from Zhong Guo. Magdy spoke, briefly and with difficulty about his best friend. When he sat back down, Gretchen was there to hold him while he sobbed. Finally we all stood and some prayed and others stood silently, with their heads bowed, thinking about missing friends and loved ones. Then people left, until it was just me and Gretchen and Magdy, standing silently by the marker.

"He loved you, you know," Magdy said to me, suddenly.

"I know," I said.

"No," Magdy said, and I saw how he was trying to get across to me that he wasn't just making comforting words. "I'm not talking about how we say we love something, or love people we just like. He really loved you, Zoë. He was ready to spend his whole life with you. I wish I could make you believe this."

I took out my PDA, opened it to Enzo's poem, and showed it to Magdy. "I believe it," I said.

Magdy read the poem, nodded. Then he handed the PDA back to me. "I'm glad," he said. "I'm glad he sent that to you. I used to make fun of him because he wrote you those poems. I told him that he was just being a goof." I smiled at that. "But now I'm glad he didn't listen to me. I'm glad he sent them. Because now you know. You know how much he loved you."

Magdy broke down as he tried to finish that sentence. I came up to him and held him and let him cry.

"He loved you too, Magdy," I said to him. "As much as me. As much as anyone. You were his best friend."

"I loved him too," Magdy said. "He was my brother. I mean, not my *real* brother . . ." He started to get a look on his face; he was annoyed with himself that he wasn't expressing himself like he wanted.

"No, Magdy," I said. "You were his real brother. In every way that matters, you were his brother. He knew you thought of him that way. And he loved you for it."

"I'm sorry, Zoë," Magdy said, and looked down at his feet. "I'm sorry I always gave you and Enzo a hard time. I'm sorry."

"Hey," I said, gently. "Stop that. You were supposed to give us a hard time, Magdy. Giving people a hard time is what you *do*. Ask Gretchen."

"It's true," Gretchen said, not unkindly. "It really is."

"Enzo thought of you as his brother," I said. "You're my brother too. You have been all this time. I love you, Magdy."

"I love you too, Zoë," Magdy said quietly, and then looked straight at me. "Thank you."

"You're welcome." I gave him another hug. "Just remember that as your new family member I'm now entitled to give you all sorts of crap."

"I can't wait," Magdy said, and then turned to Gretchen. "Does this make you my sister too?"

"Considering our history, you better hope not," Gretchen said. Magdy laughed at that, which was a good sign, then gave me a peck on a cheek, gave Gretchen a hug, and then walked from the grave of his friend and brother.

"Do you think he's going to be okay?" I asked Gretchen, as we watched him go.

"No," Gretchen said. "Not for a long time. I know you loved Enzo, Zoë, I really do, and I don't want this to sound like I'm trying to undercut that. But Enzo and Magdy were two halves of the same whole." She nodded to Magdy. "You lost someone you love. *He's* lost part of himself. I don't know if he's going to get over that."

"You can help him," I said.

"Maybe," Gretchen said. "But think about what you're asking me to do."

I laughed. It's why I loved Gretchen. She was the smartest girl I ever knew, and smart enough to know that being smart had its own repercussions. She could help Magdy, all right, by becoming part of what he was missing. But it meant her being that, one way or another, for the rest of their lives. She would do it, because when it came down to it she really did love Magdy. But she was right to worry about what it meant for her.

"Anyway," Gretchen said, "I'm not done helping someone else."

I snapped out of my thoughts at that. "Oh," I said. "Well. You know. I'm okay."

"I know," Gretchen said. "I also know you lie horribly."

"I can't fool you," I said.

"No," Gretchen said. "Because what Enzo was to Magdy, I am to you."

I hugged her. "I know," I said.

"Good," Gretchen said. "Whenever you forget, I'll remind you."

"Okay," I said. We unhugged and Gretchen left me alone with Enzo and his family, and I sat with them for a long time.

Four days later, a note from Dad from a skip drone from Phoenix Station.

A miracle, it said. *I'm not headed for prison. We are heading back on the next supply ship. Tell Hickory and Dickory that I will need to speak to them when I return. Love you.*

There was another note for Jane, but she didn't tell me what was in it.

"Why would Dad want to talk to you?" I asked Hickory.

"We don't know," Hickory said. "The last time he and I spoke of anything of any importance was the day—I am sorry—that your friend Enzo died. Some time ago, before we left Huckleberry, I had mentioned to Major Perry that the Obin government and the Obin people stood ready to assist you and your family here on Roanoke should you need our assistance.

Major Perry reminded me of that conversation and asked me if the offer still stood. I told him that at the time I believed it did."

"You think Dad is going to ask for your help?" I asked.

"I do not know," Hickory said. "And since I last spoke to Major Perry circumstances have changed."

"What do you mean?" I asked.

"Dickory and I have finally received detailed updated information from our government, up to and including its analysis of the Colonial Union's attack on the Conclave fleet," Hickory said. "The most important piece of news is that we have been informed that shortly after the *Magellan* disappeared, the Colonial Union came to the Obin government and asked it not to search for the Roanoke colony, nor to offer it assistance if it were to be located by the Conclave or any other race."

"They knew you would come looking for me," I said.

"Yes," Hickory said.

"But why would they tell you not to help us?" I asked.

"Because it would interfere with the Colonial Union's own plans to lure the Conclave fleet to Roanoke," Hickory said.

"That's happened," I said. "That's done. The Obin can help us now," I said.

"The Colonial Union has asked us to continue not to offer aid or assistance to Roanoke," Hickory said.

"That makes no sense," I said.

"We are inclined to agree," Hickory said.

"But that means that you can't even help *me*," I said.

"There is a difference between you and the colony of Roanoke," Hickory said. "The Colonial Union cannot ask us not to protect or assist you. It would violate the treaty between our peoples, and the Colonial Union would not want to do that, especially now. But the Colonial Union may choose to interpret the treaty narrowly and has. Our treaty concerns you, Zoë. To a much lesser extent it concerns your family, meaning Major Perry and Lieutenant Sagan. It does not concern Roanoke colony at all."

"It does when I *live* here," I said. "This colony is of a great deal of concern to *me*. Its people are of a great deal of concern to *me*. Everybody I care about in the whole universe is here. Roanoke matters to me. It should matter to you."

"We did not say it did not matter to *us*," Hickory said, and I heard something in its voice I had never heard before: *reproach*. "Nor do we suggest it does not matter to you, for many reasons. We are telling you how the Colonial Union is asking the Obin government to view its rights under treaty. And we are telling you that our government, for its own reasons, has agreed."

"So if my dad asks for your help, you will tell him no," I said.

"We will tell him that so long as Roanoke is a Colonial Union world, we are unable to offer help."

"So, *no*," I said.

"Yes," Hickory said. "We are sorry, Zoë."

"I want you to give me the information your government has given you," I said.

"We will do so," Hickory said. "But it is in our native language and file formatting, and will take a considerable amount of time for your PDA to translate."

"I don't care," I said.

"As you wish," Hickory said.

Not too long after that I stared at the screen of my PDA and ground my teeth together as it slowly plodded through file transformations and translations. I realized it would be easier just to ask Hickory and Dickory about it all, but I wanted to see it all with my own eyes. However long it took.

It took long enough that I had hardly read any of it by the time Dad and the others had made it home.

"This all looks like gibberish to me," Gretchen said, looking at the documents I was showing her on my PDA. "It's like it was translated from monkey or something."

"Look," I said. I pulled up a different document. "According to this, blowing up the Conclave fleet backfired. It was supposed to make the Conclave collapse and all the races start shooting at each other. Well, the Conclave is starting to collapse, but hardly any of them are actually fighting each other. They're attacking Colonial Union worlds instead. They really messed this up."

"If you say this is what it says, I'm going to believe you," Gretchen said. "I'm not actually finding verbs here."

I pulled up another document. "Here, this is about a Conclave leader named Nerbros Eser. He's General Gau's main competition for leadership of the Conclave now. Gau still doesn't want to attack the Colonial Union directly, even though we just destroyed his fleet. He still thinks the Conclave is strong enough to keep doing what it's been doing. But this Eser guy thinks the Conclave should just wipe us out. The Colonial Union. And especially us here on Roanoke. Just to make the point that you don't mess with the Conclave. The two of them are fighting over control of the Conclave right now."

"Okay," Gretchen said. "But I still don't know what any of this *means*, Zoë. Speak not-hyper-ese to me. You're losing me."

I stopped and took a breath. Gretchen was right. I'd spent most of the last day reading these documents, drinking coffee, and not sleeping; I was not at the peak of my communication skills. So I tried again.

"The whole point of founding Roanoke colony was to start a war," I said.

"It looks like it worked," Gretchen said.

"No," I said. "It was supposed to start a war *within* the Conclave. Blowing up their fleet was supposed to tear the Conclave apart from the inside. It would end the threat of this huge coalition of alien races and bring things back to the way it was before, when every race was fighting every other race. We trigger a civil war, and then we sweep in while they're all fighting and scoop up the worlds we want and come out of it all stronger than before—maybe too strong for any one race or even a small group of races to square off against. That was the plan."

"But you're telling me it didn't work that way," Gretchen said.

"Right," I said. "We blew up the fleet and got the Conclave members fighting, but who they're fighting is *us*. The reason we didn't like the Conclave is that it was four hundred against one, the one being us. Well, now it's still four hundred against one, except now no one's listening to the one guy who was keeping them from engaging in total war against us."

"Us here on Roanoke," Gretchen said.

"Us everywhere," I said. "The Colonial Union. Humans. *Us.* This is happening now," I said. "Colonial Union worlds are being attacked. Not just the new colony worlds, the ones that usually get attacked. Even the established colonies—the ones that haven't been attacked in decades—are getting hit. And unless General Gau gets them all back in line, these attacks are going to keep happening. They're going to get worse."

"I think you need a new hobby," Gretchen said, handing me back my PDA. "Your new one here is really depressing."

"I'm not trying to scare you," I said. "I thought you would want to know about all this."

"You don't have to tell me," Gretchen said. "You need to tell your parents. Or my dad. Someone who actually knows what to do about all this."

"They already know," I said. "I heard John and Jane talking about it last night after he got back from Phoenix Station. Everyone there knows the colonies are under attack. No one's *reporting* it—the Colonial Union has a lockdown on the news—but everyone's talking about it."

"What does that leave for Roanoke?" Gretchen said.

"I don't know," I said. "But I know we don't have a lot of pull right now."

"So we're all going to die," Gretchen said. "Well. Gee. Thanks, Zoë. I'm really glad to know it."

"It's not that bad yet," I said. "Our parents are working on it. They'll figure it out. We're not all going to die."

"Well, *you're* not going to die, at least," Gretchen said.

"What does that mean?" I asked.

"If things really go swirling, the Obin will swoop in and take you out of here," Gretchen said. "Although if all of the Colonial Union is really under attack, I'm not sure where you're going to end up going. But the point is, you have an escape route. The rest of us don't."

I stared at Gretchen. "That's incredibly unfair," I said. "I'm not going anywhere, Gretchen."

"Why?" Gretchen said. "I'm not *angry* at you that you have a way out, Zoë. I'm *envious*. I've been through one attack. Just one missile got through and it didn't even explode properly, and it still did incredible damage and killed someone I care about and everyone in his family. When they come for us for real, we don't have a chance."

"You still have your training," I said.

"I'm not going to be able to engage in single combat with a *missile*, Zoë," Gretchen said, annoyed. "Yes, if someone decides to have a landing party here, I might be able to fight them off for a while. But after what we've done to that Conclave fleet, do you think anyone is really going to bother? They're just going to blow us up from the sky. You said it yourself. They want to be rid of us. And you're the only one that has a chance of getting out of here."

"I already said I'm not going anywhere," I said.

"Jesus, Zoë," Gretchen said. "I love you, I really do, but I can't believe you're actually that dumb. If you have a chance to go, *go*. I don't want you to die. Your mom and dad don't want it. The Obin will hack a path through all the rest of us to keep you from dying. I think you should take the hint."

"I get the hint," I said. "But you don't understand. I've *been* the sole survivor, Gretchen. It's happened to me before. Once is enough for any lifetime. I'm not going anywhere."

"Hickory and Dickory want you to leave Roanoke," Dad said to me, after he had paged me with his PDA. Hickory and Dickory were standing in the living room with him. I was clearly coming in on some sort of negotiation between them. And it was also clearly about me. The tone of Dad's voice was light enough that I could tell he was hoping to make some point to the Obin, and I was pretty sure I knew what the point was.

"Are you and Mom coming?" I said.

"No," Dad said.

This I expected. Whatever was going to happen with the colony, both John and Jane would see it through, even if it meant they would die with it. It's what they expected of themselves as colony leaders, as former soldiers, and as human beings.

"Then to hell with that," I said. I looked at Hickory and Dickory when I said it.

"Told you," Dad said to Hickory.

"You didn't tell her to come away," Hickory said.

"Go away, Zoë," Dad said. This was said with such a sarcastic delivery that even Hickory and Dickory couldn't miss it.

I gave a less-than-entirely-polite response to that, and then to Hickory and Dickory, and then, for good measure, to the whole idea that I was something special to the Obin. Because I was feeling saucy, and also because I was tired of the whole thing. "If you want to protect me," I said to Hickory, "then protect this colony. Protect the people I care about."

"We cannot," Hickory said. "We are forbidden to do so."

"Then you have a problem," I said, "because I'm not going anywhere. And there's nothing you or anyone else can do about it." And then I left, dramatically, partly because I think that was what Dad was expecting, and partly because I was done saying what I wanted to say on the matter.

Then I went to my room and waited for Dad to call me again. Because whatever was going on between him and Hickory and Dickory, it wasn't over when I stomped out of the room. And like I said, whatever it was, was clearly about me.

About ten minutes later Dad called for me again. I went back into the living room. Hickory and Dickory were gone.

"Sit down, Zoë, please," Dad said. "I need you to do something for me."

"Does it involve leaving Roanoke?" I asked.

"It does," Dad said.

"No," I said.

"Zoë," Dad said.

"*No*," I said again. "And I don't understand you. Ten minutes ago you were happy to have me stand here in front of Hickory and Dickory and tell them I wasn't going anywhere, and now you want me to leave? What did they tell you to make you change your mind?"

"It's what I told them," Dad said. "And I haven't changed my mind. I need you to go, Zoë."

"For what?" I said. "So I can stay alive while everyone I care about dies? You and Mom and Gretchen and Magdy? So I can be saved when Roanoke is destroyed?"

"I need you to go so I can *save* Roanoke," Dad said.

"I don't understand," I said.

"That's probably because you didn't actually let me *finish* before you got on your soapbox," Dad said.

"Don't mock me," I said.

Dad sighed. "I'm not trying to mock you, Zoë. But what I really need from you right now is to be quiet so I can tell you about this. Can you do that, please? It will make things go a lot more quickly. Then if you say no, at least you'll be saying no for the right reasons. All right?"

"All right," I said.

"Thank you," Dad said. "Look. Right now all of the Colonial Union is under attack because we destroyed the Conclave fleet. Every CU world has been hit. The Colonial Defense Forces are strained as it is, and it's going to get worse. A lot worse. The Colonial Union is already making decisions about what colonies it can afford to lose when push comes to shove."

"And Roanoke is one of those," I said.

"Yes," Dad said. "Very definitely. But it's more than that, Zoë. There was a possibility that I might have been able to ask the Obin to help us here on Roanoke. Because you were here. But the Colonial Union has told the Obin not to help us at all. They can take you from here, but they can't help you or us defend Roanoke. The Colonial Union doesn't want them to help us."

"Why not?" I asked. "That doesn't make any sense."

"It doesn't make sense if you assume the Colonial Union wants Roanoke to *survive*," Dad said. "But look at it another way, Zoë. This is the first colony with colonists from the CU rather than Earth. The settlers here are from the ten most powerful and most populous Colonial Union worlds. If Roanoke is destroyed, all ten of those worlds are going to be hit hard by the loss. Roanoke will become a rallying cry for those worlds. And for the whole Colonial Union."

"You're saying we're worth more to the Colonial Union dead than alive," I said.

"We're worth more as a symbol than as a colony," Dad said. "Which is inconvenient for those of us who live here and want to stay alive. But, yes. It's why they won't let the Obin help us. It's why we don't make the cut for resources."

"You know this for sure?" I asked. "Someone told you this when you went back to Phoenix Station?"

"Someone did," Dad said. "A man named General Szilard. He was Jane's former commanding officer. It was unofficial, but it matched up with my own internal math."

"And you trust him?" I asked. "No offense, but the Colonial Union hasn't exactly been on the up-and-up with us lately."

"I have my issues with Szilard," Dad said. "And so does your mom. But yes. I trust him on this. Right now he's the only one in the whole Colonial Union I actually *do* trust."

"What does this have to with me leaving Roanoke?" I asked.

"General Szilard told me something else when I saw him," Dad said. "Also unofficial, but from good sources. He told me that General Gau, the Conclave leader—"

"I know who he is, Dad," I said. "I've been keeping up with current events."

"Sorry," Dad said. "He said General Gau was being targeted for assassination by someone in his own close circle of advisors, and that the assassination would happen soon, probably in the next few weeks."

"Why'd he tell you this?" I asked.

"So I could use it," Dad said. "Even if the Colonial Union wanted to tell General Gau about the attempt—which it doesn't, since it probably would like to see it succeed—there's no reason to believe that Gau would consider it credible. The CU *did* just blow up his fleet. But Gau might listen to the information if it came from me, because he's already had dealings with me."

"And you were the one who begged him not to bring his fleet to Roanoke," I said.

"Right," Dad said. "It's because of that we've been attacked as little as we have. General Gau said to me that neither he nor the Conclave would retaliate against Roanoke itself for what happened to the fleet."

"We were still attacked," I said.

"But not by the Conclave itself," Dad said. "By someone else, testing our defenses. But if Gau is assassinated, that guarantee dies with him. And then it's open season on Roanoke, and we'll get hit, fast, because we're where the Conclave had its biggest defeat. We're a symbol for the Conclave, too. So we have to let General Gau know he's in danger. For our own sake."

"If you tell him this, you'll be giving information to an enemy of the Colonial Union," I said. "You'll be a traitor."

Dad gave me a wry grin. "Trust me, Zoë," he said. "I'm already neck-deep in trouble." His smile disappeared. "And yes, General Gau is an enemy of the Colonial Union. But I think he might be a friend to Roanoke. Right now, Roanoke needs all the friends it can get, wherever it can get them. The ones we used to have are turning their backs on us. We're going out to this new one, hat in hand."

"And by *we* you mean *me*," I said.

"Yes," Dad said. "I need you to deliver this message for me."

"You don't need me to do it," I said. "You could do it. Mom could do it. It would be *better* from either of you."

Dad shook his head. "Neither Jane nor I can leave Roanoke, Zoë. The Colonial Union is watching us. They don't trust us. And even if we could, we can't leave because we belong here with the colonists. We're their leaders. We can't abandon them. Whatever happens to them happens to us too. We made a promise to them and we're going to stay and defend this colony, no matter what happens. You understand that." I nodded. "So we can't go.

"But *you* can, and secretly," Dad said. "The Obin already want to take you off Roanoke. The Colonial Union will allow it because it's part of their treaty with the Obin, and as long as Jane and I stay here, it won't raise an eyebrow. The Obin are technically neutral in the fight between the Conclave and the Colonial Union; an Obin ship will be able to get to General Gau's headquarters where a ship from the Colonial Union couldn't."

"So send Hickory and Dickory," I said. "Or just have the Obin send a skip drone to General Gau."

"It won't work," Dad said. "The Obin are not going to jeopardize their relationship with the Colonial Union to pass messages for *me*. The only reason they're doing this at all is because I'm agreeing to let them take you off Roanoke. I'm using the only piece of leverage I have with the Obin, Zoë. That's you.

"And there's something else. General Gau has to know that I believe the information I'm sending him is good. That I'm not just being a pawn again in a larger Colonial Union game. I need to give him a token of my sincerity, Zoë. Something that proves that I have as much to risk in sending him this information as he has in receiving it. Even if I or Jane could go ourselves, General Gau would have no reason to trust what we say to him, because he knows both Jane and I were soldiers and are leaders. He knows we would be willing to sacrifice ourselves for our colony. But he also knows that I'm *not* willing to sacrifice my only daughter. And neither is Jane.

"So you see, Zoë. It has to be you. No one else can do it. You're the only one who can get to General Gau, deliver the message, and be believed. Not me, not Jane, not Hickory and Dickory. No one else. Just you. Deliver the message, and we might still find a way to save Roanoke. It's a small chance. But right now it's the only one we've got."

I sat there for a few minutes, taking in what Dad asked of me. "You know if Hickory and Dickory take me off Roanoke, they're not going to want to bring me back," I said, finally. "You know that."

"I'm pretty sure of it," Dad said.

"You're asking me to leave," I said. "You're asking me to accept that I might not ever see any of you again. Because if General Gau won't believe me, or if he's killed before I can talk to him, or even if he does believe me but can't do anything to help us, this trip won't mean anything. All it will do is get me off Roanoke."

"If that's all it did, Zoë, I still wouldn't complain," Dad said, and then quickly held up his hand, to stop me from commenting on that. "But if that's *all* I thought it would do, I wouldn't ask you to do it. I know you don't want to leave Roanoke, Zoë. I know you don't want to leave us or your friends. I don't want anything bad to happen to you, Zoë. But you're also old enough now to make your own decisions. If when all was said and done you wanted to stay on Roanoke to face whatever came our way, I wouldn't try to stop you. Nor would Jane. We would be with you until the end. You know that."

"I do," I said.

"There are risks for everyone," Dad said. "When Jane and I tell the Roanoke colony council about this—which we will do once you're gone—I'm pretty sure they are going to kick us out as the colony leaders. When news gets back to the Colonial Union, Jane and I are almost certainly going to be arrested on charges of treason. Even if everything goes perfectly, Zoë, and General Gau accepts your message and acts on it and maybe even makes sure that Roanoke stays unmolested, we will still have to pay for our actions. Jane and I accept this. We think it's worth it for a chance to keep Roanoke safe. The risk for you here, Zoë, is that if you do this, you might not see us or your friends again for a very long time, or at all. It's a big risk. It's a real risk. You have to decide whether it's one worth taking."

I thought about this some more. "How long do I have to think about this?" I asked.

"All the time you need," Dad said. "But those assassins aren't sitting around doing nothing."

I glanced over to where Hickory and Dickory had been. "How long do you think it will take them to get a transport here?" I asked.

"Are you kidding?" Dad said. "If they didn't send for one the second I was done talking to them, I'll eat my hat."

"You don't wear a hat," I said.

"I will buy a hat and eat it, then," Dad said.

"I'm going to come back," I said. "I'm going to take this message to General Gau, and then I'm going to get back here. I'm not sure how I'm going to convince the Obin of that, but I'm going to do it. I promise you, Dad."

"Good," Dad said. "Bring an army with you. And guns. And battle cruisers."

"Guns, cruisers, army," I said, running down the checklist. "Anything else? I mean, as long as I'm going *shopping*."

"Rumor is that I might be in the market for a hat," Dad said.

"Hat, right," I said.

"Make it a jaunty hat," he said.

"I promise nothing," I said.

"Fine," Dad said. "But if you have to choose between the hat and the army, pick the army. And make it a good one. We're going to need it."

"Where is Gretchen?" Jane asked me. We stood outside the small Obin transport. I had already said good-bye to Dad. Hickory and Dickory waited for me inside the transport.

"I didn't tell her I was leaving," I said.

"She is going to be very upset about that," Mom said.

"I don't intend to be away long enough for her to miss me," I said. Mom didn't say anything to that.

"I wrote her a note," I said, finally. "It's scheduled for delivery tomorrow morning. I told her what I thought I could tell her about why I left. I told her to talk to you about the rest of it. So she might come by to see you."

"I'll talk to her about it," Jane said. "I'll try to make her understand."

"Thanks," I said.

"How are you?" Mom asked.

"I'm terrified," I said. "I'm scared I'll never see you or Dad or Gretchen again. I'm scared I'm going to screw this up. I'm scared that even if I don't screw this up it won't matter. I feel like I'm going to pass out, and I've felt that way since this thing landed."

Jane gave me a hug and then looked to my neck, puzzled. "You're not taking your jade elephant pendant?" she said.

"Oh," I said. "It's a long story. Tell Gretchen I said for her to tell it to you. You need to know about it anyway."

"Did you lose it?" Jane asked.

"It's not lost," I said. "It's just not with me anymore."

"Oh," Jane said.

"I don't need it anymore," I said. "I know who in this world loves me, and has loved me."

"Good," Jane said. "What I was going to tell you is that as well as remembering who loves you, you should remember who you are. And everything about who you are. And everything about *what* you are."

"What I am," I said, and smirked. "It's because of *what* I am that I'm leaving. *What* I am has been more trouble than it's worth, if you ask me."

"That doesn't surprise me," Jane said. "I have to tell you, Zoë, that there have been times when I have felt sorry for you. So much of your life has been completely out of your control. You've lived your life under the gaze of an entire race of people, and they have made their demands on you right from the beginning. I'm always amazed you've stayed sane through all of it."

"Well, you know," I said. "Good parents help."

"Thank you," Jane said. "We tried to keep your life as normal as possible. And I think we've raised you well enough that I can tell you this and have you understand it: What you are has made demands of you all your life. Now it's time to demand something back. Do you understand?"

"I'm not sure," I said.

"*Who* you are has always had to make room for *what* you are," Jane said. "You know that."

I nodded. It had.

"Part of that was because you were young, and what you are is so much larger than who you are," Jane said. "You can't expect a normal eight-year-old or even a fourteen-year-old to understand what it means to be something like what you are. But you're old enough now to understand it. To get an appreciation for it. To know how you can use it, for something besides trying to stay up late."

I smiled, amazed that Jane remembered me trying to use the treaty to stay up past my bedtime.

"I've watched you in the last year," Jane said. "I've seen how you interact with Hickory and Dickory. They've imposed a lot on you because of what you are. All that training and practicing. But you've also started asking more of them. All those documents you've had them give you."

"I didn't know you knew about that," I said.

"I was an information officer," Jane said. "This sort of thing is my job. My point is that you've become more willing to use that power. You are finally taking control of your life. *What* you are is starting to make room for *who* you are."

"It's a start," I said.

"Keep going," Jane said. "We need *who* you are, Zoë. We need you to take what you are—*every* part of what you are—and use it to save us. To save Roanoke. And to come back to us."

"How do I do it?" I asked.

Jane smiled. "Like I said: Demand something back," she said.

"That's unhelpfully vague," I said.

"Perhaps," Jane said, and then kissed me on the cheek. "Or maybe I just have faith that you're smart enough to figure it out on your own."

Mom got a hug for that.

Ten minutes later I was fifteen klicks above Roanoke and climbing, heading for an Obin transport, thinking about what Jane had said.

"You will find that our Obin ships travel far more quickly than your Colonial Union ships," Hickory said.

"Is that right," I said. I wandered over to where Hickory and Dickory had placed my luggage and picked out one of the suitcases.

"Yes," Hickory said. "Far more efficient engines and better artificial gravity management. We will reach skip distance from Roanoke in a little under two days. It would take one of your ships five or six days to reach the same distance."

"Good," I said. "The sooner we get to General Gau the better." I unzipped the suitcase.

"This is a very exciting moment for us," Hickory said. "This is the first time since you have lived with Major Perry and Lieutenant Sagan that you will meet other Obin in person."

"But they know all about me," I said.

"Yes," Hickory said. "The recordings of the last year have made their way to all Obin, both in unedited and digest form. The unedited versions will take time to process."

"I'll bet," I said. "Here we are." I found what I was looking for: the stone knife, given to me by my werewolf. I had packed it quickly, when no one was looking. I was just making sure that I didn't imagine packing it.

"You brought your stone knife," Hickory said.

"I did," I said. "I have plans for it."

"What plans?" Hickory asked.

"I'll tell you later," I said. "But tell me, Hickory," I said. "This ship we're going to. Is there anyone important on it?"

"Yes," Hickory said. "Because it is the first time that you have been in the presence of other Obin since you were a child, one of the members of Obin's governing council will be there to greet you. It very much wants to meet with you."

"Good," I said, and glanced at the knife. "I very much want to meet with it, too."

I think I actually made Hickory nervous right then.

TWENTY-TWO

"Demand something back," I said to myself as I waited for the Obin council member to greet me in my stateroom. "Demand something back. Demand something back."

I'm definitely going to throw up, I thought.

You can't throw up, I answered myself. *You haven't figured out the plumbing yet. You don't know what to throw up into.*

That at least was true. The Obin don't *excrete* or take care of their personal hygiene the same way humans do, and they don't have the same issues with modesty that we do when they're with others of their own race. In the corner of my stateroom was an interesting array of holes and spigots that looked like something that you would *probably* use for bathroom purposes. But I had no idea what was what. I didn't want to use the thing that I thought was the sink, only to find out later it was supposed to be the toilet. Drinking from the toilet was fine for Babar, but I like to think I have higher standards.

This was definitely going to be an issue in another hour or two. I would have to ask Hickory or Dickory about it.

They weren't with me because I asked to be taken directly to my stateroom when we took off and then asked to be alone for an hour, at which point I wanted to see the council member. I think that by doing that, I messed up some sort of ceremonial welcome from the crew of the Obin transport (called *Obin Transport 8532*, in typical and boring Obin efficiency), but I didn't let that bother me. It did have the effect I was going for at the moment: I had decided I was going to be a little bit difficult. Being a little bit difficult was going to make it easier, I hoped, to do what I needed to do next. Which was to try to save Roanoke.

My dad had his own plan to do that, and I was going to help him with it. But I was thinking up a plan of my own. All it needed me to do was to demand something back.

Something really, really, really *big*.

Oh, well, my brain said. *If this doesn't work at least you can ask this council guy where you're supposed to pee.* Yes, well, that *would* be something.

There was a knock on my stateroom door, and the door then slid open. There was no lock on the door because Obin among themselves didn't have much of a concept of privacy (no signal on the door, either, for the same reason). Three Obin entered the room: Hickory and Dickory, and a third Obin who was new to me.

"Welcome, Zoë," it said to me. "We welcome you at the start of your time with the Obin."

"Thank you," I said. "Are you the council member?"

"I am," it said. "My name is Dock."

I tried very hard to keep a smile off my face and failed miserably. "You said your name was Dock," I said.

"Yes," it said.

"As in 'Hickory, Dickory, Dock,' " I said.

"That is correct," it said.

"That's quite a coincidence," I said, once I got my face back under control.

"It is not a coincidence," Dock said. "When you named

Hickory and Dickory, we learned of the nursery rhyme from which you derived the names. When I and many other Obin chose names for ourselves, we chose words from the rhyme."

"I knew there were other Hickorys and Dickorys," I said. "But you're telling me that there are other Obin named 'Dock,' too."

"Yes," said Dock.

"And 'Mouse' and 'Clock,' " I said.

"Yes," said Dock.

"What about 'Ran,' 'Up,' and 'The'?" I asked.

"Every word in the rhyme is popular as a name," said Dock.

"I hope some of the Obin know they've named themselves after a definite article," I said.

"We are all aware of the meaning of the words," Dock said. "What was important is the association to you. You named these two 'Hickory' and 'Dickory.' Everything followed from there."

I had been getting sidetracked by the idea that an entire fearsome race of aliens had given themselves goofy names because of the names I had thoughtlessly given two of them more than a decade before; this comment by Dock snapped me back into focus. It was a reminder that the Obin, with their new consciousness, had so identified with me, so imprinted on me, even as a child, that even a nursery rhyme I liked carried weight.

Demand something back.

My stomach cramped up. I ignored it.

"Hickory," I said. "Are you and Dickory recording right now?"

"Yes," Hickory said.

"Stop please," I said. "Councilor Dock, are you recording this right now?"

"I am," it said. "Although only for my personal recollection."

"Please stop," I said. They all stopped recording.

"Have we offended you?" Dock asked.

"No," I said. "But I don't think you'll want this as part of the permanent record." I took a deep breath. "I require something from the Obin, Councilor."

"Tell me what it is," Dock said. "I will try to find it for you."

"I require the Obin to help me defend Roanoke," I said.

"I am afraid we are unable to help you with that request," Dock said.

"It's not a request," I said.

"I do not understand," Dock said.

"I said, it's not a request. I didn't *request* the Obin's help, Councilor. I said I *require* it. There's a difference."

"We cannot comply," Dock said. "The Colonial Union has requested that we provide no assistance to Roanoke."

"I don't *care*," I said. "What the Colonial Union wants at this point means absolutely nothing to me. The Colonial Union is planning to let everyone I care about die because it's decided Roanoke is more useful as a symbol than a colony. I don't give a crap about the symbolism. I care about the people. My friends and family. They need help. And I require it from you."

"Assisting you means breaking our treaty with the Colonial Union," Dock said.

"Your treaty," I said. "That would be the one that allows you access to me."

"Yes," Dickory said.

"You realize you *have* me," I said. "On this ship. Technically on Obin territory. You don't need Colonial Union permission to see me anymore."

"Our treaty with the Colonial Union is not only about access to you," Dock said. "It covers many issues, including our access to the consciousness machines we wear. We cannot go against this treaty, even for you."

"Then don't break it," I said, and this is where I mentally crossed my fingers. I knew the Obin would say they couldn't break their treaty with the Colonial Union; Hickory had said so before. This is where things were about to get *really* tricky. "I require the Obin help me defend Roanoke, Councilor. I didn't say the Obin had to do it themselves."

"I am afraid I do not understand you," Dock said.

"Get someone else to help me," I said. "Hint to them that the help would be appreciated. Do whatever you have to do."

"We would not be able to hide our influence," Dock said. "The Colonial Union will not be swayed by the argument that our forcing another race to act on your behalf does not constitute interference."

"Then ask someone the Colonial Union knows you can't force," I said.

"Whom do you suggest?" Dock asked.

There's an old expression for when you do something completely crazy. "Shooting the moon," it's called.

This was me raising my rifle.

"The Consu," I said.

Blam. There went my shot at a *very* faraway moon.

But it was a shot I had to take. The Obin were obsessed with the Consu, for perfectly excellent reasons: How could you *not* be obsessed with the creatures that gave you intelligence, and then ignored you for the rest of eternity? The Consu had spoken to the Obin only once since they gave them consciousness, and that conversation came at the high cost of half of all Obin, everywhere. I remembered that cost. I planned to use it to my advantage now.

"The Consu do not speak to us," Dock said.

"Make them," I said.

"We do not know how," Dock said.

"Find a way," I said. "I *know* how the Obin feel about the Consu, Councilor. I've studied them. I've studied you. Hickory and Dickory made a story about them. Obin's first creation myth, except it's true. I know how you got them to speak to you. And I know you've tried to get them to speak to you again since then. Tell me it's not true."

"It's true," Dock said.

"I'm willing to guess you're still working on it even now," I said.

"We are," Dock said. "We have been."

"Now is the time to make that happen," I said.

"There is no guarantee that the Consu would help you, even if we convinced them to speak to us and hear our plea on your behalf," Dock said. "The Consu are unknowable."

"I understand that," I said. "It's worth a try anyway."

"Even if what you ask were possible, it would come at a high cost," Dock said. "If you knew what it cost us the last time we spoke to the Consu—"

"I know *exactly* how much it cost," I said. "Hickory told me. And I know the Obin are used to paying for what they get. Let me ask you, Councilor. What did you get from my biological father? What did you get from Charles Boutin?"

"He gave us consciousness," Dock said, "as you well know. But it came at a price. Your father asked for a war."

"Which you never gave him," I said. "My father died before you could pay up. You got his gift for free."

"The Colonial Union asked for a price to finish his work," Dock said.

"That's between you and the Colonial Union," I said. "It doesn't take anything away from what my father did, or the fact you never paid for it. I am his daughter. I am his heir. The fact you are here says that the Obin give me the honor they would give him. I could say to you that you *owe* me what you owe him: a war, at least."

"I cannot say that we owe you what we owed your father," Dock said.

"Then what do you owe *me*?" I asked. "What do you owe me for what I've done for you? What is your name?"

"My name is Dock," it said.

"A name you have because one day I named those two Hickory and Dickory," I said, pointing at my two friends. "It's only the most obvious example of what you have through me. My father gave you consciousness, but you didn't know what to *do with it*, did you? None of you did. All of you learned what to do with your consciousness by watching me grow into mine, as a child and now as who I am today. Councilor, how many Obin have watched my life? Seen how I did things? Learned from me?"

"All of them," Dock said. "We have all learned from you, Zoë."

"What has it cost the Obin?" I asked. "From the time Hickory and Dickory came to live with me, until the moment I stepped onto this ship, what has it cost you? What have I ever asked of any Obin?"

"You have not asked for anything," Dock said.

I nodded. "So let's review. The Consu gave you intelligence and it cost you half of all the Obin when you came to ask them why they did it. My father gave you consciousness, and the price for it was a war, a price which you would have willingly paid had he lived. I have given you ten years of lessons on how to be conscious—on how to *live*. The bill for that has come due, Councilor. What price do I require? Do I require the lives of half the Obin in the universe? No. Do I require the Obin to commit to a war against an entire other race? No. I require only your help to save my family and friends. I don't even require that the Obin do it themselves, only that they find a way to have someone else do it for them. Councilor, given the Obin's history of what it's received and what it has cost, what I am requiring of the Obin now comes very *cheap* indeed."

Dock stared at me, silently. I stared back, mostly because I had forgotten to blink through all of that and I was afraid if I tried to blink now I might scream. I think it was making me look unnervingly calm. I could live with that.

"We were to send a skip drone when you arrived," Dock said. "It has not been sent yet. I will let the rest of the Obin council know of your requirement. I will tell them I support you."

"Thank you, Councilor," I said.

"It may take some time to decide on a course of action," Dock said.

"You don't have time," I said. "I am going to see General Gau, and I am going to deliver my dad's message to him. The Obin council has until I am done speaking to General Gau to act. If it has not, or will not, then you will leave General Gau without me."

"You will not be safe with the Conclave," Dock said.

"Are you under the impression that I will tolerate being among the Obin if you refuse me?" I said. "I keep telling you this: I am not *asking* for this. I am *requiring* it. If the Obin will not do this, they lose me."

"That would be very hard for some of us to accept," Dock said. "We had already lost you for a year, Zoë, when the Colonial Union hid your colony."

"Then what will you do?" I asked. "Drag me back onto the ship? Hold me captive? Record me against my will? I don't imagine that will be very *entertaining*. I know what I am to the Obin, Councilor. I know what uses you have all put me to. I don't think you will find me very useful after you refuse me."

"I understand you," Dock said. "And now I must send this message. Zoë, it is an honor to meet you. Please excuse me." I nodded. Dock left.

"Please close the door," I said to Hickory, who was the closest to it. It did.

"Thank you," I said, and threw up all over my shoes. Dickory was over to me immediately and caught me before I could fall completely.

282 | John Scalzi

"You are ill," Hickory said.

"I'm fine," I said, and then threw up all over Dickory. "Oh, God, Dickory," I said. "I'm so sorry."

Hickory came over, took me from Dickory and guided me toward the strange plumbing. It turned on a tap and water came bubbling out.

"What is that?" I asked.

"It is a sink," Hickory said.

"You're sure?" I asked. Hickory nodded. I leaned over and washed my face and rinsed my mouth out.

"How do you feel?" Hickory said, after I had cleaned myself off as best I could.

"I don't think I'm going to throw up anymore, if that's what you mean," I said. "Even if I wanted to, there's nothing left."

"You vomited because you are sick," Hickory said.

"I vomited because I just treated one of your leaders like it was my cabin boy," I said. "That's a new one for me, Hickory. It really is." I looked over at Dickory, who was covered in my upchuck. "And I hope it works. Because I think if I have to do that again, my stomach might just flop right out on the table." My insides did a flip-flop after I said that. Note to self: After having vomited, watch the overly colorful comments.

"Did you mean it?" Hickory said. "What you said to Dock?"

"Every word," I said, and then motioned at myself. "Come on, Hickory. Look at me. You think I'd put myself through all of *this* if I wasn't serious?"

"I wanted to be sure," Hickory said.

"You can be sure," I said.

"Zoë, we will be with you," Hickory said. "Me and Dickory. No matter what the council decides. If you choose to stay behind after you speak to General Gau, we will stay with you."

"Thank you, Hickory," I said. "But you don't have to do that."

"We do," Hickory said. "We would not leave you, Zoë. We

have been with you for most of your life. And for all the life that we have spent conscious. With you and with your family. You have called us part of your family. You are away from that family now. You may not see them again. We would not have you be alone. We belong with you."

"I don't know what to say," I said.

"Say you will let us stay with you," Hickory said.

"Yes," I said. "Do stay. And thank you. Thank you both."

"You are welcome," Hickory said.

"And now as your first official duties, find me something new to wear," I said. "I'm starting to get really ripe. And then tell me which of those things over there is the toilet. Because now I really need to know."

TWENTY-THREE

Something was nudging me awake. I swatted at it. "Die," I said.

"Zoë," Hickory said. "You have a visitor."

I blinked up at Hickory, who was framed as a silhouette by the light coming from the corridor. "What are you talking about?" I said.

"General Gau," Hickory said. "He is here. Now. And wishes to speak to you."

I sat up. "You have got to be kidding me," I said. I picked up my PDA and looked at the time.

We had arrived in Conclave space fourteen hours earlier, popping into existence a thousand klicks out from the space station that General Gau had made the administrative headquarters of the Conclave. He said he hadn't wanted to favor one planet over another. The space station was ringed with hundreds of ships from all over Conclave space, and even more shuttles and cargo transports, going between ships and back and forth from the station. Phoenix Station, the largest human space station and so big I've heard that it actually affected tides on the planet Phoenix (by amounts measurable only by sensitive instruments, but still), would have fit into a corner of the Conclave HQ.

We had arrived and announced ourselves and sent an

encrypted message to General Gau requesting an audience. We had been given parking coordinates and then willfully ignored. After ten hours of that, I finally went to sleep.

"You know I do not kid," Hickory said. It walked back to the doorway and turned up the lights in my stateroom. I winced. "Now, please," Hickory said. "Come to meet him."

Five minutes later I was dressed in something I hoped would be presentable and walking somewhat unsteadily down the corridor. After a minute of walking I said, "Oh, crap," and ran back to my stateroom, leaving Hickory standing in the corridor. A minute later I was back, bearing a shirt with something wrapped in it.

"What is that?" Hickory asked.

"A gift," I said. We continued our trip through the corridor.

A minute later I was standing in a hastily arranged conference room with General Gau. He stood to one side of a table surrounded by Obin-style seats, which were not really well designed either for his physiology or mine. I stood on the other, shirt in my hand.

"I will wait outside," Hickory said, after it delivered me.

"Thank you, Hickory," I said. It left. I turned and faced the general. "Hi," I said, somewhat lamely.

"You are Zoë," General Gau said. "The human who has the Obin to do her bidding." His words were in a language I didn't understand; they were translated through a communicator device that hung from his neck.

"That's me," I said. I heard my words translated into his language.

"I am interested in how a human girl is able to commandeer an Obin transport ship to take her to see me," General Gau said.

"It's a long story," I said.

"Give me the short version," Gau said.

"My father created special machines that gave the Obin

consciousness. The Obin revere me as the only surviving link to my father. They do what I ask them to," I said.

"It must be nice to have an entire race at your beck and call," Gau said.

"You should know," I said. "You have four hundred races at yours. Sir."

General Gau did something with his head that I was going to hope was meant to be a smile. "That's a matter of some debate at this point, I'm afraid," he said. "But I am confused. I was under the impression that you are the daughter of John Perry, administrator of the Roanoke Colony."

"I am," I said. "He and his wife Jane Sagan adopted me after my father died. My birth mother had died some time before that. It is on my adopted parents' account that I am here now. Although I apologize"—I motioned to myself, and my state of unreadiness—"I didn't expect to meet you here, now. I thought we would come to you, and I would have time to prepare."

"When I heard that the Obin were ferrying a human to see me, and one from Roanoke, I was curious enough not to want to wait," Gau said. "I also find value in making my opposition wonder what I am up to. My coming to visit an Obin ship rather than waiting to receive their embassy will make some wonder who you are, and what I know that they don't."

"I hope I'm worth the trip," I said.

"If you're not, I'll still have made them nervous," Gau said. "But considering how far you've come, I hope for both our sakes the trip has been worth it. Are you completely dressed?"

"What?" I said. Of the many questions I might have been expecting, this wasn't one of them.

The general pointed to my hand. "You have a shirt in your hands," he said.

"Oh," I said, and put the shirt on the table between us. "It's a gift. Not the shirt. There's something wrapped in the shirt. That's the gift. I was hoping to find something else to put it in before I gave it to you, but you sort of surprised me. I'm going to shut up now and let you just have that."

The general gave me what I think was a strange look, and then reached out and unwrapped what was in the shirt. It was the stone knife given to me by the werewolf. He held it up and examined it in the light. "This is a very interesting gift," he said, and began moving it in his hand, testing it, I guessed, for weight and balance. "And quite a nicely designed knife."

"Thank you," I said.

"Not precisely modern weaponry," he said.

"No," I said.

"Figured that a general must have an interest in archaic weapons?" Gau asked.

"Actually there's a story behind it," I said. "There's a native race of intelligent beings on Roanoke. We didn't know about them before we landed. Not too long ago we met up with them for the first time, and things went badly. Some of them died, and some of us died. But then one of them and one of us met and decided not to try to kill each other, and exchanged gifts instead. That knife was one of those gifts. It's yours now."

"That's an interesting story," Gau said. "And I think I'm correct in supposing that this story has some implication for why you're here."

"It's up to you, sir," I said. "You might just decide it's a nice stone knife."

"I don't think so," Gau said. "Administrator Perry is a man who plays with subtext. It's not lost on me what it means that he has sent his daughter to deliver a message. But then to offer this particular gift, with its particular story. He's a man of some subtlety."

"I think so, too," I said. "But the knife is not from my dad. It's from me."

"Indeed," Gau said, surprised. "That's even more interesting. Administrator Perry didn't suggest it?"

"He doesn't know I had the knife," I said. "And he doesn't know how I got it."

"But you *did* intend to send me a message with it," Gau said. "One to complement your adopted father's."

"I hoped you'd see it that way," I said.

Gau set the knife down. "Tell me what Administrator Perry has to tell me," he said.

"You're going to be assassinated," I said. "Someone is going to try, anyway. It's someone close to you. Someone in your trusted circle of advisors. Dad doesn't know when or how, but he knows that it's planned to happen soon. He wanted you to know so you could protect yourself."

"Why?" General Gau asked. "Your adopted father is an official of the Colonial Union. He was part of the plan that destroyed the Conclave fleet and has threatened everything I have worked for, for longer than you have been alive, young human. Why should I trust the word of my enemy?"

"The Colonial Union is your enemy, not my dad," I said.

"Your *dad* helped kill tens of thousands," Gau said. "Every ship in my fleet was destroyed but my own."

"He begged you not to call your ships to Roanoke," I said.

"This was a place where he was all too subtle," Gau said. "He never explained how the trap had been set. He merely asked me not to call my fleet. A little more information would have kept thousands alive."

"He did what he could," I said. "You were there to destroy our colony. He wasn't allowed to surrender it to you. You know he didn't have many options. And as it was he was recalled by the Colonial Union and put on trial for even hinting to you that something might happen. He could have been sent to prison for the simple act of speaking to you, General. He did what he could."

"How do I know he's not just being used again?" Gau asked.

"You said you knew what it meant that he sent me to give you a message," I said. "I'm the proof that he's telling you the truth."

"You're the proof he *believes* he's telling me the truth," Gau said. "It's not to say that it *is* the truth. Your adopted father was used once. Why couldn't he be used again?"

I flared at this. "Begging your pardon, General," I said. "But you should know that by sending me to send you this warning, both my dad and my mom are absolutely assured of being labeled as traitors by the Colonial Union. They are both going to prison. You should know that as part of the deal to get the Obin to bring me to you, I can't go back to Roanoke. I have to stay with them. Because they believe that it's only a matter of time before Roanoke is destroyed, if not by you then by some part of the Conclave you don't have any control over anymore. My parents and I have risked *everything* to give you this warning. It's possible I'll never see them or anyone else on Roanoke again, because I am giving you this warning. Now, General, do you think any of us would do *any* of this if we were not absolutely certain about what we are telling you? Do you?"

General Gau said nothing for a moment. Then, "I am sorry you have all had to risk so much," he said.

"Then do my dad the honor of *believing* him," I said. "You're in danger, General. And that danger is closer than you think."

"Tell me, Zoë," Gau said, "what does Administrator Perry hope to get from telling me this? What does he want from me?"

"He wants you to stay alive," I said. "You promised him that as long as you were running the Conclave, you wouldn't attack Roanoke again. The longer you stay alive, the longer we stay alive."

"But there's the irony," Gau said. "Thanks to what happened at Roanoke, I'm not in as much control as I was. My time now is spent keeping others in line. And there are those who are looking at Roanoke as a way to take control from me. I'm sure you don't know about Nerbros Eser—"

"Sure I do," I said. "Your main opposition right now. He's trying to convince people to follow him. Wants to destroy the Colonial Union."

"I apologize," Gau said. "I forgot you're not just a messenger girl."

"It's all right," I said.

"Nerbros Eser is planning to attack Roanoke," Gau said. "I have been getting the Conclave back under my control—too slowly—but enough races support Eser that he has been able to fund an expedition to take Roanoke. He knows the Colonial Union is too weak to put up a defense of the colony, and he knows that at the moment I am in no position to stop him. If he can take Roanoke where I could not, more Conclave races could side with him. Enough that they would attack the Colonial Union directly."

"You can't help us, then," I said.

"Other than to tell you what I just have, no," Gau said. "Eser is going to attack Roanoke. But in part because Administrator Perry helped to destroy my fleet, there is no way I can do much to stop him now. And I doubt very much that your Colonial Union will do much to stop him."

"Why do you say that?" I asked.

"Because you are *here*," General Gau said. "Make no mistake, Zoë, I do appreciate your family's warning. But Administrator Perry is not so kind that he would have warned me out of his own simple goodness. As you've noted, the cost is too high for that. You are here because you have nowhere else to turn."

"But you believe Dad," I said.

"Yes," Gau said. "Unfortunately. Someone in my position is always a target. But now of all times I know that even some of those who I've trusted with my life and friendship are calculating the costs and deciding that I'm worth more to them dead than alive. And it makes sense for someone to try for me before Eser attacks Roanoke. If I'm dead and Eser takes revenge on your colony, no one else will even try to challenge him for control of the Conclave. Administrator Perry isn't telling me anything I don't know. He's only confirming what I do know."

"Then I've been no use to you," I said. And *you've been no use to me*, I thought but did not say.

"I wouldn't say that," Gau said. "One of the reasons I am here now is so that I could hear what you had to say to me without anyone else involved. To find out what I could do with the information you might have. To see if it has use to me. To see if *you* are of use to me."

"You already knew what I told you," I said.

"This is true," Gau said. "However, no one *else* knows how much you know. Not here, in any event." He reached over and picked up the stone knife and looked at it again. "And the truth of the matter is that I'm getting tired of not knowing, of those whom I trust, which is planning to stab me in the heart. Whoever is planning to assassinate me is going to be in league with Nerbros Eser. They are likely to know when he plans to attack Roanoke, and with how large a force. And perhaps working together we can find out both of these things."

"How?" I asked.

General Gau looked at me again, and did that I-hope-it's-a-smile thing with his head. "By doing a bit of political theater. By making them think we know what they do. By making them act because of it."

I smiled back at Gau. " 'The play is the thing in which I shall catch the conscience of the king,' " I said.

"Precisely," Gau said. "Although it will be a traitor we catch, not a king."

"In that quote he was both," I said.

"Interesting," Gau said. "I'm afraid I don't know the reference."

"It's from a play called *Hamlet*," I said. "I had a friend who liked the playwright."

"I like the quote," Gau said. "And your friend."

"Thanks," I said. "I do too."

"One of you in this chamber is a traitor," General Gau said. "And I know which one of you it is."

Wow, I thought. *The general sure knows how to start a meeting.*

We were in the general's official advisors' chamber, an ornate room, which, the general told me beforehand, he never used except to receive foreign dignitaries with some semblance of pomp and circumstance. Since he was technically receiving me for this particular meeting, I felt special. But more to the point, the room featured a small raised platform with steps, on which sat a large chair. Dignitaries, advisors and their staff all approached it like it was a throne. This was going to be useful for what General Gau had in mind for today.

In front of the platform, the room opened up into a semicircle. Around the perimeter stood a curving bar, largely of standing height for most sentient species in the Conclave. This is where advisors' and dignitaries' staff stood, calling up documents and data when needed and whispering (or whatever) into small microphones that fed into earpieces (or whatever) worn by their bosses.

Their bosses—the advisors and dignitaries—filed into the area between the bar and the platform. Usually, I was told, they would have benches or chairs (or whatever suited their body shape best) offered to them so they could rest as they did their business. Today, they were all standing.

As for me, I was standing to the left and just in front of the general, who was seated in his big chair. On the opposite side of the chair was a small table, on which lay the stone knife, which I had just (and for the second time) presented to the general. This time it was delivered in packaging more formal than a shirt. The general had taken it out of the box I had found, admired it, and set it on the table.

Back along with the staff stood Hickory and Dickory, who were not happy with the plan the general had come up with. With them were three of the general's security detail, who were likewise not very pleased at all.

Well, now that we were doing it, I'm not sure I was entirely thrilled with it either.

"I thought we were here to hear a request from this young human," said one of the advisors, a tall Lalan (that is, tall even for a Lalan) named Hafte Sorvalh. Her voice was translated by the earpiece I had been given by the Obin.

"It was a pretense," Gau said. "The human has no petition, but information pertaining to which one of you intends to assassinate me."

This naturally got a stir in the chamber. "It is a human!" said Wert Ninung, a Dwaer. "No disrespect, General, but the humans recently destroyed the entire Conclave fleet. Any information they would share with you should be regarded as highly suspect, to say the least."

"I agree with this entirely, Ninung," Gau said. "Which is why when it was provided to me I did what any sensible person would have done and had my security people check the information thoroughly. I regret to say that the information was good. And now I must deal with the fact that one of my advisors—someone who was privy to all my plans for the Conclave—has conspired against me."

"I don't understand," said a Ghlagh whose name, if I could remember correctly, was Lernin Il. I wasn't entirely sure, however; Gau's security people had given me dossiers on Gau's circle of advisors only a few hours before the meeting, and given everything else I needed to do to prepare, I had barely had time to skim.

"What don't you understand, Lernin?" asked General Gau.

"If you know which of us is the traitor, why hasn't your security detail already dealt with them?" Il asked. "This could be done without exposing you to an unnecessary risk. Given your position you don't need to take any more risks than are absolutely necessary."

"We are not talking about some random killer, Il," the general said. "Look around you. How long have we known each other? How hard have each of us worked to create this great Conclave of races? We have seen more of each other over time than we have seen of our spouses and children. Would any of you have accepted it if I were to make one of you disappear over a vague charge of treason? Would that not seem to each of you that I was losing my grip and creating scapegoats? No, Il. We have come too far and done too much for that. Even this would-be assassin deserves better courtesy than that."

"What do you intend to do, then?" asked Il.

"I will ask the traitor in this room to come forward," he said. "It's not too late to right this wrong."

"Are you offering this assassin amnesty?" asked some creature whose name I just did not remember (or, given how it spoke, I suspect I could not actually pronounce, even if I did remember it).

"No," Gau said. "This person is not acting alone. They are part of a conspiracy that threatens what all of us have worked for." Gau gestured to me. "My human friend here has given me a few names, but that is not enough. For the security of the Conclave we need to know more. And to show all the members of the Conclave that treason cannot be tolerated, my assassin must answer for what they have done to this point. What I do offer is this: That they will be treated fairly and with dignity. That they will serve their term of punishment with some measure of comfort. That their family and loved ones will not be punished or held responsible, unless they themselves are conspirators. And that their crime will not be made known publicly. Every one outside this room will know only that this conspirator has retired from service. There will be punishment. There must be punishment. But there will not be the punishment of history."

"I want to know where this human got its information," said Wert Ninung.

Gau nodded to me. "This information ultimately comes from the Colonial Union's Special Forces division," I said.

"The same group that spearheaded the destruction of the Conclave fleet," Wert said. "Not especially trustworthy."

"Councilor Wert," I said, "how do you think the Special Forces were able to locate every one of the ships of your fleet? The only time it assembles is when it removes a colony. Locating four hundred ships among the tens of thousands that each race alone has at its disposal was an unheard of feat of military intelligence. After that, do you doubt that the Special Forces had difficulty coming up with a single name?"

Wert actually growled at me. I thought that was rude.

"I have already told you that I have had the information checked out," General Gau said. "There is no doubt it is accurate. That is not under discussion. What is under discussion is how the assassin will choose to be discovered. I repeat: The assassin is in this room, right now, among us. If they will come forward now, and share information on their other conspirators, their treatment will be generous, light and secret. The offer is in front of you now. I beg you, as an old friend, to take it. Come forward now."

No one in the room moved. General Gau stared at each of his advisors, directly and in the eye, for several seconds each. None of them took so much as a step forward.

"Very well," General Gau said. "We do this the hard way, then."

"What will you do now, General?" asked Sorvalh.

"Simple," Gau said. "I will call up each of you in turn. You will bow to me and swear your allegiance to me as the leader of the Conclave. Those of you who I know are truthful, I will offer you my thanks. The one of you who is a traitor, I will reveal you in front of those you have worked alongside for so long, and have you arrested. Your punishment will be severe. And it will be most definitely public. And it will end with your death."

"This is not like you, General," Sorvalh said. "You created the Conclave with the idea that there would be no dictators, no demands of personal allegiance. There is only allegiance to the Conclave. To its ideals."

"The Conclave is near collapse, Hafte," Gau said. "And you know as well as I do that Nerbros Eser and his sort will run the Conclave like a personal fiefdom. One among you has already decided that Eser's dictatorship is preferable to a Conclave where every race has a voice. It's clear to me that I must ask for the allegiance I once only held in trust. I am sorry it has come to this. But it has."

"What if we will not swear allegiance?" Sorvalh said.

"Then you will be arrested as a traitor," Gau said. "Along with the one who I know to be the assassin."

"You are wrong to do this," Sorvalh said. "You are going against your own vision for the Conclave to ask for this allegiance. I want you to know I believe this in my soul."

"Noted," Gau said.

"Very well," Sorvalh said, and stepped forward to the platform and knelt. "General Tarsem Gau, I offer you my allegiance as the leader of the Conclave."

Gau looked at me. This was my cue. I shook my head at him, clearly enough that everyone in the room could see that he was waiting for my verification.

"Thank you, Hafte," Gau said. "You may step back. Wert Ninung, please step forward."

Ninung did. As did the next six advisors. There were three left.

I was beginning to get very nervous. Gau and I had already agreed that we would not carry the act so far as to accuse someone who wasn't actually guilty. But if we got to the end without a traitor, then we both would have a lot to answer for.

"Lernin Il," General Gau said. "Please step forward."

Il nodded and smoothly moved forward and when he got to me, viciously shoved me to the floor and lunged for the stone knife Gau had left on the table next to him. I hit the floor so hard I bounced my skull on it. I heard screaming and honks of alarm from the other advisors. I rolled and looked up as Il raised the knife and prepared to plunge it into the general.

The knife was left out and within easy reach for a reason. Gau had already said he intended to reveal the traitor; he said he knew without a doubt who it was; he said the punishment for the traitor would include death. The traitor would already be convinced he would have nothing to lose by attempting the assassination then and there. But Gau's advisors didn't usually carry around killing implements on their person; they were bureaucrats and didn't carry anything more dangerous than a writing stylus. But a nice sharp stone knife carelessly left lying around would be just the thing to convince a desperate would-be assassin to take a chance. This was also one reason why the general's guards (and Hickory and Dickory) were stationed at the perimeter of the room instead of near the general; we had to give the illusion to the assassin that he could get in a stab or two before the guards got him.

The general wasn't stupid, of course; he was wearing body armor that protected most of the parts of his body susceptible to stab wounds. But the general's head and neck were still vulnerable. The general thought it was worth the risk, but now as I watched the general trying to move to protect himself, I came to the conclusion that the weakest part of our plan was the one where the general presumably avoids being stabbed to death.

Il was bringing down the knife. None of the general's guards or Hickory or Dickory was going to get there in time. Hickory and Dickory had trained me how to disarm an opponent; the problem was I was on the ground and not in any position to block the knife blow. And anyway the Ghlagh were a Conclave race; I hadn't spent any time learning any of their weak points.

But then something occurred to me, as I lay there on my back, staring up at Il.

I may not know much about the Ghlagh, but I sure know what a *knee* looks like.

I braced myself on the floor, pushed, and drove the heel of my foot hard into the side of Lernin Il's most available knee. It gave way with a sickly twist and I thought I could feel something in his leg go *snap*, which made me feel sick. Il squealed in pain and grabbed at his leg, dropping the knife. I scrambled away as quickly as I could. General Gau launched himself out of his chair and took Il all the rest of the way down.

Hickory and Dickory were suddenly by me, dragging me off the riser. Gau shouted something to his guards, who were racing toward the general.

"His staff!" Gau said. "Stop his staff!"

I looked over to the bar and saw three Ghlagh lunging at their equipment. Il's people were clearly in on the assassination and were now trying to signal their conspirators that they'd been discovered. Gau's men skidded to a stop and reversed themselves, leaping over the bar to get at Il's staff. They knocked away their equipment, but not before at least one of them had gotten a message through. We knew that because all through the Conclave headquarters, alarms began stuttering to life.

The space station was under attack.

———

About a minute after Il had made his clumsy attack on General Gau, an Impo battle cruiser named the *Farre* launched six missiles into the portion of the Conclave space station where Gau's offices were. The *Farre* was commanded by an Impo named Ealt Ruml. Ruml, it turns out, had reached an agreement with Nerbros Eser and Lernin Il to take command of a new Conclave fleet after Gau was assassinated. Ruml would then take the entire fleet to Phoenix Station, destroy it and start working down the list of human worlds. In exchange all Ruml had to do was be prepared to do a little flagrant bombing of Gau's offices and flagship when signaled, as part of a larger, orchestrated coup attempt, which would feature Gau's assassination as the main event and the destruction of key battle ships from races loyal to Gau.

When Gau revealed to his advisors that he knew one of them was a traitor, one of Il's staffers sent a coded message to Ruml, informing him that everything was about to go sideways. Ruml in turn sent coded messages of his own to three other battle cruisers near the Conclave station, each captained by someone Ruml had converted to the cause. All four ships began warming up their weapons systems and selecting targets: Ruml targeted Gau's offices while the other traitors targeted Gau's flagship *Gentle Star* and other craft.

If everything went as planned, Ruml and his conspirators would have disabled the ships most likely to come to Gau's aid—not that it would matter, because Ruml would have opened up Gau's offices to space, sucking anyone in them (including, at the time, me) into cold, airless vacuum. Minutes later, when Il's staff sent a confirmation note just before getting their equipment kicked out of their paws, Ruml launched his missiles and readied another set to go.

And was, I imagine, entirely surprised when the *Farre* was struck broadside almost simultaneously by three missiles fired from the *Gentle Star*. The *Star* and six other trusted ships had been put on alert by Gau to watch for any ships that began warming up their weapons systems. The *Star* had spotted the *Farre* warming up its missile batteries and had quietly targeted the ship and prepared its own defense.

Gau had forbidden any action until someone else's missiles flew, but the instant the *Farre* launched, the *Star* did the same, and then began antimissile defenses against the two missiles targeting it, sent by the Arrisian cruiser *Vut-Roy*.

The *Star* destroyed one of the missiles and took light damage from the second. The *Farre*, which had not been expecting a counterattack, took heavy damage from the *Star*'s missiles and even more damage when its engine ruptured, destroying half of the ship and killing hundreds on board, including Ealt Ruml and his bridge crew. Five of the six missiles fired by the *Farre* were disabled by the space station's defenses; the sixth hit the station, blowing a hole in the station compartment next to Gau's offices. The station's system of airtight doors sealed off the damage in minutes; forty-four people were killed.

All of this happened in the space of less than two minutes, because the battle happened at incredibly close range. Unlike space battles in entertainment shows, real battles between spaceships take place over huge distances. In this battle, however, all the ships were in orbit around the station. Some of the ships involved were just a few klicks away from each other. That's pretty much the starship equivalent of going after each other with knives.

Or so I'm told. I'm going by what others tell me of the battle, because at the time what *I* was doing was being dragged out of General Gau's advisor chamber by Hickory and Dickory. The last thing I saw was Gau pinning down Lernin Il while at the same time trying to keep his other advisors from beating the living crap out of him. There was too much noise for my translation device to work anymore, but I suspected that Gau was trying to tell the rest of them that he needed Il alive. What can you say. No one likes a traitor.

I'm also told that the battle outside of the space station would have gone on longer than it did except that shortly after the first salvo of missiles a funny thing happened: An Obin cruiser skipped into existence unsettlingly close to the Conclave space station, setting off a series of proximity alarms to go with the attack alarms already in progress. That was unusual, but what *really* got everyone's attention was the *other* ships that appeared about thirty seconds afterward. It took the station a few minutes to identify these.

And at that point everyone who had been fighting each other realized they now had something bigger to worry about.

I didn't know about any of this right away. Hickory and Dickory had dragged me to the conference room some distance away from the advisor chamber and were keeping it secure when the alarms suddenly stopped.

"Well, I finally used that training," I said, to Hickory. I was amped up on leftover adrenaline from the assassination attempt and paced up and down in the room. Hickory said nothing to this and continued to scan the corridor for threats. I sighed and waited until it signaled that it was safe to move.

Ten minutes later, Hickory clicked something to Dickory, who went to the door. Hickory went into the corridor and out of sight. Shortly after that I heard what sounded like Hickory arguing with someone. Hickory returned, followed by six very serious-looking guards and General Gau.

"What happened?" I asked. "Are you okay?"

"What do you have to do with the Consu?" General Gau asked me, ignoring my question.

"The Consu?" I said. "Nothing. I had asked the Obin to try to contact them on my behalf, to see if they could help me save

Roanoke. That was a few days ago. I haven't heard from the Obin about it since."

"I think you have an answer," Gau said. "They're here. And they're asking to see you."

"There's a Consu ship here now?" I said.

"Actually, the Consu asking for you is on an Obin ship," Gau said. "Which doesn't make any sense to me at all, but never mind that. There were Consu ships following the Obin ship."

"Ships," I said. "How many?"

"So far?" Gau said. "About six hundred."

"Excuse me?" I said. My adrenaline spiked again.

"There are still more coming in," Gau said. "Please don't take this the wrong way, Zoë, but if you've done something to anger the Consu, I hope they choose to take it out on you, not us."

I turned and looked at Hickory, disbelieving.

"You said you required help," Hickory said.

TWENTY-FOUR

I entered the storage deck of the other Obin ship.

"So this is the human who has an entire race to do her bidding," said the Consu waiting there for me. It was the only place on the Obin ship where he would fit, I guessed.

I smiled in spite of myself.

"You laugh at me," the Consu said. It spoke perfect English, and in a light, gentle voice, which was weird considering how much it looked like a large and savagely angry insect.

"I'm sorry," I said. "It's just that it's the second time in a day that someone's said that to me."

"Well," the Consu said. It unfolded itself in a way that made me want to run screaming in the other direction, and from somewhere inside its body a creepily humanlike arm and hand beckoned to me. "Come and let me get a look at you."

I took one step forward and then had a very difficult time with the next step.

"You asked for me, human," the Consu said.

I developed a spine and walked over to the Consu. It touched and prodded me with its smaller arms, while its giant slashing arms, the ones the Consu used to decapitate enemies in combat, hovered on either side of me, at just about head level. I managed not to completely lose it.

"Yes, well," the Consu said, and I heard something like disappointment in its voice. "There's nothing particularly *special* about you, is there? Physically. Is there something special about you mentally?"

"No," I said. "I'm just me."

"We're all just ourselves," the Consu said, and folded itself back into its self, much to my relief. "That is axiomatic. What is it about you that makes hundreds of Obin allow themselves to die to get to me, is what I am asking."

I felt sick again. "You said that hundreds of Obin died to bring you to me?"

"Oh, yes," the Consu said. "Your pets surrounded my ship with their own and tried to board it. The ship killed everyone that tried. They remained persistent and finally I became curious. I allowed one to board the ship and it told me that you had demanded the Obin convince the Consu to help you. I wanted to see for myself what sort of creature could so casually demand this, and could cause the Obin to fulfill it at such a cost to themselves."

It looked at me again curiously. "You appear upset," it said.

"I'm thinking about the Obin who died," I said.

"They did what you asked of them," the Consu said, with a bored tone.

"You didn't have to kill so many of them," I said.

"Your pets didn't have to offer up so many to sacrifice," said the Consu. "And yet they did. You seem stupid so I will explain this to you. Your pets, to the extent that they can think, did this intelligently. The Consu will not speak to the Obin for their own behalf. We answered their questions long ago and it does not interest us to speak further on the subject."

"But *you* spoke to the Obin," I said.

"I am dying," the Consu said. "I am on"—and here the

Consu made a noise that sounded like a tractor falling down a hill—"the death journey that Consu prepared to move forward are permitted if in this life they have proven worthy. Consu on this journey may do as they please, including speaking to proscribed creatures, and may if asked appropriately grant a final boon. Your pets have spied on the Consu for decades—we were aware of this but did nothing about it—and knew the route of the death journey and knew the ceremonial ships those on the journey travel in. Your pets understood this was the only way they could talk to us. And your pets knew what it would require to interest me or any Consu enough to hear them. You should have known this when you made your demand."

"I didn't," I said.

"Then you are foolish, human," the Consu said. "If I were inclined to feel sorry for the Obin, I would do so because they had wasted their effort and diverted me from my journey on the behalf of someone so ignorant of the cost. But I do not feel sorry for them. They at least knew the cost, and willingly paid it. Now. You will either tell me how you demand I help you, or I will go and your pets' deaths will have truly been for nothing."

"I need help to save my colony," I said, and forced myself to focus. "My friends and family are there and are under threat of attack. It is a small colony and not able to defend itself. The Colonial Union will not help us. The Obin are not allowed to help us. The Consu have technology that could help us. I ask for your help."

"You said 'ask,'" the Consu said. "Your pets said 'demand.'"

"I demanded help from the Obin because I knew I could," I said. "I am asking you."

"I do not care about your colony or you," the Consu said.

"You just said that as part of your death journey you can grant a boon," I said. "This could be it."

"It may be that my boon was to the Obin, in speaking to you," the Consu said.

I blinked at this. "How would it be a boon to them just to speak to me if you won't at least think of helping me?" I said. "Then it would be you who wasted their sacrifice and effort."

"That is my choice," the Consu said. "The Obin understood that in making the sacrifice the answer might be 'no.' This is another thing they understand that you don't."

"I know there is a lot I don't understand here," I said. "I can see that. I'm sorry. But I still need help for my family and friends."

"How many family and friends?" the Consu said.

"My colony has twenty-five hundred people," I said.

"A similar number of Obin died in order to bring me here," the Consu said.

"I didn't know that would happen," I said. "I wouldn't have asked for that."

"Is that so?" the Consu said. It shifted its bulk and drew in toward me. I didn't back away. "I don't believe you, human. You are foolish and you are ignorant, that much is clear. Yet I cannot believe that even you did not understand what you were asking the Obin for when you asked them to come to us for your sake. You demanded help from the Obin because you could. And because you could you did not ask the cost. But you had to have known the cost would be high."

I didn't know what to say to that.

The Consu drew back and seemed to regard me, like it might an amusing insect. "Your capriciousness and callousness with the Obin interests me," it said. "And so does the fact that the Obin are willing to give of themselves for your whims despite your lack of care for them."

I said something I knew I was going to regret, but I couldn't help myself. The Consu was doing a really excellent job of pushing my buttons. "That's a funny thing coming from someone from the race that gave the Obin intelligence but no consciousness," I said. "As long as we're talking about capriciousness and callousness."

"Ah. Yes, that's right," the Consu said. "The Obin told me this. You're the child of the human who made the machines that let the Obin play at consciousness."

"They don't play at it," I said. "They *have* it."

"And it is a terrible thing that they do," the Consu said. "Consciousness is a tragedy. It leads the whole race away from perfection, causes it to fritter its efforts on individual and wasteful effort. Our lives as Consu are spent learning to free our race from the tyranny of self, to move beyond ourselves and in doing so move our race forward. It is why we help you lesser races along, so you may also free yourselves in time."

I bit my cheek at this bit. The Consu would sometimes come down to a human colony, wipe it and everyone in it off the face of their planet, and then wait for the Colonial Defense Forces to come and fight them. It was a game to the Consu, as far as any of us could see. To say that they were doing it for our benefit was perverse, to say the least.

But I was here to ask for help, not debate morals. I had already been baited once. I didn't dare let it happen again.

The Consu continued, oblivious to my personal struggles. "What you humans have done to the Obin makes a mockery of their potential," it said. "We created the Obin to be the best among us all, the one race without consciousness, the one race free to pursue its destiny as a race from its first steps. The Obin were meant to be what we aspired to. To see them aspire to consciousness is to see a creature that can fly aspire to wallow in mud. Your father did the Obin no favors, human, in hobbling them with consciousness."

I stood there for a minute, amazed that this Consu would tell me, in seemingly casual conversation, things that the Obin had sacrificed half their number for so many years ago but were never allowed to hear. The Consu waited patiently for my response. "The Obin would disagree," I said. "And so would I."

"Of course you would," the Consu said. "Their love of their consciousness is what makes them willing to do the ridiculous for you. That and the fact that they choose to honor you for something that your father did, even though you had no hand in it. This blindness and honor is convenient to you. It is what you use to get them to do what you want. You don't prize their consciousness for what it gives them. You prize it for what it allows you to do to them."

"That's not true," I said.

"Indeed," said the Consu, and I could hear the mocking tone in its voice. It shifted its weight again. "Very well, human. You have asked me to help you. Perhaps I will. I can provide you with a boon, one the Consu may not refuse. But this boon is not free. It comes with a cost attached."

"What cost?" I said.

"I want to be entertained first," the Consu said. "So I offer you this bargain. You have among you several hundred Obin. Select one hundred of them in any way you choose. I will ask the Consu to send one hundred of our own—convicts, sinners, and others who have strayed from the path and would be willing to attempt redemption. We will set them at each other, to the death.

"In the end, one side will have a victory. If it is yours, then I will help you. If it is mine, I will not. And then, having been sufficiently amused, I will be on my way, to continue my death journey. I will call to the Consu now. Let us say that in eight of your hours we will start this entertainment. I trust that will be enough time for you to prepare your pets."

"We will have no problem finding a hundred volunteers among the Obin," Dock said to me. It and I were in the conference room General Gau had lent me. Hickory and Dickory stood outside the door to make sure we weren't disturbed. "I will have the volunteers ready for you within the hour."

"Why didn't you tell me how the Obin planned to get the Consu to me?" I asked. "The Consu here told me that hundreds of Obin died to get him here. Why didn't you warn me that would happen?"

"I did not know how we would choose to try to get the Consu's attention," Dock said. "I sent along your requirement, along with my own assent. I was not a participant in making the choice."

"But you knew this could happen," I said.

"As a member of the Council I know that we have had the Consu under observation, and that there had been plans to find ways to talk to them again," Dock said. "I knew this was one of them."

"Why didn't you tell me?" I said.

"I told you that attempting to speak to the Consu would come at a high cost," Dock said. "This was the cost. At the time, the cost did not seem too high for you."

"I didn't know that it would mean that hundreds of Obin would *die*," I said. "Or that they would just keep throwing themselves into a Consu firing line until the Consu got curious enough to stop. If I had known I would have asked you to try something else."

"Given what you required us to do and the time in which we had to do it, there was nothing else," Dock said. It came to me and opened up its hands, like it was trying to make me see something important. "Please understand, Zoë. We had been planning to petition a Consu on its death journey for a long time now, and for our own reasons. It was one of the reasons we were able to fulfill your requirement at all. Everything was already in place."

"But it was my order that killed them," I said.

"It is not your fault that the Consu required their deaths," Dock said. "The Obin who were part of the mission had already known what was required to get the attention of the Consu. They were already committed to this task. Your request changed only the timing and the purpose of their mission. But those who participated did so willingly, and understood the reason for doing it. It was their choice."

"They still did it because I didn't think about what I was asking," I said.

"They did it because you required our help," Dock said. "They would have thought it an honor to do this for you. Just as those who will fight for you now will consider it an honor."

I looked at my hands, ashamed to look at Dock. "You said that you had already been planning to petition a Consu on its death journey," I said. "What were you going to ask?"

"For understanding," Dock said. "To know why the Consu kept consciousness away from us. To know why they chose to punish us with its lack."

I looked up at that. "I know the answer," I said, and told Dock what the Consu had told me about consciousness and why they chose not to give it to the Obin. "I don't know if that was the answer you were looking for," I said. "But that's what this Consu told me."

Dock didn't say anything. I looked more closely at it, and I could see it was trembling. "Hey," I said, and got up from my chair. "I didn't mean to upset you."

"I am not upset," Dock said. "I am happy. You have given us answers to questions we have been asking since as long as our race has existed. Answers the Consu would not have given us themselves. Answers many of us would have given our lives for."

"Many of you *did* give your lives for them," I said.

"No," Dock said. "They gave their lives to help *you*. There was no expectation of any compensation for the sacrifice. They

did it because you required it. You did not have to give us anything in return. But you have given us this."

"You're welcome," I said. I was getting embarrassed. "It's
not a big thing. The Consu just told me. I just thought you
should know."

"Consider, Zoë, that this thing that you just thought we
should know was something that others would have seen as
something to hold over us," Dock said. "That they would have
sold to us, or denied to us. You gave it freely."

"After I told you that I required your help and sent hundreds of Obin out to die," I said, and sat back down. "Don't
make me out to be a hero, Dock. It's not the way I feel right
now."

"I am sorry, Zoë," Dock said. "But if you will not be a hero,
at least know that you are not a villain. You are our friend."

"Thank you, Dock," I said. "That helps a little."

Dock nodded. "Now I must go to find the hundred volunteers you seek," it said, "and to tell the Council what you have
shared with me. Do not worry, Zoë. We will not disappoint
you."

"This is what I have for you on short notice," General Gau said.
He swept an arm through the space station's immense cargo
bay. "This part of the station is just newly constructed. We
haven't actually used it for cargo yet. I think it'll suit your purposes."

I stared at the immensity of the space. "I think so," I said.
"Thank you, General."

"It's the least I could do," General Gau said. "Considering
how you've helped me just recently."

"Thank you for not holding the Consu invasion against
me," I said.

"On the contrary, it's been a benefit," Gau said. "It stopped

the battle around the space station before it could get truly hor-
rific. The traitor crews assumed I had called those ships for
assistance. They surrendered before I could correct the impression. You helped me quash the rebellion before it could get
started."

"You're welcome," I said.

"Thank you," said Gau. "Now, of course, I would like them
to go away. But it's my understanding that they're here to
make sure we don't do anything foolish with our Consu guest
while he's here. The ships are fighter drones, not even manned,
but this is Consu technology. I don't imagine if they opened
fire on us we'd stand much of a chance. So we have an en-
forced peace here at the moment. Since it works for me, not
against me, I shouldn't complain."

"Have you found out any more about Nerbros Eser and
what his plans are?" I asked. I didn't feel like thinking about
the Consu anymore.

"Yes," Gau said. "Lernin has been quite forthcoming now that
he's trying to avoid being executed for treason. It's been a wonderful motivator. He tells me that Eser plans to take Roanoke
with a small force of soldiers. The idea there is to show that he
can take with a hundred soldiers what I couldn't take with four
hundred battle cruisers. But 'take' is the wrong word for it, I'm
afraid. Eser plans to destroy the colony and everyone in it."

"That was your plan too," I reminded the general.

He bobbed his head in what I assumed was an acknowledg-
ment. "You know by now, I hope, that I would have much preferred not to have killed the colonists," he said. "Eser does not
intend to offer that option."

I skipped over that piece of data in my head. "When will he
attack?" I asked.

"Soon, I think," Gau said. "Lernin doesn't think Eser has
assembled his troops yet, but this failed assassination attempt
is going to force him to move sooner than later."

"Great," I said.

"There's still time," Gau said. "Don't give up hope yet, Zoë."

"I haven't," I said. "But I've still got a lot on my mind."

"Have you found enough volunteers?" Gau asked.

"We have," I said, and my face tightened up as I said it.

"What's wrong?" Gau said.

"One of the volunteers," I said, and stopped. I tried again. "One of the volunteers is an Obin named Dickory," I said. "My friend and my bodyguard. When it volunteered I told it no. Demanded that it take back its offer. But it refused."

"Having it volunteer could be a powerful thing," Gau said. "It probably encouraged others to step forward."

I nodded. "But Dickory is still my friend," I said. "Still my family. Maybe it shouldn't make a difference but it does."

"Of course it makes a difference," Gau said. "The reason you're here is to try to keep the people you love from being hurt."

"I'm asking people I don't know to sacrifice themselves for people I do," I said.

"That's why you're asking them to volunteer," Gau said. "But it seems to me the reason they're volunteering is for you."

I nodded and looked out at the bay, and imagined the fight that was coming.

"I have a proposition for you," the Consu said to me.

The two of us sat in the operations room of the cargo bay, ten meters above the floor of the bay. On the floor were two groups of beings. In the first group were the one hundred Obin who had volunteered to fight for me. In the other group were the one hundred Consu criminals, who would be forced to fight the Obin for a chance to regain their honor. The Consu looked scary big next to the Obin. The contest would be modified hand-to-hand combat: The Obin were allowed a combat knife, while the Consu, with their slashing arms, would fight bare-handed, if you called being able to wield two razor-sharp limbs attached to your own body "bare-handed."

I was getting very nervous about the Obin's chances.

"A proposition," the Consu repeated.

I glanced over at the Consu, who in himself nearly filled the operations room. He'd been there when I had come up; I wasn't entirely sure how he'd gotten himself through the door. The two of us were there with Hickory and Dock and General Gau, who had taken it upon himself to act as the official arbiter for the contest.

Dickory was on the floor. Getting ready to fight.

"Are you interested in hearing it?" the Consu asked.

"We're about to start," I said.

"It's about the contest," the Consu said. "I have a way that you can get what you want without having the contest at all."

I closed my eyes. "Tell me," I said.

"I will help you keep your colony safe by providing you a piece of our technology," the Consu said. "A machine that produces an energy field that robs projectiles of their momentum. A sapper field. It makes your bullets fall out of the air and sucks the power from missiles before they strike their targets. If you are clever your colony can use it to defeat those who attack it. This is what I am allowed and prepared to give to you."

"And what do you want in return?" I asked.

"A simple demonstration," the Consu said. It unfolded and pointed toward the Obin on the floor. "A demand from you was enough to cause hundreds of Obin to willingly sacrifice themselves for the mere purpose of getting my attention. This power you have interests me. I want to see it. Tell this one hundred to sacrifice themselves here and now, and I will give you what you need in order to save your colony."

"I can't do that," I said.

"It is not an issue of whether it is possible," the Consu said. It leaned its bulk over and then addressed Dock. "Would the Obin here kill themselves if this human asked it?"

"Without doubt," Dock said.

"They would not hesitate," the Consu said.

"No," Dock said.

The Consu turned back to me. "Then all you need to do is give the order."

"No," I said.

"Don't be stupid, human," the Consu said. "You have been assured by me that I will assist you. You have been assured by this Obin that your pets here will gladly sacrifice themselves for your benefit, without delay or complaint. You will be assured of helping your family and friends survive imminent attack. And you have done it before. You thought nothing of sending hundred to their death to speak to me. It should not be a difficult decision now."

He waved again toward the floor. "Tell me honestly, human. Look at your pets, and then look at the Consu. Do you think your pets will be the ones left standing when this is over? Do you want to risk the safety of your friends and family on them?

"I offer you an alternative. It carries no risk. It costs you nothing but your assent. Your pets will not object. They will be happy to do this for you. Simply say that you require this of them. That you demand it of them. And if it makes you feel any better, you can tell them to turn off their consciousness before they kill themselves. Then they will not fear their sacrifice. They will simply do it. They will do it for you. They will do it for what you are to them."

I considered what the Consu had said.

I turned to Dock. "You have no doubt that those Obin would do this for me," I said.

"There is no doubt," Dock said. "They are there to fight at

your request, Zoë. They know they may die. They have already accepted that possibility, just as the Obin who sacrificed themselves to bring you this Consu knew what was required of them."

"And what about you," I said to Hickory. "Your friend and partner is down there, Hickory. For ten years, at least, you've spent your life with Dickory. What do you say?"

Hickory's trembling was so slight that I almost doubted that I saw it. "Dickory will do as you ask, Zoë," Hickory said. "You should know this already." It turned away after that.

I looked at General Gau. "I have no advice to offer you," he said. "But I am very interested to find out what you choose."

I closed my eyes and I thought of my family. Of John and Jane. Of Savitri, who traveled to a new world with us. I thought of Gretchen and Magdy and the future they could have together. I thought of Enzo and his family and everything that was taken from them. I thought of Roanoke, my home.

And I knew what I had to do.

I opened my eyes.

"The choice is obvious," the Consu said.

I looked at the Consu and nodded. "I think you're right," I said. "And I think I need to go down and tell them."

I walked to the door of the operations room. As I did, General Gau lightly took my arm.

"Think about what you're doing, Zoë," Gau said. "Your choice here matters."

I looked up at the general. "I know it does," I said. "And it's my choice to make."

The general let go of my arm. "Do what you have to do," he said.

"Thank you," I said. "I think I will."

I left the room and for the next minute tried very hard not to fall down the stairs as I walked down them. I'm happy to say I succeeded. But it was a close thing.

I walked toward the group of Obin, who were milling about, some doing exercises, some talking quietly to another or to a small group. As I got closer I tried to locate Dickory and could not. There were too many Obin, and Dickory wasn't somewhere I could easily see him.

Eventually the Obin noticed I was walking to them. They quieted and equally quietly formed ranks.

I stood there in front of them for a few seconds, trying to see each of the Obin for itself, and not just one of a hundred. I opened my mouth to speak. Nothing would come. My mouth was so dry I could not make words. I closed my mouth, swallowed a couple of times, and tried again.

"You know who I am," I said. "I'm pretty sure about that. I only know one of you personally, and I'm sorry about that. I wish I could have known each of you, before you were asked . . . before *I* asked . . ."

I stopped. I was saying stupid things. It wasn't what I wanted to do. Not now.

"Look," I said. "I'm going to tell you some things, and I can't promise it's going to make any kind of sense. But I need to say them to you before . . ." I gestured at the cargo bay. "Before all of *this*."

The Obin all looked at me, whether politely or patiently, I can't say.

"You know why you're here," I said. "You're here to fight those Consu over there because I want to try to protect my family and friends on Roanoke. You were told that if you could beat the Consu, I would get the help I needed. But something's changed."

I pointed up to the operations room. "There's a Consu up there," I said, "who tells me that he'll give me what I need to save Roanoke without having to have you fight, and risk losing. All I have to do is tell you to take those knives you were going to use on those Consu, and use them on yourselves. All

I have to do is to tell you to kill yourselves. Everyone tells me you'll do it, because of what I am to you.

"And they're right. I'm pretty sure about that, too. I'm certain that if I asked all of you to kill yourselves, you would do it. Because I am your Zoë. Because you've seen me all your lives in the recordings that Hickory and Dickory have made. Because I'm standing here in front of you now, asking you to do it.

"I know you would do this for me. You would."

I stopped for a minute, tried to focus.

And then I faced something I'd spent a long time avoiding. My own past.

I raised my head again and looked directly at the Obin.

"When I was five, I lived on a space station. Covell. I lived there with my father. One day while he was away from the station for a few days on business, the station was attacked. First by the Rraey. They attacked, and they came in and they rounded up all the people who lived on the station, and they began to kill us. I remember . . ."

I closed my eyes again.

"I remember husbands being taken from their wives and then shot in the halls where everyone could hear," I said. "I remember parents begging the Rraey to spare their children. I remember being pushed behind a stranger when the woman who was watching me, the mother of a friend, was taken away. She tried to push away her daughter, too, but she held on to her mother and they were both taken away. If the Rraey had continued much longer, eventually they would have found me and killed me too."

I opened my eyes. "But then the Obin attacked the station, to take it from the Rraey, who weren't prepared for another fight. And when they cleared the station of the Rraey, they took those of us humans who were left and put us in a common area. I remember being there, with no one looking after me. My father was gone. My friend and her mother were dead. I was alone.

"The space station was a science station, so the Obin looked through the research and they found my father's work. His work on consciousness. And they wanted him to work for them. So they came back to us in the common area and they called out my father's name. But he wasn't on the station. They called his name again and I answered. I said I was his daughter and that he would come for me soon.

"I remember the Obin talking among themselves then, and then telling me to come away. And I remember saying no, because I didn't want to leave the other humans. And I remember what one of the Obin said to me then. It said, 'You must come with us. You have been chosen, and you will be safe.'

"And I remembered everything that had just happened. And I think even at five years old some part of me knew what would happen to the rest of the people at Covell. And here was the Obin, telling me I would be safe. Because I had been chosen. And I remember taking the Obin's hand, being led away and looking back at the humans who were left. And then they were gone. I never saw them again.

"But *I* lived," I said. "Not because of who I was; I was just this little girl. But because of *what* I was: the daughter of the man who could give you consciousness. It was the first time that what I was mattered more than who I was. But it wasn't the last."

I looked up at the operations room, trying to see if those in there were listening to me, and wondering what they were thinking. Wondering what Hickory was thinking. And General Gau. I turned back to the Obin.

"What I am *still* matters more than who I am," I said. "It matters more right now. Right this minute. Because of what I am, hundreds of you died to bring just one Consu to see me. Because of what I am, if I ask you to take those knives and plunge them into your bodies, you will do it. Because of what I am. Because of what I have been to you."

I shook my head and looked down at the ground. "All my life I have accepted that what I am matters," I said. "That I had to work with it. Make accommodations for it. Sometimes I thought I could manipulate it, although I just found out the price for that belief. Sometimes I would even fight against it. But *never once* did I think that I could leave what I was behind. Because I remembered what it got me. How it saved me. I never even thought of giving it up."

I pointed up at the operations room. "There is a Consu in that operations room who wants me to kill you all, just to show him that I can. He wants me to do it to make a point to me, too—that when it comes down to it, I'm willing to sacrifice all of you to get what I want. Because when it comes down to it, you don't matter. You're just something I can use, a means to an end, a tool for another purpose. He wants me to kill you to rub my face in the fact I don't care.

"And he's right."

I looked into the faces of the Obin. "I don't know any of you, except for one," I said. "I won't remember what any of you look like in a few days, no matter what happens here. On the other hand all the people I love and care for I can see as soon as I close my eyes. Their faces are so clear to me. Like they are here with me. Because they are. I carry them inside me. Like you carry those you care for inside of you.

"The Consu is right that it would be easy to ask you to sacrifice yourselves for me. To tell you to do it so I can save my family and my friends. He's right because I know you would do it without a second thought. You would be happy to do it because it would make *me* happy—because what I am matters to you. He knows that knowing this will make me feel less guilty for asking you.

"And he's right again. He's right about me. I admit it. And I'm sorry."

I stopped again, and took another moment to pull myself together. I wiped my face.

This was going to be the hard part.

"The Consu is right," I said. "But he doesn't know the one thing about me that matters right now. And that it is that I am *tired* of being what I am. I am tired of having been chosen. I don't want to be the one you sacrifice yourself for, because of whose daughter I am or because you accept that I can make demands of you. I don't want that from you. And I don't want you to die for me.

"So forget it. Forget all of this. I release you of your obligation to me. Of any obligation to me. Thank you for volunteering, but you shouldn't have to fight for me. I shouldn't have asked.

"You have already done so much for me. You have brought me here so I could deliver a message to General Gau. He's told me about the plans against Roanoke. It should be enough for us to defend ourselves. I can't ask you for anything else. I certainly can't ask you to fight these Consu and possibly die. I want you to live instead.

"I am done being *what* I am. From now on I'm just *who* I am. And who I am is Zoë. Just Zoë. Someone who has no claim on you. Who doesn't require or demand anything from you. And who wants you to be able to make your own choices, not have them made for you. Especially not by me.

"And that's all I have to say."

The Obin stood in front of me, silently, and after a minute I realized that I didn't really know why I was expecting a response. And then for a crazy moment I wondered if they actually even understood me. Hickory and Dickory spoke my language, and I just assumed all the other Obin would, too. That was a pretty arrogant assumption, I realized.

So I sort of nodded and turned to go, back up to the operations room, where God only knew what I was going to say to that Consu.

And then I heard singing.

A single voice, from somewhere in the middle of the pack of Obin. It took up the first words of "Delhi Morning." And though that was the part I always sang, I had no trouble recognizing the voice.

It was Dickory.

I turned and faced the Obin just as a second voice took up the counterpoint, and then another voice came in, and another and another, and soon all one hundred of the Obin were singing, creating a version of the song that was so unlike any I had heard before, so magnificent, that all I could do was stand there and soak in it, let it wash around me, and let it move through me.

It was one of those moments that you just can't describe. So I won't try anymore.

But I can say I was impressed. These Obin would have known of "Delhi Morning" for only a few weeks. For them to not only know the song but to perform it flawlessly was nothing short of amazing.

I had to get these guys for the next hootenanny.

When it was done, all I could do was put my hands to my face and say "Thank you" to the Obin. And then Dickory came through the ranks to stand in front of me.

"Hey, you," I said to Dickory.

"Zoë Boutin-Perry," said Dickory. "I am Dickory."

I almost said, *I know that,* but Dickory kept speaking.

"I have known you since you were a child," it said. "I have watched you grow and learn and experience life, and through you have learned to experience life myself. I have always known what you are. I tell you truthfully that it is *who* you are that has mattered to me, and always has.

"It is to you, Zoë Boutin-Perry, that I offer to fight for your family and for Roanoke. I do this not because you have demanded it or required it but because I care for you, and always have. You would honor me if you would accept my assistance." Dickory bowed, which was a very interesting thing on an Obin.

Here was irony: This was the most I had heard Dickory say, *ever*, and I couldn't think of anything to say in return.

So I just said, "Thank you, Dickory. I accept." Dickory bowed again and returned to ranks.

Another Obin stepped forward and stood before me. "I am Strike," it said. "We have not met before. I have watched you grow through all that Hickory and Dickory have shared with all Obin. I too have always known what you are. What I have learned from you, however, comes from who you are. It is an honor to have met you. It will be an honor to fight for you, your family, and for Roanoke. I offer my assistance to you, Zoë Boutin-Perry, freely and without reservation." Strike bowed.

"Thank you, Strike," I said. "I accept." And then I impulsively hugged Strike. It actually squeaked in surprise. We unhugged, Strike bowed again, and then returned to ranks just as another Obin came forward.

And another. And another.

It took a long time to hear each greeting and offer of assistance, and to accept each offer. I can honestly say there was never time better spent. When it was done I stood in front of one hundred Obin again—this time, each a friend. And I bowed my head to them and wished them well, and told them I would see them after.

Then I headed back toward the operations room. General Gau was at the bottom of the stairs, waiting for me.

"I have a position for you on my staff, Zoë, if you ever want it," he said.

I laughed. "I just want to go home, General. Thank you all the same."

"Some other time, then," Gau said. "Now I'm going to preside over this contest. I will be impartial when I'm observing it. But you should know that inside I'm rooting for the Obin. And that's something I never thought I would say."

"I do appreciate it," I said, and headed up the stairs.

Hickory met me at the door. "You did what I hoped you would do," Hickory said. "I regret not volunteering myself."

"I don't," I said, and hugged Hickory. Dock bowed to me; I nodded back. And then I approached the Consu.

"You have my answer," I said.

"So I have," the Consu said. "And it surprises me, human."

"Good," I said. "And the name is Zoë. Zoë Boutin-Perry."

"Indeed," the Consu said. He sounded amused at my cheekiness. "I will remember the name. And have others remember it as well. Although if your Obin do not win this contest, I do not imagine we will have to remember your name for long."

"You'll remember it for a long time," I said. "Because my friends down there are about to clean your clock."

And they did.

It wasn't even close.

TWENTY-FIVE

And so I went home, Consu gift in tow.

John and Jane greeted me as I jumped off the Obin shuttle, all of us ending in a pile as I ran into Mom full speed and then we dragged Dad down with us. Then I showed them my new toy: the sapper field generator, specially designed by the Consu to give us a tactical advantage when Nerbros Eser and his friends came to call. Jane immediately took to it and started fiddling with it; that was her thing.

Hickory and Dickory and I decided that in the end neither John nor Jane needed to know what it took for us to get it. The less they knew, the less the Colonial Union could charge them with at their treason trial. Although it looked like that might not happen—the Roanoke council did remove John and Jane from their posts once they revealed where they had sent me and who I was supposed to see, and had appointed Gretchen's dad Manfred in their place. But they had given Mom and Dad ten days to hear back from me before they informed the Colonial Union about what they'd done. I got back just under the wire and once they saw what I brought, weren't inclined to offer my parents to the tender affections of the Colonial Union judicial system. I wasn't going to complain about that.

After I got Mom and Dad acquainted with the sapper field generator, I went for a walk and found Gretchen, reading a book on her porch.

"I'm back," I said.

"Oh," she said, casually flipping a page. "Were you gone?"

I grinned; she hurled the book at me and told me that if I ever did anything like that again, she would strangle me, and that she could do it because she always was better in our defense courses than I was. Well, it was true. She was. Then we hugged and made up and went to find Magdy, so we could pester him in stereo.

Ten days later, Roanoke was attacked by Nerbros Eser and about a hundred Arrisian soldiers, that being Eser's race. Eser and his soldiers marched right into Croatoan and demanded to speak to its leaders. They got Savitri, the administrative assistant, instead; she suggested that they go back to their ships and pretend their invasion never happened. Eser ordered his soldier to shoot Savitri, and that's when they learned how a sapper field can really mess with their weapons. Jane tuned the field so that it would slow down bullets but not slower projectiles. Which is why the Arrisian soldier's rifles wouldn't work, but Jane's flame thrower would. As did Dad's hunting bow. And Hickory's and Dickory's knives. And Manfred Trujillo's lorry. And so on.

At the end of it Nerbros Eser had none of the soldiers that he'd landed with, and was also surprised to learn that the battleship he'd parked in orbit wasn't there anymore, either. To be fair, the sapper field didn't extend into space; we got a little help there from a benefactor who wished to remain anonymous. But however you sliced it, Nerbros Eser's play for the leadership of the Conclave came to a very sad and embarrassing end.

Where was I in all of this? Why, safely squirreled away in a bomb shelter with Gretchen and Magdy and a bunch of other teenagers, that's where. Despite all the events of the previous month, or maybe because of them, the executive decision was made that I had had enough excitement for the time being. I can't say I disagreed with the decision. To be honest about it, I was looking forward to just getting back to my life on Roanoke with my friends, with nothing to worry about except for school and practicing for the next hootenanny. That was right about my speed.

But then General Gau came for a visit.

He was there to take custody of Nerbros Eser, which he did, to his great personal satisfaction. But he was also there for two other reasons.

The first was to inform the citizens of Roanoke that he had made it a standing order that no Conclave member was ever to attack our colony, and that he had made it clear to non-Conclave races in our part of space that if any of them were to get it into their heads to make a play for our little planet, that he would personally be very disappointed. He left unsaid what level of retaliation "personal disappointment" warranted. It was more effective that way.

Roanokers were of two minds about this. On the one hand, Roanoke was now practically free from attack. On the other hand, General Gau's declaration only brought home the fact that the Colonial Union itself hadn't done much for Roanoke, not just lately but ever. The general feeling was that the Colonial Union had a lot to answer for, and until it answered for these things, that Roanokers felt perfectly justified in not paying too close attention to the Colonial Union's dictates. Like, for example, the one in which Manfred Trujillo was supposed to arrest my parents and take them into custody on the charge of treason. Trujillo apparently had a hard time finding either John or Jane after that one came in. A neat trick, considering how often they were talking.

But this folded into the other reason Gau had come around.

"General Gau is offering us sanctuary," Dad said to me. "He knows your mom and I will be charged with treason—several counts seem likely—and it's not entirely out of the realm of possibility that you'll be charged as well."

"Well, I *did* commit treason," I said. "What with consorting with the leader of the Conclave and all."

Dad ignored this. "The point is, even if people here aren't in a rush to turn us in, it's only a matter of time before the CU sends real enforcement to come get us. We can't ask the people here to get into any more trouble on our account. We have to go, Zoë."

"When?" I asked.

"In the next day," Dad said. "Gau's ship is here now, but it's not like the CU is going to ignore it for long."

"So we're going to become citizens of the Conclave," I said.

"I don't think so," Dad said. "We'll be among them for a while, yes. But I have a plan to get us somewhere I think you might be happy with."

"And where is that?" I asked.

"Well," Dad said. "Have you ever heard of this little place called Earth?"

Dad and I spoke for a few more minutes, and then I walked over to Gretchen's, where I actually managed to say hello to her before I broke down in sobs. She gave me a hug and held me, and let me know it was okay. "I knew this was coming," she said to me. "You don't do what you've done and then come back and pretend nothing has happened."

"I thought it might be worth a try," I said.

"That's because you're an idiot," Gretchen said. I laughed. "You're an idiot, and my sister, and I love you, Zoë."

We hugged some more. And then she came over to my house and helped me and my family pack away our lives for a hasty exit.

Word spread, as it would in a small colony. Friends came by, mine and my parents', by themselves and in twos and threes. We hugged and laughed and cried and said our good-byes and tried to part well. As the sun started to set Magdy came by, and he and Gretchen and I took a walk to the Gugino homestead, where I knelt and kissed Enzo's headstone, and said good-bye to him one last time, even as I carried him still in my heart. We walked home and Magdy said his good-bye then, giving me a hug so fierce that I thought it would crack my ribs. And then he did something he'd never done before: gave me a kiss, on my cheek.

"Good-bye, Zoë," he said.

"Good-bye, Magdy," I said. "Take care of Gretchen for me."

"I'll try," Magdy said. "But you know how she is." I smiled at that. Then he went to Gretchen, gave her a hug and a kiss, and left.

And then it was Gretchen and me, packing and talking and cracking each other up through the rest of the night. Eventually Mom and Dad went to sleep but didn't seem to mind that Gretchen and I went on through the night and straight on until morning.

A group of friends arrived in a Mennonite horse-drawn wagon to carry our things and us to the Conclave shuttle. We started the short journey laughing but got quiet as we came closer to the shuttle. It wasn't a sad silence; it was a silence you have when you've said everything you need to say to another person.

Our friends lifted what we were taking with us into the shuttle; there was a lot we were leaving behind, too bulky to take, that we had given to friends. One by one all my friends gave me hugs and farewells, and dropped away, and then there was just Gretchen and me again.

"You want to come with me?" I asked.

Gretchen laughed. "Someone has to take care of Magdy," she said. "And Dad. And Roanoke."

"You always were the organized one," I said.

"And you were always *you*," Gretchen said.

"Someone had to be," I said. "And anyone else would have messed it up."

Gretchen gave me another hug. Then she stood back from me. "No good-byes," she said. "You're in my heart. Which means you're not gone."

"All right," I said. "No good-byes. I love you, Gretchen."

"I love you too," Gretchen said. And then she turned and she walked away, and didn't look back, although she did stop to give Babar a hug. He slobbered her thoroughly.

And then he came to me, and I led him into the passenger compartment of the shuttle. In time, everyone else came in. John. Jane. Savitri. Hickory. Dickory.

My family.

I looked out the shuttle window at Roanoke, my world, my home. Our home. But our home no longer. I looked at it and the people in it, some of whom I loved and some of whom I lost. Trying to take it all in, to make it a part of me. To make it a part of my story. My tale. To remember it so I can tell the story of my time here, not straight but true, so that anyone who asked me could feel what I felt about my time, on my world.

I sat, and looked, and remembered in the present time.

And when I was sure I had it, I kissed the window and drew the shade.

The engines on the shuttle came to life.

"Here we go," Dad said.

I smiled and closed my eyes and counted down the seconds until liftoff.

Five. Four. Three. Two.

One.

ACKNOWLEDGMENTS

At the end of my book *The Last Colony*, I mentioned that I was likely to step away from the "Old Man's War" universe for a while, and in particular that I was going to give the characters of John Perry and Jane Sagan a rest, and let them have their "happily ever after." So, it can be reasonably asked, what is *Zoe's Tale* doing here now?

There are a number of reasons, but two big ones have to do with reader feedback. The first was that I got a lot of mail that went like this: "Hey, *The Last Colony* was great. Now write another one. And make it about Zoë. Also, I want a pony." Well, I couldn't do anything about the pony (sorry), but the more I thought about it the more I realized that I was interested in knowing more about Zoë as well. Zoë had played critical supporting roles in *The Ghost Brigades* and *The Last Colony*, and enough had happened to her in the course of the books that I thought there would be enough to tell her story and make it interesting. It's up to you to tell me if I was right about that, but I'll say that I'm pretty happy.

The other bit of reader feedback involved two criticisms of *The Last Colony*. In that book, the "werewolves," the indigenous intelligent species of Roanoke, played a role in a critical plot point, and having done that, went away for the rest of the book. I thought I had sufficiently explained their disappearance, but more than a few readers were either unsatisfied with the explanation or missed it entirely, and so I got a bunch of mail that asked "Where did the werewolves go?" This annoyed me, not because the readers were complaining but because clearly I was not as clever explaining their exit from the story as I would have liked.

To go with this, there was some (totally fair) criticism of *TLC* that Zoë going off into space and somehow coming back with a "sapper field" that was pretty much exactly what the defenders of Roanoke needed to defeat their attackers represented a complete *deus ex machina* maneuver on the part of a lazy writer. Yes, well. This is the problem of knowing more than your readers; as an author, I knew all the back story, but there was no way to get it into the book without wrenching the whole book onto a 30,000-word tangent. So I did a little hand waving and hoped I wouldn't get caught. Surprise! Apparently I have smart readers.

So in both these cases of reader dissatisfaction, writing *Zoe's Tale* allowed me a second bite at these apples, and in the process helped to make the events that take place in the "Old Man's War" universe more internally consistent and comprehensible. What have we learned here? Mostly that I do listen to feedback from my readers, both positive ("write more!") and negative ("fix that!"). Thanks for both.

Because I wanted to address reader questions, and because I thought it would be fun and interesting to do, I wrote *Zoe's Tale* to take place in parallel time to the events of *The Last Colony*, told from an entirely different point of view. Naturally, I'm not the first person to think of this clever trick (and here I perform a hat tip to my particular inspirations, Orson Scott Card with *Ender's Shadow* and Tom Stoppard for *Rosencrantz and Guildenstern Are Dead*), but stupid me, I thought it would actually be *easy*.

Indeed, I recall actually saying this to Patrick Nielsen Hayden, my editor: "I already know the plot and the characters; how hard can it be?" Patrick did not do what he should have done, which was to grab me hard by the shoulders, shake me like a maraca and say, "Good God, man, are you *insane*?!?" Because here's a little secret: writing a parallel time novel that does not, in fact, just lazily retell the story in a previous book is *hard*. Like, the hardest thing I've done as a writer to this point. And, damn it, Patrick's job as my editor is to make everything *easy* for me. So I feel he bears some responsibility for my months of complete flailure trying to write the novel (yes, flailure: "failure" + "flailing" = flailure. Look it up). So, yes: I blame Patrick. For *everything*. There, I feel better now.

(Note: The above paragraph is a complete lie: Patrick's patience and understanding and advice during this writing process was invaluable. But don't tell him that. Shhh. It's our little secret.)

The other really hard thing about *Zoe's Tale* was the fact that I was writing it from the point of view of a teenage girl, which is something I've never been, personally, and was a species of creature I can't say I actually *understood* back when I was a teenage boy (this will not come as news to my female contemporaries at high school).

For too long a time, I despaired how I would ever actually get a writing tone approximating that of an actual teenage girl, nor did I get particularly good advice from my male friends on this one. "So go hang out with teenage girls," is an I-swear-to-God actual quote from a male friend of mine, who is apparently oblivious to the social and legal implications of a thirty-eight-year-old emphatically un-Brad-Pitt-like man lurking around sophomore-aged girls.

So, I did something I think was smarter and less liable to get me a restraining order: I showed some of the work in progress to women I trust—all of whom, so I'm told, were teenage girls at one point in their lives. These women—Karen Meisner, Regan Avery, Mary Robinette Kowal, and especially my wife Kristine Blauser Scalzi—were instrumental in helping me find a voice that worked for Zoë, and equally unsparing when I got too caught up in my own imagined cleverness with the character. To the extent Zoë works as a character, you may credit their influence; to the extent that she doesn't, you can blame me.

I've already mentioned Patrick Nielsen Hayden as my editor, but there are others at Tor Books who have worked on the book as well, and I would like to offer my public thanks to them for their work. They include John Harris, who gave the book its most excellent cover; Irene Gallo, the world's best art director; copy editor Nancy Wiesenfeld, whom I pity for having to catch my many screwups; and my publicist at Tor, Dot Lin. Thanks also and as always to my agent Ethan Ellenberg, and also to Tom Doherty.

Friends! I have them, I don't even have to pay them, and they helped me keep it together when I felt like I was going to completely blow apart. Thanks in particular go to Anne KG Murphy, Bill Schafer, Yanni Kuznia and Justine Larbalestier, each of whom I spent more time chatting with on IM than I probably should have, but oh well. Devin Desai called me on a regular basis, which also helped to keep me from bouncing off the proverbial walls. Thanks also to Scott Westerfeld, Doselle Young, Kevin Stampfl, Shara Zoll, Daniel Mainz, Mykal Burns, Wil Wheaton, Tobias Buckell, Jay Lake, Elizabeth Bear, Sarah Monette, Nick Sagan, Charlie Stross, Teresa Nielsen Hayden, Liz Gorinsky, Karl Schroeder, Cory Doctorow, Joe Hill, my sister Heather Doan, and lots of other folks whose names escape me at the moment because I always blank out when I start making lists of names.

Also, an extra special set of thanks to the readers of my blog Whatever, who had to put up with quite a lot of disruptions this year as I tried to get this book done. Fortunately, they're good at keeping themselves amused while I'm banging on the keyboard like a monkey. And a fond farewell to readers of By the Way and Ficlets.

Certain names in the book are borrowed from people I know, because I'm really bad at making up names. So hat tips are in order to my friends Gretchen Schafer, Magdy Tawadrous, Joe Rybicki, Jeff Hentosz, and Joe Loong, who has the special distinction of having been murdered in two of my books now. It's not a trend, Joe. I *swear.*

One final reason that I wanted to do *Zoe's Tale* is because I have a daughter of my own, Athena, and I wanted her to have a character of mine that she could feel kinship with. As I write this, my daughter is nine, which is quite a bit younger than Zoë is in this book, so it's not accurate to say the character is based on Athena. Nevertheless many of Athena's qualities are in evidence in Zoë, including some of her sense of humor and her awareness of who she is in the world. So my thanks and love go to Athena, for being an inspiration for this book, and for my life in general. This is her book.

Visit **www.panmacmillan.com** to read more about all our books and to buy them. You will also find features, author interviews and news of any author events, and you can sign up for e-newsletters so that you're always first to hear about our new releases.